Melanie Hudson was born in Yorkshire in 1971, the youngest of six children. Her earliest memory is of standing with her brother on the street corner selling her dad's surplus vegetables (imagine *The Good Life* in Barnsley and you're more or less there).

After running away to join the British Armed Forces in 1994, Melanie experienced a career that took her around the world on exciting adventures. In 2010, when she returned to civilian life to look after her young son, she moved to Dubai where she found the time to write novels. She now lives in Cornwall with her family.

Melanie's debut, *The Wedding Cake Tree*, won the Romantic Novelists' Association Contemporary Romance Novel of the Year 2016 and her second novel, *The Last Letter from Juliet*, was a *USA Today* bestseller.

🐦 @Melanie_Hudson_
📘 www.facebook.com/melhudson7171
📷 @melly.hudson71
🆚 @MelHudson

Also by Melanie Hudson

The Wedding Cake Tree
Dear Rosie Hughes
The Last Letter from Juliet

The Night Train
to Berlin

Melanie Hudson

One More Chapter a division of
HarperCollins*Publishers*
The News Building
1 London Bridge Street
London SE1 9GF

www.harpercollins.co.uk

HarperCollins*Publishers*,
1st Floor, Watermarque Building, Ringsend Road,
Dublin 4, Ireland

This paperback edition 2021

First published in Great Britain in ebook format by
HarperCollins*Publishers* 2021

A catalogue record for this book
is available from the British Library

ISBN: 9780008420932
ISBN TPB: 9780008465810

Set in Birka by Palimpsest Book Production Ltd, Falkirk
Stirlingshire

Printed and bound using 100% Renewable Electricity at
CPI Black Print, Barcelona

For Ysabel who sent hand sanitizer and Ian
who found ten-thousand words.

Prologue

Alex

Christmas Day, 1944

This was the second memorable train on which Alex had travelled within the past year. Both had journeyed overnight, but where the first had offered a degree of spacious opulence and old-world charm, the second – the *Sonderzüg* – offered nothing at all. At least, nothing more than one hundred and fifty fellow passengers forcibly crammed into the same boxcar, with no food, no water, no latrine, no light and increasingly, it seemed, no hope.

Alex couldn't even begin to guess at the time. His watch was broken and the clock he carried in his coat pocket had, of course, long since stopped. It might as well be three-fifteen, he thought, it was as good a time as any. He guessed that they had pulled into a siding. Other trains had rattled past for hours now, but they were different kinds of train carrying different kinds of people. They

1

were trains where gentrified passengers – passengers who looked the right way, spoke and thought and behaved the right way, the accepted way – enjoyed comfort and a little warmth. They would perhaps not notice the line of cattle cars waiting in the siding, cast aside to allow their train to speedily pass, nor were they likely to notice the thousands of men, women and children forced into such cattle cars – some barely alive, some dead already, the rest utterly bewildered, hungry and afraid.

The old man to his left hadn't moved for hours but his face was pushed onto the back of Alex's head, his arm twisted awkwardly, painfully, into Alex's side. They were animals off to slaughter, except that animals would surely suffer less. Of that, Alex was certain.

He allowed his thoughts to drift to another night train, to a time when he had been the very epitome of a gentrified passenger, when life – if only he had known it at the time – had been something really and truly wonderful. The green dress, the pinched waist, that look she threw his way, as if daring him to catch it, her beautiful, wonderful smile. Where was she now? Was she safe, was she well, was she alive, even? If only he had known to grab that blessed time on the night train and to cherish it – cherish her – to tell her, the moment she sat down opposite him, that he was spellbound, that he adored the very ground she walked on, that he – yes, even at that first moment – loved her. If only, oh, if only he could go back to that moment and cherish it, revel in it, to get it right.

Chapter 1

Ellie

Present Day

It was a particularly busy evening rush hour on the Central Line when Ellie Nightingale – a violin case in one hand and a wheeled suitcase in the other – managed to catapult herself out of the Tube at Paddington Station. She tried to walk invisibly down the platform, pausing now and again to catch her breath while wending her way upstream. Getting anywhere quickly was never Ellie's forte, and as one woman – fast-footed, suited, lovely sneakers – dashed past, Ellie realised that she was the laborious tortoise to the superwoman's hare, which was one of the many reasons why she generally avoided the Tube. She didn't like that feeling of being stepped over, of being trampled on, of being undone.

And also, nobody ever seemed to smile.

But it was a beautiful spring day out there – up there

– a time when smiling at strangers was obligatory, and so Ellie smiled anyway. She smiled at the busker who was playing 'It's a Wonderful World' on his guitar in one of the underground tunnels and she smiled as she travelled all the way up the escalator at the people travelling all the way down on the other side, her fiddle case lifted, as though she was Poseidon rising out of the stormy sea.

As she stepped off the escalator, Ellie was pleased to see that Paddington railway station was not mobbed. The Salvation Army Band were just arriving at the final bars of 'The Lord Bless You and Keep You' and as she stood in the middle of the atrium and turned full circle to take it all in, Ellie realised that the spirit of spring had not only filtered into her own little soul this evening, but had also descended upon the whole station. It was as though she had stepped through the wardrobe into Narnia and felt that the very air around her, usually so electrified and frenetic in London, was softer somehow, giving the same sense of muffled peacefulness that a soft warm breeze flowing through the leafy London streets brings.

'And all is calm,' she said to herself, confusing spring with Christmas somewhat but it didn't matter, 'and all is bright.'

Ellie was particularly excited tonight as she was travelling to Cornwall, but the real excitement came because she wasn't catching any old train. Tonight she was catching the sleeper train, also known as the *Cornish Riviera*, which travelled all the way from London to Penzance, where the pirates came from. Tonight's trip was marketed as a 'themed evening of travel into the nostalgic and bygone age of the 1940s'. (In other words, a Vera Lynn-themed fancy-dress party and booze-up.) Ellie adored 1940s style and music, but she worried that she might perhaps feel even lonelier and more self-conscious tonight, likely being the only single person at a busy event.

No matter. Travelling by sleeper train to Cornwall was something that had been at the top of Ellie's bucket list for ages. Some years before, a friend of her Great Granny Nancy's had bequeathed a cottage in Cornwall to Nancy in her will. This little cottage, in a pretty fishing cove in the farthest reaches of the county, was surrounded by wild countryside and stood with its toes resting on a cobbled slipway that ran gently down to the sea. It was the place where Ellie had spent much-loved family summer holidays, for which they had all been so very thankful.

And there was a lot for Ellie to be thankful for this year, which was why, much to her family's disappointment, and for reasons only comprehensible to herself, she'd decided that it was time to return to the cottage for a holiday – to finally have the particular adventure that Great Granny Nancy had wanted her to have – and she would go on this holiday completely and utterly alone.

But the train didn't leave for a whole hour yet – not until 7.02 p.m. – which left Ellie free, now that the Salvation Army band had packed up for the evening, to take out her fiddle, position herself upwind of Paddington Bear, who sat steadfast as ever on his bench near platform one, and throw her hat – a vintage red beret kept especially for such an occasion – onto the floor. She would fill the halls with the unmatched and absolute joy of fiddle music this evening. She would become 'Ellie Nightingale, for one night only' – something else she had always wanted to do.

She took up fiddle and bow and realised that this – right now, at the beginning of the adventure – was one of those moments that marks a fabulous stepping-off point. She took a moment to savour this realisation before beginning her set with the reprise to her favourite movie of all time, *Beauty and the Beast*. Ellie had imagined playing her violin to a packed audience all of her life (albeit within the setting of a theatre, but you couldn't have everything) and wanted nothing more than to swaddle these busy passengers in good feeling. She put bow to string, paused a moment to settle, closed her eyes and began to play, and by the time she was ten bars in, the whole of Paddington Station and every last Victorian iron rafter rang out with the good cheer that only a Disney theme tune can bring. (*'Ellie Nightingale is a talented musician prone to daydreams, exaggeration and sudden lapses in concentration'* ... this from her music teacher, year nine.) But truly, at the sound of the music – because, for Ellie, there was nothing, NOTHING, more romantic and more fuelled with empathy and emotion than the sound of a fiddle in full swing – the commuters were not simply commuters anymore, they were new-found friends who were smiling at each other, and without any effort on their part, found themselves tapping their feet, jigging a little to the music, relaxed and happy and free.

She took a moment to open her eyes and noticed a stocky-looking chap sitting on the plinth with his arm wrapped around the Paddington Bear statue. He had particularly lovely wavy blond hair and was wearing – incredibly, as it was quite a warm evening – a blue duffle coat. He held out an arm to take a selfie of himself with Paddington before turning in the direction of the music. Ellie smiled at him over the top of the bow. He smiled back, and for the whole of her set the man in the duffle coat sat with Paddington and listened to the music, smiling to himself; at least, he was smiling whenever she glanced up to look at him, which was often.

With her eyes closed as she neared the end of her set, Ellie sensed that someone was standing in front of her. She opened her eyes. It was the man in the duffle coat. He put a hand in his pocket and bent to place something in her hat. Ellie nodded her thanks as she played on and watched him disappear into the crowd. She lost sight of him somewhere near the ticket office, frowned to herself, and finished the song. Looking down at the beret, she found not only a whopping twenty-pound note inside, but also a button in the shape of a toggle. Ellie very quickly gave the money to a rough sleeper who was trying to settle down for the night in a sleeping bag outside the station, but the toggle ... the toggle she saved for herself.

Chapter 2

Ellie

Departing Paddington

A car attendant called Rihanna (late twenties, blonde hair secured in a bun, kind smile) was holding a clipboard and standing on the platform next to carriage D as Ellie put down her cases and scrolled through the emails on her phone.

'Sorry about this,' she said, looking up. 'The confirmation email is on here somewhere. I won't be a minute.'

Rihanna put a hand on Ellie's arm. 'Don't worry about the reference. We don't tend to get stowaways on this train. I just need your name.'

Ellie slipped her phone into a back pocket of her jeans. 'Ellie Nightingale,' she said.

Rihanna noticed the fiddle case. 'Oh, was it you playing "Beauty and the Beast" on the platform?' she asked, looking up from the clipboard. 'I've been dancing up and down the dining carriage laying the tables for the last half an hour singing "Be Our Guest"!'

Ellie laughed.

'I *love* those songs,' added Rihanna, wistfully. 'Oh to be Belle, eh?'

Both women took a moment to think about what it would be like to actually be Disney's Belle until Rihanna scrunched her nose and burst the bubble by saying, 'A bit unrealistic though, falling in love with someone *that* ugly. Not that I'm shallow or anything, but there's ugly, and then there's an actual beast! I could get past the horns and a tail ... but the paws?' She shook her head. 'Crazy, really. A whole generation of women inspired by a "tale as old as time" about a supposedly clever woman who decides to abandon her career, her home, her friends, everything, and all because she's decided that there might just be a nice side to a grotesque sociopath who beat up her father and locked her up in a dungeon. And *these* are our role models. Is it any wonder I'm on my second husband?'

Ellie didn't respond. She had never thought of it that way. She wasn't sure she wanted to.

'Still, to be Belle though, right?' said Ellie.

Rihanna gestured her absolute agreement. 'Oh, to be sure! For the clothes if nothing else ... and the castle. Anyhow, thanks for joining us this evening!' She glanced down again. 'Let's have a little look on the list.'

Ellie peered over Rihanna's shoulder and spotted her

name straightaway. She pointed to it. 'There. There I am,' she said.

'Fab.' Rihanna drew a line through Ellie's name with a biro. 'You're in coach F, cabin number seven.' She nodded down the platform. 'That's two carriages further along. Now, you will be joining us for our musical extravaganza this evening, won't you? It all starts with dinner at eight.'

'I want to,' said Ellie, doubtfully. 'And I've brought a lovely dress – it's vintage, too – but I'm on my own and ...'

'Oh, don't worry about that!' Rihanna dismissed Ellie's uncertainty with a bat of the hand. 'Tonight's bunch seem to be very friendly, and you're not the only person travelling alone, so you should come! There's going to be a lovely quartet singing for you all, the D-Day Dames, who are – oh, my God – they're *so* amazing. Why don't you come to dinner and see how you feel after that? You'll need to eat something, at any rate.' Rihanna's eyes widened. 'I know, take a book with you! Do you have one? I never go anywhere without a book when I'm on my own.'

Did Ellie have a book?

Ellie was the master at carrying a book. Always the same one.

'Yes, I have a book,' she said.

'That's sorted then. I warn you, though, someone is *bound* to talk to you at some point. There's just something about travelling on the sleeper train. It makes even the most anti-social people want to be ... well, sociable! I love it!' Rihanna's excitement, Ellie had to concede, was contagious.

'OK, I'll be there!' Ellie was getting in the mood now. 'And where did you say my cabin is ... coach F?'

'That's the one. Cabin seven. Let me know if you need anything. The meal starts at eight so if you could be in the dining car by five-to, that would be fab. Jake – he's the barman – will sort you out for drinks and everything. It's all complimentary.'

Complimentary? Even better.

Imagining something from an Agatha Christie novel, Ellie grabbed her things, manoeuvred her way onto the train and began to work her way along the carriages. She read the door numbers out loud as she went along, counting down to ...

Coach F, cabin number seven.

She opened the door and stepped into heaven. No, it wasn't a suite at The Ritz, but it was her own little space of luxury and she imagined herself later, safe and snug in this plush little place while the train rumbled on, rocking her to sleep, the vibration of wheels on rails acting as her own personal lullaby. The lighting was subtle, the wardrobe was hidden, a sink doubled as a bedside table, the fold-down bed had a thick duvet pulled back to reveal a bag of chocolates sitting on the pillow, and although the newly refurbished train wasn't *exactly* as she had imagined (namely, the Orient Express with a beady-eyed Poirot sitting in a corner twiddling his moustache) it was, nevertheless, really quite plush and everyone she had bustled past in the aisle had an air of holiday spirit about them. She let out a contented sigh. Here she was, finally, having her very own adventure, and it felt really, really good.

She took a moment to lie down on the bed – doctor's orders – and closed her eyes but then promptly opened them again.

No, she couldn't rest. The lounge and dining cars were just a few carriages away and were probably filling up with excitable people by now. Maybe they would all be dressed in their 1940s clothes, too? Ellie smiled. A little rest could wait. She opened her suitcase and removed two things: an emerald green silk dress and a leather-bound journal. The dress she hung from the wardrobe door, smoothing it down, the journal she opened, taking out a letter from Great Granny Nancy. She kissed the paper and began to read Nancy's words for possibly the hundredth time since Nancy's death a few years ago:

Excerpt from The Last Will and Testament of Nancy Dubois.

… And finally, to my great-granddaughter, Eliza (Ellie) Nightingale, I bequeath 'Meadowsweet', my property in Penberth Cove, Cornwall, along with all the contents therein and riparian rights associated with the property. I also bequeath a vintage Christian Dior silk evening gown in emerald green. Given that both the house and the dress once belonged to my dear friend,

war artist Eliza Grey, I also bequeath Eliza's war journal and associated sketches to Ellie, in the knowledge that she will be inspired not only by the paintings, but by the courage and self-sacrifice of such an incredible woman.

I bequeath all these things on condition that, when Ellie is strong enough – fit enough, adventurous enough – as I know with certainty that she will be one day, she has the courage to travel alone to Penberth on an adventure of her own and to live there a little while, without the fuss of family and the medical profession around her. For sentimental reasons, I should also like her to travel on the night train from Paddington Station and have set aside a small amount of capital in order to pay for the ticket and to finance her stay.

I do all these things with love, partly because I know that my great-granddaughter will thrive in Cornwall, but mainly because every woman, at one point in her life, should have an exciting adventure all of her own.

Ellie sighed, popped the notepaper back into the journal and looked at the dress. It was certainly beautiful, if a little daring. It had a high halter neck, which was fortunate, as it covered her chest – which Ellie preferred, given the scar – but it was bare at the back and would skim the body in a way that left nothing to anyone's imagination, and was significantly more stylish and, dare she say, seductive than anything she would ever usually wear.

Ellie ran the fabric of the dress through her fingers and remembered that there were no second chances in life. That little humiliations meant nothing, not really. She reminded herself that tonight she was, after all, *Ellie Nightingale, for one night only*, and it simply didn't matter if all the other passengers hadn't bothered to glam up. If she was the only person dressed up at the party (her ultimate dread), who on earth would notice or care?

Ten minutes later, there was a knock at the door. It was Rihanna and she was delivering Ellie's pre-dinner aperitif on a silver tray – champagne!

'Wow!' Rihanna entered the cabin and began to speak in only exclamation marks. '*What* a fabulous dress! You look absolutely stunning!' and so on ...

Ellie was thrilled and did a little spin.

'I would literally kill to wear it! That dress combined with that fabulous pixie haircut? Incredible!'

Ellie put a hand to her hair. She had been disappointed not to have long enough hair to put into victory rolls tonight. She turned to the mirror again. 'It belonged to a friend of my great-grandmother's. They were nurses together in the war. Is it too much, tho—'

Rihanna interrupted by handing her the glass of champagne. 'Stop that, right now! Knock back your drink, and I'll pop back and get you when everyone is seated. You can walk behind me into the dining car. No one will even notice you arrive ...'

Unable to resist a force of nature such as Rihanna and

spurred on by the fizz, when the knock came at the door a little later, Eliza grabbed her gloves, her book and her clutch and followed her new friend into the dining car. As for Rihanna's conviction that Ellie could slip silently into her seat without anyone noticing her entrance ... she couldn't have been more wrong.

Chapter 3

Eliza

Early April 1944

'Coach F, cabin seven,' Eliza said to herself as she worked her way along the sleeper carriage, her suitcase in one hand, her satchel, full of charcoals and paints, in the other. An easel was wedged precariously under one arm. 'Four, five ... six ... ah, seven.' She pushed down the handle with an elbow and fell inside. She placed the easel and satchel in the storage net above the bed, plopped her case down, sat on the bed and stared at the wall, losing herself in a vacuum of thought, until the sudden jolt of the train, now departing Paddington Station, juddered her into action.

She stood, losing her balance briefly as the train crossed tracks, then turned to face the case and clicked open the locks. A carefully packed evening gown lay across the top; a long, sensuous, silk affair in emerald green, folded at the waist. It was a dress that fell off Eliza in all the right places, highlighting her slender waist and skimming her hips in a way that would make any Hollywood starlet proud. Eliza hung the dress on a hanger, sat down again and sighed. Dressing for dinner seemed ridiculous nowadays (not that she had ever thought it particularly important), the war having left her free to dress in her preferred casual style – that being her favoured artist's garb or, more recently, her auxiliary nurse's uniform. But travelling first class on the sleeper train brought with it a return to the old way of living, and although she felt too young for the tag, really, Eliza was, nonetheless, Lady Arbuthnot, Lord Arthur Arbuthnot's wife, which brought with it all the social expectations of a woman of the peerage. But could she really be bothered to dress the part of the grand lady tonight? Not really, no.

A knock came at the door.

'Yes?' she shouted, a hand automatically rising to tidy her long, glossy brown hair, curled under with a bounce at the ends.

The door opened. A silver tray entered first, followed by a smiling steward, an elderly man, whose starched shirt was too big around his slender neck and who hovered at the door, expertly balancing the tray as the train rocked on.

'Your aperitif, Madam,' he said, edging inside. 'And may I say how wonderful it is to have you travelling with us again, this evening.' He had the accent of a Londoner who was trying to gentrify his speech. 'And may I take this opportunity to welcome you aboard and say how pleased I am to see you looking so well.'

Eliza stood. She took a glass of sherry from the tray.

'Thank you, Jeffries. It's wonderful to see you too. And how is Mrs Jeffries?' Eliza took a sip.

'Oh, so, so, thank you, Madam. Her sister caught it from a whopper down the East End a couple of weeks ago. It's knocked Mrs Jeffries for six, I'd say. They were very close. But she'll get by, we all will, never you fear.' He tucked the tray under his arm and returned to business. 'I've reserved your usual table at the end of the dining carriage for you this evening.'

'Thank you.' Eliza glanced in the mirror. She tucked a stray hair behind an ear. 'And I shan't mingle in the lounge. I'll head straight to the dining car at eight,' she said.

The steward nodded. 'Very good, Madam. And if there's anything you need tonight, you just let old Jeffries know.'

Eliza watched the door close behind him before she turned to speak to her evening gown directly.

'Better take a book!'

The dining carriage was already busy when, at five minutes past eight, Eliza floated down the carriage a couple of paces behind Jeffries, making her way to her usual table. Every head turned. Eliza never intended for this to happen, nor did she ever intend to float – it was simply her way of walking – but at nearly six feet tall, with the profile, figure and lips of a movie star, she simply couldn't help it.

Indifferent to the appreciative glances (the women, as ever, catching the eye of their partners to either admonish them for staring or to agree that, yes, the woman was striking and possibly famous), Eliza arrived at her table and sat with her back to the rest of the carriage. Jeffries took the starched napkin off the table, swished it open with a flick of the wrist and laid it on her lap. The crisp white tablecloth, the silver cutlery, the crystal glasses, the single rose in a tiny vase, the candlelight, were all symbols of a pre-war age. Such things, Eliza mused as she waited for her meal, were both wonderfully decadent and inappropriately elitist during a time when depravation rampaged throughout the world.

But still. It was nice.

Eliza took a moment to gaze out of the window and watch the world pass by. The dying embers of the midsummer sun setting behind a line of tall poplar trees cast long shadows across a field of golden barley. She reached for her journal and a pencil and began to sketch the scene, an occupation which also served to prevent being drawn into conversation with the couple sitting at the table across the aisle, who had been trying to catch her eye ever since she sat down.

The train moved on from the barley fields and passed briefly into a tunnel. The darkness served to quash the image of the long shadows in her mind's eye. When the evening light returned, she put down the journal and pencil, opened her clutch and took out a book. She opened the page at the bookmark and was just settling in when Jeffries reappeared. He had the look of a disquieted man.

'I'm terribly sorry to disturb you, Madam ...'

Eliza glanced up from her book with a smile. Jeffries twitched on the spot and fixed his eyes on the empty seat opposite her.

'Yes?'

'I'm afraid that this is the last vacant seat this evening and ...' Clearly distressed, Jeffries turned to look down the aisle.

'What the dear chap is trying to say,' another man said, moving Jeffries to one side to squeeze past, 'is, would it be an awful imposition if I joined you for dinner this evening?'

The man stood by the table, his tall, broad frame towering over her, the left side of his face somewhat disfigured by what was almost certainly a burn of some sort.

Eliza put a gloved hand to her mouth. 'It's you,' she said, in a barely audible whisper.

'Yes,' he said. 'It's me. Have we met before? I do have rather an unforgettable face.'

Eliza shook her head and said, 'Perhaps I've confused you with someone else.' She gestured towards the empty seat opposite her. 'Do sit down.'

'It happens to me all the time, you see. People feeling that they know me when they don't.' He sat down and flicked out his own napkin, much to the distress of Jeffries, who handed him the wine list instead.

Eliza glanced down at her book while the man perused the list.

'What's the meat tonight?' the man asked.

'Beef, Sir.'

He handed the wine list back. 'In that case we shall have the claret, no ... the merlot. It's a better year.'

Jeffries turned to Eliza for confirmation, who glanced up to offer him a reassuring smile.

'Very good, Sir.' Jeffries side-eyed Eliza and shuffled away.

'And you needn't worry about becoming embroiled in any chatter nonsense,' added the man, addressing Eliza again, despite her having placed her nose very firmly in her book. 'I've brought something to read, too.' He took a small book from the inside pocket of his dinner jacket.

Eliza smiled another brief acknowledgement and returned to her book, glancing up now and again, just to be sure. Yes, it was definitely him. She had seen his picture in the society pages; the same eyes, the same handsome face (on one side, at least), and the same dark hair, ever so slightly unkempt, coming forward in a devil-may-care quiff across his brow.

'Unless, of course, you want to?' he said, throwing his book onto the table.

'Want to?'

'Talk,' he confirmed.

'I'm happy with my book,' she said, offering another polite smile. 'But thank you for the offer.'

She glanced down again.

'No matter.' His tone was matter of fact. 'One doesn't want to appear rude, you see. It would be dreadful for us to behave like one of those couples where the man sits reading and ignoring his companion all night, while the bored lady sitting opposite him stares blankly into space wondering how on earth she became lumbered with such an arrogant ass!'

Eliza let out a laugh. 'Well, I should say it's very gallant of you to be concerned for me, and really quite selfless, but I can assure you that I am more than happy with my own company, and luckily you have come prepared, so we shall both survive the journey without falling into such a pitfall, thankfully.' She glanced down again, the conversation over. Not that she wanted it to be over, not really, but there were conventions to consider. She was Lady Arbuthnot, he really *was* an arrogant ass (she knew this for a fact) and also the couple across the aisle were listening.

He tapped the table absently. 'I'm not sure that I'm exactly in the mood for reading.' He picked up the paperback, looked at the cover, sighed and threw it back onto the table dismissively. 'I chose this because I thought the subject would be fitting for the evening. But ... with hindsight, it was probably a mistake.' He sighed again.

'Agatha Christie,' she said, nodding towards the book and reading the dust jacket. '*Murder on the Orient Express.*'

The man suddenly held out his hand across the table. 'Let's do the thing again, properly, shall we? I'm Joseph Alexander Levine, but everyone calls me Alex, including you, I hope. And you are?'

Eliza removed her glove and offered her hand. 'Lady Arbuthnot.' She glanced towards the book again. 'Tell me, Mr Levine, do you know something the rest of us do not?' Her mouth, she knew, had taken on an angle of amusement.

'I'm sorry?'

Jeffries arrived with the wine.

'You said you thought the book might be fitting for the evening,' she said. 'Do you believe, then, that we are to have a murder on the train this evening?'

Jeffries glanced at her. Eliza shook her head to reassure him.

'If I did, I would hardly own it,' said Alex, his eyes challenging Eliza to respond in a similar, spirited manner. 'Especially if I was involved in the doing of the thing.'

She placed her bookmark on the page, closed her book and accepted the challenge. Jeffries edged away.

'Doesn't that rather depend upon whether you are to be the murderer or the murdered? Then again, maybe you would set yourself up as the detective in the scenario, or would you prefer to be one of the many suspects?'

Alex glanced out of the window. He scratched his chin, feigning deep thought, before looking back at her. 'I would probably place myself as ... either the detective or the man least likely to have committed the murder. Let's go with the latter.'

'Why?'

'Isn't it obvious? If I was the man least likely to have committed the murder, I would clearly be placing myself as the character who, in point of fact, is most likely to have done the thing – that's how such novels are written, I believe. It's quite straightforward.'

Eliza picked up her glass. 'I see.'

'I would insist upon having a wild and unadulterated past, of course,' Alex went on. 'And a fabulous reason for doing the deed.'

'A crime of passion,' Eliza suggested.

'I doubt it.'

Alex sat back and adopted a satisfied expression, his explanation complete.

Eliza nodded, her eyes narrowed. 'You wouldn't place yourself anywhere in-between, I suppose. Wouldn't see yourself as the red herring fellow who has a passionate motive but then doesn't quite have the courage to go through with the deadly deed?'

Alex looked at Eliza quite decidedly. With a mischievous twinkle in his eye he said, 'Offer myself up as the inconsequential sap in the corner, you mean?'

'If you like.'

'Never. Such characters are always the ones who just so happen not to have an alibi. Never suspect a man without an alibi. It's never him!'

'Or her, of course.'

Alex acquiesced with a shrug.

'Well, I'm glad we sorted that out.' She returned to her book. This dialogue – the beginnings of chatter – needed to be switched off. These were the types of conversations that women really did need to steer away from, especially with men who had a certain twinkle in their eye. And especially Alex Levine. She scanned for her place on the page. Her heart, however, wasn't in it. She held the book aloft so that Alex could not see her face. It would give away her amusement.

'What's it about?'

Eliza closed the book once more and sighed.

Alex didn't seem to notice the sigh, which left him with an inquisitive expression on his face and Eliza in need of an answer.

'I should have thought that was perfectly obvious ...' she began, but Alex was already talking.

'Of course, when I say, "What is it about?", please don't think that I mean for you to answer in any deep, existential way. Rather, quite literally, I ask, what is the basic premise of the story – or stories, by the looks of the title?'

Eliza opened her mouth to offer a brief precis but was prevented from doing so by the arrival of the first course, which was half a sliced boiled egg on a salad leaf. Eliza couldn't help but smile at Alex's clear disappointment.

'To put it very simply,' began Eliza, 'this book is a

collection of twelve individual stories about women who lived remarkable lives, which is why it is called *Women in History That Other Women Should Read About.*'

'Hmm. I bet the first three chapters cover Florence Nightingale, Grace Darling and Marie Curie, and maybe that other one, what's her name, that famous nurse in the first war?' He picked up his cutlery.

'Edith Cavell.'

'That's the one; terrible business. So, am I right?'

Eliza scrunched her nose. 'Not so well known, perhaps, but even so, they led the sort of exciting lives that women who do not feel the need to conform seem to live. Some did good works, some had scandalous affairs, some displayed incredible courage. That, in a nutshell, is what the book is about.' Eliza placed the book on the seat beside her and picked up her knife.

'And?' he said, a slice of egg hovering halfway to his mouth.

Eliza shrugged. 'There is no "and". You asked for a brief precis and that is precisely what I have given you.'

He placed the egg in his mouth and shook his head with an associated 'Hmm.'

'There must be a little more to it than that,' he said, swallowing.

Eliza put down her knife.

'Any book – even a memoir – to be truly interesting, requires ...' Alex glanced out of the window again, considering. It seemed to be a habit. 'A degree of ... angst. Difficult decisions, tragedy.' He gestured his knife in her direction. 'Fitzgerald said— Are you familiar with Fitzgerald?'

Eliza nodded.

'Fitzgerald said, "What people are ashamed of usually makes a good story". What do you think of that?'

Eliza, deciding that answering his question would be the fastest route to being able to eat her meal, said, 'I would say that I agree, in part, and as I mentioned, the women in the book have all pushed boundaries in their lives, taken risks. As for being ashamed of one's life ... it all depends on the individual's moral standpoint, one presumes.' She picked up her cutlery.

'Ah, now we're getting somewhere,' he said, pausing to eat another mouthful, which was basically the whole dish on a fork. He flourished his knife again while swallowing. 'Go on ...'

'Go on?' repeated Eliza.

'Give me an example, from the book.'

Eliza took a deep breath, thinking. 'Well ... take Hatshepsut, for example ...'

Alex laughed. 'Hatshepwho?'

'Sut,' said Eliza, also laughing now. 'She was a ruler of Egypt in the Eighteenth Dynasty. Incredible woman. She built temples, prevented civil war, all kinds of things. Egypt was prosperous and at peace under her leadership.'

Alex sniffed. 'And?'

Eliza looked at him squarely. 'Isn't that enough?'

Alex shook his head. 'No, it isn't. Where's the conflict?

It all seems like nothing more than a happy little success story to me. How very dull.'

'Perhaps the fact that she had to wear a false beard might placate you.'

Alex roared with laughter. 'A beard?'

'Yes!' said Eliza, rather enjoying his reaction to her story. 'The idea of having a woman as a ruler was offensive – nothing has changed much there, clearly. So ... she wore a beard. It's a perfectly simple solution. Does that spice things up enough for you?'

Alex took a sip of his wine.

'It certainly does. Fabulous!'

'I doubt it was fabulous for her,' clarified Eliza. 'A false beard can give one the most terrible rash, you know, not to mention the obvious itch.'

Alex's shoulders began to shake with more laughter. His eyes sparkled and his head tilted to one side. 'And from whom did you hear that titbit?' he asked.

Eliza had picked up her glass and was about to sip. She paused.

'Let's just say I know some very interesting people ...'

Alex laughed out loud again and picked up his glass. 'A toast!' he said, suddenly.

'To what?' Eliza felt herself sliding into the slipstream of his joviality.

'To interesting people!' he said.

Eliza smiled. 'To interesting people,' she repeated as the glassware chinked.

'You'll be on your, what, third reading of it now?' Alex nodded towards the book where it sat on the seat next to her.

Eliza's fork paused once more. 'Considerably more, probably,' she confessed. 'But how do you—'

'Because of the way you hold it,' he interrupted.

'Which is?'

'Tenderly. Also, it's well-thumbed.'

'I may have borrowed the book from someone else,' she said. 'Or from the library.'

Alex dabbed his mouth with a napkin. 'True,' he said, 'but I don't think so. It's a book that is important to you. So the question is, what happens within those pages that has driven you to read it over and over again through the years?'

Eliza took the opportunity to eat before answering.

'I thought you said you did not want me to discuss the book in any deep – how did you put it – "existential" way?'

Alex placed his elbows on the table and rested his chin on his hands. 'Has anyone ever told you that your eyes are incredibly beautiful when you're having fun?'

Eliza glanced at the couple opposite.

'Mr Levine,' she said. 'Please ...'

'But in answer to your question,' he said, sitting back and seemingly not giving a jot about the couple across the aisle, 'I asked for a simple answer because I didn't want you to feel under pressure to answer in an academic way.'

'Under pressure?'

'Yes. To offer the kind of critique a literature student might give. Such an answer may have proven to be ...'

'Longwinded?' Eliza answered for him. 'Or perhaps you thought deeper consideration would be beyond me?'

'Worse,' he said, sitting back once more. 'To be perfectly honest, I was concerned your answer may prove to be dull. You're an attractive woman and the aura of intrigue around you is really quite something – ask anyone in the carriage. The image I have painted of you in my mind would have been dashed for all eternity if you had answered in a dull manner. And it would also be dashed boring for the couple opposite, who are having a jolly time listening to our conversation.'

Eliza heard a loud, 'I say!' from across the aisle.

Alex winked and rested his chin on his hands again.

Eliza shook her head in wonder. 'Do I look like the sort of woman who would feel under pressure to perform?' she asked.

He sat back and took her in. 'On reflection, no. Perhaps the dress was a distraction. I apologise for putting you into a stereotype.' He leant forwards again. 'But you were saying about the book ...'

Eliza glanced longingly at her first course, which although meagre, remained unfinished.

'As I said, the book is simply a compilation of stories about interesting women. One is a slave, another is a sailor. There is a woman who decides to dress as a man to get on in life, an anarchist, a Byzantine Empress and two explorers, one of whom is Nellie Bly, a fascinating woman who circum-navigated the world in seventy-two days just to see if Jules Verne's book was possible. She also pretended to be insane in order that she might have herself committed to a lunatic asylum, simply to expose the horrors of such places – she wrote a book about it.'

'I've read it,' said Alex, taking Eliza by surprise. 'It's called *Ten Days in a Mad-House*.'

Eliza was beginning to wonder if she hadn't entered into a madhouse.

'And that, in a nutshell, is what the book is about,' she concluded. 'Endeavour, derring-do, and dare I say it, a significant degree of pizzazz!'

'Ah, I see.' Alex nodded, his expression one of under-standing – understanding of what, however, Eliza had no idea.

'You see what, exactly?'

'I see why it resonates.'

Although apprehensive as to his answer, Eliza felt compelled to say, 'And why would that be?'

'It resonates with you because you are a woman of intel-ligence who feels trapped by convention.' He glanced quickly at the band of gold on her wedding finger. 'You are wearing a stunning gown which was probably bought for you by your husband. The way it drips off you high-lights the bits that should be highlighted and has brought you a great deal of interest within this carriage alone. But is this ...' He made a flourish in her direction. 'This image of perfection, is it the woman you really are? I am not asking the question, by the way. It is you who are asking yourself the very same question, by the act of reading the book.'

Eliza's expression was one of amusement, rather than offence, which only served to spur him on.

'The war has begun to emancipate women,' he continued, 'to really emancipate them, and you are beginning to wonder what your future role might be. You are caught in the tangled net of a marriage to an influential man. Lord Arbuthnot is considerably older than you – don't worry, you're not unusual in this – and that, no doubt, is why you are drawn to such a book.'

Explanation complete, he celebrated his genius with a sip of wine.

Rather than shake her head in wonder and take great offence (he was right, after all, damn him) Eliza laughed out loud, as though channelling Katherine Hepburn laughing at Spencer Tracy in *Woman of the Year*. 'You sound like a detective of personalities, Mr Levine, a veritable Sherlock Holmes. Should I expect you to notice a fray on my collar which leads you to draw conclusions as to how I spent the day?'

Alex bowed theatrically in his seat. 'I accept your teasing. But tell me, was I incorrect in my reasoning?'

Eliza looked out of the window. It was twilight now and the light across the fields was a crimson glow.

'No, you were not. But to return to the original point,

I am fond of the book because my mother bought it for me. She wanted me to break boundaries in life, I think.'

'But that's wonderful!' he said, showing more warmth and genuine interest now, which pleased her.

'My mother died when I was a child,' she explained. 'The bookmark inside was hers, too. Just having this book with me makes me feel safe in troubled times, but also, I love it because the women inside the pages are the sort of strong women I admire. I admire their relationship with landscape, with society, with a refusal to conform. Ultimately, I enjoy it because every single one of them made mistakes but survived to tell the tale. The accounts are frank and honest and, for the most part, true. So yes, I feel a sense of resonance with the story, I will give you that, although I shall not own as to why. I spend a great deal of time examining nature – people ...' Eliza trailed off. 'But further than that, I do not wish to discuss.' She picked up her cutlery once more. 'Let us draw a line on the subject in order that I might eat before the steward arrives to collect our plates. I do so hate to hold Jeffries up and I am hungry. Feel free to return to your book.'

Pleased to have silenced him for good, Eliza gathered food onto her fork and began to eat. Alex had touched a sensitive nerve. The book, after all, was about women who lived the kind of life Eliza would have liked to live, would still like to live. Alex was right, it was the conflict and the drama in the stories that drove Eliza to keep turning the page, to seek out the inspiration, because after the hell of witnessing London in the Blitz, something had changed in her and God knows how she now yearned for excitement – for freedom – in her own life.

Several moments of the sound of Eliza's clicking cutlery along with silent glances out of the window passed by. Starters complete, Jeffries appeared. He removed the plates and topped up the wine. He fussed over Eliza like a protective grandparent. Eliza's right hand was just reaching down to retrieve her book again when Alex, after taking a sip of wine, said, almost shyly now, 'Have I been frightfully direct this evening?'

Leaving her book on the seat, Eliza smiled and said, 'You have, rather.'

'I am sorry. Truly. It's a professional habit. I'm a newspaper reporter, you see, and I forget to ease off, sometimes.'

'I see.'

'I'm actually a war correspondent, or hoping to be, at least,' he added. 'No doubt you're wondering for whom I write?'

'Not particularly.'

'Ha!' he exclaimed. 'I shall tell you anyhow! I write for *The Times* and *The Tribune* on the whole, but I'm submitting to American newspapers more and more these days.'

The following words were out before Eliza could rein them in. 'I hear the editor of *The Tribune* is a frightful dragon.'

Alex almost spat out his wine. 'Yes,' he said, 'I suppose she is. Are you really not the least interested in who I am or are you trying to appear mysterious and aloof? If so, you're very good at it.'

Their eyes met in the middle of the table and danced a mischievous little dance before returning to the window. Eliza decided it was probably best to finally offer the truth and be done with it.

'If I seem to be disinterested it is because I already know who you are.' She did not leave a long enough pause for him to comment. 'I know, for example, that you are an ex Battle of Britain pilot who returned to the newspaper world following a nasty burn-up in a Spitfire over the English Channel. You have an inflated opinion of yourself, one which is roughly the size of Belgium, or maybe Wales, even. You also once had your pay docked for overflying a village so low that you missed the church spire by a whisper.' She picked up her glass and toasted it in Alex's direction. 'And I know all of this because you are also the man who, in a national newspaper, criticised – quite harshly, I might add – my artwork, which was commissioned on behalf of the War Office.'

There was the expected momentary pause while the cogs turned in Alex's mind. He shuffled in his seat. 'But your name is Arbuthnot, and I have never, to my mind, criticised an Arbuthnot. The editor wouldn't allow it, I assure you.'

'I sign my work with my maiden name.'

'Which is?'

'Grey. Eliza Grey.'

The cogs finally fell into place and Alex had the good grace to look sheepish. 'Oh. In that case, I can see why you might be a little cross with me,' he said. 'And I think you've been a damn good sport to engage with me so far!'

'Cross? Not at all.' She was determined to respond in as nonchalant a manner as possible. The last thing any artist should do is allow a critic to get the upper hand. 'In fact, I quite liked being given the handle of – what was it you called me, again? "A delusional and misleading optimist"?'

Alex bit his lip, clearly trying to suppress laughter. It didn't work. He laughed out loud.

'Well, that does sound exactly like the sort of thing I would say. I am guilty of all charges, but with regards to the church spire incident, the truth is that there was a clock on the spire and I desperately needed to know the time.'

Eliza laughed then, she just couldn't help it, and certainly couldn't keep the quarrel going. His face was just too ... wonderful. Too full of devilment. And anyway, it wouldn't do to have a scene in the dining carriage, especially with the pair across the aisle smirking away. Also, the evening light filling the carriage was far too soft for angst, and the journey was passing by far too quickly. They had already passed the small Somerset town of Castle Cary. She leant towards him across the table and whispered. 'Between you and me, I had been placed on a bit of a pedestal in the art world, and it was beginning to feel rather uncomfortable. I was more than pleased to be toppled off.'

Alex smiled again. 'Well, that's very gracious of you, Eliza. What a gent you are! And thank you for letting me off the hook so pleasantly. May I call you Eliza, by the way? Lady Arbuthnot seems a little formal for such an intimate setting.'

'You may,' she said quietly, after a pause.

Both parties proceeded to glance out of the window and wait in a companionable silence for the main course to arrive – slivers of beef with carrots and boiled potatoes.

Eliza looked down at her food and picked up her knife and fork once more. It was time to return to conversation which, like the food, was being served in rounds. Despite herself, she was rather looking forward to round two.

Chapter 4

'And what is it that takes you to Cornwall this evening, Mr Levine?' Eliza began. 'A holiday or ...?'

Alex picked up his wine rather than his cutlery and hesitated before answering.

'The simple answer is that I'm going to Cornwall for both work and a holiday and I thought the night train would be the most sensible use of my time. But please, do call me Alex.'

'And the more complicated answer ... Alex?'

He looked at her straight. His eyes no longer danced, instead they were full of ... what was it? Worry? Regret? Despair? If she were to paint a portrait of Alex right now, there would be long, desperate, black shadows dripping off of him. She would have to fight the brush in order to offer him some kind of hope.

'I'm running away,' he said, before knocking back his wine. 'Actually, that's banal. Forget I said that. I hate that kind of mysterious nonsense. In truth, I'm going to stay with old friends in order to have a bit of a think.'

'I see. You have been to Cornwall before, then?' She offered him the kindness of not probing further.

'Yes, I adore Cornwall, the western tip in particular. It's my go-to place in times of ... well, uncertainty ...'

'Really?' Eliza dropped her aloof repose. 'But ... me too!'

They smiled then. 'There's nowhere quite like it, is there?' he asked.

She shook her head. 'No,' she said, 'there really isn't.'

Alex offered no more on the subject and after taking a moment to begin his meal, dabbed his mouth with the napkin, sat back in his seat and said, 'What about you? What takes you to Cornwall on this fine evening, other than the fact that you adore it?'

Jeffries arrived and gave her the opportunity of a moment to consider by topping up Alex's wine. Eliza placed a hand on top of her glass and as Jeffries moved away she glanced at the couple opposite, who had finally turned their attention to their dinner. 'I have a decision to make and I'm hoping that, once I am safely home in Cornwall, I shall find some clarity.'

The train's brakes began to screech, halting conversation as a row of houses appeared outside of the window. Children played in a cottage garden backing onto the railway line while others ran along the embankment chasing the train. The children became engulfed momentarily in a cloud of steam and disappeared from view.

They returned to the occupation of eating dinner, now and again passing the occasional pleasantry about the countryside, the warm spell of weather, or the pleasantness of eating off-ration on the train. Dessert arrived – steamed pudding and custard.

'Your favourite, Madam,' Jeffries said, placing a bowl of pudding in front of each of them.

'The staff all seem to know you quite well,' said Alex as Jeffries walked away and Eliza picked up her spoon. 'I'm assuming – in the manner of an Agatha Christie genius sleuth, of course – that you travel to Cornwall by the night train fairly often? Either that or you have shares in the railway and the staff have no choice but to be kind to you.'

Eliza laughed. 'Nothing so grand. I have a little cottage by the sea and I stay there when I'm painting. I prefer to travel by night train to get there.'

'And this cottage you are headed to, is it the place you referred to earlier as "home"?'

Eliza paused. Had she said that?

'Yes,' she said, 'it is.'

'Which is where your husband also resides?'

Eliza swallowed. 'No, it's my own place.'

Alex scratched his nose. 'I hear that the light in Cornwall is particularly good for artists this time of year – *all* year, in fact.' He laughed a little. 'Of course, I'm only saying that to try to appear knowledgeable when, in truth, I have no idea if or why the light is good in Cornwall, or what "good" is, in fact. Is that why you go there so often, to paint?'

Eliza shook her head. 'I was born at my cottage. It's in a little cove called Penberth. That's why I refer to it as home, I suppose.'

Alex put down his spoon. 'But I know Penberth! It's close to where I stay.' He shook his head in wonder. 'Which cottage is it?'

'The last one on the lane, opposite the stepping stones, facing the slipway?'

'I know it! I've often wondered who lived there. It is not – you'll forgive me for saying – the kind of residence where I would expect Lady Arbuthnot to have been born.'

Eliza turned the spoon in her hand. 'I was not born to privilege. I lived in Penberth when I was a young child, and I'm sad to say that I don't remember much about my early childhood.'

'Your parents moved away? Was it their summer cottage, or ...'

'Summer cottage?' Eliza laughed good heartedly. 'I'm from far too humble a stock for such luxuries. My accent has become significantly more refined since my marriage and subsequent move to London. When speaking with my neighbours next week, however, I'll slip back into my Cornish vowels, I assure you. No, this evening dress – as you alluded to earlier – is a façade. In reality, I'm nothing more than a simple Cornish maid. My parents both died of the Spanish Flu in 1918, two weeks apart, and I suppose

the cottage is my only connection to them. When I ...'
Eliza was just about to say, 'when I married' but stopped
herself. 'When I was in a position to buy the cottage, I
persuaded the local estate to sell it to me.'

'You must have been very young when they died?' he
said.

'I was eight.'

'I'm sorry.'

Eliza shook away the sadness. 'Don't be. Perhaps you
think me a fraud playing out the role of the grand lady.'

'We're all playing roles, Eliza,' said Alex, gently. 'Tonight,
you're a society lady and a famous artist – mysterious,
alluring, beautiful – while I have tried to pass myself off
as a clever, somewhat aloof but – dash it all – irresistible,
insightful and attractive man. If I were lucky enough for
you to walk away from the table tonight thinking of me
that way then you would be mistaken. In reality, I am a
man who has difficulty coping with his physical and
emotional injuries, who has not one clue where to turn.
A man who still feels that he needs to prove himself in a
war in which he is, in fact, no longer allowed to fight. I
am a fake, Eliza. A pure fake. The roles we choose for
ourselves, which are interchangeable, don't always suit our
true character, which is not interchangeable; at least, I don't
think so. I have come to the conclusion that it is not a
failing to discard an old costume and choose another role,
in another play, if the one you chose originally is now too
difficult for you to play out with true conviction.'

Eliza looked down at her uneaten pudding.

Alex followed her gaze. 'Perhaps we should eat,' he said, his voice soft and gentle. 'It is your favourite pudding after all.'

Chapter 5

Ellie

Paddington to Reading

All heads turned as Ellie, looking every bit the starlet and humming 'The Arrival of the Queen of Sheba' in her head, attempted to float down the aisle behind Rihanna, which was difficult as the dress was too long. She lowered herself onto the seat in the way she imagined Ingrid Bergman would – demurely. A shiver of a thrill flashed through her when she saw the table, set beautifully with a crisp white tablecloth, silver cutlery, crystal glasses, a candle and a single red rose in a tiny vase. Each table was named after a place associated with the war, and she was equally thrilled to see that hers was named 'Berkeley Square', which was apt, given her surname of Nightingale. It was all thanks to Rihanna's delicate touch, no doubt.

Ellie smiled at the couple seated opposite (dressed as a woman in the Land Army and a soldier) and allowed Rihanna (who winked at her) to flick out the napkin and place it on her knee. So what if she was alone? There were great delights to be had in enjoying her own company – the peace, the time for reflection, the food – and anyway, she had Eliza's journal to read, which was just what she needed to get herself in the mood for Cornwall. She took the journal out of her bag, sniffed the leather cover and opened the first page just as Rihanna reappeared. She knelt down in the aisle next to Eliza's seat and whispered, 'If I was to put a *really* sexy man opposite you, would you mind?'

Eliza glanced around nervously. 'How sexy?'

'Very.'

'It might be awkward ...'

But Rihanna was already walking away.

The couple opposite were a little too quiet suddenly. Ellie turned her back on them to look out of the window as a Rihanna reappeared with a man dressed as a fighter pilot ace wearing a leather flying jacket over overalls (which must have been roasting, Ellie thought) and a white scarf held out at an angle by a coat hanger as if being blown in the wind. A leather helmet and goggles, and a fake moustache, finished the ensemble. He placed a stuffed black Labrador dog on one of the seats on the other side of the table and sat down beside the dog. Without looking at Ellie, he delved into a jacket pocket and took out a tiny antique brass clock. He put the clock on the table and searched through every other pocket until a pair of glasses appeared. Ritual complete, he glanced up to acknowledge

Ellie's presence, at which point his face took on an expression of genuine surprise.

'It's you,' he said, as Rihanna – watching on, her face now the epitome of professionalism – flicked out the napkin and lay it on his lap.

'It's me,' Ellie repeated, smiling.

The man, who was staring at Ellie in wonder, regained his composure.

'You're the woman from the platform, aren't you? You were playing the violin. I could have stayed and listened to you play all day.'

Ellie blushed a little, flattered. 'Yes, it was me. Thank you for the tip.'

'Tip?'

'Yes, the money you gave me. You popped a note into my beret.'

The man tapped his forehead. 'Oh, of course! You meant *that* kind of a tip! I thought you meant that I'd told you how to get mould off the grout in your bathroom, or something. No worries, it was my pleasure.'

Ellie rolled down a glove. She removed it in the manner of an Austen heroine and held out a hand with perfect grace. 'I'm Ellie Nightingale,' she said, 'and I'm very pleased to meet you.'

'And I'm Joe,' he said, offering his own hand across the table. 'Joe Burton, from Leeds, as you can probably tell from my accent.' He cocked his head and looked at her – really looked at her, which was a bit odd. 'It's weird,' he said, his eyes narrowed, assessing her, 'but I have the strangest feeling that I know you, like, properly know you. Do I? Know you, I mean?'

Ellie shook her head.

'I don't think so,' she said. 'Perhaps I have one of those faces. Are you a doctor?' Most of the men Ellie had ever met had been doctors.

Joe laughed. 'With *my* exam results? Not likely!'

'Must have been a past life, then,' stated Ellie, feeling it to be the only plausible answer.

'Clearly,' agreed Joe. 'Perhaps you were a glamorous society woman,' he said, 'and I was a pilot ace and we met on the train and fell desperately in love ...'

Ellie blushed and looked down at her book.

Joe blushed and picked up the clock.

Rihanna – still standing beside the table – beamed!

'But seriously,' he said, putting down the clock and gathering himself by taking off his leather flying helmet and goggles and running his fingers through his mop of baby blond hair. 'I know that having a stranger sit opposite you is the last thing you probably want to have forced onto you tonight, and you must be thinking, "Oh, no, who is this random bloke they've plonked in front of me now!"'

'Not at—'

'But don't worry. I have my clock to mend, and you have your book, so we'll be fine.'

Ellie smiled politely and looked down once more at her book.

'Unless you want to talk, obviously,' Rihanna chipped in. 'It *is* a party train after all.'

Joe pushed his glasses up his nose, the sweat from the helmet having run down his forehead. 'Well I'm game if you are,' he said to Ellie. 'Although I'm not sure I can keep up the act of the dashing RAF fighter hero. I'm sweating like a pig! When I put this uniform on, I thought I looked pretty bloody brilliant, to be honest; a sophisticated, dashing and yet intriguing man of mystery.' He looked at Ellie over the top of his glasses, which had slid down his nose again. 'But I think we all know that I blew that the moment I sat down!'

Rihanna mouthed, 'I. Love. Him!' at Ellie and handed Joe the wine menu.

'Ellie can choose,' he said, offering her the menu across the table.

Ellie looked at the list but shook her head. 'I have absolutely no idea about wine,' she said. 'Red, white, rosé ... it's all the same to me.' She handed the wine list back. 'It will feel more authentic – more 1940s, like – if you choose. I'm a confident enough millennial to allow it.'

And so he did. A deep and intoxicating merlot.

'We need to toast something,' said Joe, as Rihanna poured the wine five minutes later.

Ellie scratched her chin as Rihanna excused herself. 'How about ...' She turned to look at the people sitting at the table behind her. They were dressed as a nurse and a surgeon (the surgeon's outfit being a little close to the bone on the garish front). 'How about, to the greatest generation?'

Joe wasn't so sure. 'Hmm. They deserve it, obviously,' he said, 'but I was thinking of something closer to home.' He raised his glass.

'To unexpected encounters!' he said, clearly pleased with himself.

Ellie put a hand to her chest, thrilled. 'To unexpected encounters!' she repeated.

Joe pushed the clock to one side and waited for Ellie to speak. And she did. Happily.

'So, what's brought Joe from Leeds to the night train this evening?' she began. 'Are you a 1940s buff or going on holiday to Cornwall? Or is it something else?'

Joe opened his mouth to answer, then closed it again. He put a hand to his fake moustache to twiddle it. 'It's difficult to know where to start,' he said. 'The thing is ...'

Rihanna arrived with the pâté starter. 'Ah, saved by the bell,' he said.

'So, the thing is ...' Joe began again '... I went to Berlin a couple of days ago to buy this clock ...' He picked up the little clock.

'All the way to Berlin?' chimed in Rihanna, who had stayed exactly where she was after delivering the starters to listen to Joe. 'Just for a tiny clock?'

Joe shrugged. 'Yes.'

Rihanna flashed Ellie a quick side eye.

'So, anyhow, long story short ...' Joe paused to glance

down to assess his pâté. He looked disappointed. 'But when I got there, it turned out to be broken.'

'Berlin or the clock?' asked Rihanna with a laugh.

'The clock.' Joe gave the thing a little shake to prove the point. 'But I felt sorry for it, like it was desperate to start ticking again, so I bought it anyway.'

'And what has the clock got to do with why you're going to Cornwall?' asked Rihanna, now fully committed to the conversation.

Joe glanced up at Ellie. 'Erm ... I'd tell you but you'd think I'm nuts. Maybe later, when I've had a drink or two.'

Rihanna shrugged and moved on.

He put down his glass. 'And you?' he said. 'Why are you on the night train this evening? Did you just fancy a party night?'

Ellie had lots to potentially say on the subject of why she was on the train this evening. It was a trip that had been planned *for* her rather than *by* her, and a long time ago at that, by her great-grandmother, Nancy. Nancy was a woman of wonderful spirit who believed that one day Ellie would be well enough to experience a kind of independence more suited to a woman her age. And oh, how Ellie wanted to feel that way, to have some space – some blessed space – to feel free of it all, free of a condition that meant her pulse went tickety tick tock, rather than tick tock.

But she didn't want to talk about that right now, she just wanted to behave like any other twenty-nine-year-old independent woman. She wanted to feel like the wild, reckless, spirited soul she wished she'd been born to be. She wanted the Cornish wind to whip her hair into an invigorated frenzy, not that that would be easy with a pixie cut, but anyway, just for a moment she wanted to live a life where she felt absolutely free. Damn it all, she wanted to be Belle.

Ellie glanced around, her eyes bright, her spirit soaring. 'I suppose I'm looking for a taste of adventure. And the sleeper is *so* nostalgic, especially tonight, don't you think?'

'It's great, yeah ...' Joe looked down to assess the pâté again. He picked up the toast and examined it. 'Bit of a misnomer, though, being called the sleeper train,' he said, taking up a knife.

'Misnomer?'

Joe scraped pâté onto the toast. 'If this really is a party train, then I'm going to do lots of things tonight, but sleeping isn't one of them!' He smiled and took a bite of toast.

Ellie flashed him her best 'Oh, really!' look before sipping her wine and turning to smile at the people on the table opposite. The woman winked at Ellie, having heard what Joe had said.

'I mean, obviously, I'm not expecting to ...'

Ellie let him dig himself out of a hole while wondering what he would look like without the fake moustache – better, was her conclusion.

'I thought we would be given spam fritters and Ovaltine for starters,' she said. 'I doubt they would be able to get their hands on much salmon pâté during the war.' The toast paused between the plate and her mouth. 'Except for Scotland,' she added quickly. 'They probably could get it there, a black market kind of thing.'

'Just like *Whiskey Galore!*' said Joe. 'But with salmon.'

Ellie put the toast down altogether. 'You've seen *Whiskey Galore!?*'

'I have. About ten times.'

'But I *love* that film!'

What she was really saying was, 'We are so right for each other, Joe from Leeds!' but remembering that she was supposed to be playing the part of a demure temptress – and deciding it was probably best not to start planning the wedding on the basis of the fact that they both liked the same film – she returned to her food.

'The original black and white version, obviously,' confirmed Joe.

'Obviously,' agreed Ellie. 'Where will you be staying?' she asked.

'I pick up a hire car in Penzance in the morning and I'm staying at ...' He paused, thinking. 'It's marketed as a boutique hotel, but I can't remember what the place is called. I've got the confirmation on my phone. It's at a little place called ...' His knife hovered over the plate as he thought about it. 'Lamorna Cove. Is that right?'

It was.

'No! I mean yes. My place is just along the coast from there. I'm staying in a cottage at Penberth and—'

Rihanna appeared, interrupting Ellie. She excused herself for leaning across the table while pulling down the window blind. 'For the blackout,' she said, clipping the blind down securely. 'Can't have the Luftwaffe blowing us up as we trundle along, can we?'

Adopting a BBC news anchor accent, Eliza said, 'Ah, frightfully good idea, old chap, what! Loose lips sink ships and all that!' before returning to her normal voice to talk about the cottage with Joe. 'It belonged to a friend of my Great Granny ... Nancy.' Ellie loved telling this story. 'She – this friend of Nancy's – was a famous war artist, called Eliza Grey. Isn't that a wonderful name?'

Joe opened his mouth to speak but closed it again because four women dressed in US Army-style uniform (skirts, jackets, chip hats, red lipstick, pinup hair) had begun to walk the length of the carriageway saying, 'Hi there! Good to see y'all,' in American accents to everyone. Ellie reckoned they were about as American as she was, but still, it was great fun.

At the far end of the carriage, where tables had been removed, the quartet each took hold of a microphone (Joe and Ellie agreed they couldn't believe they hadn't noticed the microphones earlier) and one connected an iPad to the PA system, and hey presto, there was a band! The tallest woman did an introductory speech announcing that they were the D-Day Dames and that they were delighted to see everyone looking so wonderful this evening. They quickly launched into their opening number, 'Sentimental Journey', in full harmonic bliss.

Ellie, who had turned in her seat to watch the women sing, turned back to face Joe, feeling bright and joyful.

'Oh, I *love* this one!' she said. 'And how apt for tonight. Aren't they fabulous? This is turning out to be The. Best. Evening. Ever!'

She smiled.

Joe smiled.

The people across the aisle, listening in, smiled.

Somewhere down the carriage, Rihanna smiled.

The train swayed, the guests swayed, and at that moment Ellie had absolutely no doubt that even the cows in the passing fields would be swaying.

The main course arrived – Beef Wellington – just as the train slowed to pass through the small town of Castle Cary. Joe, clearly also washed through with merriment, picked up his glass once more and said,

'To sentimental journeys!'

'To sentimental journeys, it is!' Ellie repeated.

Chapter 6

Eliza

'Time to pull down the blinds, Madam,' Jeffries said, leaning across the table to secure the blind for the blackout. The carriage had begun to take on the aroma of a gentlemen's lounge, or that of an intimate nightclub, languishing in a haze of smoke as the women relaxed with coffee and the men lit cigarettes, or, if very lucky, cigars Jeffries paused before leaving the table. His expression was one of uncomfortable doubt, like a sentence was struggling to form a tight hold in his head.

'Is everything all right, Jeffries?' asked Eliza, looking up at him.

'It's just that you usually retire to your cabin before coffee, Madam. But I was wondering if tonight ...'

Jeffries glanced from Eliza to Alex and back again.

'You're right, of course.' Eliza began to gather herself together. 'It really is time that I was ...'

Alex took charge and spoke to Jeffries directly.

'Ms Grey is doing me the great honour of making an exception to her usual routine this evening,' he said, his dark brown eyes offering kindness to Jeffries and yet casting a look that said that there was to be no room for discussion. 'Do you have brandy?'

'Yes, Sir.'

'Then please could we have a brandy each, one with ice …' He turned to Eliza. Eliza knew that the questioning glance was not to ask if she would mind staying in the dining carriage with him – that was a given – but simply to ascertain if she wanted ice with her brandy. Eliza turned to Jeffries.

'No ice for me, thank you,' she said, thinking, as Jeffries nodded and turned away, that it really was time to take a hold of this man, or if not the man, then the conversation, at least.

'I'm from London,' he said. 'Not that you've been wondering but I thought I would tell you anyhow.'

'Which part?'

'Belgravia – well, originally.'

The brow raise from Eliza was infinitesimal but it was there and Alex didn't miss it.

'You have just judged me, Ms Grey,' he said.

'You're right. I'm sorry. Although, in point of fact, I'm not sorry. Not really. Not a bit of it.'

Alex smiled, amused.

'Why? Why are you not sorry?'

'Because I didn't judge you at all. I made a snap decision about your background that is probably correct.'

'Which is?'

'That you were born into a wealthy family.'

'And you, Lady Arbuthnot, married into one.'

Eliza laughed. 'All right, you win,' she said. 'I did judge you, a little. And where do you live now?' she asked.

'Hampstead,' he said, dully.

A quick sip of coffee caught in her throat. 'Hampstead?'

Alex really did laugh out loud this time.

Eliza dropped her head. 'I just did it again, didn't I?'

Alex smiled sweetly at her. 'You did, rather.'

'I'm sorry, I just couldn't help it. I'm merely surprised, that's all. Hampstead is not usually the playground of men who come from a background of considerable wealth.'

'I like it there,' he said. 'It suits me. And the wealth was my father's, not mine. All such wealth has gone, along with my parents.'

'I'm sorry,' she said. 'You're an orphan too, then ...'

He laughed out loud and shook his head. 'No. They live in America. Father is in aluminium these days; he's trying to recoup a lost family fortune.'

'And you like your job?' she asked.

Alex took time to consider this. 'Yes, on the whole. It gives me a purpose for living, I suppose.'

Eliza, who had always felt her purpose for living was merely to wonder at the beauty of the world, found this to be a woeful statement.

'I fell into journalism before the war because of my sister – my twin, in fact.' At this, a devilish smile edged across his lips. It was a smile he was trying to hold in, Eliza saw, but no matter how hard he tried, it continued to spill out.

'Because of your sister?' she repeated.

'Yes. She's a reporter too. We're quite competitive, the two of us, although she is the more ambitious, for some reason.'

'Your sister is perhaps more ambitious because she is a woman and feels the need to prove herself in a man's world.'

'You are most certainly right,' he said.

'Would I know of her?' asked Eliza, smiling up at Jeffries, who had arrived with the brandy.

'Perhaps. Nora Levine,' he answered. 'She's the editor at *The Tribute*. You mentioned her earlier, I seem to recall ...'

His words hovered in the air between them until the penny dropped. A hand rushed to Eliza's mouth.

'Oh, of course!' She was unable to stifle a laugh. 'And I called her a dragon! I'm so sorry. Why didn't you say something earlier?'

Alex leant forwards across the table cloth and whispered, 'Because I think she's a bit of a dragon, too.' He sat back. 'But I'm grateful to her. She got me my first job, and then pushed me back into the throng after my spell in the RAF. And although she may be a dragon, I do respect her, mainly for her part in encouraging America into the war.'

'You make it sound as though she were singlehandedly responsible. I thought Pearl Harbor was the catalyst?'

Alex glanced at the cigarette in his hand. He seemed to consider it, then placed it on the ashtray. 'It was, but Nora had been working hard on ensuring that her stories made it past the censors in the States before that. No, she's a very good woman, deep down, if, as you say, a bit of a dragon.'

Who was this man, Eliza wondered? This man who was savagely blunt one moment and the epitome of humanity the next. The man with danger, kindness and despair in his eyes all at once. 'You're from a passionate family, then?' she asked.

'We're Jewish. Not that either my sister or myself are practising now, but the kinship is still there, pushing us on to do more.'

Eliza wasn't sure how to follow that. Sometimes, it was better to say nothing at all. Alex filled the gap.

'What's happening in Europe,' he said, 'not just to the Jews, but to anyone Hitler happens to regard as inconsequential vermin ...' He shook his head. 'How can we do anything but fight it? I'm not one of these sops who will gloss over a story for the sake of propaganda. For the sake of keeping everyone's chipper up!' His jaw, his face, his very soul, hardened.

Eliza looked down at her glass.

'By "sop", I take it you are referring to me and my propaganda art.'

He shook his head. 'I didn't say that.'

'You didn't need to, you already said it in your review.'

Alex took a deep breath. 'See here, I hadn't any wish to

offend, but we have family in Austria, friends in Germany, and have had not a word from any of them for over two years. I – we – don't want that watered down by press censorship or sickly propaganda posters.'

Eliza felt a knot in her stomach develop and tighten. 'I take it you don't agree with keeping public spirits high – through artistic media, for example – in order that we might strive to maintain a sense of national strength, a positive collective effort?' She no longer had difficulty meeting his gaze. She was proud of her artwork. It was iconic. It was cheery. It helped to motivate, to encourage, to keep the faith ...

'No, I don't,' he said. 'Do you?'

'Yes,' she answered, holding his gaze. 'I do. I have faith that ...' She glanced down at her mother's book.

'That?'

'That in the end, all shall be well, and I want others to feel that way, too.'

The couple on the table opposite were clearly enthralled. Eliza no longer cared.

'I'm sorry to correct you,' he said, his voice tired, his shoulders sagging now. 'But in my opinion, you're wrong, and I'm not exactly sure that in the end, whatever "the end" is, all actually shall be well, as you put it.'

'Look.' Eliza lowered her voice. 'It's already been a long war, and I won't apologise for choosing to be optimistic. I can't physically fight in the war, so my artwork and my other voluntary work are the best I can do. And trust me, after the things I've seen in London, the wounded I've tended, the ...' She stopped. It was the wounded and dead children that shattered her the most. She would not show this man her pain, her sorrow, her utter exhausted despair. She sat back. 'Let's just say that I think we owe it to the ones who are gone to stay as positive as possible.'

'So it's all going to turn out dandy and with your jolly posters you feel as though you are doing your bit.' He said it not as a question, but as a statement.

'It is, and I do.'

He shook his head and lit another cigarette, which hovered in his fingers by his mouth. He used it as a pointing tool.

'You've sold out,' he stated. 'That scene you painted ... the one in the hospital of the downed airman?'

Eliza held her breath.

'You painted the man in the bed like an angelic, peaceful hero. No pain, no tremors, no scream of despair. Just heroic valour.' He indicated the burnt side of his face and turned it towards her. 'Look at this!'

Eliza's immediate reaction was to look away.

'Look at it.' He said it quietly but she couldn't mistake the feeling behind it. '*This* is the ugly reality of war.'

Alex sat back in his seat, Eliza's silence acting as water on a flame.

'Propaganda is simply another word for censorship, which I abhor,' he said, quieter now. 'I do not agree with misinforming one's own people, with dampening down the truth. What I yearn for, so very much, is for everyone – correspondents, et cetera – to report the cold hard facts – no more, no less. To be informative but remain non-political, non-agenda-driven. To allow the public to make up their own minds about things, not to be manipulated. When I wrote that article about your artwork it was because I think that art, literature, film, the press – when used by a government office, I might add – have a responsibility to be non-agenda-driven.'

Eliza saw a big chink in his argument and aimed for it. 'I think you're being naïve,' she said, 'and hypocritical. What you're talking about is simply another form of censorship, which you disapprove of, apparently.'

Alex shook his head. 'You paint scenes to be used as propaganda posters. They are images of stoic people doing jolly well and keeping their spirits up. Let's everyone keep calm and carry on. Meanwhile, millions of Jews are being incarcerated, murdered. I don't want people to keep calm, Eliza, I want them to fight!'

'But that's what I want, too. And can't everyone do that more effectively when they have faith?' she asked, bitterly.

'Faith.' He spat out the word, but surprised her by suddenly putting down his cigarette, leaning across the table and taking her hand. 'Why don't you have a raging desire to truly make a difference with your art? Before the war you were a genre-defying artist of note. I remember seeing one of your exhibitions and I was blown away. Surely it is the responsibility of all artists to seek to make a difference during a time of crisis? To find that thing others cannot see. Something deeper than folly. To experience a single moment in history and capture the very essence of it – not a photographic reproduction, but the very essence, so that that moment lasts a lifetime, and when people look at the painting they don't just see it, Eliza, they feel it.'

'But if I see something in a different light to you – *feel* something in a different way – will you criticise me for it still? It seems to me that what you really want is for everyone to see the world through your eyes and your eyes only. Forget Hitler. Perhaps it is you who are the ultimate egomaniac?'

This last comment took the wind out of Alex's sails. He slumped back in his chair, the image of a confused and troubled man. Eliza was left with the feeling that the last thing he had really wanted to do was to offend, and yet hadn't she gone out of her way to wound him, too – to kick the dog that had bitten her? Eliza was about to offer a truce when Alex knocked back the rest of his drink, looked down at her wedding finger and said, 'Maybe you are too comfortable to desire any real ambition, Lady Arbuthnot.' He emphasised the 'Lady'.

Eliza was side-swiped. Criticism of her artwork she could take, she was used to it, she even enjoyed it. And the criticism of her pro-propaganda stance she could also endure, just about, but a direct question hitting at the heart of her marriage, she could not – would not – tolerate.

It was too close to the bone. Too close to the rub of why she was here. She stood, put on her gloves and glanced down at him.

'Sir, you have said and drunk far too much. It is best, I think, if I leave you to your empty glass. It will, no doubt, be filled up again very quickly.' She stepped into the aisle. He grabbed her arm. She ignored the desperate expression on his face. 'Do you know something, Mr Levine,' she began. 'When I look at people I can see an aura of colour around them, I can't help it. It's like I can see their emotions displayed in a visual sense right before my eyes. It is the colour of the aura that subsequently dominates my paintings. I won't apologise for the fact that I don't like it when I see the dark shades around people as I go about my day, which is why, sometimes, I improvise – I turn their faces towards the light. When I look at you, all I see is darkness. A darkness so deep that even I could not lighten the pain within the portrait – or the grief. These are strange times and you have suffered a great deal. I am very sorry that you are experiencing all of this horror with such deep anger, but there is absolutely no need to take it out on me, or my work.'

Alex had no answer. The anger in his eyes had been replaced with a nothingness that did not award Eliza any pleasure.

'We have all experienced horror of some sort. You say my artwork should be more real ... I have seen enough of this so-called "real" life as a nurse in London to last me a lifetime. Why do you think I run to Cornwall? To get away from reality, just for a moment. To have a second to not be overcome with the strain of it all. And yes, I am privileged, and you no doubt think spoiled, to be able to do this – I think that myself – but if I don't go to Cornwall, if I don't try to cling on to a last breath of optimism, I will go under. I am weakened to the point of giving up – giving in – by this war, but I know that I cannot. And yes, I would like to become one of the strong women in my book, and I chide myself every day that I do not have their courage, their bravery, their stamina. I try to be more than I am constantly, but I never seem to meet my own expectations. I do not, therefore, need you to tell me of my weaknesses, my failings, because I am already more than aware of them myself. Maybe if you saw it as vulnerability rather than weakness, you would have more compassion, more heart, more understanding of others who fail to reach the bar that you have set so high. You said that you appreciate F. Scott Fitzgerald. So do I. You may recall that he also wrote, "To be kind is more important than to be right". Kindness is all that matters. It's the only thing to remember to be. I simply believe that if you are kind, then all of that kindness builds up in the universe and then one day, when you need that kindness to be returned the most, it will come back to you in abundance and probably from the least expected source. And now I am cross with myself because I am not, perhaps, being kind to you, but as I say, I am flawed.'

Eliza did not hesitate before walking away. She had spoken far too much and had not given him a single second to interrupt. Had she given herself a moment to consider, however, she would have realised – as she did later – that the anger in her speech, which she abhorred, was directed at herself as much as at Alex, because everything Alex had said about her work, Eliza thought already and simply hadn't wanted to admit to it. In chiding Alex she was really chiding herself, telling herself that she was more than the woman that appeared before her. Alex had merely acted as the means of holding up the mirror. She might also have remembered to pick up her book, which by the time she reached her cabin and had locked the door behind her, was in the hands of a terribly sad and most repentant man. A man who did not order himself another brandy, as he usually would, but who sat alone in the dining carriage for the rest of the night, a frayed embroidered bookmark with an optimistic quote written across it in his left hand, a book about adventurous women in his right, while occasionally looking up from the text deep in thought, glancing at the bookmark and the empty seat across from him and remembering the vision in green who had filled his heart with joy.

Chapter 7

An omnibus dropped Eliza in the village of St Buryan, a couple of miles short of the tiny fishing cove of Penberth, where Eliza's cottage, Meadowsweet, was situated. Her front door was only a few marching paces from a cobbled slipway, a slipway that hurtled brightly painted fishing boats into a turquoise sea. She travelled the rest of the way on the back of old Mr Pengelly's cart, Mr Pengelly – better known as Uncle Bill, although they shared no relation – having been telegrammed to expect her arrival by the first omnibus departing Penzance that morning.

It was a beautiful day and Eliza's shoulders began to relax as the morning sun seeped into her aching, sleep-deprived limbs. After her quarrel with Alex, there was no possibility of sleeping on the train. She stifled a yawn as the old carthorse, Teddy, clip-clopped his way down the meandering lane to the cove. Stone hedges sprinkled with wildflowers flanked the lane and were particularly lovely this spring, with pink campions, wild garlic and ground lilacs all offering the perfect welcoming bouquet. Eliza smiled as she reached out a hand now and again to collect a flower, only to then be handed an actual posy by Mrs Cardew, the flower farmer who lived at the entrance to the hamlet, who had been watching out for Eliza for over an hour.

But Eliza's broadest smile was reserved for the moment she passed Mrs Gwennap's thatched cottage and the pretty stream and stepping stones of her childhood came into view.

Penberth.

She took a deep breath and sighed.

Home.

Eliza spent several hours busying herself, flitting between airing the place, sorting through a food parcel collected in town with her ration coupons (and the little extras of vegetables supplied by Mrs Cardew) and catching up with welcoming neighbours. It was all exactly the same and exactly as it should be. Her neighbour's lobster pots and a collection of bright orange buoys were scattered, as they always were, outside her house on the cobbles. The front door – the blue paint flaking now – was flanked by large sash windows, which was unusual for such a small cottage. Inside, the staircase located directly in front of the door led to two bedrooms upstairs, while to the left led to a light, airy kitchen that ran the length of the house, with windows front and back. The door to the right of the entrance led to a pretty lounge, not so light as the kitchen, but all the cosier for it, especially when the fire was lit. The windows to the front faced out across the cobbled cove, perfectly situated to watch the comings and goings of the fishermen and their families.

In the late afternoon, dressed in faded blue dungarees and with her hair held back with a powder-blue headscarf, Eliza pushed the pine kitchen table out of the way and pulled up a chair to sit at the front window. Arthur – Lord Arbuthnot – had given her a gift of a new leather-bound journal when she had last spent time with him – which was so long ago now she could barely remember it – and she had begun to keep a record of the war (better late than never), but since she was more of an artist than a writer, the journal was soon filled with sketches rather than words. She intended to return to the sketch of the poplar trees from the train, but her mind, drifting all by itself without any help from Eliza, turned to Alex, and the pencil hovered above the page as if looking up at her and waiting for instruction as to what to sketch. She stared at the page and saw nothing but his face.

'Come on, Eliza,' she said aloud. 'Alex Levine is not a man of consequence and so his opinion is certainly of no consequence. And your life is all the better for knowing that.'

She decided that it would perhaps be better to begin the journal with a new painting not associated with the train. Yes, she would paint the posy of wildflowers, which she had plonked quite haphazardly in a green jug and which was looking all the prettier for the lack of fuss. She fished a nib of charcoal from a little tin box, but then glanced out of the window and became distracted by activity on the slip. A lugger, a Cornish fishing boat, was being hauled out of the sea and pulled up the cobbled slip by means of the capstan. A handful of men and women pushed on the levers, walking in slow, steady circles, while pulling the boat up the slip. Eliza loved watching this simple symbiosis at work; it was both soothing and comforting at once to know that, in this frightening world of change and confusion, in a tiny corner of England, everything remained exactly as it was. She focused on the paper, but her mind's eye returned once again to last evening, and rather than draw flowers, Eliza began to sketch a face.

Alex's face.

She sat back and laughed. 'Eliza Grey, you are such a fool!' she said to herself, looking closely at the few lines she had sketched already – his jawline, the beginnings of a brow, a trace of his eyes – realising she was sketching the burnt side, rather than the untarnished, youthful one. She put down the charcoal, her thoughts drifting to what horrors Alex must have witnessed during his time as a Spitfire pilot in the RAF.

She had been at a field hospital near Dover during the worst days of the Battle of Britain in September 1940. One day she painted a sky scene of aircraft in a dogfight being waged over the English Channel, where lines of aircraft contrails drew squiggles in the sky like a child's doodle.

The fight ended as it always ended – badly – with twisted, burning metal and some poor man, whatever his nationality, either trapped inside a fated aircraft or floating under a parachute. It was after one such parachute appeared that she packed up her easel and headed to the hospital, where she managed to gain access to a ward as a Home Front War Artist. She painted a man lying unconscious in a hospital bed, his face bandaged. He was a man expected to die very shortly but, with the use of much light, she had brought him back to life in her portrait. After painting his soul rejoicing in great beams of beautiful light, she had sat next to his bedside all through the night and rested one of her warm hands on one of his cold ones. The next day, when he woke, she smiled at him, placed a kiss on his forehead and walked away.

It was the criticism of this scene by Alex that had hurt Eliza the most. She had never, in all of her life, met such an arrogant, self-opinionated, curt and, quite frankly, rude individual as Alexander Levine. 'And God willing,' she said in a mutter, picking up the charcoal and progressing with his jaw, 'I shall never lay eyes on the damn foolish man again!'

Which was when there was a knock at the door.

'Hallo.'

It was Alex, a book tucked under his arm, a straw sun hat in one hand, a posy of flowers in the other, a contrite look on his face. 'I was inexcusably rude last night.'

Eliza put a hand to her hair in horror.

He was here. At her house. On her step.

And she looked a complete fright!

'If it was inexcusable ...' she said, rallying, but doing that thing people sometimes do only to regret it later: unnecessarily perpetuating an argument for the sake of it when they already have the upper hand '... then why are you here?'

So much for kindness, she thought.

He tried to hand her the flowers, but they were left hanging. His body language remained repentant, his smile incorrigible. 'You left this behind on the train, too,' he said, showing her the book. 'I thought the bookmark in particular might be special to you.' He took out the book-mark and read the quote written down the length of it. '"*And all shall be well*." I see where you got the idea from now. It's very ... you.'

Eliza didn't speak. He was here. Holding her book. Reading her bookmark. She was delighted and immensely annoyed in equal measure – although the delight edged ahead by a nose, perhaps. She had forgotten all about the book – her mother's special book! – until after she left the train and had resolved to contact the relevant lost property department, but here it was, with him, standing in her doorway.

He handed over the book, which she took, and then the posy, which she also took.

'I was assured by the woman up the lane there that

these are your favourites.' He nodded towards the posy. 'Odd name for a flower, though. A bit macabre, if you ask me. What is it again? Bleeding love, or something ...'

'Love Lies Bleeding,' she said, glancing past him up the lane. Kindness was all well and good, Eliza thought, but she had a reputation to uphold locally and now rumours would be rife about Eliza receiving flowers from a man that was not her husband.

Alex began to edge forwards in the manner that a lion tamer might approach an injured animal, leaving Eliza in the unusual situation of being both delighted to see him but cross nonetheless from the conversation on the train, the fallout from which still clung onto all the exposed parts of him like sticky buds. The light around him, she noticed now, was lighter and edged with gold, although that was probably the sun, which was beginning to filter in through the door. The combination of the book, the posy and the contrite manner left her with no option but to say, 'Do come in.'

Eliza ushered him into the kitchen, closing the door behind her, but not before looking out into the cove to see if anyone was watching. She tipped paintbrushes out of a jam jar, refilled it with water from her drinking jug, and placed the flowers very carefully inside. She smiled at them, the happy little flowers, her back to Alex, her heart prancing like a giddy child. Moving the other jug of flowers out of the way, she placed the new posy in the middle of the table.

Alex was looking at the sketch in her journal, left open on the windowsill.

'Interesting sketch,' he said.

Eliza looked up from the flowers and froze. Damn! The sketch was clearly of him! The only thing to do was brazen the thing out. She joined him at the windowsill.

'Yes, it is,' she said, offering no more by way of explanation.

'And what will you call this one, do you think?' he asked, his eyes still transfixed on his own portrait.

Eliza felt a sudden urge to be very naughty. 'It's difficult to know,' she said. 'I'm not overly familiar with the subject. Perhaps ... *Insufferable Arrogance?*'

Alex laughed. He turned his gaze from the sketch to Eliza. 'Perhaps if you become more familiar with the subject, a more fitting title will come to you ...'

There was a holding of breath, then. A pause between two people of the like Eliza had only read about. There are moments in life at the beginnings of things when looking at each other is too much; this was such a moment.

Alex turned to look at the sketch again. 'I painted a very poor picture of myself yesterday,' he said, touching the paper gently. 'From the moment I sat down I was edgy and opinionated. I'm not sure what I was trying to prove.' He looked up. 'All I can say in my defence is that I was not expecting company – especially company that ...' He paused. 'Let's just say that I tried to impress you, but the wine, the brandy and my own bloody-mindedness turned me into a damn silly fool, and for that I am truly, truly sorry.' He nodded towards his portrait. 'I hope that, sometime soon, you will be able to paint this miserable fellow in a better light.'

Eliza hesitated. In her heart she wanted to say, 'I hope so, too', but it would encourage discourse, and she really oughtn't to encourage discourse. Friendship with this man could – would – lead her down a dangerous road. She was married. She had decisions to make and she needed absolutely no complications right now.

'It's certainly a pretty cottage,' he said, wandering to the back of the room to look out of a window, which faced onto a small rear garden where vegetables once grew but was now covered over with grass and weeds. 'And I love the colours,' he added, turning around to take in the room and the contrasting shades of French green, ochre and light yellow Eliza had used to decorate some of the walls and furniture. 'It's so wonderfully peaceful here.'

An ornate little clock sat on the windowsill. Alex picked it up.

'Is it really three-fifteen?' he asked, looking at his watch and then back at the clock. 'I make it closer to four.' He put down the clock and tapped his watch.

Eliza left her perch on the opposite window and joined him.

'I found it in the rubble during the worst of the Blitz. I painted it.'

'But I know that painting!' he said. 'You called it *The*

End of Time. It was frightfully good, more like your older ...' He paused.

'The hands must have stopped when the bomb hit,' she said.

He picked up the clock, an intricate thing and turned it over in his hands. 'London has been really rather bloody, hasn't it?'

With his words, a kaleidoscope of London scenes ran windmills in Eliza's mind. Death, destruction, blind fear, desolation ... some she had painted, some she had not.

'It's been a living hell,' she agreed.

'And yet you stayed.'

Eliza nodded. 'I stayed, but I'm afraid the only way I've found to deal with the horror of it all – to come to terms with all the waste – is to either paint it or run away from it.' She shrugged and smiled. 'There goes the story of my life.'

Alex crossed the room towards her. 'See here, I'm sorry, again, for what I said – what I wrote – about your work ...' He ran a hand through his hair. 'I've not been myself, and that painting you did of the downed airman ... I've lost so many friends, you see. So many good men gone, and I just found it to be far too ... well, far too optimistic. They died terrible deaths and I would know. I watched it happen while waiting for it to happen to me.'

Despite herself, Eliza placed a hand gently on his arm.

'But back to that little clock of yours!' he said. 'Wouldn't you like to get it fixed?'

Eliza dropped her hand and considered this. 'Yes, and no. Time is an irrelevance to me when I'm in Cornwall. I quite like the fact that I live my day by the rising and setting of the sun, by the movement of the tides.' It was Eliza's turn to pick up the clock. 'Mother would have asked Father to fix it, though, if she were here. I'd like to think so, anyhow. Mrs Cardew says that Mother was a stickler for keeping good time and having things *just so*.'

Alex rested his back against a larder cabinet. 'You remember them?' he asked.

She shook her head. 'Nothing more than a flash of a memory, the occasional image that has probably been embroidered by time. The way I remember them now is more a feeling than an image – a feeling of security, of being wanted ... loved, which seems better somehow than an actual image. I try to convey a similar feeling in my paintings ... in my earlier work, I mean, and the work I do privately.'

Alex allowed Eliza the space to keep talking.

'I want to stimulate the viewer's senses. I want them to be equally, if not more, aroused by my interpretation of the subject than if they saw the scene for real themselves. I don't want my artwork to be a photograph, but a *feeling*, although I think a clever photograph can – does – produce very emotive feelings, too.'

She edged towards the door. He was asking questions again, leading her in, and she mustn't be encouraged. Having Alex in her Cornish home was confusing. He was both a perfect stranger and incredibly familiar all at the same time.

'Thank you again for the flowers,' she said, arriving at the door and smiling up at him. 'You're staying with ...?'

'The Trewiddens? At Black Gate Farm?'

She nodded her familiarity with the place. 'Is that how you found out where I live? Were your detective skills put to good use after all?'

Alex laughed. 'Not at all. You told me, remember? The last house in the hamlet. And also ... your address is written on the inside of the book cover.' He picked up the book from the table and opened the front cover. 'See. "*This book is presented to Eliza Grey. Meadowsweet Cottage, Penberth, on the event of her seventh birthday*."'

Eliza smiled at the thought of her mother's neat handwriting. 'I'm grateful to you for returning it,' she said. 'Truly.'

Alex lay the book on the table and joined her in the doorway. 'Do you mind that I came, really?'

Eliza stepped outside. 'As I say, thank you for returning the book. It was very kind of you.' Alex didn't move. He just scratched his head, thinking.

'You see, the thing is,' he began, 'I was hoping that you would come for a walk with me ... show me your favourite places? There's lots left of the day. And it is a lovely day.'

Eliza bit her lip.

'Only, I should so very much like to show you that I'm actually quite a decent chap. You could call it research ...' He nodded towards the kitchen. 'For the portrait.'

Eliza blushed slightly.

He rested a hand gently on her arm. 'Mightn't we be friends?'

She wanted to say, 'Oh, all right. We can be the best of friends and I'd love to come!' But it was impossible. Simply impossible.

'I'm afraid my husband ...'

'Wouldn't know,' Alex finished for her. There was a pause then. A definite moment of acceptance that this was, or could be, something more than friendship, although his following words denied it. 'It's only a walk to the beach after all,' he said with a shrug.

'Even so,' she said, 'Arthur wouldn't understand, and ...' She was about to say, 'He's such a dear old thing, and I owe him a great deal ...' but stopped herself. Such placid words would show the reality of her relationship with Arthur and she left the sentence unfinished. 'I'm sorry, Alex,' she said, 'but I think it's best that you go.'

The use of his first name seemed merely to add to his determination to stay, however. 'You said you had come to Cornwall to make some decisions,' he began. 'I think I know what those decisions are about.'

She shook her head. 'No,' she said, glancing up the lane once again. 'You don't.'

'Only, one hears rumours,' he went on, 'especially in my profession. Your husband is a recluse. He's hidden himself away in Scotland for the duration of the war. He took you with him but you came back to London. To paint, to volunteer as a nurse, when you could have hidden away in safety … why?'

Why, why did he push her so? And oh, how she did so want to grab her sun hat, leave the door ajar and run out into the lovely Cornish breeze with this enigmatic stranger. Would it really be so very bad to forget her responsibilities and do just that, just this once?

'Thank you again for the flowers,' she said, 'but I really do need to get on.'

Alex stepped out into the sunshine and put on his hat. He began to walk away but turned back to face her. 'If I could turn back time, just for twenty-four hours,' he said, 'I would make every second on that train count. I wouldn't have been an ass. I wouldn't have tried to impress you. As soon as I sat down I would have told you how beautiful you are. I would have told you that the very sight of you took my breath away. We would have talked all night about beautiful things, optimistic things, wonderful things. We would have gotten that Jeffries fellow to sing and we would have danced in the aisle all evening. Life is clearly a wonderful thing to you, and I bitterly regret chiding you for it. For the past couple of years I've become nothing more than a bitter, cynical and judgemental man, but since last night … I wish – I do so wish – I could have the chance to show you the man that I would like to be – the man I can be.'

And with that he walked away, leaving Eliza to slowly, silently, close the door.

Chapter 8

The following morning, dressed and ready for the day, Eliza walked into the kitchen and put some water on to boil for washing. She picked up her journal absently and looked at the sketch of Alex, which was now a little further along. The morning sun began to refract light through a small crystal elephant, a trinket of her mother's, across the room. All the colours of the rainbow arched towards the sketch in her hand. Eliza shook her head and smiled. Was Alex to be her pot of gold, she wondered? She poured herself a glass of milk and glanced at the sketch again. How unbearably embarrassing. To be caught 'in the act', as it were, thinking of him, and so intimately as to sketch a portrait. She must have seemed quite mad. But wasn't she, just a little bit?

She shook her head. These thoughts were not the thoughts she had come to Cornwall to ponder over. Eliza had other decisions to make – decisions about her marriage, her career, her whole future. She had come so far, she couldn't let everything slip through her fingers now.

After the death of her parents, Eliza had been 'taken in' by distant relatives who lived in a cramped terraced house on a busy street in Penzance. The house operated with an atmosphere of constant anxiety, dominated by the bad temper of an older son who was far too fond of the sauce and quick to raise a hand. Eliza's prospects had never looked particularly rosy, but she had one advantage over her foster siblings (two of each) that would prove to be her ticket out of there – her love of art. Mrs Kelly (two doors down and a landlady in her own right) had no children, but she did have a vast collection of books and loved to draw and paint. Eliza, benefitting from the looser rein a younger child has, especially living with an exhausted guardian who had no maternal fondness for her foster child whatsoever, spent many hours sitting in Mrs Kelly's parlour, which was a dusty place with red velvet swags and aspidistras everywhere. Eliza devoured just the kind of books a young girl with a vivid imagination ought to devour – and some she probably oughtn't have – and she sketched and painted too. Oh, how she sketched and painted.

With the benefit of natural beauty combined with immense artistic talent on her side, Eliza was awarded a scholarship with the Newlyn School of Art and very quickly blossomed into the golden girl of the Cornish art scene, which was where she had met her future husband, Arthur Arbuthnot, a Scottish Lord and peer of the realm, who was a benefactor at the school (and almost three times her age). They married quickly and before long he whisked her off to his house in London and introduced her to all the right people. From that moment on he had managed her career to perfection, ensuring that her artwork was on show at all the best galleries. By the time she was twenty-five, Eliza Grey was the artist's name on everyone's lips.

It was a marriage of intellects rather than a marriage of great love or passion, but in those early days she hadn't minded so much. Arthur was not demanding physically, nor did he expect her to devote much of her time to his attention. Art was everything – everything – to Eliza. Not sex, not passion, not youth. And in marrying Arthur, a man she genuinely did love, she had secured herself the means by which to have the freedom to paint without worrying about working in any other way. In marrying Eliza, Arthur had secured for himself a project, a pleasing trinket on his arm, and a nurse for his old age, which was not too far away. The situation worked well for both of them. But when the bombs began to fall on London, Arthur, who was of a fragile disposition, fled to his Scottish castle for safety while Eliza, who wanted to do her part for the war effort, volunteered as a nurse and was commissioned as a Home Front War Artist, staying behind in town. Arthur returned to London now and again as the war progressed, but not often, and these days it seemed to Eliza that she was living an entirely separate and utterly liberated life.

The War Artists Advisory Committee had been chasing

after Eliza since the outset of the conflict. Determined to concentrate on her nursing role, however, she agreed to produce just a few 'women on the home front' pieces to promote the role of women in the war effort. But Eliza soon learned to love – relish, really – her work for the committee and realised that she had a unique opportunity to empower future generations of women by encouraging them to really grasp the nettle in a way she never had; not really, not independently. Her success as an artist before the war took on a bittersweet taste knowing that, without the patronage of her husband, it was unlikely that she would ever have been discovered. She was realistic enough to know that this was the way of the world, but at the same time felt the need to encourage a rebalance, especially now. She also felt a desperate need to find the humanity, the courage, the colour and the love in the war, and put it all down on canvas. And until Alex's review of her work was published, she had thought herself to be doing a good job. Now ... she wasn't so sure.

Yes, she had painted the propaganda posters that the government eventually persuaded her to paint (having someone as talented and famous as Eliza Grey designing and painting their posters had been somewhat of a boon) but now, with the War Artists Advisory Committee, a new opportunity had been offered that both thrilled and petrified Eliza to the core. The committee thought that Eliza might consider taking a new post overseas – as a bona fide war artist. She would be the first woman artist to follow along with the troops after an invasion – when they would (hopefully) liberate France.

The thought of such an opportunity was frightening ... but thrilling. She didn't know if she had the mettle for it, and there was Arthur to consider, of course. Lady Arbuthnot had a reputation as an eternal optimist, keeping everyone's jolly spirits up singlehandedly, but Eliza Grey was a lonely, saddened woman who had never known real passion in her life, and who wanted – oh so very, very much – to laugh and dance and sing and have the courage to make a real difference, to be like the women in her book. Alex had said that it was never too late to step out of one role if it no longer fit. But what about Arth—

No, she wouldn't finish that sentence. Eliza glanced around the kitchen, her home. Alex had loved it here, felt at home here, *looked* at home here ...

And after all, he had only asked her for a walk ...

Pushing Arthur into the deepest closed-off section of her mind, Eliza – buzzing suddenly with a kind of frenetic energy – grabbed paper and a pencil and scribbled a note:

Please meet me at Porthcurno Beach at 3.15 today. Time does not exist here, except for 3.15 (ask the clock). We can meet, therefore, as friends in a separate space and time without any feelings of guilt or reference to regret. Eliza.

Not allowing herself a moment to reconsider, Eliza rushed out of the door and headed up the lane to where she knew she would find the perfect messenger – Mrs Cardew's grandson. The note and a halfpenny were promptly pressed into his hands with instructions to deliver the note immediately to the man with the scar staying at Trewidden's Farm, and to run. Run like the clappers until his heart felt fit to burst!

At two forty-five, a halfpenny the poorer and wearing her nicest Oxford bag trousers, a pretty check blouse, a woollen cardigan and stout shoes, Eliza grabbed her sunhat, journal and pencil, and set out for the beach.

Chapter 9

While scrambling up the coastal path heading away from Penberth, Eliza paused now and again to take in the view and to catch her breath. The path, a familiar friend, weaved its way past wind-ravaged hawthorn thickets and around the headland, the Atlantic Ocean constantly in view far below to the left. Eliza glanced at her watch as Porthcurno Beach came into view ahead – 3 p.m. A sudden feeling of terror combined with the thrill of the possibility that Alex might be there caused her to stop and consider for a moment. She stared down at the beach, a triangle of pure white sand, fine as dust, each grain precious as a diamond. The triangle broadened towards the sea, away from the village, which was flanked by high rocks. It was the unique colour of the sand that gave the sea such a special shade of blue, and the light helped too. Such a soft and gentle light that added a warm and cosy filter to the landscape, to the people.

When away from Cornwall, Eliza often yearned for this romanticised idea of home. The wild blue sea, the gothic moors, the timeless farmsteads, the Celtic stone crosses littering the roadsides, the characterful people living uncomplicated lives working the land or fishing the sea ... They were all right here at the edge of the world, carrying on. As she rounded the corner and looked down towards Porthcurno she saw the distinct whitewashed buildings of the Telegraph Station and School. Porthcurno wasn't simply a beautiful beach, it was the main telegraph cable hub for the whole of Great Britain. Nearly all of the telegraph cables that crossed the Atlantic made landfall at Porthcurno. It was where news of the war – the good, the bad, the political, the intensely personal – became real by being printed onto tape in the big white building she currently overlooked. Since the invention of the telegraph, millions of messages had passed through those cables under the sea. So many truths, so many lies, so many stories had washed ashore, stories of great battles, of loves lost, of loves won. She had painted the beach many times – the beach of messages – imagining the thick steel cables arriving from far out to sea, running aground like electric eels beneath the white sand and all that information pulsing along them. It was a never-ending stream of dots and dashes, to be passed through a machine and, in turn, interpreted by men and, increasingly, by women. Women who would have read messages of such tragic news over the course of the war so far. Try as she might, she couldn't help imagining the postman walking down the lane, or road, or farm track, or city street with a black-edged telegram in his hand, ultimately handing over terrible news to a loved one. News that had travelled under vast oceans to be handed to a poor woman (it was always a woman) who would see the telegram in the postman's hand, and fall to her knees, her hand clutched to her chest, wailing. At least, that was how Eliza always imagined it.

But there were, she reminded herself, considerably more messages of love floating around under the oceans than people realised, which buoyed her. It was the light to brighten the darkness. The good news story to balance the bad. To Eliza, the telegraph was nothing short of magic, and the telegraph operators, with their dials and tape and dots and dashes, were the magicians, working tirelessly while surrounded by the beautiful light that Cornwall was famous for.

With such positive thoughts in mind, Eliza turned a final corner on the cliff tops. As she began her descent towards the beach there was a renewed skip in her step – and a growing flutter in her stomach.

But her heart fell to her boots when the beach came into better focus. Two impenetrable fences, with rolls of barbed wire running along the top of them, ran along the entrance to the beach, and a concrete gunning pillbox had been built into the rockface on the far cliff. Even worse, a line of ugly machines were stretched right across the beach, a series of black scorch marks fanning out in the sand in front of the machines.

'Flamethrowers,' murmured Eliza.

The whole beach was now clearly off limits to the public and it was at this point that she saw him.

Alex.

He was on the beach, on the far side, beyond the flame-throwers, arranging a blanket as if he were on Brighton Beach. Next to him was a basket and a very large umbrella.

'Well, I'll be!' she said, shaking her head in amusement. How on earth had he gained access? She looked along the length of the beach. The only way on was via a barrier, which was guarded by a sentry. Eliza concluded that Alex must have simply asked to be allowed entry – as a war correspondent, perhaps? Deciding to be equally as brazen, Eliza straightened herself up, took out her identification papers, marched down the path, approached the sentry guard and began to speak ...

Which proved fruitless.

The sentry said he didn't care who she was, or where she lived, or what she 'bloody well painted'. The beach was far too dangerous a place for any 'daft woman' and she wasn't getting on, not on his watch.

Eliza hid her frustration and walked on along the ugly fence that ran across the back of the dunes at the edge of the beach, swinging her arms with her straw hat in her hand as if simply out for an afternoon stroll, while looking back now and again to see if the guard was watching. He wasn't. She followed the footpath around the perimeter of the beach.

It was just at the moment when the path began to

meander away from the beach and she was about to give up hope when she heard a 'Psst!' coming from the dunes behind the fence. Alex was poking his head out from behind a dune beyond the wire. 'Go a little way further up the path,' he said, in a sort of half-shouted whisper. He gestured with his hand as if batting off a fly. 'There's a gap in the wire. You'll be able to get through along there.'

Eliza glanced up the hill longingly, then down towards the sentry, and finally back at Alex.

'But what if we get caught?' she asked in a whisper, her eyes both laughing and fearful.

Alex laughed. 'Then we get caught. Come on, it's your special beach, you said so yourself, and I've got a surprise for you, so do hurry up!'

What to do?

Arthur, who had been nothing more than a shadowy translucence during her walk along the cliff path from Penberth, would become a solid apoplectic lunatic if she were to be caught on a forbidden beach and subsequently summonsed by the police. The disgrace! But dear Arthur wasn't here, Alex was, and she felt an overpowering sensation of needing to burst out, to be young and bloody well free of it all.

Eliza threw her hat and journal over the fence towards Alex before laughing out loud and scampering up the road, where she quickly found the gap in the fence. Two minutes later, with her trousers rolled to the knee and her shoes and stockings in her hands, she stood on a dune looking down at Alex, on the beach, who was smiling up at her with equal amounts of joy. She looked at her watch. Three-fifteen.

'You came,' he said.

She nodded, holding up a hand to the sunlight. 'I came,' she repeated softly.

No other explanation was given or necessary.

The surprise was the picnic. Eliza was appropriately surprised and delighted. Alex reached a hand across the blanket. 'Let's start again,' he said. 'I'm Alex Levine, and I'm really very pleased to meet you. And you are?'

Eliza, with her newfound desire to accept his badinage and to run with it, but also determined to begin again as herself – not as Lady Arbuthnot, not in the fake role she had played out on the train – held out her hand and said, 'I'm Eliza Grey. And I'm really very pleased to meet you, too!'

Alex began to open the picnic hamper, looking, if Eliza wasn't much mistaken, a little nervous. 'I've rustled up a few eats,' he said, 'thanks to my landlady, and there's some lemonade, too ...' He glanced up. 'Or there's tea in a flask, if you would prefer?'

'Lemonade would be lovely,' she said. 'Can I help at all?'

Alex shook his head. 'No, no, just enjoy the scenery.' He glanced along the beach. 'Not the blasted flamethrowers, of course. They're dreadful, so perhaps position yourself

to look the other way – wistfully – it will match the ambi-
ence.'

Eliza laughed again, equally joyful, happily shaded underneath the umbrella, while Alex, a smile on his face, fussed
with the general preparation of the picnic. She was happy
to glance out to sea as a distraction, because Alex Levine
was looking particularly dashing today in casual slacks, a
short-sleeved shirt and a jaunty hat. He had positioned
himself on purpose, she knew, to her right, so that she could
see the unmarked left side of his face, but he needn't have
bothered. The burn on Alex's face meant nothing to Eliza
– that's not how she saw people. Eliza saw beauty in people's
light, and today, the sun having caught him already, the man
seemed to positively shimmer.

'Shall we get into serious trouble, do you think?' asked
Eliza, unfolding bread and butter from a napkin and
popping it onto a plate.

'Well now, that all depends.'

Eliza cocked her head to one side. 'Depends? On what
exactly?'

'On whether or not you're a spy. The sergeant on the gate
said that some suspicious characters have been roaming
around the place, trying to get onto the beach ... and I've a
feeling that you might just come under such a category.'

Eliza laughed out loud. 'Me? A spy? In this blouse?
Surely a spy would wear a Mackintosh?'

Alex flipped the lid of a glass bottle of lemonade and
began to pour.

'A Mackintosh?' he repeated, handing her a glass. 'No. That's the last thing a spy would wear.'

'Well, it all seems a little clandestine to me, but anyhow ...' She raised her glass. 'Bottoms up!'

Alex laid out the rest of the picnic while he offered happy-go-lucky anecdotes of his memories of Cornwall.

'Do tuck in,' he said, offering Eliza a china plate with a pretty flower pattern around the edge. 'I wanted to bring a gramophone with me, too, but my landlady said the plan was starting to "border on the ridiculous".'

'Wouldn't the music have given the game away, rather?'

Alex laughed. 'Yes,' he said, 'I suppose it would have.'

Eliza watched a plover land on a stretch of barbed wire and dart off again. The conversation bobbed along easily, naturally.

'Your landlady must be very fond of you,' she said. 'There's quite a chunk out of a ration book here. It's Mrs Trewidden, isn't it? Up in Lamorna?'

'Yes, marvellous woman. She's the mother of an old RAF pal of mine ... That's how I first came to know about this place. He invited me for Christmas – two Christmases in a row, in fact – '39 and '40.'

'That was good of him, but I suppose you all became very close on the squadron. And where is he now?' Eliza picked up her lemonade again. It was all such a perfect treat.

'I'm afraid we lost him in '41.'

Eliza could have bitten out her tongue. 'I'm so sorry.

How foolish of me to ask. But how lovely that you still visit his family.'

Alex picked up a sandwich. 'Yes, I've found a kind of second family with them. And I love it on the farm. It's odd but I feel that Peter – my old pal – wants me to come up here. I always make sure a great parcel of as much food as I can lay my hands on is sent up ahead of me on the train ...' The sandwich hovered by his mouth. 'So you needn't worry that you're taking food from the mouths of babes.'

Eliza picked up a fork and helped herself to some fish. 'And I suppose pilchards are more plentiful around here than elsewhere just now ...' She was getting into the spirit of enjoying the food and the beach without guilt, pushing all thoughts of the war and other inconveniences right out of her mind. 'The fishermen in my cove still have a huer. Isn't that wonderful?'

'I have no idea what a huer is.'

Eliza screwed her glass into the sand to prevent it from toppling over. 'Ah, right. Well, here's something to tell you about. A huer is a clifftop lookout. It's the person who cries out when he – or she – spots a pilchard shoal. The cry goes out, "Hevva! Hevva!" It's wonderful.' She looked down the length of the beach and sighed. 'That's what this place should be like, full of fisherman and their families, or children enjoying a lovely day on the beach, not barbed wire, or scorched black sand and gunning towers.'

Alex topped up her lemonade. 'Now, none of that,' he

said, 'not today. I've taken a leaf out of your book. And today is a day I've set aside only for optimism and good cheer!'

'*You* have?' she said, doubtfully.

He nodded his answer.

'The man who only wants the world to be real? No fake good cheer?' she went on.

'That was yesterday,' he said. 'Today, I'm a new man.' He edged his way out of the shade of the umbrella, rested on his elbows and tilted his face towards the sun. 'No, I'm in Cornish holiday mode now. It only ever takes me half a day to get back into the swing of it. The sun is out. The sea is blue. I'm wearing my very dashing new sunhat – what do you think of it? Dapper?'

Eliza laughed. 'Very dapper.'

'We're in heaven, Eliza Grey, and one can only be perfectly happy in heaven – if not, what's the point of it?' He sat up again and bit a strawberry in half. 'Now then, tell me more about this cove of yours ...'

And she did, at length and with great enthusiasm until summarising with, 'Basically, it's the most magical place on earth. You've seen it so you must agree, surely?'

Alex repositioned himself to lie on his front in the sand. 'I have and I do. Tell me more about the fishing.'

Eliza examined the rest of the picnic to choose her next bite. 'Well, they go out early each day from the slip – it's mainly mackerel and crab now, rather than pilchards – and the lobster pots go out, of course, but the valley that runs down to the cove is special too because of the flower farm. I pop up there quite often with my paints. What else is there to tell you?' She took a deep breath and thought. 'Oh, before the war we held an annual rowing and swimming race, which was great fun. It will be a happy day when we can hold the competition again and laugh freely without fear of suddenly remembering all of the pain ...'

Alex turned onto his back again. 'Well, I'll say hallelujah to that!'

He picked a long blade of grass out of the dune and tried to whistle with it. Eliza returned to the picnic. There was a rather good-looking sponge cake filled with raspberry jam ...

'Do you miss it?' she asked. 'The flying?'

Alex didn't pause to answer. 'Not a bit. I miss my friends. I miss the camaraderie. But that kind of life, it changed me. I could never go back. I swore to myself after that last trip that I would never use any kind of weapon, in any form, for any reason ever again.'

'You're a pacifist, then?' she asked.

He shook his head. 'No, not really. We still need to win the thing. But when you kill a man – men – it changes you. I can't go down that road anymore. I'll simply have to write about it now.'

Eliza saw for the first time the kindness and the gentleness that had not been visible on the train. Something had happened to Alex over the past twenty-four hours. She guessed that that something was Cornwall.

'The pen is mightier than the sword, eh?' she said.

Alex smiled. 'Something like that. What about you? Do you miss your society life?'

Eliza frowned at him over imaginary spectacles. 'Not particularly. Anyhow, I may be going away soon,' she began, 'although when I say soon, I'm not entirely sure how soon that will be. The War Artists Advisory Committee have suggested that I might go to France; you know, when the big push comes. My appointment is yet to be approved by the chairman of the committee though.'

'Is he likely to block it?' Alex asked.

'War artists are usually men as the military commanders like it that way, or so I've heard.'

Alex opened the flask and began to pour tea into two cups. He paused to look up. 'It's the same with correspondents – women reporters don't get the same look-in, but that doesn't stop them, not these days, anyhow. Well, if it happens, it will be an exciting opportunity for you, which makes my comments on the train even more ridiculous.'

Eliza touched his arm.

'Don't. You already apologised and you only vocalised what I'd been thinking for some time. I *do* want to push myself – my art. To be experimental. I also think that a woman – women – should be allowed to see it all, to record it from their own viewpoint.'

Alex nodded and handed a cup and saucer to Eliza. 'There's no sugar, I'm afraid.'

'Thank you,' she said, taking the cup.

'You and I aren't so dissimilar as you may think,' he began, while running a napkin through his fingers.

'In what way?'

'I was hoping to be affiliated as a war correspondent, too. But I've recently been offered a position in Boston ...'

'In America?' she asked. Eliza knew this news should not affect her so, and yet ...

'Yes.'

'That's a long way away,' she said.

'Yes,' he agreed softly.

'When are you due to go?'

'In a couple of weeks. It's where my parents are, so at least that's one silver lining. I suppose I came to Cornwall to say goodbye.'

'Goodbye?'

'To the Trewiddens.'

'Of course. So we are both to leave on adventures,' she said. 'Me to Europe – possibly – and you to America.'

'Will you send me a postcard from Berlin?' he asked.

'Of course,' she answered – a little too quickly, a little too brightly – smiling. 'Of course I will.'

'Let's make it a deal, then,' he said, sitting up onto his knees. 'Berlin is a beautiful city. It needs artists and poets, not jackboots. Let's meet there one day, you and me, when the Allies have marched on Europe and stormed the citadel!' He held out his hand. 'Is it a deal?'

Eliza shouldn't encourage him, she absolutely shouldn't ...

'It's a deal,' she said, and shook his hand.

'So anyhow, Ms Eliza Grey.' Alex didn't let go of her hand. His mouth was twitching with fun. 'I'm curious to know something ...'

Eliza removed her hand and picked up a second slice of cake. 'Go on.'

'Of all the incredible women in that book of yours, which one would you most like to be? Are you a warrior or a princess or a nun? Or perhaps you are a savage! They're all in there.'

Eliza snorted. 'How do you know?'

'I read it.' Alex picked up an apple and rubbed it on his trouser leg.

'You read it?'

'I certainly did.'

Eliza shook her head and picked up her teacup.

'So, come on, whose story do you love the most?' he asked again. 'Which woman would Eliza Grey like to be?'

Eliza put down her teacup again and put a hand to her chin, playing along with him. 'Hmm,' she began. 'Let's see ... I suppose it would be great fun to be as free and adventurous as Lilian Bland – the one who built her own plane. Did you see that she fashioned a fuel tank from nothing more than a whisky bottle and an ear trumpet!'

'I did,' he said, starting on his apple. 'Fabulous!'

'She *is* fabulous. And did you see that her hobbies are listed as martial arts, motor racing, swearing and gambling?

She lives in Cornwall, too, apparently. Must be as old as the hills by now, but I'd love to meet her.'

Alex coughed out a piece of apple. 'You want to swear and gamble and fly planes?'

'No!' she exclaimed. 'Well, not all of the time,' she added playfully. 'So there's her, but, in all honesty, I see myself as a bit of a queen.'

'A queen?' Alex repeated, clearly enjoying himself. 'Wouldn't that be rather dull? All that reverence.'

'Dull? Never! Take Theodora, the Byzantine Empress. Now I quite fancy being her.'

'I don't really recall that one. What did she do?'

'She was a Machiavellian rebel! Her father was a bear-keeper in Constantinople's hippodrome, and she was on the stage too, dancing, mime and even comedy. Anyhow, one thing led to another and she eventually became Empress of Rome.'

'Just like that?'

Eliza shrugged. 'It's a classic rags to riches story ...' At this, Eliza, self-conscious of her own similar story, paused, before adding less enthusiastically, 'And she went on to make many improvements for impoverished women. The end.'

'Not a bad role model,' he agreed, 'although now you've sparked my memory. The way I read it, she wasn't exactly averse to the occasional poisoning of her enemies, or torture, either ... so, perhaps she's not such a wonderful role model after all.'

Eliza laughed. 'Oh, I glossed over that bit. And anyway, as a woman in power she would have had to resort to pretty much any kind of dirty trick not to get toppled – it came with the territory.'

'I suppose it would,' he said. 'I dare say even now. Anyhow, back to Eliza Grey. If you were to paint this beach today, how would you paint it?'

The apple Eliza was about to crunch paused at her lips. 'What do you mean?'

'Would you ignore the hardware, or would you include it, and if you included it, would you paint it in a positive light?'

Eliza considered her answer. 'It depends. Is this to be a fictional painting for the War Office, or something for myself?'

Alex opened his mouth to answer but Eliza added. 'Because if it is for myself then I would want to paint a memory, something special to me, in which case the thing I would paint may be fairly abstract ...'

'But I thought you were a realist?'

'I am, but it doesn't mean to say that I don't dabble in other forms.'

'And what if you were painting for the government?'

'Then I would be recording history. And this is where your idea of propaganda comes into play. There is a huge responsibility – as you know from your writing – to be careful of how much one's own feelings and political leaning goes into a painting, which is why realism is perhaps the best style for war art. I could, for example, paint the flamethrowers with a very dark feel, and give the nature around it a menacing touch. When I looked down at the beach from the cliff earlier and saw what had happened, how it had been closed off and militarised, I felt such a dark, desperate anxiety about the place. But now I'm sitting here with you, I see that nature is finding a way to work around the machines. Although there is a fence and wire and horrid concrete and harsh metal, the sea is unchanged, the cliffs are unchanged and even you and I have not been kept from the beach. Nature has a way of getting through the gaps in things, of softening everything, so I would not paint a horror picture, but a softer one – of us, having a picnic on the beach, with the plover standing on the wire, and the seals bobbing their heads out of the water, and the wildflowers and the sunshine, all finding a level together, because that, today, is the truth of it all – *our* truth.'

With this last statement Alex looked at Eliza and said, 'Paint it for me.'

'What?'

He grabbed her journal, which was sitting on the blanket, and handed it to her.

'Paint it for me, in your book.'

His eyes were so soft (and so close – too close), how could she refuse? She shuffled back a little, taking the book.

'Very well,' she said, batting him away. 'But I have only

a pencil so all I can offer is a rough sketch. Go and act naturally on your side of the blanket and I'll see what I can do.'

An hour later, Alex awoke, having slept a while, his straw hat covering his face, as Eliza closed the journal, sketch complete.

'Finished,' she said, filled with contentment.

Alex sat up. He held out his hand. 'Already? May I ...?'

'No, you may not. Not yet. I want to add some colour at home. *Then* you may see it.'

But this was not the answer Alex wanted to hear. He edged his way quickly to Eliza's side of the blanket and wrestled with her in roars of laughter before she finally let him have the book.

'You seem to have taken on some collateral damage during the invasion of the beach,' said Alex, sitting shoulder to shoulder with her now, holding the journal and nodding towards Eliza's left shoulder. Her cardigan was ripped slightly.

She turned her head to look. 'Oh, I'll stitch it up later, or wear it while I'm painting. Most of the clothes I wear to paint in would look good on a scarecrow, so it will fit into my wardrobe perfectly.'

'You're not at all the woman you appeared to be on the train,' he said, softly.

'Never judge a woman by the clothes that she wears,' she said, 'it's like judging a book by its cover ...' She leant away.

He was too close to her. In every possible way, he was too close. 'So anyway, I thought you wanted to see the sketch?'

Alex opened the journal.

'It's perfect,' he said, smiling. 'Just perfect.' He turned to face her on the beach. 'And was it worth it?' he asked, his eyes dancing, his dark hair shining in the sunlight.

'What, exactly?' she asked.

'Ripping your clothing apart to sit with me on the beach?'

'Oh, I think so,' she said, turning away to gaze out to sea. 'I think so.'

It was time to put some distance between them, and there had been enough chatter. Too much chatter could be worse than no chatter at all on some occasions; it might give her away.

She stood and lowered herself into a starting position for a running race. 'Race you to the sea,' she said, while glancing up at him mischievously.

Alex frowned. 'We'll be seen.'

'I doubt it. That sentry is all the way beyond the dunes. Now, take off those socks and shoes, roll up your trousers, take my hand and we'll run into the sea together.'

Alex glanced towards the flamethrowers.

'They won't go off now,' she said. 'And didn't I tell you I'm a nurse? Red Cross Auxiliary. So if anything happens to you, I know exactly how to bandage you up!'

'And can you bandage up my ego when I lose to a woman?'

107

Eliza's face took on an expression of mock horror. 'Joseph Alexander Levine, that is not the attitude of a self-professed modern man! And here I was thinking that I'd spent a wonderful afternoon with a fellow suffragette. Now, come on!' she said, bending down to roll her trousers above the knee. Let's see those legs!'

Eliza didn't stop when they reached the water's edge, but carried on running, dragging Alex straight into the particularly cold water with her. And soon, with trousers wet to above the knees and with splashed arms and faces, the two new friends forgot all about the fact that the beach was, in fact, out of bounds. They built sandcastles, collected shells, walked and talked, laughed and joked, pushed and pulled, until Alex turned suddenly, ankle-deep in water, took Eliza by the hand and said, 'If they do ask you to go to Europe, will you?'

Eliza, surprised by his sudden change of manner, pushed her hair from her eyes and asked, 'What would Theodora do?'

Alex laughed out loud. 'I'm pretty certain she would go,' he said, just as quite a large wave hit them side on, soaking them through.

'In that case,' she said, laughing and suddenly more sure of herself than she had ever been in her whole life, 'yes! I do believe I *would* go! *Shall* go!' she corrected.

The sound of a whistle pierced the moment.

They looked towards the dunes. The sentry from the

gate was standing on the top of a dune at the far end of the beach. 'Oi, you two!' he shouted. 'Stay exactly where you are!'

Alex told Eliza to run. She started at a pace towards the picnic. Still laughing, Alex shouted to Eliza to save herself, to run – 'run like the clappers!' And so she ran, laughing all the more as she tripped over the sand, trying to catch her breath. She ran away from the approaching sergeant who, by luck, was of a portly stature, and headed towards the picnic blanket, grabbing her socks and shoes and journal on her way before continuing on towards the gap in the fence. And when all of her bits and bobs were gathered and she was safely away, soaked through, she looked down on the beach from the coastal path and saw Alex being escorted off at gunpoint (of all things) by the over-zealous sergeant. He looked up at her and waved his arms about wildly.

'So long, brave Theodora! Queen of the beach!' he shouted. 'Save yourself, be free!'

And for the first time in a very long time, that was exactly how Eliza felt ... absolutely and completely free. She turned on her heel and ran home, laughing all the way.

Chapter 10

Ellie

Reading to Castle Cary

Ellie spent much of the main course talking about Eliza's artwork, and her journal, and Eliza's sojourn with a war correspondent called Alex at the cottage in Cornwall in April 1944. She explained how Eliza and Alex met on the train – the very same train they were on now, she stressed – and had gone on to spend several days together in Cornwall. Ellie ran her hand gently over the leather cover and smiled at the thought of Eliza's story, which she had read many times before.

'It must have been wonderful,' she said, her voice full of wistful regret.

Joe took off his glasses and rubbed his eyes. 'And did she ever finish it?'

Ellie took a moment to register his meaning. 'The sketch

of the picnic on the beach? Yes. I'll show you.' She opened the journal to the portrait.

'This is Alex,' she said.

'And his face ...'

'Was burned in the war. He was a pilot and was shot down in the Battle of Britain.'

'Really? What a hero.'

Ellie nodded. 'I know. Can you even imagine? The other side of his face doesn't seem to have been burned, though. There are lots of pencil or charcoal sketches and little paintings of him throughout the journal, but there are only three where she didn't add any colour: this one and two near the end – a portrait of a German soldier called Leo, and another of a lady called Francine.'

Joe put on his glasses. 'Are the pages in chronological order?' he asked.

'Yes,' Ellie said.

'So, the first sketch she did of him was without colour. I wonder why?'

Ellie shrugged. 'She doesn't say why. She doesn't go into much detail about the whole week, to be honest. She was married at the time, you see.'

Joe lifted his eyes from the portrait. 'Married?'

'I know. Shocking, eh!'

Joe looked at the sketch. 'Don't you think he looks a bit ... serious?'

Ellie, feeling the need to defend this man called Alex, quickly flicked over to the next page. 'This is him, too, looking more relaxed this time. Look, there's a straw hat covering his face.'

Joe peered closer. 'It's lovely,' he said. 'Just looking at it makes me feel ... I don't know, like everything is all right in the world. They must have had a lovely time on that beach. Which beach is it, do you know?'

'Porthcurno ...'

'Porthcurno? You don't mean ...' Joe looked at the clock, '*the* Porthcurno, where the Telegraph Museum is ...?'

Ellie shrugged. 'Yes, it's not far from my cottage.'

Joe ran a hand through his hair, shaking his head, clearly amazed. He picked up the little clock.

'You're not going to believe this,' he said, still shaking his head in wonder, 'but when I opened it up to fix it ...'

'The clock?'

'Yes, I'm an engineer, didn't I tell you that?'

Ellie shook her head.

'I like to fix things. Anyway, that's not important right now. What is important is that I found a note inside it.'

'Inside the clock?'

'Yes.'

'What kind of a note?'

'Money?' asked Rihanna, who had been topping up the glasses of the couple opposite and had been listening in.

'No, a handwritten note, dated 1945. I've put it in a sandwich bag to keep it protected. It's in my cabin.'

'What does it say, this note?' asked Rihanna, who was

ignoring a passenger two tables down who was trying to catch her attention.

'Say? Nothing much ... except that the hands had been purposefully set to rest at three-fifteen, because that's apparently when two lovers met, on a beach in Cornwall – Porthcurno Beach. Whoever wrote the note wanted to stop time so that the two lovers could be together for ever ... That's what it says, anyhow.'

Ellie looked at Rihanna.

Rihanna looked at Ellie.

'I think that is absolutely and totally the most romantic thing I've ever heard of,' said Ellie.

Rihanna nodded her head in agreement. 'It really is,' she said.

'Anyhow, this fella,' Joe went on, 'there's no name on the note but I think it's the sort of note a man would write ...'

Rihanna snorted. 'Not any man I've ever met.'

'... Anyway, he urged the next person who opens the clock – me – to also go to Cornwall. To go to the beach at three-fifteen, just in case she's there ...'

'Is that the real reason you're on the train?' asked Ellie, quietly.

Joe blushed crimson. 'Yes, I suppose it is.'

'In case who's there?' asked Rihanna.

'The love of my life, I guess.'

'Oh! I totally get that!' said Rihanna. She looked down at Ellie and mouthed, 'Definitely single' before wandering off.

Joe scrunched up his nose. 'It's all a bit of nonsense, really.'

'And you're sure it said to go to Porthcurno Beach? And at three-fifteen?' Ellie's face was flushed red with excitement. 'Only, there's this painting in Eliza's journal ... and the clock hands are set at ...'

'Three-fifteen.' He picked up the clock. 'You don't think ...?' He paused.

'That the clock belonged to Alex?' she said.

They looked at each other, then at the clock, and then the journal, and then at each other.

'Nah!' they said together, laughing. 'As if that could be true!'

They sat back then and took a moment to have a bit of a think in silence, but their thoughts were interrupted by the D-Day Dames, who had launched into a new number, 'Begin the Beguine'. Ellie felt the vibration of Joe's foot tapping under the table. He picked up his wine glass, took a sip and shouted across the table, 'What is a beguine, exactly?'

Chapter 11

Penberth, April 1944

Sitting like a couple of contented garden gnomes, Eliza and Alex perched themselves on the stepping stones that led across the stream at Penberth. Their bare feet were dipped into the water, and they tipped their faces to the sun, basking in the spell of fabulous weather that had yet to break. Eliza hadn't been the least bit surprised when he'd appeared at her door the day after their picnic on the beach. He was carrying a flask and the makings of afternoon tea. 'Scones are obligatory in Cornwall,' he had said. And she hadn't been surprised the next day, when he had appeared again, this time empty-handed, which meant that Eliza would be obliged to invite him in for refreshment. She hadn't, and they had walked out instead, with Alex regaling her – for the third time, but she did so enjoy it – with the story of what happened with the sentry on the beach, and how he'd been marched through the village like a Nazi spy to the commanding officer's house, only to be asked in for supper, both men having gone to the same school in Rugby, much to the chagrin of the sentry. And now, this being the fourth day since they'd first met on the night train, they sat in companionable silence, having settled into the easy association of close friendship, not feeling the need to fill in any gaps in conversation or in the story of their lives.

Alex threw a pebble into the stream. 'Tell me about your work as a nurse,' he said. 'I take it you trained at the start of the war to support the effort in town?'

Eliza nodded. 'Yes, I'm just a basic auxiliary, that's all – bedpans, dressings, cleaning, that sort of thing. I volunteer at a command post at Paddington Station. A friend of mine is a nurse there too, Nancy. She lives in her aunt's house, close to the station, and I sleep there after shifts – I have my art studio there, too.'

Alex hesitated before saying, 'You don't return home, to your own home with your husband, I mean, after duty?'

This was the first time either of them had referred to anything outside of their Cornwall bubble, and certainly it was the first reference to Eliza having any home other than *Meadowsweet*.

'No,' she said, offering no more in the way of explanation. She glanced around. 'It's so hard to imagine all those bombed-out streets right now, isn't it, sitting in this little piece of heaven.' With this she returned to waggling her hands in the water. 'I've decided something today,' said Eliza.

'And that is?'

'When the big push comes I'm going to tell the committee that I'll go to France – if they want me – and guess what else I'm going to do?'

'What?'

'I'm going to march my way with the troops right into the heart of Berlin.' She nudged his shoulder. 'All of which is inspired by you, by the way. And I'll paint the whole sorry mess as I go, every bit of it, just so that you will be proud of me and everyone all over the world will know the truth of it – and I promise you that I won't even paint what I see with a golden glow.'

Alex dropped his head, which wasn't the response she had hoped for. 'Listen, Eliza ...' He took her hand out of the water and held it. She glanced around to see if any wives were watching. 'Don't go to France because of something I said. You don't have to prove anything, least of all to me.'

Eliza smiled to reassure him. 'I came to Cornwall to make some decisions and I've made them. The war needs women's voices, and it needs their artwork too. Perhaps your being on the train was ...'

'Fate?' he asked.

'I was going to say destiny, but yes, fate.'

'Next stop Berlin, then?' he said, releasing her hand.

'Absolutely. Next stop Berlin. And hey ...' She nudged him again. 'Don't forget now. We made a pact to see each other there, God willing.'

'It's a deal,' he said. 'But I don't believe that God will have much to do with it, willing or not.'

Eliza lifted her head and tilted her face towards the sun. She closed her eyes. 'You're Jewish,' she said, 'but you don't seem to be religious in any way.'

'Being Jewish is more deep-rooted than I can ever explain. I'm proud to be a Jew. But I believe in solid things, like mathematics, which is explicably true. I studied mathematics at university, did I tell you that?'

Eliza lifted her head. 'No, you didn't. You don't have any kind of faith at all, then?'

'You could say that believing in the order of things in a mathematical way is a kind of faith, I suppose,' he conceded. 'What about you?'

Eliza's hand reached immediately for a chain around her neck. It carried a crucifix. She held it while considering her answer.

'The bookmark, the one you returned to me?' she said.

'The one with the quote?'

'Yes, "*all shall be well*", originally written by Julian of Norwich.'

'Julian of where?'

Eliza laughed. 'Norwich.'

'Never heard of him.'

'Her,' corrected Eliza.

'Who was she, another woman from your book?'

'No, not quite. I suppose you could call her a spiritual counsellor, from centuries ago – fourteenth century, I think.

Anyhow, Julian wasn't her real name, it was taken from a church local to her. She was a recluse, but people would go to her for advice and guidance. It was a time of plague and poverty and pandemics, so I suppose she'd be quite busy back then, but despite all the suffering of the time, her writings were full of nothing but faith and hope and love. The bookmark was my mother's – did I tell you that? The full quote reads, "*And all shall be well, and all shall be well, and all manner of things shall be well.*"'

Alex picked up another stone and threw it into the stream. 'A nice idea,' he said, 'but I'm not sure I could ever have such blind faith – everything can't be well all of the time, that's just not possible.'

Eliza shook her head. 'I don't think that's what it means. I think it's about choosing to live life with an open heart and an attitude of hope rather than one of dread and fear. It's about just knowing, I suppose, that all will be well ...' she placed a hand on his chest '... in here. Julian wasn't saying that bad things won't happen to you, she wasn't even saying that you won't come to a sticky end. I think she was saying that, no matter what is going on around one, all can be well within. I suppose if I believe in anything, it's in that kind of thing.'

'You have faith in having faith,' he said, softly. He glanced down at the hand still resting on his heart.

Eliza removed her hand. 'I never really thought about it before but, yes, I do. I like the idea of simply believing. It keeps me going.'

'I wish I had your faith,' said Alex with a sigh. 'But Pandora's Box has been well and truly opened with this war, unleashing nothing but misery. I can't see any happy endings coming along any time soon.'

Eliza shook her head and smiled. 'It wasn't a box, you know,' she said.

'What wasn't?'

'The thing Pandora opened. It was a kind of Greek jar. Do you know what was left in the jar, after all the evils of the world had flown out of it?'

Alex's expression turned from melancholy to amusement. 'No?'

Eliza's eyes twinkled brighter than the stream. 'Guess?' she said.

'I have absolutely no idea. Tell me, and make it something good.'

'It is,' she said. 'It was Hope. She got stuck under the lip, or something like that.'

Alex laughed.

'Hope is a woman, then?'

'Of course! And the good news is that we still have her, saved securely in the jar. It's a nice thought, really.'

Alex scratched his nose. 'Well, maybe it is and maybe it isn't. Do we have access to the jar?'

Eliza shrugged. 'I have no idea. Does it matter?'

'Of course.'

'Why?'

'Because if Hope remains in the jar, not out in the world

with us, we don't have her to fall back on at all, do we? How cruel,' he said, 'and how depressing, to set all those evils free to rampage around the world and not give us Hope.'

Eliza frowned. 'That can't be right. Perhaps I'm looking at it too simplistically. This is the Greeks we're talking about, and do remember that "hope" in Greek does not have the same positive connotation as it does in English. In Greek, "hope" means to anticipate something – which may turn out to be good or bad.'

Alex scratched his cheek this time. 'So, it was anticipation that was left in the jar, not hope.'

'Exactly.'

'And was that a good or a bad thing?'

Eliza shrugged. 'Now *that* is something that scholars have been arguing about for years. I don't think we're likely to solve the conundrum today.'

Alex sighed and put an arm around her shoulders. He pulled her in closer.

'Do you think if we both wish hard enough,' said Eliza, resting her head on his shoulder, 'that it will all just go away?'

She glanced up at him. Tears edged her lower lashes and he reached out a hand to brush a stray tear from her cheek.

'One day – though I don't know when or how – I promise you, Eliza, all shall be well.' He took her face into his hands and for the first time, she didn't shy away. 'All shall be well,' he repeated as he leant forwards to kiss her.

Then a cry went out. 'Hevva!'

Eliza gasped and snapped her face out of his hands. She looked up towards the cliff top. A man was waving and shouting, 'Hevva! Hevva!' and the hamlet suddenly came alive. Aproned women with floured hands and toddlers hanging off their hips dashed out of cottages. A baby holding a wooden teething ring was pressed into Eliza's arms. With her tears quickly quelled, Eliza became fuelled with excitement.

'Quickly,' she said to Alex, dashing towards her cottage, holding the baby close to her chest. 'Help fetch my easel. I can hold the baby while I paint.'

Alex followed, but was gesturing towards the slip where boats were being made ready for the off. 'But oughtn't I offer to help the men?' he asked, looking startled.

'Yes, of course, but it will only take a moment to get my things. I can watch all the children while I paint. That's what I usually do if I'm here when the cry goes up. Come on, catch up! You'll have plenty of time to stand and stare later!'

By early evening, the first of the boats were in. Alex rolled his sleeves to help the men haul the catch home and Eliza looked on, painting, while seeing to the baby and watching over several small children.

At nine in the evening, just as the sun set behind the high cliffs that flanked the cove, Eliza, wrapped in a turquoise shawl, handed Alex a bottle of cider as he ambled up the cobbled slipway. The smile he gave her then – his face and arms golden brown, his shirt covered in grease from the boats – was a smile of utter contentment. It was the smile of a weary man who had spent a long day doing manual labour in the sunshine and had loved it. The meditative quality of the work combined with the speed at which it needed to be done had clearly taken away previous feelings of angst or melancholy. And Eliza couldn't help but think – as she stood in front of her cottage with a sleeping baby in her arms, watching the older women of the hamlet hand out pasties and ale to the men who, the catch now in, relaxed on the slip with their womenfolk – that this man, this place, this house, all seemed to fit together, and that not only did Alex belong here, but he was thinking the exact same thing too.

A fiddler began to play on the slip. It was time to celebrate.

'I'll just take little Molly here back to her mother,' whispered Eliza, so as not to wake the baby. 'Why don't you go inside and clean yourself up, open the window and listen to the music? They will probably all get very merry and light a fire on the slip soon. You'll find water in the jug and a cloth and so on in a box at the top of the stairs.'

Alex looked into the house and then back at Eliza.

'You're inviting me in?' he said.

Eliza looked down at the baby. 'Yes, I'm inviting you in.'

She wrapped the shawl a little tighter around herself and Molly and walked towards the hamlet folk. Her neighbour held out her arms to take the baby with a wide smile and a thank you. A jug of cider was pressed into Eliza's hands, which she took with gratitude, and as she turned towards the cottage, she noticed Alex stepping inside, reminding her of a stray dog who has been slowly encouraged indoors.

Dinner consisted of pasties and cider and it was all the more delicious for being eaten while ravenous. Alex pulled the table towards the open window. Their faces were tight and glowing from their day in the sun and they watched the tide lap against the cove while smiling at the hamlet folk, who celebrated their haul with muted echoes of chatter and song, Molly's father having knocked at the door, asking to borrow Eliza's gramophone and collection of records.

There was no need for conversation – Eliza and Alex were beyond that now – and at any rate, the only topic left to discuss concerned their real lives, their lives outside Penberth. Eliza told herself over and over that it didn't matter that they had become friends, and then she told herself to stop being ridiculous, because the truth of the matter was that she had fallen in love with Alex Levine.

Alex turned to her. It was twilight. A breeze danced with the flowers on the table.

'The thing you came here to think about,' he began. 'It wasn't simply about going to Europe, was it?'

'No,' she said,

'Are you going to end it?' he asked, both of them knowing perfectly well that he meant her marriage.

'I don't know' was her simple answer.

Eliza wondered how on earth she could begin to explain her marriage. It was a marriage of ideas, of expression, of companionship, but not of souls, of touch, of sense or of body.

'In my flying days,' Alex began in a whisper, 'there was a very pretty field – a meadow – next to the airfield, and every morning I would rise early with the express purpose of walking around that meadow on my bare feet, just to listen to the birds and really appreciate the specialness of being allowed to see it all, even if it was just for one more day, because I really did believe that every day would be my last. Then the scramble would go up, and when I jumped into the cockpit and headed out over the Channel I never expected to make it back alive; none of us did.'

Eliza took his hand.

'Since then, I've been a shadow of the man I used to be, but not anymore. The only things I intend to regret are the things I didn't say, didn't do.'

Eliza let go of his hand. She took a deep breath and looked around her. 'The woman that you see now, in this place,' she said, 'is not the woman you would have known several years ago. That woman was penniless and homeless. She had nothing but a few paintbrushes and a degree of talent to her name. So she married a man nearly three times her age so that she could feel secure. Looking back now, I should have been more like the women in Mother's book – fearless, determined, brave enough to go it alone – but though that's all very well in books, or when one has money, the reality is that it isn't always possible. I have made a commitment to Arthur that no longer suits me – so what do I do? Leave? And what do I become if I do? I can't go on with the old regime after the fighting ends. But to change things now, when Arthur is so frightened by the war? I don't know if I can.'

'And as for the rest of our evening?' he probed.

'We will carry on exactly the same. Two friends, enjoying a quiet moment in all of the madness.'

The music drifted in through the window, the fast-paced American music that had monopolised the evening so far slowing to a melancholy tune. With twilight fading to darkness, Vera Lynn began to sing 'The White Cliffs of Dover' and they sat together and listened in silence. Then came Artie Shaw and 'Begin the Beguine'. Ultimately, as she knew they would, nightingales flittered into the room, nightingales who were being serenaded by angels in Berkeley Square.

Alex put down his bottle of cider, stood, smiled down at her and held out his hand.

'Shall we?' he asked.

Eliza rose and fell into his arms.

'Do you think angels really do dine at The Ritz?' Alex whispered into her hair as they swayed to the music.

Eliza glanced up, puzzled.

'The words,' he explained. '*There were angels dining at The Ritz ...*'

She rested her head on his shoulder. 'I do hope so,' she whispered, feeling utterly at home in his arms and thinking that in all of her life, she had never felt more secure and happy than this. 'I do hope so.'

He stopped dancing and stepped away from her a little. 'Just one word from you, and America can wait, or we could go there together. Come with me! To hell with the whole damn shooting match. Come to America with me, Eliza. I don't care what anyone thinks ... Will you?'

His eyes were so bright, so loving, so alive. He brushed her hair away from her face. She didn't answer. She couldn't answer. He took her into his arms again. 'I'm being unfair. But I know one thing ... I'm glad that old clock isn't fixed,' he said. 'Because for a few wonderful days we've been able to freeze time and just enjoy the moment. Yesterday has gone and tomorrow is yet to come.'

'And now?' Eliza whispered into his chest, before looking up.

'Now,' he said, pulling her closer, 'is only for us. Only ever for us.'

That was at 11 p.m. By 7 a.m., Eliza was sitting by Mr Pengelly's side as he flicked the reins for his best mare to trot on. He was taking the morning milk to Penzance, as Eliza knew he would. She had woken early, entwined with Alex on her bed, and had panicked. What on earth would she say to him when he woke? How would the people of Penberth react to her – a married woman – having allowed Alex to stay the night? Where would – where could – Eliza and Alex move on to now?

No, she couldn't have faced him when he woke. She couldn't face anyone. She had been swept away by Cornwall and Alex and the fishing party and oh, the very romance of it all, and she had, in the end, despite her best efforts to hold back, been unfaithful – wholly and completely unfaithful – and she had loved it. Her time with Alex had held up a mirror to show just how dreadfully woeful her marriage was. Oh, how desperately she had yearned for passion, to feel young again. In fact, there was no 'again' about it. She had never felt like this before, never. This unbridled yearning for touch. Yet in the cold light of day she hadn't been able to deal with what she had done, and like a thief in the night she had fled. But in doing so she had made a bad situation worse, hurting yet another person with her selfishness.

She didn't leave a lengthy note, there hadn't been the time, and anyway, it was too dark to write. She had simply ripped a scrap of paper from her journal and written, *I am sorry, my darling love. Forgive me*. The letter she wrote from the security of the milk train later that morning, however, was more explanatory, and as the train rattled onwards, speeding her away from Cornwall, she knew the very last thing she should have done, after all, was leave him. But it was too late. The deed was done.

My darling, Alex

You will have woken at Meadowsweet by now and found me gone. This is not how I wanted to part from you, but I woke early with an overpowering fear that today would become a day of reckoning and of guilt.

I have allowed my life to be shaped by my relationship with Arthur. Every decision made concerning my life before the war was made for me and not by me. Now, however, I have freedom and a sense of real accomplishment. I am a person – finally – in my own right. There is no doubt that I am about to step into a new chapter, but any decision I make now should not be influenced by my feelings for another man.

If I had stayed, I'm certain I would have asked you to leave. We might have argued, or become melancholy, and I absolutely did not want our time together this week to end that way. Talk spoils things. It seems to me that the more sound a person is morally, the more likely they are to find a way to talk themselves out of happiness. Guilt is like the most pernicious of weeds. It wends its way through the cracks until it turns something beautiful into something quite ugly. I did not want that to happen to us, or to allow my guilt to sully the time we have been gifted this past week, which does, indeed, feel like the very best of gifts.

In sum, I have obstacles to work through before I can consider where my life might lead me now, and such obstacles need to be navigated with a gentle hand at the tiller, and at my own pace. This is my chance to become an independent woman, but until that woman exists, I am not in any way free to be with you, nor should I behave so. I wish I could have made our moment last for ever. I wish the clock really could have been stuck at three-fifteen; but try as I may, the only way I have ever found to capture time is with paint and a brush. For mere mortals, the clock will insist on ticking on.

Please do one thing for me, take the little clock as my gift. Fix it. Give it life again, and maybe one day you can give it back to me, and our moment can resume: our lives – our hearts – can beat again.

With dearest love, Eliza

Chapter 12

Eliza

London, 1 May 1944

Eliza took a seat on a hard bench in the vestibule of the offices of the War Artists Advisory Committee, rested the portfolio of her most recent paintings on her lap and tried not to fidget. She knew she looked smart, although perhaps too smart, in her dark-green fitted suit and silk blouse. She took off her hat and put her gloves inside her clutch. Why on earth had she ever begun to wear such clothes? They sat uncomfortably on her, like a dinner suit on a clown. This was an environment for artists, not society ladies. She examined her hands. They were cracked from turpentine. Inspecting them deeper she smiled at the sight of a fleck of burnt umber embedded in a cuticle, such a lovely colour. She tried to remember why she'd used it – ah, yes: to enhance the blood on an arm she'd painted just that morning. The arm had protruded from a pile of rubble after a bombing raid. The smile faded. Would any colour ever represent true beauty again after the horror of the war?

It was the perfect moment to run through interview tips she'd been given the day before by her friend Nancy. Nancy, an actress-cum-nurse, was exactly the kind of woman who instinctively knew how to perfect that tricky balance between assertiveness and femininity. Not that Eliza was being interviewed, as such; at least, she didn't think so. The chairman wanted to meet to discuss Eliza's options, one of them being that she might transition from the Home Front to a deployed war artist. Nancy 'had people in common' with him and said not to bother flirting because he was really old, at least fifty!

Eliza opened her clutch again and took out her journal. Inside was a letter from Alex. Less than a month had passed since those beautiful days in Cornwall, but it seemed like forever. She read the letter again, which was a mistake before an interview, but just seeing his words – words that he himself had written on paper that he himself had touched – brought her closer to him, and yet what was written served only to tear them further apart.

Dear Eliza
Thank you for your letter. My first reaction when I found you gone on that last day was anger, and then disappointment and confusion. But I see now that it was wrong and unfair of me to feel that way. You are

*married and I am not. I have no right to expect anything
other than to be grateful for the time we were given.*

*But know this: you have shown me the importance
of kindness and the importance of optimism – of faith.
With that in mind I will endeavour to be a better man
– a kinder man – in the hope that one day soon, as
you say, all of that kindness will be returned to me in
the reward of you (although I can hear you now warning
me that it does not work that way, and that there is
no such thing as conditional kindness).*

*The thought of bumping into you in town or seeing
your name or photograph in the society pages brings
me no pleasure, and so I have accepted the offer of
employment in Boston. I expect that I shall be more
than ready to come home after a couple of years, but
in these uncertain times who knows where the future
will lead us.*

*I told you on the train that I admire F. Scott
Fitzgerald. Well, here is a final quote. He wrote, 'I love
her, and that's the beginning and end of everything.' I
have never really understood the depth of those words
until now.*

Alex

Eliza ran her fingers across the words and blinked back
tears. She had confessed about her time with Alex to
Nancy, who spoke (and looked) as though she still had
a hockey stick in her hand. 'Cripes, Eliza!' Nancy had

said. 'You're such a rebel! He's definitely keen, I'd say. Sailing to America, though, that's a bit drastic! And what about dear Arthur?'

And that was the point, of course: what about dear Arthur? Eliza had thought of nothing else but dear Arthur since Cornwall. One part of her brain – the practical part – wanted to push Alex Levine as far away as possible. Another part, the greater part – the part that was drawn to Empress Theodora and a life of adventure – wanted to throw Arthur to the wind and rush to America.

And yet, the question remained: what about dear Arthur?

Arthur had been waiting at their home in London on her return from Cornwall. He seemed different. He was inquisitive, but vague. Watching, yet distant. Eliza felt sure he knew, but how? No one of significance – significance in terms of 'people in common' – had been on the night train, she was sure, and even if they had been, it was obvious that her dinner companion had been forced upon her. But perhaps in Penberth? Who was Arthur in contact with in Penberth? Paranoia crept in. Maybe Arthur was not so dear after all. Maybe, for years, he had paid someone in the village to watch over her? No, it wasn't possible. The Penberth folk were her people. They would never tell. But there was certainly 'something' in his manner, and the very fact that he had returned to London early ...

But what of it? What if he did know? The beginning of the war had heralded the end of her marriage, and hadn't she known this long before she stepped onto the night train at Paddington? What of her house, though – *Meadowsweet* – would she lose it?

Eliza shook her head. It sounded, even in her thoughts, mercenary. But weren't these the things that women who were dependent upon their husbands had no choice but to consider? There was no right answer. The 'what if's were innumerable and kept her awake at night. What if Alex appeared at her home and asked her to leave with him? That would be unconscionable, but anyhow, the possibility of such an occurrence – which she dreaded and longed for in equal measure – disappeared the moment his letter arrived. He was going to America, and so the only question that now remained was: what if she never saw him again? That was even more unthinkable. But why? Why was it unthinkable? She had only known him for a week, after all. On the return journey from Cornwall, Eliza realised that, at some point in every woman's life, she should know the fire and passion and ecstasy of falling desperately in love with a mysterious man, even if that man subsequently proved to be unsuitable. There was nothing, she knew now, to match the first throes of falling in love. If only she could bottle that feeling. If only she could paint it – really do great justice to it. Love. The simple act of loving someone and being loved back. Every painting she had ever done felt incomplete and inadequate. How could she possibly have ever captured love in her paintings, which she had always striven to do, when she hadn't really known it? But what was this kind of love anyway? Was it real? Was it obsession? Was it lust? Was it temporary?

In marrying Arthur she had been naïve and foolish – selfish, even – and the price she paid now was to live with the knowledge that she had never, not until that last night with Alex, been kissed with vigour, with urgency, with (although she hated to admit it) anything other than sedate affection.

'Lady Arbuthnot.'

Eliza didn't respond.

'Lady Arbuthnot,' the receptionist said, louder. 'If you please?'

Eliza came back to the present with a jolt.

'Mr Cartwright is ready for you now. It's down the corridor all the way to the end, then up the stairs and second on the right.'

Eliza stood, brushed down her skirt and said, 'Thank you'.

The meeting was over before it began. Mr Cartwright smoked his cigar while she chatted away animatedly. He asked few questions, leaving Eliza plenty of room to dash down rabbit holes about how she suddenly felt compelled to do much more for the war effort, almost to the level of a religious calling, and how she longed to move away from her propaganda work, to attempt to paint the truth of the war, to find the sorrow and the pain and the love and light in it, and how she had decided to accept their offer to be accredited and do her bit ...

Five minutes in, however, she knew he had no intention of sending her to Europe. At the ten-minute point, when the secretary knocked on the door with what Eliza knew was a fake and planned interruption, she decided to ask him outright.

'Mr Cartwright. Some weeks ago I received a letter suggesting that I might consider progressing my role to become a deployed war artist, yet everything you have said today leads me to believe that such a proposal is no longer on the table. So I ask you straight: have you any intention of sending me away with the troops or are we wasting each other's time?'

A flicker of something more promising flashed across his face. But after resting his cigar on an ashtray, placing his elbows on the table and crossing his hands in the reverent way that men who are about to deliver a sermon might cross them, he said, 'Tell me, Lady Arbuthnot, would you be able to dig yourself a latrine, do you think, or a deep bunker?'

'Well, I ...'

'Can you carry a backpack matching your own weight, maybe more, while also carrying your cot bed, paints, paper, respirator, helmet? Basically, are you physically able to carry all the kit you would need to survive *and* to do your job?'

'I don't know.'

'You have a maid at home?'

'Well, yes, I did, before the war, but not rec—'

'And this is why I am reluctant to send women, particularly women of your standing, to the front. Believe it or not, it is to protect you, and the men you would ultimately be reliant upon. Most generals do not want the bother of it – of having women with them. But I do like the cut of your jib, I'll give you that, and your paintings are very good, I'd say. Yes, very good indeed.'

Eliza stood and put on her hat. She was going to say, 'Why did you waste my time, you old fool?' and 'Are you aware that I am also an auxiliary nurse, that I was not born a lady, that I ...' But she looked at his face and realised there was simply no point.

'It would have been nice – sorry, not nice,' she corrected, 'that's the wrong word. I should have appreciated it if I had been given the opportunity to at least try, especially as it was your department who raised the notion in the first place. My opinion, for what it is worth, is that it is high time the war was painted through the eyes of a woman.'

'There is a naivety to you which is endearing, but if it is of any consolation, there are limits to what I am allowed to release to the public and you would not, in any case, be allowed to paint the absolute "truth of the war" as you put it.'

Eliza began to argue but Cartwright raised his hand.

'Does an American mother want to see the absolute truth of the fate of her baby GI on the front cover of her newspaper or woman's magazine as she pours her coffee in the morning? What if the mood in America changed and they pulled their troops out of Europe? Where would we be then? Finished, that's where we'd be. I'm sorry but that is the end of the matter. Also, I shall not have the death of a woman on my hands.'

Eliza put on her gloves and crossed the room. She placed a hand on the door handle.

'Please do me the service of answering this question honestly,' she said, looking back. 'Did my husband have a part to play in your decision to keep me at home?'

His ensuing silence was the only answer she needed.

Nancy was waiting for her in the office of *Lady and Home*, chatting away to her Aunt Sheila, the editor of the magazine, who had her feet on her desk and was smoking a cigarette when Eliza walked in. A bottle of sherry and three crystal-cut glasses sat on Sheila's desk and they looked up expectantly as she entered. Eliza saw the light in their eyes and the sherry on the table and realised that feeling disappointed was one thing, but having to see the drop in the faces of excited friends when they only wished the best for you was even harder.

Eliza moved a pile of papers from a leather chair that ran on swivel wheels and flopped down. The chair scooted across the room a little.

'Blast. You didn't get it,' stated Nancy. 'But I thought you were a shoo-in? They asked for you, didn't they, not the other way around?'

Eliza sighed out her disappointment. 'Yes, they asked for me, well, someone did, but not the head man, apparently.' Eliza began to fiddle with a glass paperweight in the shape of a tortoise.

'But ...?' Nancy's ability to speak ran out of steam. 'Why?'

'Because I am a woman, apparently.'

Sheila took her feet off the desk and harrumphed. 'That's rot! I mean, yes, you are a woman, but your portfolio is incredible! Did you tell him about your huge following in America?'

Eliza smiled. 'I wouldn't say my following is "huge", exactly, but he wasn't interested in me anyhow. And that, I'm afraid, is the end of the story.'

Sheila was on an ill-tempered roll now. 'I'll tell you this,' she began, using her cigarette as a pointer, 'it wasn't Churchill that persuaded Roosevelt to send the troops over to Europe. No siree! It was the American housewife that got them moving, and all because of your paintings!'

Eliza smiled. If only Alex could hear this conversation. He'd thought it was his sister who got America into the war. Truth was, it had been a whole host of things. Her propaganda paintings may have cajoled and courted sympathy in the States, but that was all. Nancy, still wearing her Red Cross uniform, having just come off duty, was playing absently with the stopper on the sherry decanter. 'I thought it was Pearl Harbor that got America into the war,' she said, thereby twitching her nose very firmly down a rabbit hole.

Sheila rolled her eyes. 'That too, but just shush, Nancy!'

Nancy surprised the others by suddenly kicking a small pouffe halfway across the room and saying (quite aggressively for Nancy), 'I do believe that the only thing missing from your portfolio was ...'

The other two looked on, waiting in wonder for the pronouncement.

'Was?' Sheila prompted.

'Well ... quite frankly a ... a ...'

'A?'

'A penis! There, I've said it!'

'You certainly have' was Sheila's only response.

'I've a feeling that the chairman knows Arthur from his club,' said Eliza. 'He looked the type, and Arthur won't admit it, but he doesn't want me to go, so ...'

Nancy looked at Sheila. Sheila looked at Nancy.

'Well, it's done now,' offered Sheila, her tone soothing. 'And in a way, I'm relieved. Oh, I know you had your heart set on it, but being out there, on the front line, it could be – *would* be – well, to be honest, a bloody nightmare. And crossing the Channel with the troops if they go ...'

'*When* they go,' corrected Eliza.

'All right, when they go, would be hellish. Simply hellish. And you've always got your studio here with me, you know. Please don't lessen the merit of the artwork you do in this country over this, because you'd be lessening the role of women on the home front, I'd say. That's vital too, you know.'

At this, Eliza simultaneously pushed herself out of her depressed state and her seat and threw her arms around her friends.

'You're the best friends in the whole world, you two. Do you know that? The absolute best. Have I told you that before?'

Sheila batted her off while Nancy, glassy-eyed, clung on. 'Oh, just a couple of times,' she said. 'But tell me again anyway.'

Feeling slightly better, Eliza rested her backside on the desk and breathed a relaxing sigh. Sheila nodded towards a book that sat on the edge of Eliza's desk. 'What would Empress Theodora do now, do you think?' she asked.

Eliza shrugged. 'I'm not absolutely sure, although I have a feeling she would somehow find a way to go anyway, most likely.'

'Sod it!' said Nancy. 'Sherry?'

Sheila handed out the three small glasses and said, 'Here's mud in your eye,' before turning away and picking up an unopened telegram from her desk. With a wink in Nancy's direction, she turned to Eliza and held out the envelope.

'Is it from the Cornwall chap?' asked Nancy.

Nancy edged closer to peer over Eliza's shoulder and said, 'Come on, old thing, what does it say?'

Eliza read the telegram. It was the best and worst news.

LAST MINUTE CHANGE (STOP) AMERICA OFF
(STOP) AFFILIATED WITH FIRST ARMY (STOP)
HAVE BEGUN FIXING YOUR CLOCK (STOP) SEE
YOU IN BERLIN (STOP) ALEX

Eliza handed the telegram to Nancy and kicked the poor pouffe further across the room.

'The First? Who are they?' asked Nancy.

'Americans,' answered Sheila.

'What he's really saying,' explained Eliza, 'is that he'll be going with them to Europe when they go, as a reporter, into France … and that he'll see me there.'

Nancy glanced at Sheila. 'But you aren't going to be there …' she said softly to Eliza.

Eliza sat back in the chair and closed her eyes. For four long years, via millions of brush strokes, she had catalogued the role of women in the war. Her portfolio was full of stories of courage, bravery and derring-do. She realised that she didn't need to ask what Theodora would do in the same situation, but to ask what Eliza Grey would do. She focused on the red cross stitched onto Nancy's armband. Still holding the telegram, she felt the beginnings of a plan start to ignite. She knocked back her sherry and with a reinvigorated bright smile said, 'You know what, you two, I think I might just find a way to get there after all.'

Chapter 13

Ellie

Castle Cary to Crewkerne

'It's a dance,' said Ellie, who had just returned from refreshing her lipstick in the powder room, an act that was not easy on a moving train. She glanced down at her beef dinner.

'What is?'

'The beguine,' she said, cutting a baby carrot in half. 'It's a dance, from the Caribbean. At least, I think that's what it is. A bit like a foxtrot.'

'You must be the only person under sixty to know that.' Joe popped a whole baby carrot into his mouth. 'Do you dance?'

Ellie shook her head. 'No, I'm just a nostalgia geek.' She ran her tongue over her top teeth (no woman wanted to ruin The Best Night Of Her Life with lipstick-covered teeth).

'Really? So am I!'

Lace sleeves, that's what the wedding dress would have.

Joe took a knife to his beef, which was a little stringy. It struck Ellie that either one of them could sit there and tell each other anything – spin any kind of fantastic yarn – and the one would simply believe the other without question, saying things like, 'No! Really? You tame lions for a living! Incredible!'

She said as much to Joe. He laughed.

'Yes, I missed a trick there,' he said, wiping his mouth with the napkin. 'I should have told you that I did something fabulously brave for a living, although clearly I'm a daring fighter pilot ace tonight.' He glanced down at his clothes, and then patted and held up the Labrador. 'What do you think of my dog? Every pilot has to have a dog, I think.'

'Adorable,' she said.

'And the moustache?' He turned his head to one side to allow her to assess it fully.

'Well, what can I say? It's ...'

'Suave? Debonair? Irresistible?'

Ellie shook her head. 'Actually, it's a little crooked; you knocked it with your napkin. And there's ... well, there's quite a bit of gravy on it ...'

Joe used a spoon as a mirror, adjusting the moustache for a moment before eventually giving up and ripping it off.

'Better?' he asked.

'Better,' repeated Ellie, smiling. *Much better.*

'This is terrible, by the way.' He started on his food again.

Ellie frowned. 'The beef?'

'No, not the food, just the fact that we're on the main course already and I still don't know anything about you other than that you play the violin. Is that what you do, are you a professional musician?'

Ellie poured water into two tumblers. She needed to slow the drinking down; she'd be under the table by Exeter if not.

'If busking is counted as a profession,' she answered, 'then yes, I'm a musician.'

'It is in my book,' he said, protectively. 'I, for one, think that the world would be more than a bit rubbish without buskers.' He returned to his beef.

'Thanks. I also teach the violin and guitar online ... oh, and the cello, and the ukulele for kids.'

'Cello? Impressive. Although, to be honest, I never know if the cello is something you put between your legs or in your mouth.'

Ellie spat out her wine. 'Between your legs,' she said, laughing.

'Ah, right. That big violin thing. And do you busk regularly or was tonight a one-off?'

Ellie scrunched her nose. 'A one-off. I was pretending to be a famous soloist in an orchestra. I was "Ellie Nightingale, for one night only"! Daft, really.'

149

Joe swallowed his last mouthful and shook his head. 'It's not daft at all. I thought you were fabulous. You could have told me that you are the special violinist to the Queen and I would have believed you.' His cutlery hovered above the plate, his expression taking on the look of a sudden dawning. '*That's* what I wanted to ask you!' he said. 'One of the songs you played was familiar but I couldn't put my finger on it. It reminded me of being a kid.'

Ellie smiled, nodded and swallowed. 'Disney,' she said.

'Disney?'

'*Beauty and the Beast.*' She hummed the first couple of bars to 'Tale As Old As Time'.

'Ah, of course. Wonderful.' He leant forwards and whispered, 'Although, clearly, I'm far too butch and manly to have seen the film or remember the music ...'

'Clearly,' she whispered conspiratorially, throwing in a knowing wink.

He put down his cutlery. 'Here's a question then. Favourite Disney film?'

Ellie let out a sigh, thinking. 'Impossible question. But if pushed, I'd say it's a close call between *Beauty and the Beast* and *Cinderella*.'

Joe shook his head. 'Too much scrubbing in *Cinderella*, and she's not much of a twenty-first-century woman. The whole Prince Charming thing ...'

'Not very modern thinking, is it?'

'I suppose the only question left is ... have you found him yet?'

'Who?'

If Ellie wasn't mistaken, Joe blushed beneath his glasses. 'Your Prince Charming,' he said, eating another baby carrot whole.

Ellie rubbed her nose and glanced under her lashes at the couple across the aisle, who were also waiting for her answer.

She shook her head. 'No, I don't suppose I have.'

Joe leant in. 'If it's any consolation, I hear Prince Charming is an absolute arsehole – a bit vain, if you know what I mean?'

Ellie laughed. 'I think you're probably right.'

It was time to change the subject, before she looked completely soppy. She kicked herself under the table for behaving like an excited schoolgirl rather than a great lady. She was on her big, grown-up adventure after all, and sitting across from ... OK, a bit of a geek, but a handsome, really quite kind geek at that, who was, if you squinted and looked at him from a certain angle, a bit of a Clark Kent.

'You do realise you keep encouraging me into talking about myself while giving very little away about yourself,' she said, running a finger around the rim of her glass and trying her hardest to look like an alluring and sophisticated woman.

Joe glanced up cheekily, but with a mouthful of food he had to wait to swallow before saying, 'That's probably because I'm sitting across from an enigmatic woman who has a beautiful ... talent, and I'm worried that my own little life won't match up to expectation.'

She repeated the words in her head. Enigmatic? Beautiful? That would do.

'And I'd rather you thought of me as a bally hero fighter ace for a while than pull away the mask too soon.'

Ellie snorted into her drink. So much for sophistication. 'Oh, don't worry. Pull away,' she said before polishing off her second glass of wine (which was definitely against doctor's orders). 'I've never seen the big attraction to men in uniform.' *Utter lie*. 'After all,' she babbled on, 'strip the uniform away and what are you left with?' She considered this a moment before saying, 'Just a sexy, ripped bloke sitting around in his boxer shorts ... which I don't suppose would be all *that* bad, come to think of it ...'

Joe laughed at this. A proper belly laugh, not just a titter.

Ellie, pleased to have inadvertently caused him to laugh – and he did look so bloody lovely when he laughed – said, 'So come on, drop the veil. Who is the man behind the moustache? Who is Joe from Leeds?'

Joe rolled his eyes. 'All right. But if I suddenly appear above you and start shaking your shoulders violently it's because I think you've slipped into a coma. My assistant, actually she's more like my mum – Gloria – always gives me strict instructions not to bore anyone to ...'

'Just tell me!'

He put down his glass. 'I own a curiosity shop – a shop of memorabilia. It's nothing, really.'

'An antiques dealer, no way! Have you got a bowtie? Do you have a guest slot on *Antiques Roadshow?*'

Joe put up a hand.

'Stop! I am not now, nor have I ever been, an antiques dealer. Also, do I look like a man who could carry off a bowtie?'

He did, actually. Ellie bit her lip and swallowed a laugh.

'I collect things, unusual things. You could say that I'm a bit of a kleptomaniac, I suppose.' He picked up his glass.

Ellie glanced at the doctor and nurse across the aisle, who glanced back at her, before they all turned to stare at him. 'You steal things?' she blurted.

Joe spat out his wine. 'What? Steal? No!' He turned to the other couple. 'Ignore her. She's been drinking. I'm not a thief, honestly.' He turned back to face Ellie. 'Why on earth would you think that?' he whispered.

Ellie shrugged. 'Probably because you said you're a klep-tomaniac ...'

'And?'

'*And* a kleptomaniac is someone who is addicted to stealing things.'

'No, it isn't. A kleptomaniac is someone who's addicted to collecting nostalgia ... aren't they?' He turned to pose the question to the doctor, who shook his head, as did the nurse. 'Shit,' Joe whispered, leaning forwards across the table. 'I've been calling myself a kleptomaniac for years! No wonder I've been getting so many funny looks.'

Ellie shook with laughter. She used the napkin to wipe

away the tears while Joe polished off the rest of his meal in two mouthfuls.

'See,' he said, placing his knife and fork neatly on his plate. 'I knew I shouldn't have told you. You think I'm dull.'

'Not at all,' she said. 'I love it! Didn't I say I was a nostalgia geek? Please, please tell me yours is the kind of shop that has a Dickensian-type frontage, with a bell attached to the front door and lots of dark wood and dusty shelves of things you never sell, and pots of aspidistras everywhere ...'

'Yes!' exclaimed Joe, his smile lighting up the carriage. 'My shop is *exactly* like that!'

And the skirt of the wedding dress would be exactly like Cinderella's.

Ellie nodded towards the clock.

'And what about this sweet little thing? Is it for sale? Only, my kitchen in Cornwall hasn't got a clock in it. Will you fix it, do you think?'

'I was going to set about fixing it on the train ...' Joe picked up the clock and looked at it fondly before passing it to Ellie. 'But I don't know, maybe it doesn't want to be fixed.'

'Is it valuable?' she asked, spinning the clock around in her hands.

Joe shook his head. 'Nah, it's not even worth what I paid for it, to be honest.'

Ellie looked up and smiled, intrigued. 'So, why ...?'

'Did I buy it? I suppose I liked the idea of making it tick again.'

Ellie put a hand to her chest. 'That's a wonderful thing to want to do,' she said, handing the clock back. 'Just wonderful.'

Rihanna arrived to take orders for dessert, which was a choice between raspberry pavlova covered with a chocolate cage and cherry jus, or plain and simple raspberry crumble.

'Ooh, raspberry crumble, please,' said Ellie.

'Any chance of both?' said Joe.

Rihanna tapped her nose. 'I'll see what I can do.'

Chapter 14

Eliza

'I'm just looking for a bit of a change, a fresh challenge,' Eliza had said to Matron at the Paddington depot the day after Cartwright had refused to deploy her as a war artist. 'Perhaps to France after the invasion,' she suggested. 'They're going to need all the nurses they can get, I should think. I mean, if they go, obviously.'

The request was noted and Eliza, who was beginning to wonder if she oughtn't to have been more careful what she wished for, was very quickly given her orders to deploy. Where to, however, was secret. All she knew was that she was to take all the kit she had ever been issued and report to her depot at 1600 hours on 28 May. She would find out the location of her deployment later that evening, upon arrival.

The telegram she sent to Arthur was brief.

AM BEING DEPLOYED AS A NURSE (STOP) NO IDEA WHERE (STOP) TAKE CARE (STOP) ELIZA

It had been cowardly to send a telegram rather than to phone, but they hadn't spoken since her return from Cornwall and the thought of speaking to Arthur now felt awkward. When had her marriage become so strained as to not even want to speak to him, she wondered? After Cornwall or before? Before, she decided, definitely before. Making up her mind to do the right thing and telephone, not just to speak to him before leaving London but to suggest that there really were things they needed to discuss on both of their returns, she made a trunk call to Scotland. But Arthur was out with his ghillie and was not available.

At least I tried, Eliza thought. At least I tried.

She barely recognised herself when she looked in the mirror that last morning in London. She looked excessively tired. The starched, somewhat uncomfortable nurse's cap secured firmly to her head didn't help. The white pinafore over the nurse's dress, the newly issued shoes not yet worn in, the big red cross on the front of the pinafore, were all things she was more than used to wearing, and yet the uniform still felt alien to her. And that was just her working dress. Her army-style fatigues and helmet were also stashed in her kitbag, as ordered, waiting to go. It was like playing at dressing-up – like a child pretending to be a nurse one minute and a soldier the next.

And yet, if anyone had earned the right to wear a nurse's apron it was Eliza. She had tended to many shocking injuries during the Blitz, stoically carrying on, often with Nancy by her side. She sometimes wondered if nursing didn't offer more reward than her art. From the beginning of the Blitz, from the very moment she slipped on the distinctive uniform for the first time, in fact, she had experienced this feeling of needing to be there, of *having* to be there, with the wounded, risking her own life by sticking her nose up to Hitler like the other Londoners who felt a defiant need to stay and carry on. There were times, of course, when she was bowed down by the savagery and the inhumanity of it all, and times when the thought of one more laceration, one more burn, one more severed limb or decapitation – she turned away from the image – was too much to bear. There was still, nevertheless, an excitement to it all, as dreadful as that sounded even to her own ears. And that excitement, like it or not, was addictive.

But Alex was right, she was lucky. When it all got too much, Lady Arbuthnot could simply step onto the night train and remove herself from the horror, stepping off the train as Eliza Grey, the artist, the local Cornish girl done good. But who was she really? Eliza often wondered, always arriving at the conclusion that she was all of these versions of herself, and that was all right.

But for all of her bluster with Alex in Cornwall she was afraid. Perhaps it was this constant juggling between being a nurse in the morning and artist in the afternoon – painting pictures full of positivity where, in reality, she found none – that had unbalanced her, and yet, didn't the one enhance the other, as macabre as that might seem?

Eliza didn't know answers to any of these questions and

came to the conclusion that it was better not to ponder on anything at all, but to simply put one foot in front of the other and carry on.

The strangest thing happened on the morning of her departure: Eliza received a telegram from Nora Levine, Alex's sister, asking her to lunch at The Savoy Hotel.

Gobsmacked, and more than a little apprehensive, Eliza agreed to the meeting.

The waitress escorted Eliza to a table in the corner of the dining room, where a woman dressed in high-waisted trousers and a smart blouse stood and held out her hand. It was quite a shake.

'Hallo, there. I'm Nora. Look here, you don't mind if I *don't* refer to you as Lady Arbuthnot, do you?' She gestured that Eliza should take a seat. 'Only I'm not a fan of pomp?'

Nora's smile, despite her words, was warm and welcoming.

'I'd rather prefer it if you didn't.'

'Right ho!' Nora slapped Eliza on the back, sat down, and without drawing much of a breath, said, 'I hear you know my brother.'

Eliza blushed despite herself. 'Yes,' she said, but her answer had to hover in the air a moment because a waitress, an older lady, arrived with a slice of bread and butter for each of them. The lady's hand shook slightly as she placed the plates on the table.

'Tea for two, please, Doris,' said Nora, before quickly

adding, 'oh, and bring along any other small eats you have, I'm absolutely starving!'

Eliza, who realised that the Levine family were obviously used to taking charge of any social situation, smiled her thanks to the waitress, who edged away.

Nora flicked out a bright white napkin.

'You met in Cornwall?'

'Who?'

'You and Alex.'

'No.'

'Oh, that's not what ...?'

'We met on a train,' clarified Eliza.

'How romantic.' There was definitely a sardonic edge to Nora's tone. 'Truth is, and I'll get straight to the point, I understand you're having a spot of trouble.'

'Trouble?' repeated Eliza, with no clue as to where Nora was going with this.

'Yeeess,' Nora said, dragging out the word so that the noise came out like a deflating balloon. 'A friend at the War Artists Advisory Committee tells me you're having trouble getting properly accredited – as a deployed artist.' Nora flashed Eliza a matter-of-fact stare. 'Apparently, you're after doing the thing properly now, rather than playing around with that flimsy stuff you've been churning out.' Nora took a bite of her bread and butter and waited for a response.

Eliza gave some thought to taking offence, but Nora had a way of stating a fact without any particular malice.

'Yes, I am,' she said, relieved, frankly, that the 'trouble' in question was not Alex.

'The Artists Committee won't let you go because you're a woman,' stated Nora, just as the tea arrived.

'But how—'

'Oh, one can find out anything in London, Eliza – may I call you Eliza? – if one knows all the right people.'

'And you know the right people?'

Nora laughed. 'Yes. I'm afraid I do! Including this Mr Cartwright of yours. What happened?'

Over tea and sandwiches, Eliza told Nora the story of being asked to consider travelling abroad by the Committee, until the meeting with Cartwright where he had taken a sharp about-turn. She also told Nora that none of that mattered anymore because she had volunteered for forward duties in a nursing capacity and was being dispatched 'somewhere' forthwith. She would, of course, find a way to sketch and ultimately paint upon canvas on her return, whatever she saw, wherever she ended up.

Nora's expression turned from marginal indifference to delight. 'Well, I say,' she exclaimed. 'Good for you! Good for you!' Nora leant in and lowered her voice a little. 'When Alex told me about you, I thought you'd turn out to be a bit of a flimsy flop.' Nora tilted her head to one side, seemingly assessing Eliza from top to toe. 'But there's a quiet determination about you that is really quite impressive, I should say. Yes, quite impressive.'

Eliza laughed. It was impossible to take offence with Nora, and she did so remind Eliza of Alex.

Nora edged her chair closer. 'See here, not that we know exactly when it's going to happen, the big push and all that, but one hears rumours. How do you feel about sending anything you sketch directly to me – should you be deployed with the troops, of course – and I'll see what I can do about getting your work published? No promises, mind you, but I'll certainly get your paintings into print – if they're any good, of course. And then I'll speak to people I know at the ministry, see if we can't get you that accreditation sorted out.'

Eliza was stunned.

'Goodness ... I'd love to.'

'And where did you say the Red Cross are sending you?' asked Nora, taking a cigarette case out of her bag. 'Is it to the south coast?'

Eliza shook her head. 'Haven't a clue.'

'Come on ...'

'I haven't, truly.'

Nora lit a cigarette and took one long drag before sitting back in her seat and looking searchingly at Eliza. 'And they're sending you away as a nurse?'

Eliza nodded. 'A VAD nurse.'

'I bet it's the south coast,' said Nora.

Eliza secretly hoped so.

'And you're certain you know nothing else?' Nora's newspaper reporter eyes raked Eliza for a crack. 'Nothing about any invasion date or anything?' She was whispering now.

'I am a nurse. Why on earth would I know anything of note?'

Nora sniffed. 'You'd be surprised what nurses know. The Americans have been arriving in droves. I heard that a hundred and fifty thousand Americans arrived in England last month alone.'

Eliza began to take note. 'This really must be it, then?' she said.

Nora flicked ash into a metal ashtray. 'We'll find out soon enough. I'm thinking of going over there myself. You know ... when it all kicks off.'

'To France?'

'Where else?'

'Why?'

'The same reason as you. I want to be part of it. Respect to you for setting yourself up as a nurse, by the way. Crafty devil! You'll be sent to France quite quickly, I shouldn't wonder.'

The waitress brought more tea, but Eliza looked at the clock on the wall and leant down to pick up her bag from the floor. Nora shooed the waitress away and pulled her chair closer to Eliza's.

'I'm sorry, Nora, but I really must go. I've to be at Paddington soon.'

'Yes, yes, but before you go,' Nora began, 'I wanted to speak with you about another matter, one that is a bit personal. Don't mind, do you?'

Eliza was sure that she probably did mind. 'Go on.'

Nora blew smoke away from Eliza's face before resting her cigarette on the ashtray and leaning forwards to speak quietly, for which Eliza was grateful. Nora's voice could give the town crier a run for his money.

'See here, this thing you have going, your ... let's call it friendship, with a certain twin brother of mine ...'

Eliza bit her lip.

'Truth is, I've never seen him so happy, although looking at you, it's not difficult to see why. There isn't a man in the room who hasn't glanced over ...' Nora took up the cigarette again. 'No, credit to you, he came back from Cornwall a changed man, which, you can imagine, was a relief. I've been so worried as there had been such a lot of talk of pointlessness, and so on ... Bad show, that ...' Nora sniffed back her emotion.

Eliza, who had been holding her breath, breathed out.

'You're married to Arthur Arbuthnot, of course.'

Eliza looked at her wedding ring as an automatic response.

'Yes.'

'I shan't beat about the bush. My brother, he's a special soul. Don't misunderstand me, he can be a prig and an ass sometimes, but his heart ...' Nora paused. 'Let's just say it's an open wound and I've been stitching it up. Thing is, I rather think you and your lovely looks have opened it up again somewhat. Talk of you leaving your husband for him one day, et cetera. Wouldn't you rather miss being the venerable Lady Arbuthnot, if you left?'

Nora had, in one moment, transitioned from being an amenable and very likeable friend to a brutal newspaper hack. Eliza felt her heckles rise.

'Why – *why* – is it acceptable for perfect strangers to ask me such personal questions?' she spat, clearly taking Nora by surprise. Her voice was calm, but her eyes flashed.

'Steady on, old thing.' Nora put a hand on Eliza's arm but Eliza shrugged it off.

'I am not old,' corrected Eliza, 'and I assure you that I am perfectly steady. All of my life, people have thought it all right to say whatever they bloody well think – to have opinions on my life – when I don't give a fig what anyone else does or how they live their lives.'

Eliza took a steadying sip of tea.

'That's all well and good,' said Nora, 'but you might like to know that Alex is intending to throw over his chance of a new life in America – and his well-earned safety – to go to France.'

Eliza regained her composure. 'So I understand,' she said, looking away.

'And do you also "understand" that it was your husband who oiled the wheels for him to do this – to be deployed with the First Army? His plan being to keep you at home by nobbling Cartwright, while dispatching Alex to France. It's all very tidy.'

'But my husband doesn't even know about ...'

Nora rolled her eyes. 'What a naïve fool you are. Oh, he knows, Eliza. Trust me, he knows.'

Eliza had to take a moment. She sat back. It all seemed too incredible. How on earth could Arthur possibly know?

Nora put out her cigarette. 'I can't work you out,' she said. 'My brother says you are the very best of women, but I wonder if you aren't a little ... calculating. One hears things.'

Eliza couldn't help but laugh at this.

'You seem to base your entire life on "hearing things",' she said. 'It's a wonder you are not deaf!'

Nora laughed at this.

'You think me calculating,' said Eliza. 'That would be because of my marriage to Arthur, I suppose?'

Nora didn't respond, simply shrugged.

'You believe me to be mercenary because I was poor and then I married Arthur and now I am rich.'

There was not a trace of embarrassment to Nora. The opinion stood. 'Quite so,' she said.

Eliza looked away. She needed to gather herself. This whole meeting had been surreal. She buttered half of a dry scone she had intended to leave. Nora Levine could jolly well wait. Eventually, Eliza said, 'I was eighteen and an art student when I met Arthur. I had been told to leave the house I was raised in – a woman took me in when I was eight – as they needed the room for a lodger. I slept on a sofa in a friend's studio in Newlyn. I lived off the benevolence of others. All my life, my shoes were too tight and my skirts were too short because I couldn't buy new ones. I owned two things of my own – a book and a crucifix. Arthur was a benefactor at Newlyn and a regular visitor – I think he liked the sea air and the kudos of being involved with a progressive art school. He gave me brushes and canvas. He was very kind and it was the first time I had known kindness since my parents died. Yes, I admit it, he became my own personal benefactor – judge me as you will, it's nothing to me – and after a short time he asked me to marry him. He was forty-nine and I was nineteen, he didn't seem to be particularly old at the time and marrying him seemed to be the most natural thing to do. I wasn't in love with him, but I did love him. I can see why part of that story, in your opinion, would portray me as a calculating woman, but perhaps try not to judge someone until you have walked a mile in their – very tight – shoes. Basically, think what you will, I don't care.'

Nora's expression remained impassive.

'I haven't been in contact with your brother since Cornwall and though I will own to having become extremely fond of him, beyond that I will say no more.'

Nora stubbed out her cigarette and smiled.

'Then let us say no more about it.'

Eliza gestured to the waitress for the bill and picked up her bag.

'My treat,' said Nora, putting on her jacket. 'And the offer still stands. If you do get to France, do make sure you send your sketches back to me. I pay well and if you leave him you will need the money. Shall you send them, or are you too much offended by my manner?'

Eliza was savvy enough to appreciate Nora for her professional capability, if not her private interference.

'I shall.'

'Than may I give you some advice?'

'You may.'

'I was in North Africa last year. It was damn awful, but I learned something: not to look away, but to look within, and to record it. There will be times when all you wish to do is turn away, to not see the horror. But you need to record it, Eliza, all of it. Yes, the censors will not approve some of your work for now, but those paintings won't disappear completely, not in the long run. You are expected to record what happened with impartiality and yet in a way that will evoke great feeling in the viewer. Future generations need to look back with horror and wonder at this war, and hope and pray that it will never happen again. Wherever you go, whatever you see, think about which style is best to convey the emotion – the horror, the beauty, the truth. You're a realist, yes?'

'Yes.'

'Think about everything you were taught at art school and push yourself. There will never be another opportunity as exciting as this one for you in your lifetime as an artist – at least, I hope not. I want you to be bold. Take the person who cannot be there and put them right into that moment. That is your challenge, Eliza. Your responsibility, your quest.'

Nora stood. It seemed the advice had come to its conclusion. 'And ... if Alex gets in touch, do tell him to go to America. When the war is over, the two of you can do as you please, but if you love him ... for now, please, just let him go.'

Eliza arrived at Paddington later that afternoon to find that she was part of a tranche of medical support personnel who were detailed to the naval base at Portsmouth. On arrival, she discovered that the port was packed to the gunnels with troops and playing host to an armada of ships. Nora was right, the long-awaited Allied assault into France was no longer a pipe dream but real and, more importantly, imminent.

And the surprises did not stop there. Eliza was to be deployed as a nurse auxiliary onboard a hospital ship, presently docked at the naval base. Ship and staff were standing by to sail across the English Channel alongside the troopships in order to provide care for the thousands of wounded men expected to be shipped back from the Normandy beaches once the first assault pushed through. It was simply a matter of waiting for General Eisenhower to order the off.

Eliza had never before seen a hospital ship, and when she was taken dockside on that first evening, she paused with one foot on the gangplank looking up in absolute wonder. The ship was an incredible sight in its white-painted livery, a ghostly, pristine marvel with its iconic red crosses and a long, striking, green line running the length of the sides. It wasn't until her third day in Portsmouth that she began to feel even slightly familiar with either life onboard or the terminology used by the regular members of staff, who were a mixed bag of English and American medical personnel.

The medical training onboard was not as thorough as Eliza had hoped it would be. She took time to familiarise herself with the ship and its facilities – the areas set aside as wards, the well-equipped operating theatre, the storage facilities for all the blood and plasma, and the cupboards full of the drugs and bandages that would be required – but what worried her was that none of the nurses had worked on a ship before and so there was no single person to refer to as a voice of experience.

'What's to know?' one doctor said to her. 'It's just the same as any old hospital, except it floats.' But his flippancy only masked his anxiety and with the Normandy beaches heavily defended, the nurses were told to expect the worst kind of injuries. And so it was inevitable that the wards that stood silent and pristine just now, with pure white bedlinen pulled tightly across the cots, would soon become a bloodbath. Eliza thought of the flamethrowers and wire fences at Porthcurno and shuddered as she imagined the men, their heads down, running onto the beaches, laden with ammunition and backpacks full of kit. All of which meant that Eliza had an awakening the likes of which she had not imagined possible just days earlier, when she expected to take on nothing more than basic duties at the shoreside hospital. Whether there would even be time for her to sketch what she saw – the whole reason she had volunteered – was another worrying matter.

With the ship and the crew waiting for the off and the atmosphere at the dockyard becoming increasing sombre yet also frenetic, Eliza couldn't help but feel nervous – frightened, even. The chatter of her fellow nurses in the mess decks didn't help. Would the Germans honour the Geneva Convention and leave the hospital ship untargeted, or were they to be seen as simply another Allied ship to be shelled from the beaches or bombed from the air? She didn't know, no one did. All she knew was that she was a part of it now, and she had been the one to make it happen.

On 5 June, Eliza woke to a particularly blustery and unseasonably cold morning. She stepped off the hospital ship and took a walk along the dockside, trying to take in the sheer scale of it all – the number of ships, the hardware, the personnel, all amalgamated and waiting for the off. She paused alongside HMS *Belfast*, her sketchbook in her hand, a pencil in her pocket. The Solent – the narrow stretch of water between Gosport and the Isle of Wight – had become one of the many gathering points for the armada, which she discovered was dotted all along the south coast of England. It was an armada the likes of which no one in her lifetime had ever seen. Ship after ship was full to the brim with military hardware and men – mainly American, British and Canadian troops. Eliza had been in Portsmouth for less than a week, and during that time she had watched tractors, jeeps, personnel carriers, and row after row of what she'd heard referred to as LCTs – Landing Craft Tanks – and all manner of things, winched on to the ships in a relentless operation to prepare for the ultimate battle for liberation – the invasion of France. She had watched the men at work and sketched them when she could, although most were simply hanging around the dockyard, smoking, or playing cards and waiting. The dockyard was in lockdown. Once in, no one was allowed out. It was the biggest secret ever kept – the hiding from Hitler of an invasion force gathered in the south of England – and it needed to be kept at all costs. With the absence of Luftwaffe bombing raids on ports such as Portsmouth over the past few weeks, it seemed they had, by some miracle, and lots of counter-intelligence, accomplished their goal.

The size and complexity of the operation had been almost too great for Eliza to comprehend when she had arrived in Portsmouth. Speaking to Nora about rumours of the off was one thing, but seeing it for real, meeting the men who would do the thing, was another, and she had begun to feel overwhelmed, to worry that she was simply not up to the task. She confessed such fears to her ward sister, who, after telling Eliza in no uncertain terms to pull herself together, had also said that Eliza had been specially recommended by her last unit and to remember that nursing through the horror of the Blitz would have been the perfect training for whatever was to come.

Feeling a little calmed, Eliza spoke to some of the GIs and asked their permission to sketch them as they waited in the dockyard. She sketched a group of four young men who were playing craps. A red blanket had been rolled out and the men had laughed and teased each other as they rolled the dice, gambling for cigarettes and dollars. They were from Idaho, Eliza discovered, and had enrolled together, trained together and would now fight together. Not one of them was over twenty-two. Eliza drew their helmets and weapons laid out on the floor next to the blanket. On returning to her mess quarters later she added colour to the sketch. It was only when she stood back and looked at the finished painting she realised that she hadn't painted a blanket, but a pool of blood around the helmets. She called it *Waiting to Die* because, after all, that was the real game they were playing and the most heartbreaking thing was that they all knew it, too.

Despite the crippling anxiety felt by all, the optimist in Eliza's soul refused to bow down completely, and so as an antidote to the painting, she sought out the young men again and asked them to stand together, with their arms around each other and smiles on their faces, one with a cigarette hanging from the corner of his mouth, one with a shining gold tooth. She called it *Brothers In Arms*, and they loved it.

The one question on everyone's lips was, when would they go? Tonight? Tomorrow? It was late afternoon and a large group of GIs had gathered around a chaplain who stood on a crate on the dockside, his white robes a stark contrast to the battle fatigues of the infantrymen. He held up his right hand, a bible in his left, and began to pray. The men – boys, really – dipped their heads in reverence. It was a moment that put a halt to any tomfoolery. It must almost be time to go, then, Eliza thought, the very air around her charged with fear and adrenalin. She would cope with whatever was to come, she told herself, by doing exactly what she'd been asked to do – nurse the wounded – but after that she would record it all for ever.

Eliza was sitting on a coil of rope, sketching, when a Petty Officer she knew from the hospital ship dashed past her. She was concentrating on the detail of a small boat, an LCT, which was loaded on a ship and was full to the gunnels with American soldiers. She'd watched them embark. Some were silent, some joking, some praying. The distinct clanking noise of anchor chains being coiled in began to echo through the dockyard. It was a simple noise with a deafening impact and could only mean one thing.

'What's happening?' she asked, quickly gathering up her bits and pieces.

'We're only bloody well off!' he shouted back, with an expression somewhere between an inane grin and abject fear. 'And never sit on a rope or a chain in a dockyard, you'll get your bloody leg ripped off!'

Eliza, flushed with fear at the thought of her own ship sailing without her, was just about to turn tail and run across the dockyard when she heard her name called out.

'Eliza! Eliza Grey! Up here! Look up. Up here! It's me!'

Eliza followed the direction of the voice. A man was standing waving his arms at her from the port side of the departing HMS *Belfast*. Eliza ran towards the water's edge. A sailor barked at her to stand back, but the departing ship was still close enough to see that the man was definitely Alex. Who else would be wearing an RAF flying jacket over army fatigues while standing on a Navy ship?

'I can't believe it's you!' he shouted across the water. 'I was just thinking about you. What are you doing here?'

Eliza pointed to the red cross on her armband. The ship began to turn in earnest away from the dockside and put on some steam. 'I'm here to nurse,' she shouted. 'On the hospital ship.'

'But aren't you painting?'

'Yes and no,' she shouted back. 'Too difficult to explain. What about you?'

'I'm covering the landings. I got billeted on here. Did you get my telegram?' he shouted.

She ran along the jetty. 'Yes! I did! Thank you!'

A happy realisation crossed his face.

'You didn't send anything back. I thought you'd forgotten me.'

'Not a bit,' yelled Eliza, beaming up at him.

Alex cupped his right ear with his hand to indicate he couldn't hear. He began to walk quickly along the deck to keep as close to Eliza as possible. 'But listen,' he yelled. 'May I see you again?'

'What?'

'I'll not be gone for long. I'm covering the landings and then I'll be back. I'll come and find you, shall I? Are you staying here?'

He ran around the deck, trying to keep Eliza in view as the ship turned onto course, but his way was blocked by one of the ship's guns.

'I want to tell you something ...' she shouted.

'What?' He put his hands up in frustration.

'I miss you!'

But Alex couldn't have heard because he shrugged and shouted back, 'Goodbye, Theodora!' and began to wave instead.

She shouted, 'I miss you,' again, across the water, but the ship turned hard to broadside, and as Alex edged out of view, Eliza did not have time to dwell in melancholy and stand to watch the ship sail away. She had her own part to play.

She set off at a pace towards her own ship. 'And all shall be well,' she said to herself while running towards a big red cross. 'And all shall be well.'

Chapter 15

Ellie

Crewkerne to Taunton

'And how was your dessert, Sir?' asked Rihanna, clearing away Joe's two pudding bowls.

'Delicious, thank you. But I think the crumble had the edge,' said Joe, bobbing his head from side to side, considering, 'but only by a whisper.'

Ellie couldn't help but smile. Joe looked so much more content now that his belly was full.

Rihanna turned to Eliza. 'Would you like tea or coffee, Madam?'

'Is it Yorkshire tea?' asked Joe, not giving Ellie time to answer. 'Because that's a deal-breaker with me on the tea front, I'm afraid.'

Rihanna shook her head. 'It's not Yorkshire tea, Sir.'

Joe sniffed dismissively. 'In that case, make that two coffees and feel free to throw in as many chocolate mints

on the tray as you can muster, to make up for the tea issue!'
He threw Rihanna a thousand-watt smile and turned to
Ellie, suddenly frowning. 'Shit. Sorry. Is that OK? It must
be the uniform making me all ...' he struggled to find the
word '... domineering. Anyway, to do it properly ... would
you care to join me in the partaking of a little coffee, Ms
Nightingale?'

Ellie looked up at Rihanna and was just about to say
that that would be lovely, when Joe added, 'But do say yes.
The rest of the evening would be rubbish if you went to
bed now.'

The eye contact between the two women said everything.

'Two coffees, please, my good woman,' said Ellie. 'And
like the gentleman said, as many chocolate mints as you
can muster!'

At around 10 p.m. the D-Day Dames took a break and
decamped to the bar. Joe and Ellie didn't mind. It gave
them an opportunity to talk, which had been an almost
impossible task while the Dames were singing.

'So, you never actually met the lady who left your granny
the cottage?' asked Joe, nursing an Irish coffee.

Ellie shook her head. 'No. But I do have her journal, so
I feel I know her quite well.'

Joe glanced at the clock and the journal sitting together
on the table.

'It's funny, isn't it?' she said, looking around and taking

in the costumes on show. 'Here we all are, dressed up like 1940s finest, all having a great time playing out our roles, but when you read the journal and look at her sketches, you can't help but wonder how on earth they got through it all.'

'It must have been hell,' Joe agreed.

'Eliza was at the Normandy landings. Did I tell you that?'

Joe shook his head. 'Did she write about them?'

Ellie opened the journal, turning the pages carefully. 'It's funny, but before I read this, the war was something that seemed to have happened off-stage, or if not off-stage, exactly, then something romanticised in my mind in an image of black and white. But when you read this ... you realise that it happened to people just like us, and although it seems to have happened years and years ago, it was just yesterday, really. I don't suppose you'd like to ...'

'Read it? I'd love to!' Joe pushed his glasses up his nose.

'Her D-Day entry appears fairly early on.' Ellie carefully flicked through the pages. 'Ah, here it is. June 1944. Oh, and there's a letter pasted in after her entry, it's from Alex. He was there too. Imagine that?'

With his eyes on Eliza's beautiful handwriting and Ellie's eyes on him, Joe began to read. Ellie sat back, her thumbnail between her teeth, and watched his reactions as he read.

11 June 1944

Dear Eliza

It's late, at least I think it's late, but you'll no doubt understand when I say that time has lost all meaning. This is the first moment I've taken for myself other than to eat and sleep and write my pieces since the invasion began, and I'm dizzy with exhaustion.

HMS Belfast has been nothing short of incredible in her role to support the troops. From before dawn on that terrible first day, her guns pounded the shoreline from zero hour, shaking the ship to its very core. Casualties began to arrive onboard pretty quickly, but Eliza, the bodies in the water ... They were just floating past the ship, many of them not actually shot, but drowned, unable to swim ashore in the bad weather. As I saw them I thought of what you would be witnessing too, and I would have done anything to shield you from the horror of it all at that moment. The only thing to say with certainty is that this is – it must be – the beginning of the end.

I shall be reporting from the ship for a while yet, but I hope to get back to Portsmouth at the end of June or the beginning of July, at which time I have decided that I shall come and find you. I don't care what the consequences are. If we are vilified then we shall go to America. I am certain they will not be so judgemental over there. Life is too fragile, too transient,

*too frail to not say the things we need to say to each
other at the time we need to say them.*

I love you, Eliza.
Yours, as ever,
Alex

Joe shook his head. 'It must have been a living hell,' he
said, not taking his eyes off the book as he studied a sketch
Eliza had drawn on the leaf opposite the letter. It was of
HMS *Belfast* drifting away from the dockyard. A figure
was waving from the deck. He turned the page to find
another painting, again in a realist style, of two nurses,
one with a hand on the shoulder of the other. Both were
standing on the rear deck of a hospital ship, a line of
golden sand sitting beyond a stretch of blood-red sea.
Barrage balloons flew above them. It was called *Sisters*.
The next page was Eliza's journal entry for June 1944. Joe
read on.

*I am far too exhausted and … numb, I suppose, to
write, but if I don't get something down on paper now,
the immediacy of the memory will be gone. The consequences of D-Day ripped through the hospital ship like
a tidal wave. Back at Portsmouth, what was once a
dockyard of anxiety and anticipation became a place
of suffering and mourning as the dead and the dying
were shipped home.*

Guns pounded the shoreline relentlessly from the off,

*targeting gun batteries, installations, foxholes and every-
thing in between. Casualties arrived onboard by
lunchtime. We heard that when the ramps lowered some
LCTs were not yet close enough to shore to allow the
men to run onto the beach, and so they found themselves
in freezing water above their heads.*

*Arthur wrote to say that I was a naïve little fool,
volunteering to transfer to the front line, and he was
right, although where would we be if there weren't lots
of naïve little fools like me around? Nothing – not even
the horror of the Blitz – could have prepared me for
the sights, sounds and smells of all those young men
brought onboard. With a pen in my hand rather than
a brush, I find it difficult to know where on earth to
begin to paint the scene. All I can say is that I was not
prepared for the reality of the Normandy beaches – who
could be?*

*On the second day, I was required to assist on the
water ambulance, which meant wading out to the
beach to help the stretcher-bearers while the battle
waged on around us. Some men were dead where
they fell, some were checked for life quickly and left
behind. Bodies, bloated out of recognition, were
washed in by the tide and would nudge up against
my leg as we repeatedly waded into the terribly cold
water to carry the wounded onboard. And once
onboard, what hell. What to say of the burns and
fractures and blast injuries, the jaws rewired, the*

missing eyeballs, the missing limbs, all of which I helped to treat with what was nothing more than Girl Scout medical training.

What we witnessed on those beaches has set for me a new bar, I think, in the witnessing of human suffering. It seems that there is no end to the unfathomable waste of human life our generation must witness. The road to Berlin is upon us, and I, more than ever, despite everything – or perhaps because of everything want to paint it. It's late but I feel more invigorated than ever and know that it is time to put down this pen and pick up a brush. It's time to show the world what I have seen, and there will be no sugar coating.

Joe stopped reading. He turned page after page of the sketches that followed. He took off his glasses and rubbed his eyes.

'It's impossible to know how they coped,' he said. 'I can see why you treasure the journal.'

Ellie leant towards him, her knee touching his knee under the table as she turned the next page, revealing a painting of a beach that Eliza had called *Red Sea*.

'This next picture is of the wounded strewn on Normandy beaches,' Ellie explained. 'It's in a different style to most of the others. I think it's impressionism, but I'm not sure, but it's more of a *feeling* of the place than a reproduction of a picture of it.'

Joe nodded his agreement.

'There's a collection of her artwork at the Imperial War Museum. Some of those pieces are from her time on the hospital ship and they're all … It's difficult to know how to describe them. Harrowing, and yet beautiful and tender at the same time. But this one,' Ellie nodded towards the journal, 'seems more desperate than the others somehow. The museum wanted to remove it from the journal and put it on display, but my granny wouldn't let them. As the journal progresses many more of her paintings take on an impressionist style, until right at the end, when they're different again – quite modern, really. Cubism, according to Great Granny Nancy.'

Joe closed the journal. 'I guess she felt she could express herself best in art,' he said. 'It's like you and your music, isn't it? We all find the best outlet for our emotions, one way or another. Thank you for showing me.' He handed the journal back. 'You must know her words off by heart by now.'

Ellie was about to say that she did, absolutely she did, and that, yes, whenever her life had been at its most diffi-cult, she had turned to the expression of music, not the written or spoken word, but she didn't have the time to explain because Rihanna appeared.

Looking fraught, Rihanna crouched by the table to address Ellie face to face.

'Now, tell me to bugger off if it's too much of an impo-sition,' she said, 'but I'm up the proverbial crap creek without any kind of paddle and – oh, my God, I hate to

186

ask – but do you think you could do me a ginormous favour?'

Rihanna had the pallor of someone about to be sick. Ellie sat back a little in surprise and waited for an explanation.

'Could you play your violin while we try to fix the music system? The PA has broken so the D-Day Dames are refusing to resume their set. But it shouldn't take too long to get going again.'

Ellie's hand rushed to her chest. 'What?'

'It's just, the passengers are getting restless. Some are drifting off to bed chuntering about refunds. And the bloody D-Day Dames don't care a toss! I've asked them to sing without backing but they just laughed.'

'Where are they now?' asked Joe.

'Getting truly blathered at the bar. And I wouldn't mind but they're not even American! They're from Bolton, apparently. I had no idea.'

Ellie's hand went from her chest to her mouth in an attempt to stifle a laugh.

'I've gone from hero to zero in the space of five minutes. Could you possibly fill the void? Please? Just for ten minutes. I'll pay you, obviously. The train company won't cough up but I've got forty quid in my purse ...'

Ellie put a hand on Rihanna's shoulder to calm her, then glanced at Joe for his thoughts.

'I suppose you did say that tonight's performance was your big break,' he said, throwing in a shrug. '"Ellie Nightingale, for one night only" and all that.'

'Please?' This from Rihanna.

On the one hand, she would be delighted to play along – so long as the train didn't bounce around too much, which could be problematic – but she was enjoying her evening with Joe so very much, and it would be such a shame to spoil it now, to break the flow. This had been her very best First Date ever (not that she had been on many dates, or that Joe even realised that it was a date), but it was magical. It was perfect. For once in her life, she had got to play the heroine ...

But Rihanna had been so kind and the passengers *were* beginning to grumble ...

'Oh, all right, then,' she said, standing. 'I'll just get my things. Won't be a tick.'

Ellie returned with fiddle and bow and positioned herself in the aisle by the side of Joe's seat at the end of the carriage. She did this for two reasons: firstly, so that she could lean against something as the train swayed, and secondly, so that she couldn't look at him as she played, because what if he wasn't looking up adoringly at her while she enjoyed her moment? What if, instead, he was picking at his fingernails, bored stiff?

Rihanna tapped a glass with a teaspoon.

'Ladies and gentlemen, soldiers, nurses, doctors, women of the Land Army, and even you over there in the Yoda costume ...' (There was always one.) 'While we take a few minutes for the engineer to fix the PA system – and get the party train really rocking again – I have a surprise and a real treat for you, because tonight, for one night only, we are very lucky to have dining among us one of the brightest stars of the English classical music scene, and she has kindly offered to play for you all as you enjoy your coffee. Ladies and gentlemen, sit back, relax a moment and put your hands together for the unique and truly dazzling enigmatic angel that is Ellie Nightingale.'

Polite applause.

Ellie, who had taken off her heels to balance, stood in a pool of green. She lifted bow to violin and waited to begin. The train juddered over a crossed line, causing her to stumble a little, which was when she felt a strong arm wrap around her waist to steady her. She glanced down.

'I've got you,' whispered Joe, smiling.

She took a deep breath, smiled at her audience and began to play.

Chapter 16

Eliza

Field Hospital, Rennes, late July 1944

Wearing her already tatty Women's Army Auxiliary Corps (WAAC) fatigues, and tired out to the brink of exhaustion, Eliza stood in the nurses' wash tent and wrung out her underwear above a bowl of cold water.

Where on earth was Lady Arbuthnot now, she wondered?

She thought suddenly of Mrs Kelly from her childhood back in Penzance, wringing out clothes above the kitchen sink. Mrs Kelly would scrub Eliza's face with a starched, rough cloth until her poor skin glowed red. 'Cleanliness is next to Godliness, Eliza, remember that!' she would say, her gentle eyes attempting sternness while Eliza stood on a box next to the high enamel sink. Such simple times. Times that were always so underappreciated at the moment they happened for their calm and comfortable security. But it wasn't too late to appreciate them now, when she needed the warmth of those memories the most.

Eliza had been released from the hospital ship in early July. She returned to London, briefly, only to find that Arthur remained squirrelled away in Scotland and Nancy had been deployed to a field hospital in Berkshire. There had been no word from Alex. Nora had been as good as her word and had quickly found exposure for Eliza's D-Day paintings, even securing a feature in the July edition of American *Life* magazine, with the emotive *Brothers in Arms* painting taking pride of place on the cover. Eliza's work became a cause of controversy, being criticised as too 'real' for public consumption. But Nora had devoured them and whatever the critics said didn't matter, because Eliza had never been so proud of any work she had released before.

The pace of her life, Eliza realised, had shifted up several gears. She was busy, she was in demand, she was the darling of the London art scene once more, but it was the cover of *Time* that led to the next extraordinary turn of events. A request was sent, via Mr Cartwright, from the British Red Cross organisation for Eliza to become their own particular War Artist. Cartwright, it seemed, on having seen Eliza's work and hearing that she had, somehow, made it to the Normandy landings, had altered his opinion regarding the possibility of female war artists deploying to the front. The fact that Arthur seemed to have given up trying to keep Eliza home didn't harm matters either. Cartwright explained how impressed the 'higher-ups' of the Red Cross had been by Eliza's work. As they were also aware of her impeccable record in her nursing capacity, they asked if she might consider recording the remainder of the war from their perspective – or more particularly, from the perspective of the medics in a field hospital as it moved eastward through France.

Would she go, Cartwright asked, when she visited him in London? Or was it perhaps time to concentrate on her home life?

Eliza did not hesitate with her answer. It was yes.

And the surprises did not stop there. A second meeting with Nora Levine was arranged – not at The Savoy this time, but a summer stroll in Hyde Park. Despite her annoyance at Nora's previous comments about Alex, Eliza was surprised to find that she was pleased to see his sister. After all, the reason for Eliza's sudden exposure and acceptance as a war artist of merit was in no small part down to Nora. Eliza was keen to tell her new – no, it would be too much to call her a 'friend' – her new colleague the news: that she was going to France! Eliza could barely believe it, but the facts were there. Eliza Grey was to be an actual war artist. After all these years, she had made it.

But Nora already knew of her news, and the reason Nora already knew was because Nora – Eliza should have realised sooner – was the person who had arranged it all.

'You're to act as ... let's call it my "go-between",' she explained, as the two women wandered through the park. 'You'll be given messages – codes, ciphers and whatnot –

don't worry about how you'll receive them for now, just accept that this will happen – and you're to find a way to put the … message, or whatever, into your latest painting, which will then be dispatched to me for processing.'

Eliza stopped walking and took a deep breath. This took her task to a whole other level.

Nora noticed her hesitancy. 'It's a boon, Eliza! Honestly! Just think, you'll be published nationally and internationally without question. This is the big league. No scrubbing about in the periodicals after this …'

'But how …?'

'Oh, leave the hows and the wherefores to me and don't overthink it, there's a good girl. And remember that some bits and bobs are decoys so don't start second guessing what any particular message is all about. It's best you don't know, at any rate.'

Eliza's furrowed brow betrayed her anxiety. Nora punched her arm. 'Smile! Your art will be synonymous with the war! And don't even think about telling me that you don't care about that kind of thing – that you're all about the art, Ms Grey – because I simply won't believe you!'

Eliza laughed and carried on walking. Nothing surprised her anymore, least of all when it involved Nora Levine. But then another thought crossed her mind. She looked over her shoulder across the park and whispered, 'Then you're a … sp—'

'Spy?' exclaimed Nora with a laugh. 'No. Well, not quite.

I work for the intelligence services now and again, that's all.' She patted Eliza's hand. 'Just remember, all you have to do, you lucky thing, is to paint – and try to stay alive, of course!' She added the latter as if it were something fairly low down on her order of priorities. 'Anyhow, don't worry about it now. I'll touch base with you as soon as I get over there.'

Eliza stopped walking again. 'Over there? You?'

Nora shrugged as if she'd just confirmed she was taking a cottage in Brighton for the summer.

'Yes, me. I've been affiliated.'

'With whom?'

'The WAACs of all things. Can you imagine it, me, bunking up with a load of American women?' Eliza couldn't, not for one minute. 'It'll be hell!' concluded Nora.

'But why the WAACs?' asked Eliza.

'It was all I could get. You know how it is. They're still not letting women reporters affiliate with the forward battalions. Bad show all round, I say.'

'Even though you've got your other ... tasks to sort out? They still won't let you bunk up with the men?'

Nora shook her head. 'Nope, not even then.' She put an arm through Eliza's. 'Doesn't matter. I'll get myself bunked up with the right people once I'm over there, never you worry. The WAACs are simply a quicker way of securing a ticket across the Channel, and anyhow, it looks more normal that way. If I got special privileges the other women reporters trying to get over there would smell a rat. Anyhow,

I've a few things to sort out this end and then I'll be off – you can't keep all the fun to yourself, you know!'

Nora wasn't the only person keen to cross the Channel. *Everyone*, it seemed, was heading to France. Having visited the Normandy beaches during the landings, Eliza was surprised on her return to see how different it all looked. The strewn bodies that had carpeted the beaches during her first Channel crossings were gone, and as for those poor souls bobbing along in the sea where they fell, who knew where they were now, or if their dog-tags would ever be recovered. It seemed odd to think that she was here again, walking around in the relative safety of the beaches, beaches that had witnessed so much bloodshed and terror just weeks before, the young men mown down in their thousands ... The boys from Idaho, where were they now? She shuddered. How could a place that had experienced such horror ever be quite the same again? Ships were everywhere, people were everywhere, makeshift floating harbours were everywhere. Barrage balloons floated above line after line of trucks and tanks and jeeps, all of which flowed continually onto the beaches from LCTs that worked shuttle services from ship to shore.

Once ashore, it seemed that the whole of northern France was tiptoeing around landmines. White tape marked out safe passages through the sand. The field hospital staff, with Eliza in tow, were taken by convoy to their first location, which was about five miles inland. As the truck moved on and Eliza gazed in wonder at the scenes playing out around her, she saw tired, dirty and bewildered troops hanging around along the roadside, awaiting their orders. The trees in one area along the way were littered with parachutes, abandoned as part of the disposable detritus littering Normandy after the invasion. Dead bodies, mainly German bodies, and notices reading *Achtung Minen* – 'Caution, Mines' – littered the roadside and became a sight so common that it soon failed to shock anyone.

Two miles into the journey, an orderly sitting in the back of one of the forward trucks in the convoy was shot dead by a stray bullet. From that point, Eliza was crippled with fear as they rumbled along the country lanes, her jaw stiff, her eyes alert. She saw a surgeon she knew from the hospital ship tending to another unfortunate Red Cross volunteer by the side of the road, shot in the chest, no doubt, by a rogue sniper hidden in the trees. The Germans may have been pushed back from the beaches, but not by far. Eliza had naively imagined 'the front' as a defined line, forward of which were Germans. But there was no clear line with good people on one side and bad people on the other. The front was nothing more than farmyards, and crop fields, and tree-lined avenues, and crumbling church spires. It was a non-existent place, a place of shifting sands, an ephemeral dune in a vast, wide desert.

It was clear that the place was being systematically decimated, plain and simple. It was as if nothing that existed here – not buildings, not animals, not people – was sacrosanct, and as the allies moved inland and the medics picked up the pieces, the civilians who found themselves and their few remaining possessions in the way soon realised that, for them, the liberation was not so much a blessing as a nightmare.

With her art supplies limited, Eliza had to be selective in what she drew, which focused the mind somewhat. Often without the time or the space to set up her easel and paints, she would disappear into a discreet corner and sketch the scene first with charcoal or a pencil, and complete the final painting later on, either in the chow tent or back at her own billet. She began to feel a sense of unworthiness – of a kind of fake godliness – in deciding which of the things she saw were more important to capture than the next. Because, to Eliza, every last bit was important, from the patients lying on the ground between beds due to overcrowding, to the pails of water boiling away on an open fire outside the surgery tent for sterilising needles. And then the coded messages began to arrive via a motorbike courier. Sometimes two per week, although sometimes none. They were always different. Sometimes colours, sometimes a book title, other times numbers and often a set scene. Eliza never understood what on earth the messages might mean, or who they were destined for, and realised it was almost certainly better that way.

Despite her tenuous involvement with espionage, it was, nevertheless, a simple life. Eliza's worldly possessions consisted of Army-issue trousers and jacket (slightly too big), waterproof leggings, a woollen sweater (smelly and snagged), boots (that rubbed), a gas mask, a helmet, a foldable spade and a camp cot (which was heavy). A bed roll and, of course, her art supplies completed the inventory of her possessions.

The field hospital was established at an apple orchard outside Rennes. Eliza spent her time nursing at night and painting during the day – they were simply too short staffed for her not to help – securing only a few hours here and there to manage a little sleep, or to eat. Polish, Canadian, British and American wounded were brought in, as well as injured German POWs. Eliza soon rediscovered how to live by forced emotional distance, having been taught the rudiments of survival in the Blitz. She kept her emotions in check by maintaining a friendly, kind and helpful persona, but keeping a detached distance from colleagues and patients; the reserved Lady Arbuthnot, it seemed, was not quite dead after all.

Eliza pegged up the last of her clothing and smiled at the thought of her week in Cornwall. It was just a couple of months ago now but it seemed so much longer. Where was Alex right now? she wondered. She lay back against the bark of a gnarled apple tree and took a moment to rest in the shade. Glancing across at the empty pastures beyond, where cattle would once have grazed in the sunshine and horses would have enjoyed a gallop, she shook her head in an attempt to push away the memory of all the animal corpses she had seen lying by the roadside, their stiff legs in the air, their big brown trusting eyes staring into oblivion. It hurt her more to see a dead animal than a dead German. What had happened to her soul, she wondered, for this to be so? Not to even flinch at the sight of a dead man just so long as he was wearing a German uniform? This demarcation, this compartmentalising of death ... it was savage, but it was, she knew, necessary.

There was no doubt that her artwork was becoming darker by the day, but now and again, Eliza made an effort to rebel against the war, to rebel against Alex and Nora and their desire to keep everything real, and found something lighter to paint for her journal. It was this work, the work she did for herself to keep her thoughts from crashing into oblivion, that became increasingly more enjoyable and expressive, and with a desire for such pleasant thoughts in mind, Eliza, feeling a kind of swaddled security while sitting in the lush familiarity of the grid of trees, took out her journal and began to sketch a couple of nurses who were also taking moment for themselves in the orchard. It was then, while trying to capture an image of women enjoying the comfort of great friendship, that Eliza began to feel a longing for Nancy's company. Yes, keeping distance from others reduced the risk of pain, but it brought with it limited joy, too.

She was interrupted from these thoughts by a familiar voice calling her name through the trees. A nurse was staggering towards her, her helmet lopsided and her back bowed by the huge backpack. Extra kit was strapped on the pack in the manner of a pedlar trading her wares on the street.

'Man alive!' shouted the woman. 'If it isn't Lady Bloody Arbuthnot lounging around like a bally princess. No change there, then. Don't you know there's a war on!'

With her arms open and her smile wide showing pearly white teeth, the young woman, her long, hockey-toned legs striding confidently, picked up her pace towards Eliza, who rose to her feet, staring, not able to quite accept the sight of this friendly, laughing face. Could it really be Nancy? Here? But how could she be ...?

'You don't look in the least pleased to see me!' Nancy caught her breath as she spoke.

But Eliza couldn't answer for a moment. She simply couldn't take it in. Her life in France was a removed bubble, a place to paint and work, not a place where loved ones should be. But then hadn't she just been thinking about Nancy – wishing for her? Whatever the case, Eliza was suddenly overcome with a sense of belonging and an outpouring of emotion and found herself enfolded by Nancy's embrace. Resting her head against her friend's shoulder, Eliza allowed her body to melt into Nancy's, and for the first time since Cornwall, she finally took a deep breath, and relaxed.

The newly arrived Nancy, having shed her heavy backpack on the ground outside Eliza's tent, sat on a cot and sipped a cup of tepid black coffee from her new, and very clean, issued tin cup.

'The landmines are a bit grim,' she said, swishing the muddy water around in the bottom of the cup and looking down at it with disappointment.

Eliza, still in shock somewhat at the arrival of her friend, could only say, 'But ... how come ...?'

'I'm here?' finished Nancy. 'Oh, I asked to be posted with you. Couldn't let you get all the action, old thing. But I never expected it to happen. One of the orderlies said that if I couldn't find you in the hospital than you would probably be in the orchard by the mess tent. And there you were, sketching away. Nothing really ever changes, does it?'

Eliza shook her head and smiled. It didn't, not really. Not the things that mattered. She took Nancy's cup out of her hand and wrapped her arms around her friend once again. The two women held on, one fresh, the other exhausted, offering that kind of silent comfort that one woman can pass on to another so well.

'I'm worried that I'm out of my depth now that I'm here,' said Nancy, breaking away from the embrace and looking down at her boots. 'It's pretty bloody awful over here, isn't it? But wait a minute, I've got something for you ...' Nancy opened a front pocket on her jacket and took out a folded square of brown paper. She handed it to Eliza. 'It's from Sheila,' she said. Eliza opened the paper to find a crumbly mess – a piece of broken shortbread. 'I'm afraid I've already eaten the other four, but do tuck in. Might be the last you'll see of a home-made treat in a while.'

Eliza, delighted at the offering, devoured the sweet treat. 'I can give you some quick pointers if you like?' said Eliza, licking a finger to dab at the remaining crumbs. 'Things I've learned the hard way over the past couple of weeks. It might save you the bother.'

Nancy nodded. 'I think you better had.'

'Have you found the lavvy yet?'

'No, a few of us told the chaps to look the other way when we jumped off the truck.'

'Right, well, it's an eight-hole latrine at the back of the orchard. We all sit side by side on a plank of wood and get on with it. Don't be coy, just go for it, or you'll get constipated. Personal hygiene is everything – I shouldn't have licked my fingers just now, come to think of it. Wash your hands and your mess tins *really* well or you'll get the trots. Carry any water for washing inside your helmet – it's enough, trust me – and the Germans tend to strafe the most at night-time, so there's a decision to be made there ... Have you found a place to put your cot yet, by the way?'

'Not yet.'

'Good. I'll budge up in here and you can bunk up with me.'

This brightened Nancy.

'And whatever time you do eventually go to bed,' continued Eliza, 'day or night, you need to decide whether to sleep with your helmet on or if you're just going to rest it over your face. The next thing to decide, when the attack comes, is whether to hit the trench or not. I've already dug

203

a trench next to this tent so at least you won't have to do that, but the blackout means you can just about stumble out and fall into it. During the day, though, it's better to run to the main trenches behind the orchard, beyond the latrines. I'll show you where they are. They were dug out by the army so they're much deeper.'

Nancy's face went from ashen to whitewashed. 'Crikey. What do you do?'

Eliza shrugged. 'It depends. The girls who have only ever lived in the countryside all hit the deep trench, but I suppose we've been hardened by living in London. A bit silly, really, but I suppose not hitting the trench is a little like the attitude of the shelter dodgers back home – you know, the "it will never happen to me" kind of an attitude. But I head for the big trench if I can, and most nights I sleep with my helmet on, just to be on the safe side. Sometimes though, you'll be so exhausted you'll stay where you are just to get a good sleep. Oh, and watch out for tent talk.'

'Tent talk?'

Eliza nodded knowingly. 'Some of the newer nurses chatter on. Ask them to pipe down if they start. The best medicine out here is to sleep when you can. We can all talk about it later.'

'If we ever want to,' added Nancy with a sigh.

'Quite. Let's see, what else? Check your boots for snails in the morning, and the occasional lizard. Oh, and never let a fellow carry your kit unless you're tired to the bone, it looks bad on the rest of us, a chap doing the heavy work.'

Eliza tightened the laces on her boots, brief complete.

'Gosh, well, that all seems to make sense, I suppose. But what about the actual nursing? Any tips there?'

'It's interesting,' began Eliza, 'but now that I'm painting more than nursing, I see things that I didn't notice before. When the men are brought in, be extra nice to the ones who are crying, and also, try to remember that many of the medics have been here a while and are beyond exhausted, as you will be too. They may snap at you, but don't take it personally. It's not so different from London, and at least there are no injured children to nurse here.'

Eliza put her arm around her friend. 'But I'm just so glad to see you! I thought you'd spend the whole of the war at home, but you're actually here. With me.'

Nancy nudged Eliza and nodded down at Eliza's arm, smiling. 'And look at you, all grown up with your new armband.'

Eliza patted the white band on her arm with pride. It had a large W and A written on it.

'You're an actual proper war artist now,' said Nancy, with such pride in her voice. 'We thought the day would never come. How does it feel? Is it all you hoped it would be?'

Eliza thought about it. 'Yes, and no. I have such contradictory emotions depending on what's happened or how tired I'm feeling. But yes, I'd say I'm glad I'm here, although "glad" isn't the right word, I shouldn't think ...' Eliza winked at her friend. 'Although I *am* proud of the armband, I have to say! I do miss home though ...' Eliza thought of Alex and Cornwall, not Arthur and London, she noticed. 'So tell me, how are things back in Blighty?'

'Oh, same old, same old ... except for the doodlebugs, of course. They're bloody awful! The East End is taking such a pounding. Bad show that. Everyone goes around with an ear cocked to the sky to hear if it's a motorbike trundling down the road or a bally bomb! I suppose it would be a funny sight if it wasn't all so shocking. I begged Aunt Sheila to get out of town, but she won't. You know what a trooper she is.'

'Is she still doing the spotlight operator job?' asked Eliza, draining the bottom of her cup.

'Yes. She says that if *she* doesn't do it, who will? A damn brave thing to do though, standing on a rooftop lighting up the Luftwaffe, not sure I'd have the nerve.'

Eliza laughed suddenly and shook her head, mainly at the madness of their conversation. Here they were, two young women whose everyday conversation was not about men, hair and fashion, but bombs and derring-do. Nancy knew instinctively what she was laughing at and soon they were both in complete hysterics.

'I suppose it's either laugh or cry.' Nancy stood. 'You're looking thinner, by the way,' she added, stifling a yawn.

Eliza looked down at her uniform. The belt was pulled to the tightest hole, but that was no longer tight enough. 'That's living in the field for you,' she said. 'It isn't so bad, although God help us when winter kicks in. The good news is that having the Americans here means there's a decent supply of tins so at least we're not hungry all of the time now.'

'I just can't believe what a mess the place is,' said Nancy. 'Looks like the poor Frenchies have been bombed to smithereens!'

'I know,' agreed Eliza. 'I sometimes wonder if ... well, I wonder if the local people wouldn't rather we hadn't come. They seem to love us and hate us, all at the same time.'

Nancy scrunched her mouth into half a smile. 'Whatever the case,' she said, 'next stop, Paris – I've *always* wanted to go to Paris – and then, before you know it, we'll be ... how does the song go? *Hanging out the washing on the Siegfried Line?*'

Eliza smiled. 'I remember dancing to that song with you a few months ago at the Five Hundred Club. Who would ever have thought the two of us might actually cross it for real?'

'Cripes,' said Nancy. 'Who'd have thought it.'

'So, any broken hearts left behind in London, then?' asked Eliza. 'Last time I saw you there was talk of a date with that chap from Air Command ...'

Nancy's eyes misted over. 'Why do you think I'm really here? He copped it somewhere over Germany. Lancasters. Same old story.' Nancy used her cuffs to wipe each eye in turn before rallying. 'Poor show on my behalf. Should have known better than to get involved with a chap on a bomber crew. But he was such a good sport, and didn't seem to mind my silly old ways or big hips one bit!'

Eliza took Nancy's hand but Nancy stood and batted her off. 'Why didn't you say something earlier?' asked Eliza.

Nancy sniffed away any pity. 'Because there's simply nothing to say.' She stepped out of the tent into the fading sunshine. Eliza followed her. 'Right then!' said Nancy, brightly. 'Let's go and see if those lovely woollen smalls of yours are dry yet, and then we can have something to eat before I report to Matron. I'm starving.' She looked down at her backpack, doubtfully. 'Help me on with this, will you? I feel like I'm hauling coals to Newcastle with this thing on my back!' Each grabbed a strap and manoeuvred the heavy backpack onto Nancy's bruised shoulders. 'As for eats, I've got a little bit left from my ration pack and a tin of beans.' Nancy returned her thoughts to her empty stomach. 'What have you got?'

Eliza dipped back into the tent and reappeared with a tin of Spam. 'A GI gave me this,' she said. 'I've been saving it for a special occasion.'

Nancy laughed out loud. 'Spam fritters with beans it is, then!' She turned away suddenly to look beyond the orchard towards the hospital tents. 'Hold on, what's that?'

The horn of a jeep was being sounded in short bursts over and over again. Other nurses who had also been relaxing around the orchard began to run towards them.

'Drop your pack and grab your helmet, quickly,' said Eliza, while shooting into the tent. Fastening her own helmet as she reappeared, she grabbed Nancy's hand and the pair began to run to the far side of the orchard, to the deep trench. 'It's an air raid,' shouted Eliza above the sound of the horns beeping.

'But aren't we running away from the closest trench?' asked Nancy, looking back towards the orchard as she ran.

'We'll have time to get to the bigger one, so long as we're fast.'

But they were still running when the drone of Luftwaffe engines came into earshot. Eliza looked back, only to duck as an aircraft flashed past, flying very low.

'Damn!' She stopped running and let go of Nancy's hand while looking around for shelter, but Nancy already had them covered, grabbing Eliza by the shoulders and throwing her under a nearby hedge, landing on top of her a moment later, just as more aircraft sped past. Both women put their hands on their helmets and waited for impact.

It didn't come.

Some minutes later, a long beep of a horn from the direction of the hospital sounded the all-clear. The women stood and began to brush themselves down.

'That's quite a throw you have,' said Eliza, rubbing the shoulder that had taken the brunt of the fall.

Nancy winked. 'I was village shotput champion, Horton on the Green, 1934. It's all in the technique, you see.'

Eliza laughed. 'Well,' she said, 'you just survived your first strafing run. How do you feel?'

Nancy let out a long whistle of relief. 'I don't suppose it's much different to dodging the doodlebugs back home, and yet it feels so much the worse for being away from London and the shelters, doesn't it?'

Nancy nodded towards something in Eliza's hand. 'You kept hold of the Spam, then? At least we can still have dinner, or were you intending to throw it at Jerry and take him out with a fritter?'

Eliza laughed, a big, full belly laugh. Her first one in quite a while.

'Hold on, what's that?' asked Nancy, cocking an ear towards the hospital. 'Is it … singing?'

They listened a moment and the noise became clearer.

'It is,' agreed Eliza. 'Women singing, and quite a few of them by the sounds of it.'

They ran along a dusty track that led to the main road, beyond the hospital.

'Well, I'll be dashed!' said Nancy, coming to a halt at the end of the track. 'It's only the bloody WAACs and they're marching this way! This is probably the same troop I met on my crossing, bless them.'

Eliza thought of Nora. She'd heard nothing from her so far, but with the arrival of the WAACs, Nora Levine surely wouldn't be far behind.

'What are they singing?' asked Eliza. 'I can't make it out?' She peered down the road towards the approaching women.

'What else?' said Nancy. '"The Marseillaise"!'

The WAACs soon reached them and began to stride past, their uniforms covered in dust.

'They obviously got caught out by Jerry, too, then!' said Nancy, who threw up a salute to a broad-hipped WAAC carrying an armful of roses, her blonde curls escaping from under her helmet.

'Hey there! British girls!' shouted the blonde. 'Come on. March with us!'

Eliza and Nancy exchanged amused glances and fell into step alongside.

'You all seem very merry,' said Nancy.

'We sure are,' the blonde answered, slapping Nancy on the back. 'Haven't you heard the good news?'

Eliza and Nancy shook their heads.

'Rennes has fallen!' The WAAC nodded towards the red cross on Nancy's sleeve. 'It sounds to have been a hell of a battle, and sister, you've got a whole lotta wounded headed this way. Here,' she said, 'have a flower.' She handed Nancy a yellow rose. Nancy took in the scent. Eliza, still marching along, looked around, trying to comprehend the scene.

With the arrival of Nancy, and now marching women, and roses ... her war had suddenly become utterly surreal, and so much the better for it.

'We were marching through a village a way back when some of the local gals came out of their cottages and showered us with flowers. Here, honey,' she said to Eliza. 'You have one, too.'

Eliza and Nancy stepped away from the troop. 'You ladies take care, now,' said the WAAC before marching on.

'Where do you think they're going?' asked Nancy as they watched them walk away. She held her rose with her left hand and saluted the sun with her right.

'No idea. But they've just arrived here, I know that much for certain.' Eliza broke the thorny stem from her rose and gently pushed the flower between Nancy's helmet strap and her hair.

'Just arrived? What makes you think that?' Nancy bent to pick up more roses that had fallen by the wayside. The rose fell out of her hair. She picked it up and popped it back in.

'Their uniforms are too fresh,' said Eliza, looking down at her already shabby-looking battle dress. 'And see that blonde over there?' She pointed to a woman in the last row of the WAACs.

'The one who's taken her helmet off?' Nancy asked.

'That hair is bleached or I'll be a horse's arse. And she doesn't have any roots yet so they must have just arrived. Easy deduction.' Eliza thought of Alex and their night on the train, when he had joked about his powers of deduction.

'Horse's arse?' repeated Nancy, bringing Eliza back to the moment. 'I think you've been spending too much time with those GIs you paint, Ms Grey!' Nancy put a hand to her own platinum hair. 'Oh, damn,' she said. 'I completely forgot. My blasted roots will be showing soon too, I suppose.'

Eliza placed an arm around her friend's shoulders. 'It doesn't matter. You'll look beautiful anyhow.'

Nancy shrugged her off. 'It's all right for you with your naturally glossy hair, Lady La-di-da. If I had your hair I wouldn't think it mattered either!'

Eliza bit her lip. 'You'll simply have to find yourself a blonde WAAC to become friends with, that's all. A little bottle of bleach will have been the first thing she packed in her backpack.'

This idea chirped Nancy up to no end.

'God bless America!' she said.

As the last of the WAACs disappeared from view, Eliza linked arms with Nancy and they turned back towards the hospital. As she walked, Eliza found that she was carrying with her not only the beautiful roses but also a sense of happiness she hadn't felt for some time. Her smile, however, was short-lived. Down the track, the first of the ambulances were arriving from Rennes. Eliza and Nancy quickened their step and the rose fell again from Nancy's helmet as they broke into a run. It was abandoned on the dusty track this time, just as the setting sun disappeared behind a church spire in the distance.

Chapter 17

That night, the night after the WAACs marched past the hospital and Rennes fell, was a night Eliza knew would be etched in her mind for a long time to come, if not for ever. As darkness fell on the hospital so did the wounded. Two hundred and fifty of them – at a four-hundred bed hospital that was already close to full. Eliza had no time to paint. Some wards were being left for long periods with no nurses in attendance. The IV drips ran out for some patients without anyone noticing. Urinals and bedpans lay scattered on the floor. Outside, the wounded waited to be seen, some on stretchers but many lying on the ground. The lowest ebb was the hour she spent helping to put the dead into mattress covers, having run out of body bags, ready for transportation.

Troops were received direct from battalion aid stations. Those who required urgent surgery were sent to the preoperative tent to wait for a table to become free, which is where Nancy spent the night. By 3 a.m. the doctors were so overwhelmed they instructed the nurses to use their own initiative to issue plasma and blood. As the sun rose, Eliza found herself helping out in triage. She found difficulty coping at the moment of pulling back the men's clothing to see what horrors lay beneath. The only true ray of light Eliza could find for the whole night was that there were only twenty-four deaths in total, each one a tragedy nonetheless. As she pulled the mattress cover over each face, she thought of Porthcurno and all the telegrams that would be heading home, and prayed for the women that would receive them.

The following morning, Eliza positioned herself in the abdominal ward with her canvas and paints. She had received a message to place the numbers 2, 4 and 7 in a painting, which wasn't easy, but she managed it. She was beyond sleep, they all were. She painted two symmetrical lines of stretchers, the white sheets stained red in patches with rubber tubes draped like vines along the length of the tent, feeding plasma to the men. A medicine bottle sat on a table in the foreground. Inside the bottle was a yellow rose. Nancy brushed by and paused to look at the painting, smiling a bittersweet smile. Eliza watched her walk away, her head high, a smile for the men despite the fact that she hadn't slept a wink. That was Nancy.

It was lunchtime before either woman retired to the tent for a bite to eat.

'I don't know how you have the energy to sketch,' said Nancy, flopping onto her cot.

Eliza put down a nib of charcoal. She had returned to
the orchard with the intention of putting the finishing
touches to her painting of the ward, but, taking up her
journal to write some notes, had become distracted by the
small sketch of Alex she had started, all those weeks before,
in the kitchen at Penberth. It was interesting how in the
dark of her closed eyes she could see him most clearly, as
if the mind's eye only needed to create a negative to truly
capture the shot.

'I don't have the energy, really,' answered Eliza, stretching
upwards. She took a deep breath and then exhaled slowly,
as if rationing her breaths. 'It helps, though.' She rubbed
her neck. 'Painting draws me in but it also distances me
at the same time. I'm lucky to have the outlet.'

Nancy took a compact out of a pocket and held the
mirror to her face. She puckered her lips and admired
herself from all angles. 'I've just been chatting to the most
awfully dapper chap,' she said, before looking at Eliza and
adding, 'I think he was interested, too.' She frowned. 'But
just look at the state of me now.' Nancy closed the compact
and pulled a face. 'Dracula's bride, I should say!'

Eliza laughed. 'I thought you said it was best to steer
away from romantic attachments during the war?'

'That was last week. He's called Javier. Javier Dubois.'

'Javier? He sounds ...'

'French, I know. But he's not, he's Canadian. Just arrived
from North Africa, poor lamb. Fancy surviving all of that
and then being sent straight here. He's a doctor ... and you

know how I love a man in a white coat. We met at the brew tent and then, guess what? Afterwards – after we'd had a bit of a chat – he turned to smile at me and said, "Bye for now," and he emphasised the "for now" part. And we all know what that means!'

Eliza smiled. How on earth had she coped before Nancy came along?

'And he has the *best* accent! I'm going to engineer it so that I bump into him later, although I'll pretend to look efficient and clever when I do ...' Nancy tipped her head to look at Eliza, considering something. 'Maybe I'll try to be more like you, that might draw him in a touch ...'

'Like me?'

'You know, aloof.' Nancy dipped her head and sighed. 'Tell me, just how bad *are* my roots? Are they awfully brown?'

Eliza tucked a stray hair behind Nancy's ear. She couldn't help but envy her friend. What it would be to have those moments – the beginnings of love – in Cornwall with Alex again ...

'Not a bit,' offered Eliza, a soft melancholy reflecting in her voice. 'But ... I'm not so standoffish, am I? I don't mean to be.'

Nancy scrunched her nose. 'Only a bit. And not standoffish; that's the wrong word.'

'You said "aloof". That's even worse.'

'That's the wrong word too,' assured Nancy. 'I should have said "reserved". That kind of thing.'

'Well, for what it's worth, I think you should enjoy his company,' said Eliza. 'Lord knows we get precious little relief here.' She patted Nancy's knee. 'And he sounds wonderful.'

Nancy stood and prepared to leave. 'I'm off shift in an hour or so. Why don't you pack up here and get some rest? I'll make you a nice cuppa when I get off. You're all in, Eliza.'

Eliza yawned but shook her head. 'That would be lovely, but I can't. I'm going on a trip with the chief surgeon. He wants me to go with him to a collecting station this afternoon. There's something he wants me to paint. Seems important to him.'

Nancy grimaced. 'Really? A collecting station? It will be bloody.'

Eliza raised her brows. 'I know.'

'Well, must get on.'

'Oh, but Nancy ...' said Eliza, calling after her as she ducked to leave the tent.

Nancy poked her head back through the flap. 'Yes?'

'I've been asked to assist with an airlift evacuation this evening, so I'm flying back to England tonight.'

Nancy's jaw dropped. She slumped back into the tent. 'What? Really? Tonight? Why didn't you say?' Nancy looked as though her best toy was being taken away.

'I only found out an hour ago. They haven't enough nurses to cover the airlift, and the chief surgeon knows that I want to paint some airfield scenes. It's such a massive undertaking, sending the guys home. It would be wrong not to paint it. I'll be gone a few days, I should think.'

Eliza knew this would be a blow to Nancy, just as, if Nancy left, it would be a blow to her.

Nancy screwed her face into a disgruntled ball. 'But, you will come back, won't you? We'll probably move on soon. What if the hospital moves forward and you don't make it back in time for the move?'

'Oh, don't worry about that,' said Eliza, cheerily. 'I'll find a way to get to you. This is the hospital I'm affiliated with. I have to.'

Nancy rallied at that. 'Right ho!' she said.

Eliza squeezed her friend's hand tenderly as she turned to leave the tent. 'Take care of yourself, if that's at all possible over here.'

Nancy smiled. 'You too, old thing. You too.'

The chief surgeon was called Major Smythe. He was a tall, thin, kind man who had noticeably aged in the weeks Eliza had known him. He felt passionately that the work of the medical profession should be captured in art form, which helped when she wanted access to a ward or theatre. She had sketched him without him noticing her on her second day at the hospital and then again on the tenth. The amount of charcoal she used for the dark patches under his eyes increased significantly by the second sketch, and his uniform had developed a looseness about the waist and shoulders that was previously unseen. She gave him the first sketch to send to his wife. She didn't show him the second one.

The collecting station was nothing more than a group of abandoned stone cottages on the outskirts of Rennes. It took no more than half an hour to get there and it was a pleasant day. Eliza set up her small easel outside the collecting station, facing towards the open doorway. Pleased to be able to paint something straight onto canvas while having the luxury of taking her time, and also pleased to have the freedom of her own interpretation without the need to add any kind of coded message, she smiled to herself as she prepared to start work. It was a pretty cottage, with yellow hollyhocks growing in the garden and by the door. How lovely, she thought, to be away from the hospital for a while, and what a wonderful scene to paint. Faded green shutters hung lopsided from the windows and fragrant roses in blushing pink rambled across the roof. But it was the juxtaposition between cottage and crisis that the major wanted her to capture and so the door was left open, and through the door, Major Smythe, now robed in white, was working on a recently arrived GI who lay on the kitchen table. The surgeon was preparing to amputate his leg.

The roses no longer seemed so pretty, or smelled so sweet.

'And all shall be well, Eliza,' she said to herself, trying to block out the man's screams as she painted. 'And all shall be well.'

Eliza and Major Smythe did not head back to the field hospital before departing for England that evening as there wasn't time. Instead, with the early evening sun streaming through the jeep windscreen, they accompanied yet another convoy of ambulances to the airstrip, a requisitioned flat field on the outskirts of Rennes. Major Smythe would return to the field hospital later, once the wounded had boarded the waiting Dakotas, and Eliza would help to attend to the soldiers on one of the aircraft during the short flight home.

She was standing by the door to the aircraft, which was low and behind the wing, gathering her things so she was ready to board, when another Dakota pulled alongside and its engines wound down to a stop. Major Smythe, the image of an exhausted man, stepped out of the aircraft and said his temporary goodbyes to Eliza – '*Au revoir, dear Eliza. Haste ye back*' – and she put her arms around him to offer a comforting hug. They held each other for some time – in the manner that two people who have experienced something terrible together do – before the major, having recharged his soul by absorbing Eliza's warmth and bright spirit, stood back, smiled at her warmly and, with a renewed purpose to his step, strode across the airstrip to a waiting jeep.

A man was standing in the open doorway of the adjacent Dakota, watching Eliza. When she looked properly, she knew exactly who the man was – the burn mark, the dark hair coming forward across his brow, the flying jacket. It was Alex.

A young airman appeared at the aircraft door.

'Better hurry on, Miss,' he said, his face gaunt, the weight of responsibility bearing heavily on young shoulders. 'We'll be off in a moment.'

Timing really was her nemesis. 'Could I just have a second, please?' she asked. 'Only, that man over there is an old friend and I ...'

The engines flashed up. The airman looked from Eliza to Alex and back again. 'One minute, but then we really must close the door.'

Eliza kissed him on the cheek. 'Thank you!' she said, before dashing across to Alex, who by now had disembarked and was standing on the grass, looking stunned.

'I ... My goodness ... It's wonderful to see you,' gasped Eliza, shouting above the noise of the engines. Propwash blew her hair across her face.

'Hallo, you,' he said, shaking his head in wonder and lifting a hand to brush her hair from her eyes.

Eliza noticed a 'C' for 'correspondent' on his armband, which answered all she needed to know. Despite Nora's efforts to prevent it, then, he had come.

'They're waiting for me,' she said, glancing towards the aircraft, her voice betraying her disappointment. 'But I'm just so surprised to see you! What happened to the American job?'

'America can wait. I'm to be attached to General Patton's staff,' he explained, glancing across at the airman who was still standing by the open door, waiting for Eliza.

'General Patton? But that's ... incredible. Lucky you. His troops are headed to Saint-Malo, I think.'

Alex nodded, his face still a portrait of surprise. 'I believe so, yes,' he said.

Eliza's mind couldn't help but flash back to the last time she had seen him – up close, at least. It was in her cottage. Not just in her cottage, in fact, but in her bedroom, just before she had run away. Why, *why* could she not say something more intimate to him than this?

She heard the medic shout again for her to come.

'I'm so sorry, Alex, I have to go. But listen, I wanted you to know ... Your sister said that I should—'

'Forget my sister ...'

'But, what I said to Nora that day, at The Savoy, I ... She ...'

Alex took Eliza's arm. 'The letter I sent to you, about going to America. The moment I sent it, I knew I shouldn't have. Knew I couldn't go. The thing is ... When will you be back? In fact, *will* you be back?'

'I'll be gone a few days, that's all. I'm helping out with the medivac and hoping to find more art supplies.'

Alex nodded towards her armband and touched her arm. 'You don't know how I've lain awake, regretting encouraging you to come. If anything happened to you ...'

She put a hand on his. 'I'm glad I did.'

'Has it been as you expected?'

As she had expected? How naïve she had been.

'No. I had an idealised vision of war. I thought I'd be

224

safe behind the forward line of troops and trip along to do some nice paintings of war heroes and victorious armies.' She paused and Alex waited. 'It's been ... barbaric, and yet, it feels right to be part of it. To capture it.'

A voice called for Eliza to hurry again.

'Listen,' began Alex, 'about Cornwall ...' He took her arm. 'I don't feel any differently, and I ...'

'Miss, Miss! We really do have to go!'

Eliza shook her head in frustration. Alex followed her to the aircraft door. She handed her backpack and helmet to the airman before climbing in. She stood just inside the doorway as the airman leant out to close the door.

'I would have come to America to find you,' she shouted. 'Eventually. I would have come.'

Eliza turned before he could respond and though Alex shouted something as the door closed, she couldn't make it out. The senior aircraftsman directed her to her seat. She strained to look through the window, but the aircraft had already begun to taxi.

Eliza looked around at the wounded men and remembered why she was there. She needed to focus now. But as the Dakota lifted from the grass strip and France fell away beneath her, all Eliza could pray for was that she would find her way back to this place of chaos and carnage very quickly. Because to Eliza, it was better to burn in hell with Alex by her side than to languish in heaven without him.

Chapter 18

Ellie

Taunton to Exeter

'Who would have thought Beyoncé, a violin and a D-Day Dame would go so well together?' said Rihanna as Ellie returned to her seat and the applause died down. Ellie, flushed, flopped down and sipped from a glass of water. 'She really belted that last one out!' added Rihanna, referring to the D-Day Dame who had accompanied Ellie for the tail-end of the set. 'And to manage the "Single Ladies" dance in such a narrow aisle, too?'

Ellie, Joe and Rihanna didn't have time to discuss the matter further because just then a woman dressed as a schoolgirl evacuee, carrying a snake in a caged basket, drifted past their table and departed through the far door.

'Did I just see what I thought I saw?' asked Ellie, leaning into the aisle to watch the woman depart.

Rihanna, the consummate professional at all other times, allowed herself the lapse of an eye roll.

'She says the electric socket in her cabin isn't working and she has to plug in the cage to keep the thing warm. It's a baby boa. Can you believe it? A baby bloody boa constrictor!' said Rihanna, *sotto voce*.

Ellie and Joe both bit their lips and said that they truly couldn't.

'We get all sorts on here!' concluded Rihanna, before wandering off and leaving Joe and Ellie where she found them – in stitches – as a waiter arrived with two Irish coffees and a selection of chocolate mints. Joe unwrapped a mint and handed it to Ellie.

'Here, eat this,' he said, before unwrapping another and handing her that one, too. 'I think the performance has taken it out of you a bit. The sugar will help.'

Ellie took the mints gratefully.

'That really is a beautiful dress, by the way,' said Joe. 'It was made for you.'

Ellie looked down at her dress and was going to say, 'This old thing?' but decided to take the compliment – the dress deserved it after all – and went with a simple 'Thank you' instead.

'I wish we lived in clothes like these all of the time,' said Ellie as she unwrapped another chocolate. 'We've lost all sense of day-to-day style, don't you think?'

'I know what you mean,' agreed Joe. 'But as I live in jeans, a T-shirt and my duffle coat, I'm not really in a

position to comment on style.' He tipped his head side-
ways to look down the carriage, taking in all the different
outfits. 'They were more stylish back then, that's for sure.
I wonder what it was really like, though?' He sat back,
full-bellied, tipsy, content.

'During the war? I should imagine it was hell on earth,
with occasional bits of heaven thrown in, depending on
who you were and where you were. Take Eliza,' began Ellie,
nodding towards the journal. 'She must have experienced
such extremes of emotion, I think. It's all there, in her
paintings. After the war, a book was published of all of
her war work and she wrote notes to accompany each one.'

'I'd like to see that,' said Joe.

Ellie sat up. 'Oh, but there's a copy in the cottage ...' she
began, but tailed off. It would have been the most natural
thing in the world to add, 'Come round. I'll show it to
you, if you like.' But Eliza left the sentence hanging, like
a speech bubble waiting to be completed. 'And, er ... there's
a wonderful portrait of my Great Granny Nancy in the
book. She's wearing her nurse's uniform and looking very
proud. It's a fabulous painting. Really fabulous.'

Joe clearly didn't suffer from Ellie's reluctance. 'Maybe
we could meet up and you could show me the book while
we're both in Cornwall ...' he suggested, his wide eyes a
picture of innocent optimism.

Ellie floundered.

'Although clearly,' added Joe, quickly, 'you'll be busy
doing your own thing, so don't worry, you're off the hook!'

Ellie found some courage. Not much, but enough to attempt the beginnings of what might even have been considered a flirtation. 'What if I don't want to be ...' she began, but one of the D-Day Dames started chatting on the PA system, now fixed, at the most inconvenient moment. Joe rolled his eyes at the interruption and they returned to sipping their coffees while waiting for a quiet moment to finish the conversation. When one came, Ellie was the first to speak, but she felt awkward. Too much time had lapsed to return to the notion of them meeting up. Oh, these tangles and awkward half-honesties. Why couldn't she simply find the confidence to say, 'So, where were we? About meeting up. I'd love to!' rather than returning to some inconsequential chatter about something neutral, something safe – in this case, the war.

'We know it turned out well, but at the time it must have felt like a never-ending life of uncertainty. How would you feel, do you think, if it really was 1940 and you were just about to scramble for your Spitfire and dive into a dogfight over the Channel?'

Joe unwrapped a mint. 'Life expectancy was pretty much zero for the pilots during the Battle of Britain,' he said, the mint hovering halfway to his mouth. 'So, to be perfectly honest, I'd be crapping myself. Such a terrible waste. All of your mates being killed around you every single day. If only all those scientists who spend their time working out the origins of the universe turned their attention to human behaviour, we might get somewhere ...'

'In what way?'

'We're all made of the same stuff, aren't we – all part of the same universe, made up of particles and atoms and whatever? And if everything that makes up the universe was created at the moment of the big bang, then all the other things – things that matter but have no "matter", like love and hope and joy and fear and hate – must also have been created then, in that first millisecond of the big bang. It was like the opening of Pandora's Box. And if we had the same amount of people looking into the creation of love that look into, say, the creation of the universe, and if they applied the same scientific and non-scientific argument to it, then humanity might actually begin to get somewhere, to understand ourselves better.' He scratched his forehead. 'I'm waffling now.'

Ellie smiled. 'We do have people like that,' she said. 'They're called artists.'

'Ha!' laughed Joe. 'You're right!' He leant forwards across the table towards her. 'And I'll tell you something else, too. If I listened to you play long enough, Ellie Nightingale, I could probably work some pretty universal things out all by myself. It's all there, in the music.'

Ellie mirrored him and leant forwards, her eyes dancing in the candlelight. 'You like my music?'

'I *love* your music.'

There was a most delicious pause.

'I think it's time for a toast ...' she said, sitting back.

'A toast?' he repeated, with – Ellie flattered herself – a loving kind of a smile thrown in. 'Another one?'

231

'Yes, another one. Can you ever have too many?'

'No. You're absolutely right. You can't.'

'In that case,' she began, 'to Great Granny Nancy and to Eliza, who – by the looks of her journal – were true heroes of the Western Front ... which got them into *all kinds* of bother!'

Joe raised his glass. 'To Nancy and Eliza,' he said, before leaning forward with his elbows on the table and his glasses halfway down his nose and saying, somewhat coquettishly, 'Would you like that, Ellie?'

'What?' asked Ellie, mirroring Joe again by resting her elbows on the table.

'To get into all kinds of bother?'

Ellie tilted her head to one side and said (quite seductively, she thought, although she probably just looked tipsy), 'I certainly would, Joe from Leeds. Oh, you have *no idea* just how much I would!'

Their eyes held. The train rocked. Their faces moved towards each other ... And then the carriage door opened and Rihanna reappeared, just as the music fired up again. Ellie shot back into her seat and blushed. Rihanna winked as she walked past and when Ellie glanced down the aisle towards her, Rihanna – who was topping up the glasses of a group of Land Army women – took a moment to nod her head towards Joe and mouthed, 'Ask him to dance!'

The doctor and nurse opposite stood to join the other couples down the carriage who were already dancing, and began to smooch in the aisle. Joe shuffled in his seat. Ellie bit her lip and turned to watch the others dance.

Joe leant forwards, 'Do you think ...' he began. But then the train slowed to pass a station and Ellie, desperate to dance and yet feeling oh so bloody awkward, lifted the blind to see where they were.

'Oh, no!' she exclaimed with more than an edge of melodrama. 'That was Exeter! How can we have passed Exeter so quickly? It's all going by far too fast ...' She lowered the blind and sat back, looking down at her silk gown, finding the stitching rather interesting all of a sudden.

'So,' he began again, but Rihanna shimmied up to the table with a champagne bucket in her hand and a pleased smile on her face.

'*Pour vous!*' she said, holding the champagne in the manner of a wine waiter offering her best Bordeaux to Ellie for assessment. 'As a thank you for the music.'

'Champagne? But that's far too much!' said Ellie, wondering how on earth she could possibly pour more alcohol down her neck. 'You don't need to give me anything. It was my pleasure, so there's no need, truly.'

But the gift was not from Rihanna. 'It's from Winston Churchill,' she explained. A Royal Navy Captain beckoned her from further down the carriage. She plonked the bottle into the ice bucket and blew away down the aisle as fast as she had blown in.

'Sweet of him,' said Ellie.

'Hmm,' muttered Joe. He moved the champagne to one side so that he could see Ellie across the table. 'So,' he began again, but couldn't tag a sentence onto the 'so' because Winston Churchill – along with an unlit cigar – appeared by their table.

'I wonder, old chap,' said Winston, addressing Joe with a perfect 1940s accent, 'if you would mind awfully if I asked your beautiful wife to dance with me? The lounge car has turned into something of a dance hall and, what with me being Prime Minister and all that, it's only fitting that I ask the most beautiful lady on the train to dance.'

Ellie looked at Winston in surprise, and then at Joe, who, by the look on his face, clearly *did* mind. He minded very much.

Without a moment's hesitation, Joe pushed his glasses up his nose, put his napkin on the table, stepped out to the aisle and looked down on Winston with a bit of a scowl.

'I'm frightfully sorry, old chap,' he said, 'but if anyone is going to dance with my companion this evening, then it's going to be me.' Joe held out a hand to Ellie and she took it – what else could she do? She rose from her seat in the manner of a Hollywood starlet taking to the stage. He smiled down at her, 'Shall we?' he asked.

A new song began. Ellie's favourite. 'A Nightingale Sang in Berkeley Square'.

That certain night, the night we met, there was magic abroad in the air, there were angels dining at The Ritz and a nightingale sang in Berkeley Square.

'Oh, Mr Burton,' she said, her smile bright, her big trusting eyes gazing up at him. 'We most certainly shall.'

Chapter 19

Eliza

Four days after the wheels of the Dakota lifted from the airstrip near Rennes, they touched back down again at the same airstrip with a bounce and a judder. Eliza was the only passenger on the return journey. She had taken the opportunity to go home while in London, not to the offices of *Lady and Home*, but to her real home – her home with Arthur – with the intention of having it out with him, to tell him she wanted a divorce. But the maid – one who had a great loyalty for her mistress – said that Arthur had booked himself on the sleeper to Edinburgh just that afternoon, adding, 'And he seemed to book it the very moment he heard you were on your way, Madam.'

He had run away, then, as was Arthur's way. And could she really blame him? All he wanted to do, perhaps, was to hold onto her – or the concept of her, for they were never physically together now – for all the same reasons that Eliza wanted to let go. She couldn't blame him for

235

wanting to cling on to a sense of belonging to the person you love most dearly in the world. And so, as the wheels touched back down, nothing at all had been finalised with Arthur. As they said in the women's columns she had once had time to read: life is complicated.

Eliza realised that she was relieved to be back, which was almost certainly a result of an addiction to being part of the war, part of the collective effort for good. The adrenalin, the busyness, the danger ... It was her life now and she had never felt so free – so useful. In those brief days back home, London had unnerved her. She had felt a very odd sensation just being there, a sensation of being disconnected from the city, of no longer belonging anywhere but at the hospital in France, with Nancy, where she was loved and needed. Walking alone along the Strand she had suddenly felt overcome by a desperate need to get back to the action, to Nancy and also (she might as well admit it) to Alex. Indeed, she spent the whole of the return flight thinking only of Alex, replaying their time together, from that first 'hello' on the train to their last evening together at Penberth.

The aircraft door opened. The weather was not as fair today as on the day she departed and the rain came down in fat droplets, dripping off her helmet as she trudged across the airfield, her heavy pack on her back and her satchel full of art materials hanging from her shoulder. With a rallying smile she approached a Red Cross nurse she knew from the hospital who was organising yet another long line of ambulances, the wounded waiting to be stretch-ered onto the aircraft.

'Welcome back to hell!' the nurse said brightly. 'How was Blighty?'

The journey back to the hospital in the convoy of empty ambulances was not without incident. A horse had collapsed on the road and shot where she lay, blocking the narrow dusty track leading towards Rennes.

Eliza jumped down from the ambulance to see what was going on. The scene was distressing – there was nothing worse than witnessing the death of innocence because of the idiocy of man – but Eliza didn't shy away. She grabbed a folding stool, set herself up in the rain, draped a tarpaulin over her head and sketched. She would paint the scene on canvas later.

A rope was positioned around the horse – rather in the manner of a parcel tied up with string – but the ambulance trying to move the beast was not meaty enough to gain traction and its wheels slipped on the muddy track, leaving the convoy with no choice but to stay where it was, surrounded by field after field of uncleared mines. But it was a busy, necessary track and before too long a dispatch motorbike rider found his way to the front of the line and was sent forward by Eliza to ask for help.

For over an hour the medics huddled in the ambulances while Eliza sat in the rain alone with the horse. She felt that the horse's spirit – or soul, or essence of being, or whatever else that elusive thing was – hadn't quite left yet, that it was still close by, soothing her. She pulled the tarpaulin back over her head with her left hand while the charcoal nib moved rapidly in her right, trying all the while to capture the beauty and the sadness of the moment, to make sure that the waste and the tragedy of it all would be remembered. It was the only way she knew of saying to the horse, 'You mattered.'

A sharp noise cut through the silence of the moment and Eliza glanced up to see a motorbike and a covered jeep speeding down the track towards the convoy. Both vehicles stopped short of the horse and the pillion passenger jumped off the bike. The passenger took off her goggles while walking towards Eliza.

Well, well. It was Nora Levine. Arrived at last. Nora, a little breathless, approached her.

'Good, it *is* you,' she began, not bothering with any kind of formal welcome. She pulled the tarpaulin away from Eliza's head. 'It's stopped raining, by the way.' Nora didn't look at the horse. 'Damn inconvenient of you to disappear off like that, just as I arrived. You should have sent word. I had some work for you to do. Never mind, this is a stroke of luck anyhow. I was asking after you at the hospital when this chap,' she nodded towards the motorbike driver who was now leaning against an ambulance lighting a cigarette for a nurse, 'pitched up all flustered and said there was a commotion with an artist and a horse on the road. It could only be you. Do you have your bits and bobs with you? Paper, paints and whatnot?'

Eliza looked down at her sketch pad and the charcoal in her hand. 'No.'

The sarcasm slid off Nora like melting snow. 'Jolly good. In that case, send on any surplus kit to your billet at the hospital and come along with me. I've brought a jeep and driver.' Nora turned to walk away. 'And your helmet,' Nora shouted back, still walking. 'You'll definitely need your helmet. We'll be gone a couple of days, shouldn't wonder. Sort out your things and do hurry along!'

'But, where are we going?' shouted Eliza, taking to her feet. 'Nora!'

Nora turned to face her while walking backwards. 'Where else? Saint-Malo. It's fallen, didn't you know? You don't want to paint hospital wards for the entire war, do you? Come on! Get into the action, woman!'

Saint-Malo? But Saint-Malo was a town in turmoil – at least, it had been before she left. It was also where Alex was. Eliza's pulse jumped from the slovenly beat of an old nag to that of a racing thoroughbred. Without a moment's hesitation, she closed her sketchpad, grabbed her things and ran to the jeep. She did not notice the soul of the horse flitter away into the ether, as she ran.

A French guide, Julien – a Romanesque type of a man – drove the soft-topped jeep, chatting to Nora while Eliza tucked herself away in the back. She allowed her eyes to blur against the passing charred and beleaguered country-side. It looked so different from above. From the air one could almost pretend that the decimation had never happened. It was too depressing. So much to paint. So much to tell.

After less than an hour they reached a checkpoint and Nora jumped out to speak with the American guard. Julien turned in his seat to face Eliza with a smile.

'You're quiet, my friend,' he said. 'You're thinking of a man, no?' He swirled a finger close to his head. 'I hear the wheels of your mind turning.'

Eliza shrugged good-heartedly. 'Is it that obvious?' she said.

'To me? Yes. But, is it a husband or a lover you think of? No, don't tell me, I can guess. It is a lover!'

Eliza laughed. 'What makes you say that?'

Julien shrugged the way only men whose gene pools are soaked to the core with Gallic DNA can shrug. 'Madam, no woman I ever knew seemed so regretful about her husband.'

'It's my brother she's thinking of,' said Nora, jumping into both the jeep and the conversation with a thud.

Eliza held up a hand. 'Listen, Nora, if you're going to lecture me about Alex ...'

Nora tapped the dash and said, 'Drive on,' before turning to face Eliza and adding, 'Now, about Alex.'

Eliza sighed as the jeep stopped again, thankfully causing Nora to delay her speech for a moment as she watched Julien jump out to speak to a small group of soldiers standing next to a truck that was blocking the road. 'Mines,' he said, jumping back inside and putting the jeep into gear. 'We need to find another route.'

Nora, taking this in her stride, turned to begin her conversation again.

'He's here, in France,' she said, blankly.

'I know that,' said Eliza, waiting for the fallout.

Nora didn't miss a beat. 'He could have been safe in America – he was definitely going to go, you know – had his ticket booked and everything. Then he met you. Against all the odds,' Nora went on, her voice impassioned now, 'he survived one of the most significant battles of the war. Our parents are abroad, our dear aunt and uncle and half our family are missing in Germany. He wants to protect the world, *save the* world, but he doesn't need to. He's done enough, and I can't help feeling that he's already pushed his luck as far as it should go. Do you know what the chances were of surviving those dogfights over the Channel?' Nora didn't allow time for an answer. 'Zero. Well, practically.' She reached a hand back and rested it on Eliza's knee. 'Please,' she begged, 'tell him you won't leave your husband. Let me find a way to send him home. Then, after the war, you can run away to America to find him. I promise I will tell you where he is. You will have all the time in the world, but right now ... now is no time for romance.' Nora turned away, brief complete. 'Wait! Stop the jeep!' she shouted, causing Julien to screech the tyres and Eliza to shoot forwards.

'There,' said Nora, nodding to her right and opening

her door. '*That's* why we're here – why you're here.' She jumped out.

'Keep to the road, Nora,' shouted Julien as they watched Nora walk towards a mass of something grey-coloured that was piled like a mound of manure in the field beyond.

Eliza jumped out of the jeep and it only took her brain a second or two to realise what the mound was.

'Germans,' she said.

'Dead Germans,' corrected Nora as they watched local men pull another body across the field by his boots and add him to the pile. Meanwhile, a third man attached a plough to the harness on a horse.

'It's their way of taking back control,' said Nora. 'Nothing more than clearing up so the crops can be sown.' She turned to Eliza. 'This is why you're here. Not for Alex, not for yourself – well, maybe for yourself too, hell, why are any women here? – but to paint it.' Nora took Eliza's face in her hands. 'You have an amazing gift. How you catch a moment on canvas, it's incredible. Time for you will come later ...'

'You're preaching to the wrong person, about Alex and about my artwork, and it's bloody insulting, too. Haven't I been doing all you asked? And while we're on the subject, I don't know how many of my paintings I've ruined by daubing your bloody messages into them!'

Nora scoffed. 'You haven't seen the half of it yet.'

'I'm out of my depth,' whispered Eliza, staring at the bodies.

'We're all out of our depth.'

Nora patted Eliza on the shoulder and returned to the jeep with a sigh.

The ancient, towering walls of Saint-Malo may have been highly effective against previous enemies, but they were nothing more than the fortifications of a toy when faced with the ravages of modern warfare. First, the Germans had come and set up a garrison there. The local people had capitulated but at least they kept their city in one piece. Then, the Allies came, by sea, air and land, and brought with them overwhelming firepower. What was clear to Eliza, as the jeep edged slowly inside the now crumbling walls, was that Saint-Malo in many ways no longer existed. The assault had all but destroyed what must once have been a beautiful and safe place to live. The Nazis needed to be defeated, yes, but Eliza couldn't help but wonder if the shock and awe of this particular attack hadn't simply gone too far.

Julien knew the city well, and edged his way through what was left of the narrow streets, having been briefed on a safe route to the proposed location of a press camp, which Nora intended to set up in a small hotel in the Saint Servan district. Save the occasional emaciated dog, the streets were deserted, and all was going well until a collapsed building blocked the road. As Julien jumped out of the jeep and looked around, Eliza took advantage of the moment to step out into the late afternoon sunshine and stretch.

Long shadows of splintered building fell across the detritus strewn street. Having chewed on Nora's words,

Eliza wanted to set up her easel right here and now and show Nora Bloody Levine her metal.

'There is no way to pass,' said Julien, walking past her to speak with Nora. 'We will have to walk,' she heard him say.

'How far?' asked Nora, tightening her helmet and pulling up her kitbag from beneath her knees.

'Half a kilometre, maybe more.'

Julien turned away to assess the rubble. He rubbed his forehead. 'This is bad,' he said, jumping back into the jeep. Eliza followed his lead. Julien started the engine. 'I have a bad feeling.' He put the jeep into reverse.

Nora was not impressed. 'What?' she said, leaning over in an attempt to turn off the engine. Julien grabbed her arm. 'But we're only a short walk from the press camp. The place must have been cleared, surely ...'

'I am an animal,' he said. 'You are an animal. Stop and listen to your instincts. I have, and I say to you, we need to leave.' He began reversing down the road. A shot rang out. And then another. 'Get down!' shouted Julien while pressing harder on the accelerator.

Eliza put her head in between her knees and hands over her helmet and waited for the jeep to be hit, but like that day in the orchard with Nancy when the Luftwaffe had flown by, luck was on her side, and the impact never came.

Julien drove well and soon they had retreated to the outskirts of the city, to a small hotel where he knew they would be offered shelter and assistance, if it was still standing. A young woman opened the door but only by a crack. On seeing Julien, the door flung open fully and so did her arms, which she wrapped tightly around him. She closed the heavy door behind them and explained that Saint-Malo had not fallen, not quite. Armed marauders ransacked and pillaged. German snipers lay in wait around every corner – trapped and outnumbered, but fighting on. Saint-Malo, she concluded as they stood in the dark foyer, was still very much in the thick of it all.

Eliza looked to Nora for a response, which was just one word, 'Damn!'

The rules for women non-combatants such as artists and reporters were quite clear: under no circumstances were they to be allowed near combat, which even Eliza found to be a little ridiculous, given the horrors that scores of women nurses faced every day at the hospital units. It was the severest of situations. If caught by the Germans, they would be shot. If caught by the Allies, they would be stripped of their armbands and sent home. Nora's opinion was that the latter would be the worse outcome.

'No general has the gumption to have a dead woman on his conscience,' said Nora, flopping down into a chair while unfastening her helmet. 'Oh, they're happy to allow the local women to be caught up – killed, sorry – in the bombardment, but that seems to be acceptable – simply an unfortunate consequence of war.'

'It's acceptable because they are French,' said Julien. 'Not British.'

'Well, whatever the case,' said Nora, 'I'm going nowhere.'

They hunkered down at the hotel that night, opening the shutters now and again to allow in the breeze. It seemed that Nora had no intention of trying to leave the city. They lived on the K-rations Nora had been issued and slept in beautiful, elaborate beds under eiderdown comforters, but like a caged animal Nora became increasingly agitated. With wild eyes she spoke of the possibility of scoops and the fact that she was almost certainly the only reporter this close to town – to the action. Despite the risks, it was an opportunity for them both, she said, stressing the 'both'. To Eliza's surprise, Julien agreed.

'I have borne witness to the destruction of a beautiful city,' he said. 'This is my city and I want the world to see what happened here, and in the hands of both sides. Liberation is one thing, but this ...' He shook his head and turned to Eliza, his eyes pleading. 'If I find safe areas, will you come with me, tomorrow?'

'Well, I certainly bloody well shall!' said Nora.

Eliza, for her part, said nothing.

But the next day the Allies began to bomb the town again and even Nora knew the only course of action was to stay holed up. Columns of billowing smoke rose above the skyline from across the city – from the district where the Germans were thought to be holding out. It was only when Nora looked more closely at the smoke from their hotel window that she realised the Allies had used napalm. She could barely believe it. She insisted that Eliza paint the scene immediately. Both women knew that if they submitted work showing the use of napalm in a civilianised area, it would be deleted by the censors immediately – she couldn't even smuggle it through via the Red Cross connection – and yet they wrote and painted it anyhow, which was the point at which Eliza suddenly understood everything Alex had said to her that night on the train; it was also the moment she began to respect Nora. The censors could delete whatever the hell they liked, but now that they had witnessed this, the two women wouldn't – couldn't – start censoring themselves.

And so she painted. She painted scenes from the hotel windows and scenes from memory. On the afternoon of the third day, Julien returned from a recce with news that the remaining Germans were now cornered in the Ile du Grand Bé fortress and had just flown the white flag of surrender.

The town, he was sure, really had now fallen.

Eliza watched on, cleaning her brushes, while Nora, stir-crazy from three days of being trapped in the hotel, began to pack.

'You have to get us there,' said Nora, closing up her portable typewriter into its case. Every bit as headstrong as Nora, Julien needed no persuasion. Eliza, however, did.

'But as women ... we're not allowed in, Nora. You know

that. Just being here, in town, has put both our careers at risk.' She glanced at Julien for support. She got none. And Nora wasn't listening, she was still packing.

'I have additional clearances,' she said, 'so we'll be fine.' Nora flashed Eliza a look that said, 'And you know what I'm talking about, so shush.' She began to dismantle her cot bed.

'But think about it,' continued Eliza. 'Once you submit this kind of story to the censors at the press camp they will know that you – we – were here and I for one absolutely do not want to lose my accreditation with the Red Cross. They asked for me personally, Nora. Their story is important, too, and helping at the hospital is everything to me! There are other war artists out here – male artists. They can do it. It's not a competition, Nora.'

Nora turned to look at her. 'You're a coward,' she said, which served as a slap in the face. 'And I'm not welcome inside the male press camp either, remember?' she added. 'Which is why I was setting up my own. Did you know there aren't even women's latrines at the press camp? I'm a damn bureau chief and I can't even take a ...'

She didn't finish the sentence.

'I do not care about your damn latrines and I am not a coward,' said Eliza, finding her voice against the bullish Nora. 'The truth of the matter is that you are risking our positions here simply because you want your name to be at the bottom of the best scoop in a British paper since D-Day.'

Nora looked at her as if she'd just arrived from Mars and had no clue about the run of things.

'Hello? Of course I want my name attached to my work, and of course I want the satisfaction of the kill, and yes, *of course* I want to tell the people at home the truth of what really happened here – you saw the napalm!'

Julien shook his head and began to walk away before suddenly turning back. 'I want the story to be covered, but perhaps Eliza is right, Nora,' he said. 'If you submit a Saint-Malo story, you will lose your accreditation with the WAACs.'

Nora shrugged. 'I don't like being with women, anyhow,' she said. 'I prefer to be with men. I grew up with men. It's what I'm used to ...'

'The rules are there for your protection, Nora,' said Eliza. 'Why can't you just try to go *with* the system to get what you want, not against it? I know you're used to being a big shot in London, but it is different out here.'

Nora put up a hand. The conversation was over.

'I am going,' she said, picking up her backpack, 'with or without you. Either of you. I'll find my own way there if necessary.' She approached Eliza. 'This is your chance to make a difference. Are you really only ever going to do the things other people say you can do, Lady Arbuthnot, or are you going to be the woman you really want to be?'

Eliza allowed silence to fill the void until she could gather together a sentence.

'First of all,' she began, her tone firm, her manner

bordering on angry, 'being a considered person, being cautious, being sensible of one's situation, is not the same as being a coward. There are many who do not have your strength – or perhaps foolhardiness – to be able to battle on regardless, to emerge from the trenches brandishing a weapon in one hand and a typewriter in the other. You are flying in the face of ...' She floundered because she was going to say 'God', but changed it to 'danger'. 'But does that mean that such a person is any less courageous, any less of ... a woman, in this instance, simply because of a healthy regard for one's own life? I was not a coward when I was a stretcher-bearer on the Normandy beaches and I am not a coward now.'

Nora sighed. 'Very well, I take the coward comment back. But I hold fast that you're still lacking sufficient ambition, sufficient oomph, to ever be truly great at your art. Anyhow, it matters not. I haven't time to argue. I'm off!'

Looking at Nora's defiant face as she packed the remainder of her things, Eliza couldn't help but think of Alex, and that day on the beach, when she had played the role of Empress Theodora and run off laughing. Why did she keep turning away from that woman and returning to this role – this safe role – she wondered, when the truth was, she wanted to go to the fortress every bit as much as Nora. Wanted the scoop every bit as much as Nora. She thought of Alex's words on the train ... *I have come to the conclusion that it is not a failing to discard an old costume and choose another role, in another play, if the one you chose originally is now too difficult for you to play out with true conviction.*

Nora headed for the door.

Eliza, incredibly, began to laugh.

Nora stopped at the door and also fell into laughter as Julien looked on, utterly confused.

Eliza turned to Julien. 'I cannot possibly allow this crazy woman to travel across town alone. Give me five minutes to pack and then we'll go.'

'Women!' he said, rolling his eyes and shaking his head. 'Women.'

On arrival at the fortress, Eliza could hear Nora's tirade from across the courtyard.

'Don't patronise me, you damn sonofabitch. I can go in there if you take me in there with you and you damn well know it!'

She was standing outside the Ile du Grand Bé sketching the scene silently while Nora bargained with an American major for access – at least, that was the original plan, but it had clearly turned into something else. A troop of GIs were preparing their weapons with the intention of entering the fortress to take the German surrender. No other correspondents or artists were there.

'Now listen, Missy,' the major began, towering over Nora, who, despite her efforts to stand tall, stood not a chance against a man who had, Eliza couldn't help but notice, the look and sound of John Wayne about him. 'Those Nazis in there might be playing us for fools,' he said.

Nora began to argue. He closed her down by turning to walk away. 'The answer is no,' he said, over his shoulder. 'There could be a stand-off. It could be booby-trapped. It's no place for you and that's final.' He turned to speak to his aide. 'Damn woman.'

'If I were a man you'd let me in,' spat Nora. This hit a chord. He turned back, but to Eliza's surprise his face was soft.

'I get it. You're a modern gal. And hey, it's your life you're risking, but I've been given strict orders that no women – women writer folk like you – should be allowed to get themselves into trouble. Nobody wants a dead woman on their patch,' he said. 'No siree, Ma'am.'

Nora dropped her shoulders and turned away. Eliza couldn't help but feel for Nora. And really, why shouldn't she go in? No other reporters were here.

It was time for solidarity. Enter Lady Eliza Arbuthnot, who, despite the raggedy uniform and dishevelled hair, still maintained an aura of utter loveliness about her few men could resist. Eliza had never – not once in her life – played on her charm, her looks or her ability to sway until now when, despite Nora being nothing short of a niggling pain in her backside, she saw the look of utter frustration on her face and decided it was time, finally, to help. Nora had gotten Eliza the cover of *Life* after all, and the truth was, Eliza was growing rather fond of the irrepressible Nora Levine. She stepped forwards.

'That's understandable, Sir,' she said. 'My colleague is one keen reporter, that's for sure. It gets us into all kinds of bother, I can tell you.'

Nora opened her mouth to argue but closed it again when Eliza held out her sketch pad to show him. 'What do you think?' she asked. He cocked his head to look at the drawing. A smile crept across his lips. She had sketched him in a particularly flattering light (truth be told, she had given him a distinct John Wayne appearance) and he had a definite look of command and a rugged handsomeness about him. 'It may make the cover of American *Life*. Would you mind if it did?'

'I wouldn't,' he said. Damn right, he wouldn't.

A captain appeared with a look of concern about him. He tapped the major on the arm and led him aside, but not far enough for Eliza to miss the gist of the report. Incredibly, the Americans had no one with them who could speak fluent German.

'You can speak German, right?' she whispered to Nora. 'I get by, but ...'

Eliza approached the major.

'We speak German and French between us,' she said, closing the sketch pad. The captain whooped. The major looked unsure. 'And I'll paint it – the moment you take the surrender, I'll paint it. I guarantee you'll be on the cover of the next edition of American *Life*, if not every other journal and newspaper on both sides of the Atlantic.' She flashed him her best smile.

Five minutes later, the two women, their helmets tightened, one with a notebook in her hand, the other with a sketchpad, followed behind the forward party of troops who had been tasked to enter and accept the surrender from the Nazis. A run of tunnels led into the fortress.

'I can't guarantee the cover of *Life*, by the way,' whispered Nora as the light of the courtyard turned to muted darkness.

'Doesn't matter,' said Eliza. 'We're in now, aren't we?'

Eliza heard Nora snort before falling silent, because what they found within the warren of tunnels, dimly lit and dripping with water, shocked them to the core. The disorder and complete inhumane depravity within the curved walls of those damp tunnels was like nothing Eliza had ever seen. German soldiers – some badly wounded, some dead – littered the wet ground, while the rest were slowly corralled like sewer rats into a grand hall and disarmed by the Americans. Nora and Eliza, now side by side with the American major, exited the last of the tunnels and stepped out into an open courtyard. Eliza placed a hand to her eyes as an automatic response against the bright sunlight. When her eyes adjusted she saw the German Commandant and a handful of German officers standing in the centre of the courtyard, surrounded by the first tranche of American soldiers. Their heads were bowed, their hands were raised and their weapons were scattered across the dusty floor.

'And to think, I might have missed this ...' thought Eliza. Nora was right, she did want the thrill of the scoop. She watched and sketched while Nora introduced herself to the Commandant and began to act as interpreter for the surrender. Eliza stood off at a distance, watching with pride as Nora stepped into her element. As with the tunnels, the courtyard was littered with German dead. It was at this moment that she glanced down and noticed a rabbit's foot and a packet of cigarettes on the ground close to a hand of one of the dead men. Deciding to put the image down on paper before it left her memory, she turned to a fresh page and began to draw, which was when a flash of grey caught Eliza's peripheral vision across the courtyard. The grey flash belonged to a German soldier, who dashed out from behind a rocky fortification to her left. She saw the grenade in his hand just as Nora's voice screamed out 'grenade' across the courtyard. A shot rang out and the man was grappled to the floor, leading the grenade to travel on a different path. A fraction of a second later, the whole world went dark for Lady Eliza Arbuthnot.

Chapter 20

Ellie

Exeter to Plymouth

Rihanna carried the champagne and two glasses through to the lounge carriage on a silver tray while Joe and Ellie followed, flushed from the fizz and the fun, chatting about how quickly the evening was progressing. The D-Day Dames (nothing short of workhorses, they agreed) were to have another short break, but they would reconvene shortly for a 'finale to remember'.

'"We'll Meet Again",' said Ellie, who was carrying the journal and the clock.

Joe stopped. Ellie turned to see why. He was smiling. He touched her arm. 'Do you think so?' he said. 'I'd really love that.'

Ellie saw the misunderstanding and fluffed through her explanation. 'Oh, sorry, I er ... I meant, that's the song they'll sing, for the finale. "We'll Meet Again" ... you know, Vera Lynn.'

Embarrassment flushed from Joe's boots to his hair. Ellie could have gouged out her voice box with a blunt spoon. Why did she have to correct him? Why couldn't she had just gone with it? Basically, what the hell was wrong with her?

With his cheeks fading from scarlet to simply rouged, Joe laughed off the gaffe. 'Oh, right. Of course.' They walked into the lounge car. '"I'll Be Seeing You".'

It was Ellie's turn to flush. 'Really, I'm sorry, I didn't mean to ...'

Joe laughed. 'The song they'll finish on,' he said with a wink. '"I'll Be Seeing You". Twenty quid on it.'

Rihanna placed the champagne tray on a table for two just inside the door. 'I'll leave you two lovebirds to it, then,' said Rihanna, before sliding away.

They smiled awkwardly and sat down.

'So, I know that you're a Nightingale,' he said, 'and we've just been dancing in Berkeley Square ... but do you sing like a nightingale? That's the question.' Joe picked up the bottle and wiped the base with a napkin before pouring. They watched it fizz in the glasses.

'I love to sing,' answered Ellie, picking up her glass and smiling at a WAAF who sidled past. 'But I haven't always found it easy.'

This was her in. Her moment to tell him. To explain

how, many years ago, Eliza (Ellie) Nightingale had been born with a broken heart and that her poor exhausted parents had trailed her in and out of hospitals over the years in an attempt to prolong her life. That she had endured operation after operation, that her quality of life, even now, depended on how her poor old ticker was doing, and it was often stretched to capacity, fighting to keep up with her body as she grew. What she needed was a heart transplant. But that day might never come.

'I've had a problem with my heart, *have* a problem with my heart,' she said. 'There were times when I couldn't even walk up the stairs, let alone sing. Playing the violin has saved me, I think. I used to dream that one day I'd play in an orchestra, like my parents, but that isn't to be. I'm much better now, though,' she added brightly. 'Much better.'

'Is that why you often put your hand to your chest when you're talking?' he asked. 'To protect your heart?'

Ellie wasn't aware that she did, and no one had ever said. She smiled. 'I suppose it must be.'

Joe squeezed her hand to show his empathy. She was pleased that he didn't dwell, but tactfully changed the subject.

'So, big question?' he said.

'Go on.'

'How was my dancing? Not too shabby?'

Ellie winked. 'Let's just say that Fred Astaire had nothing on you!'

Joe took on an air of being pleased with himself. He

fluffed up his feathers. 'And I'm guessing that I didn't step on your foot too often, as you didn't shout out in pain.'

Ellie laughed. 'No, you didn't. I loved it.' She was going to carry on and say, 'And, for the record, Joe from Leeds, tonight has been the most wonderful night of my life, and I'm so pleased to have shared this wonderful journey with you.' But then she would seem like a woman who was falling in love, and that wouldn't be cool. It also certainly wouldn't be channelling her inner Ingrid Bergman in *Casablanca*, either, which was what she was aiming for.

They turned to watch the Dames walk in, which gave Ellie a moment to wonder ... should she hold back? After all, if anyone had waited for a romantic moment like this for ALL OF HER LIFE, it was Ellie. And even if she never saw him again – and she knew, somewhere deep, deep down in her soul that even though she wanted to, she couldn't, not really – then she wanted him to know just how wonderful it had been. But it not being quite the right moment – there being several hours left until the train pulled into Penzance – she held back.

'Twenty quid on it, you said?'

He laughed. 'I did say that, yes.'

'In that case ...' She held out her hand. 'It's a bet!'

Chapter 21

Eliza

'You must remember this, a kiss is still a kiss, a sigh is still a sigh ...'

Eliza's eyes, responding to the sound of singing, began to open. She turned her head on the pillow to find Nancy sitting on a chair by her hospital bed, holding her hand. The two friends took a moment to take each other in, to smile, to acknowledge the moment. 'It seems I've survived to paint another day,' she said, turning her head on the pillow again to take in the scene of the ward.

'Ah, well, that's because of this.' Nancy let go of her hand and reached down to the bare ground that constituted the tent floor to pick up a book – *Murder on the Orient Express*. Nancy took out a small leaf of paper that had been popped inside and showed it to Eliza, but Eliza couldn't quite focus.

'What is it?' asked Eliza, trying to sit up.

'He drew life back into you, apparently.' Nancy handed the paper to Eliza.

'Who did?' Eliza tried to focus.

'Alex. He came in – rushed in – to see you, last evening. I did try to tell him that you must have been *miles* away from the grenade when it landed, and that other than a few cuts and bruises – don't look at your face for a few days, by the way – and a headache, you would be absolutely fine, but he wouldn't have any of it. He stayed with you all night and guess what?'

'What?'

'He held your hand and look ...' Nancy leant on the bed and pointed to the sketch in Eliza's hand, 'he's put all these little angels into the drawing, floating around you, singing and dancing and such like. I think that little one in the corner there might even be drunk!'

Eliza tried to laugh but her ribs hurt. Everything hurt, especially her head. She tried to sit up further but changed her mind.

'I blame the "Dragon", of course ...' said Nancy, straightening her uniform across her legs. 'Damn woman. Alex was awfully cross with her.'

Eliza shook her head on the thin pillow. 'He shouldn't have been. It may have been her idea to go to the fortress, but I got us in.'

'Yes,' said Nancy, doubtfully. 'I heard all about that. What on earth were you thinking?'

'Perhaps I wasn't. How is she? Nora? Did she get caught in the blast?'

'The Dragon? No such luck. From what I've seen of her,

she's too sturdy to be knocked off her feet. She did pop by before she left – a tad worried, I'll give her that – but Sister told her to leave.' Nancy laughed. 'Sister thought she was far too annoying a person to have on the ward for more than five minutes.'

'And where is Alex now?' asked Eliza, handing Nancy the drawing.

'A rider came for him. There's some brouhaha by some bridge or another – there's always some brouhaha by some bridge or another – and General Patton (*the* General Patton, no less) wanted him there. Nora wanted him to take her along as well, so that was another row.'

'Might I have some water, please?'

Nancy tipped water into Eliza's mouth from a beaker before sitting back in her chair and suggesting that Eliza rest. But Eliza wouldn't have it.

'No, I'll rest in a moment, but I need you to do something for me first.'

'Anything,' said Nancy, taking her hand again. 'What is it?'

'Write a letter for me, to Alex.'

Nancy waited, her forehead puckered.

'Tell him ... tell him that I'm desperately sorry, but while I was at home with Arthur, I realised that I have to stay with him ... No, no, please, don't try to stop me. It's the only way. Write that he is to go to America. Write that ...' the tears began to flow freely but Eliza battled on '... that the time we had in Cornwall was the best time of my life and that I'll treasure it – and him – always. But that was all I ever had to give. Tell him to leave this place; to go away as fast as he can and not to look back. He shouldn't be some general's personal scribe. He hates being told what to write. He's only here because ... because I'm here.'

Nancy nodded. 'All right, my love.'

'And you promise you'll get it to him?'

'I promise. He's bound to pop back when he can, the poor lamb was distraught at the sight of you.'

'If he does, tell Sister I don't want to see him.' Eliza turned her head away to allow the tears to fall onto the pillow. 'I've suddenly got such a terrible sense of dread.'

Nancy stood. 'Shh, now. Sleep,' she said. 'It's just the concussion making you feel odd. All will be well in the morning.'

All will be well.

Eliza closed her eyes. 'Will you look in on me while I sleep?' she asked. 'Only, it's odd to find oneself suddenly on the other side of the sheets.'

Nancy leant forwards and kissed her. 'Of course I will.' She placed Alex's sketch under Eliza's pillow. 'And when you wake up next, I'll bring you something to eat and we'll have you on your feet again in no time.'

'When I do wake,' she said, 'will you bring me something to draw with, too? I want to sketch a scene, well, not a scene exactly, but something from this perspective, as a patient, from the inside looking out. I realise now, that Cartwright was right to ...'

'Cartwright?'

'The man from the War Artists Advisory Committee. The man who sent me here. He was an artist in the last war, did I tell you that? He told me that a moment would come ...' Her voice caught. 'That a moment would come when something would click. When I wouldn't be painting a photograph anymore, but capturing a feeling. A moment when I'll know how to capture the essence of a single moment, so that the person looking at it is right there with me. I don't want to paint the war as I have been doing anymore, I want to paint the light and the colour, so that, just for a moment, whoever looks at it in the years to come, is precisely and completely here.'

Nancy gathered her things and turned to walk away. Eliza reached her hand under the pillow and took out the sketch. She called Nancy back.

'What do the words say?' she asked. 'I can't quite make them out.'

Nancy smiled. 'It's the title of the picture,' she said. '*My Love Lies Bleeding*.'

Eliza squeezed her eyes to hold in the tears. 'Of course,' she said. 'Of course.'

Chapter 22

Eliza

Paris, 28 August 1944

The Red Cross truck came to a grinding halt just as the Arc de Triomphe came into view. Liberated just two days before and littered with the burnt detritus of combat, Paris had morphed from Nazi-occupied hell to Allied-liberated heaven, with a street party in full swing that encompassed the whole of the city. Crowds of joyful people spilled out onto the streets, welcoming each Allied truck as it arrived. It was a party likely to run on for days – weeks, even – and right there, stuck in the middle of it all, in a gridlock of field hospital trucks entering the busiest part of town, were Eliza and Nancy. After ten minutes of not moving, a soldier sitting at the rear of the truck removed the pegs holding up the tailgate and allowed the metal plate to fall. He winked at Eliza and jumped out.

With the liberation of Paris, the heady days of summer

in Normandy had come to an end. Eliza's unit was tasked to establish itself for a short time in the grounds of a dilapidated hospital on the banks of the Seine. Nancy had been granted three days' leave and Eliza, now fully recovered from the explosion at the fortress, decided it would be the perfect time to do the same thing. They intended to bunk up with the other nurses at the hospital at night and gallivant around Paris by day. The war was far from over, but to be in Paris at this moment, at this page in history, just for a little while, was sublime, and as the truck moved into town, Eliza had gasped with delight at the party atmosphere, taken out her sketchpad and captured every last drop of it.

With a sense of bittersweet melancholy, Eliza put her sketch book away. Her 'scenes from Paris' showed the light and the dark again, the flowers and the destruction, the joy and the pain, which despite the party atmosphere hung heavy in the very air around them. Yes, Alex had made a good argument about only painting the truth of the war, and she did that, but it was the truth as she saw it – as she felt it – not seen in the way either Alex or the War Office wanted her to see it. Her paintings were now entirely her own interpretation, a female interpretation. And there had been lots to paint. The price in human suffering to liberate France on both sides had been so very high. There were no real winners in this. The road to liberate Paris had been a bloody and destructive one, especially for the French, who often had no fresh water, fuel or food to live by. The nurses had thrown a little of what they had for themselves down from the truck to the cheering locals, who must have stood for hours – days, even – cheering the troops on, despite their own desperate hardships. For the sake of her own sanity, her own resilience, Eliza tried to paint one good thing per day, and so, shortly before entering Paris, she had forced herself to paint a scene of a French farmer who was filling in a German trench, preparing the field for new crops, for fresh green shoots. Humans didn't take long to regroup and start again, Eliza realised ... minutes, in fact.

She fastened the buckle on her art satchel, put on her WAAC chip hat, turned to Nancy with a broad smile and said, 'Shall we, darling?' Nancy, who was apoplectic at the thought of a full three days of leave in Paris, jumped to her feet and said, '*Certainement je vais, mon petit canard!* We certainly bloody well shall, my duck!'

They jumped down from the truck with a synchronised thud. Nancy took Eliza's arm. 'Now, I know you always pretend to be such a smiley happy thing with the others, but I – your best and truest friend, by the way – know just how hard it must be to keep painting all the horror we see day after day. It buries itself away in that delicate soul of yours and tears you apart.' Eliza was about to say it was only the same for Nancy, being a full-time nurse and all ... but Nancy went on before she could interrupt. 'Once upon a time in London, Lady Eliza Arbuthnot was the brightest star in the sky – whose name and face filled all the society pages and ...'

'Society pages? I never ...'

Nancy wasn't listening. She began to speak in an affected accent. 'And here is Lady Arbuthnot now, seen here at The Ritz, baring her porcelain shoulders in a daring Givenchy gown, and here she is again, at the Pally, in Dior this time ...'

Eliza shook her head. 'I would never wear Dior to the Pally ...'

Nancy laughed and returned to her normal voice, which wasn't so far from the affected one.

'But isn't it wonderful? We're actually in Paris! And here really is the ravishing Lady Arbuthnot, looking dashing as ever in tatty army fatigues, heading into the biggest street party the world has ever seen.' Nancy took Eliza's hands. 'So, let's not feel guilty about what's been before, or what's yet to come. Let's not think about those fellows who have gone before their time, or those fellows we've gone and fallen in love with, either ...' – Nancy and her Canadian doctor friend, Major Dubois, had become something of a serious item – 'Let's have the best three days of our lives. Just the two of us. What do you say?'

Eliza hugged her friend tightly. She forced the image of Alex that had been branded into her thoughts right out of her head. 'Oh, Nancy, I say, yes! You're absolutely right. Let's make this the time of our lives, definitely.'

'And the first thing I'm going to do—' said Nancy, standing on her toes to look around above the heads of a mob of jubilant people massing around them.

'Is?'

'To find a beauty parlour. There is absolutely no way I can be seen in public until my hair has seen a bottle of bleach!'

A fellow nurse passed Eliza her kitbag from the back of the truck. 'What? A beauty parlour?' Eliza hauled the kitbag over her shoulder. 'Are you crazy? There's no way ...'

But Nancy would have none of it. She grabbed her own kit from the truck and they began to push their way through the crowd, with Nancy taking the lead. 'This is Paris, Eliza,' Nancy shouted back. 'The home of chic. No war could *ever* stop Paris from being chic.'

They linked arms and headed down the road giggling.

That was at 1 p.m. By 7 p.m., Eliza and Nancy were barely on the right side of tipsy and had found themselves a table in a bistro near the Notre Dame cathedral. A man played the piano. A woman sang Edith Piaf. The scene could not have been more quintessentially Parisian if it had been set on a stage.

'This being in uniform is a real boon,' said Nancy, arriving back at the table, a brimming champagne glass in each hand, bright-red lipstick kisses on each cheek. 'They're falling all over themselves to dish out the drinks.' She sat down and glanced around. 'Put that sketchpad away and tell me which film this place reminds you of.'

Eliza put down a nib of charcoal. 'What? The bistro?'

Nancy took a sip. 'Ah, that's bloody good stuff! Yes, this

scene, here, right now, the thing you're sketching ... the piano player, the smoke, the atmosphere, everything.'

Eliza thought for a moment then shook her head. 'No idea.'

Nancy let out a gasp of frustration. 'For goodness' sake. It's exactly like *Casablanca*, you ninny! The film. Remember?'

Eliza smiled and nodded. 'Ah, yes. *Play it again, Sam*.'

'Exactly! And you're Ingrid Bergman, all glassy-eyed and gorgeous. I wish I looked like Ingrid Bergman, but to be honest, I could look like the back end of a cow in this uniform and still get plenty of attention.' Nancy caught another fellow's eye. She raised her glass to him. 'I bloody love this!' Putting her glass down she leant in with a whisper. 'I just had my bottom pinched by one chap and had a proposal from another!' She glanced towards the bar covertly. 'Don't look now but it was that chap there ...' Nancy nodded towards a GI. He noticed her looking and waved.

Eliza placed an arm around her friend. 'You're loving this, aren't you?' she said.

'Aren't you? Please say you are? This is the thing with falling in love – when it's not going to plan, everything good in life is tarnished, which is such a waste. Please do have a lovely time, Eliza, please ...'

Eliza hugged harder.

'I *am* having a fabulous time!' she said earnestly.

'Prove it!' said Nancy, her eyes full of mischief.

'All right, I will. What would you like me to do?'

Nancy sniffed and thought. An accordionist began to accompany the piano.

'Oh, I love this one!' said Eliza. '"I'll Be Seeing You".'

Nancy took Eliza's glass, put it down on the table and grabbed her hand. 'Come with me,' she said. 'We're going to sing for our supper.'

'Oh, no! Please, Nancy, anything but that ...'

But it was no use. Fighting Nancy when she was in full swing was like swimming against a tidal wave – impossible. And anyway, Eliza knew that Nancy was right. Her aching for Alex should not taint this special time. She stopped fighting and went with the flow, which felt wonderful.

The pianist soon got into the rhythm of their singing, as did the rest of the bistro, who loved it. Nancy had a fabulous voice and carried the whole song, while Eliza was happy to sing along quietly.

It was on their second rendition when Nora Levine walked in. Alex was only two marching paces behind her, his mouth having fallen to the floor. Nancy didn't notice, but Eliza did. She stopped singing and elbowed Nancy, who now noticed the pair and, ever the consummate professional, carried on singing while waving in their direction.

As the song came to an end, Nancy grabbed Eliza's hand and rushed her back to their booth. 'She's seen me,' whispered Nancy, a little too loudly for Eliza's satisfaction. 'She must have recognised me from the hospital.'

'She recognised you because you were singing your heart

out and you waved at them, you chump!' said Eliza, her heart racing away like a train.

Nancy dipped her head. 'Don't look now but they're on their way over. Of all the gin joints in all the world, they had to walk into yours, eh?'

The utter surrealness of the day, the pent-up tiredness and the champagne, led Eliza into an immediate and uncontrolled bout of hysterical laughter. Nancy was just trying to shush Eliza when Nora strode up to say, 'Hallo, there.'

Nancy spoke for the two of them. 'Well, hello again. Fancy seeing you two here.' She gestured across the table. 'You know my friend, Lady Arbuthnot, of course?'

'Hello, Nora,' said Eliza, wiping her tears away with a paint-splattered handkerchief. 'How's tricks?'

'Oh, all is just dapper with us. It's good to see you looking well again.' The noise from the cogs of Nora's quick brain echoed around the noisy bistro. 'The last time we were together you were looking a bit of a mess, frankly!' she said, referencing the grenade attack at the fortress. 'Bad luck, that. Did they tell you I came to the hospital, to check that you were ... alive, that sort of thing?'

Eliza laughed. 'Yes, I heard. Thank you. It was good of you.'

Nora flicked a dismissive hand to say, 'It was nothing' and kicked Alex in the shin. 'Isn't she looking better, Alex?'

Eliza found great difficulty in looking at Alex. Despite her note saying that she wouldn't leave Arthur, here he was, in Paris, not in America, where he was supposed to be. And so neither Nora nor Eliza had got their way and dispatched him off to safety after all. When she eventually looked at him, he smiled to reassure her. It was a wonderfully warm smile. 'Hello, Theodora,' he said softly.

'Well, isn't this jolly!' said Nancy, breaking the moment. 'We heard there was a party going on here in Paris so we thought we'd better catch a piece of the action. And here we are. Where are you two staying, by the way?' Nancy asked this in the way polite people might break an uncomfortable pause in conversation by asking about the state of the roads or the weather.

'At The Scribe,' said Nora, who was looking, Eliza thought, noticeably uncomfortable. She was glancing away to find a table, clearly anxious to move on. 'It's where all the journos are,' she added. 'I sent you a note at the hospital saying where to find me, did you get it?'

Eliza had. She was still sending all of her paintings home via Nora, but what Nora had failed to mention in her note, of course, was that Alex was in Paris too, with her.

'And you? Where are you two bunked up?' asked Nora.

'Oh, just this little place called The Ritz,' said Nancy quickly. 'We thought we'd have a real treat. Splash out a bit. And what with Eliza being a proper lady and everything, it was easy to get in.'

At the mention of The Ritz, Eliza couldn't help but look directly at Alex and smile. The smile said, *I wish we'd had more time.*

'The Ritz?' repeated Nora with just a trace of derision. 'Very fancy. Well, you'll have to excuse us.' Nora turned to Alex. 'We've just popped in to say hello to a couple of pals from home, haven't we? Best be off.'

Alex nodded a regretful goodbye and they had only moved away by two marching paces when Nancy pushed her champagne glass across the table and dashed around to sit next to Eliza in the booth. She budged Eliza along the seat with her bottom. 'Well,' she began, her eyes bright as a freshly polished petri dish. 'What do we have to say about that little fiasco? Do we hate that woman, or what?'

Eliza smiled, put an arm around her friend and picked up her glass. All she wanted to do was weep, or run after Alex and tell him she loved him. But that would never do, not now. She held the glass aloft for a toast.

'I only have one thing to say to you right now, Nancy ...'

'And that is?'

'Can't you guess?' pressed Eliza. 'Go on, guess.'

Nancy laughed. 'Tell me.'

'Here's looking at you, kid!'

Chapter 23

Ellie

Plymouth to Bodmin

'It's been such a wonderful evening, a real sentimental journey, and I can't thank you enough for taking this journey with us.' This from the lead singer of the D-Day Dames, her West Midlands accent breaking through nicely now. 'The gals and I want to thank you all for being such a wonderful audience, but don't worry, we've got a few numbers left, so grab your partners and dance along with us. And just to be serious for a moment – health and safety and all that – it's not that easy to dance on a moving train, so do be careful.'

Ellie looked at Rihanna who was standing by the door. Rihanna flashed Ellie an encouraging smile.

'Please do sing along – you'll all know the words to this one, I'm sure.' She gathered herself and turned to the other

Dames. The music started and they began to sing – in perfect harmony, which was a surprise to Ellie as they really had had quite a skinful – '*You must remember this, a kiss is just a kiss, a sigh is just a sigh, the fundamental things apply, as time goes by ...*'

Ellie swayed to the music, her hand on her chest. The blinds in the lounge carriage had not been drawn for the 'blackout' and a broad river, far beneath them, the full moon highlighting many yachts bobbing about on the water, came into view.

'Oh, look!' she said. 'We're crossing the Tamar!'

The train cleared the bridge and the windows descended into darkness again. Ellie unbuckled her shoes and stretched out her feet. 'That's it then,' she said with a sigh, returning to her occupation of swaying to 'As Time Goes By'. 'We're in Cornwall. I think this is usually the point where the train slows down and the passengers go to bed.' She glanced regretfully at Joe.

The clock and the journal, which in their own way had added a certain intimate nostalgia to the trip, sat on the table. The stuffed Labrador sat obediently by Joe's legs.

Ellie picked up the journal. 'We didn't need the props as backup plans after all,' she said.

Alex smiled fondly at the clock. 'No, we didn't.'

'It's so beautiful,' she said, picking up the clock and turning it around in her hands. 'Will you be able to fix it, do you think?

'I'll give it my best shot.'

Ellie sighed. It was a sigh full of melancholy. 'Do you think that the last owner would have wanted it to tick again, though, given the note?'

'You can't stop time, Ellie,' he said. She handed him the clock. 'Freezing time at three-fifteen only meant something to the last people who owned it. The one thing I've learned with antiques is that things are supposed to be enjoyed. They're only antiques if you feel separated from them, if you revere them. I want the people who buy the things I sell to enjoy the history of the piece but also to feel like they're just as special to them as they were to the original owner. Things should be used. And this little clock ... I think it should tick again, not be a museum piece.'

'Would you sell it to me, please?' Ellie was surprised when the words tumbled out of her mouth.

He paused a moment. 'I'd already made up my mind to give it to you as a present, just as soon as it's fixed.' He turned to her. 'Ellie, I know we've known each other for like,' he glanced at his watch, 'four hours—'

But Ellie suddenly couldn't allow him to say whatever it was he was going to say. Despite her childish imaginings of a wedding dress, she was suddenly frightened.

'Crazy, isn't it,' she interrupted, feigning brightness, 'I feel like I've known you for ever. But I suppose the big question is ... will you go to Porthcurno Beach at three-fifteen tomorrow? See if anyone's there, waiting for you? The love of your life type of thing?'

Joe shrugged his answer, his face betraying his disappointment. 'Depends.'

Ellie picked up the journal and began absently leafing through the pages. 'I think you should go,' she said.

'Do you?'

Ellie nodded. 'God, yes. I would. It's a lovely idea.'

Joe leant down to stroke the dog. 'Well, old Fido here will need a stroll at some point, so I'll probably take him down to the beach. And three o'clock is as good a time as any. Hey, how about—?'

'Would you like to see some of Eliza's other paintings of Porthcurno?' she interrupted again, with an urgency to her voice. 'There are a couple more in here.'

Joe edged his seat towards Eliza. The dog fell over. He placed it on his knee.

'Great Granny Nancy said that it's not so much a memoir as a gathering together of Eliza's thoughts and ideas as she moved through Europe. It was her own way of escaping the hell of it all, of trying to make sense of it. Well, that's what Nancy thought, anyhow.'

'Moved through Europe?'

'She was an auxiliary nurse as well as being a war artist. The Red Cross asked her to go with them as the Allies progressed through Europe – D-Day, the liberation of Paris, the Battle of the Bulge, she saw everything. Ah, here's one of Porthcurno ...' She opened the page on a watercolour painted from a vantage point above the beach.

The turquoise sea was perfection, as was the sky and the contrast of the deep sided cliff beyond.

Joe peered in. 'What's all that? On the beach?' he asked. 'Is it a smudge?'

Ellie shook her head. 'No. This was painted in 1944. That smudge is a line of flamethrowers.'

Joe's eyes widened. 'Flamethrowers? In Cornwall?' He looked again.

'It's where all the telegraph cables came in from the Atlantic – some still do. They would have needed to protect it, I suppose.'

Joe nodded his understanding.

Ellie turned the pages with care, flicking past Eliza's scribbled notes. 'Here's another one of the beach ... It's one of my favourites, actually.'

Joe smiled down at the painting. 'A picnic scene,' he said.

'It's a self-portrait; well, kind of.' Ellie tipped her head to assess it with him. 'If you look closely, you can see two figures playing in the sea. See, here.'

'How on earth did she manage to make stick people look so happy?' he said. 'So clever to be able to express the emotion of it with just a couple of flicks of a brush. You can really see the fun and energy in their play.'

Ellie smiled. 'They do look happy, don't they? I think that's what makes it such an emotional painting for me. So much love, so much said about the two of them, but communicated entirely without words.'

281

'Like your music,' said Joe, sitting back.

'Ah, but I didn't write the music, that's where the clever-ness, no, the art – the true artist – really comes into play.'

Joe shook his head. 'I disagree. Eliza didn't create the things she painted – the earth, the sea, even the picnic – she used her talent to express what was there in paint. It's the same with music – it's how it's played that matters.'

Ellie smiled up at him. 'Would you like to see some more of her work?' she asked.

Joe leant in again. 'Definitely.'

As the train rocked on, Ellie carefully turned the pages, showing paintings not of battle, but of the people and places that were important to Eliza. There were images of Nancy, a doctor called Major Smythe, a man digging a field, Paris, Nora, a ward sister and, most of all, Alex, who, in most of the paintings, was wearing a leather flying jacket similar to the one Joe had been wearing tonight (though Joe had taken his off as he was 'baking-up like a jacket potato').

'You said she began the journal on a train, on this train ...'

Ellie closed the journal. 'Yes, she did. That's why I'm here, really. Great Granny Nancy wanted me to follow in her footsteps. I think she was trying to inspire me.'

'And how did she meet Alex?'

Ellie looked towards the D-Day Dames rather than at Joe.

'They met on the train, but she doesn't say much about

it, or about her time in Penberth during that particular trip.'

'They fell in love on this train, then?'

Ellie finally looked at him. 'I guess so ...' She grabbed the journal again. 'I think that when you look at some of the paintings of Alex, though, there's an obvious ...'

'Ache,' said Joe.

Ellie turned to him. 'Isn't there? It's the same with the paintings of her cottage. Sometimes I ...' Ellie paused. The Labrador fell off Joe's knee. She picked him up, placed him on her own knee and began to stroke him. 'I dream about her. It's as if I *am* her. And when I play the violin, it's as if she's with me – in me – helping me to feel my way into the music.'

Joe joined in stroking the dog. 'Do you know why she comes to you?' he asked.

Eliza shrugged and held the dog up to her face to kiss him. 'She wants to go home. To Alex.'

'And tonight, you're giving her her wish,' he said. 'If she's with you – in you – then you're taking her home. Maybe you're both going home?'

A stray tear fell down Ellie's face.

Joe wiped the tear from her face with his thumb.

'So, about this clock!' began Ellie. 'Who do we think wrote the note – does it say?'

But Joe took Ellie's hands in his. 'Forget the clock,' he said. 'How about we enjoy the rest of the evening just for us, not for Eliza, not for the person who wrote the note ...

or for anyone else in the whole world. Just for us. What do you think?'

Ellie smiled, though it was not the thousand-watt beamer she had wanted to emit. More like a low energy bulb glow. Because the truth was, as much as she would like to have been, she was not a princess in her own Disney movie. She simply didn't have the energy to pull it off. If anything, Ellie was Cinderella, her heart a ticking clock, the hands counting down to her unknowable fate. The real clock in the carriage, the one glaring at Ellie from behind the bar, showed that time was well on its way to midnight, a time beyond which Ellie never stayed awake, much as she often tried.

Ellie picked up the little clock again. Maybe it would be best not to have it. Although she adored the idea of stopping time, Joe was right. It simply wasn't possible, and when you lived your life from one day to the next – one minute to the next – there was no benefit of owning something that confirmed what you knew already.

She suddenly felt extremely tired and more than a little emotional.

Joe must have noticed. He nudged her. 'Hey, it's been at least half an hour since our last toast!' He poured more champagne into their glasses. 'And I've got the perfect one. To going home,' he said, raising his glass.

'To going home,' repeated Ellie, softly.

They fell quiet then and a D-Day Dame began to speak. 'We're going to sing a song now that is very special to me.

It's not from the 1940s but it's my favourite song, perfect for a journey like this one because it's about two drifters, off to see the world, and there is, as the song says, such a lot of world to see ... it's the wonderful, the iconic, "Moon River". Take it away, girls.'

Joe smiled as the music began. 'This was my mum's favourite song, too,' he said.

'Was? You mean ...?'

His eyes glazed. 'We lost her last year.' Not waiting for Ellie to respond or to offer sympathy, he stood and held out his hand. 'Dance with me?' he said.

Leaving her shoes abandoned on the floor, Ellie fell into Joe's arms, rested her head on his shoulder and began to sway.

The mood had changed. They were in Cornwall now, the final leg of the journey. The train had slowed and yet to Ellie it seemed to be running out of control, steaming ahead way too fast to its final destination. Ellie knew that life was not about the destination but the journey, and yet, tonight, the destination was all she could think of, and it was suddenly closing in on her far too fast.

Chapter 24

Eliza

Paris, August 1944

The Parisian determination to party was unrelenting and Eliza and Nancy were caught up in liberation mania, fulfilling Nancy's desire for them to behave like society girls for a couple of days. Food and alcohol emerged from secret hideaways all over the city, and the locals were more than happy to share with their liberators. The fact that Eliza and Nancy were women in uniform seemed to make them doubly appealing as recipients of gifts, and after the horror of the Normandy landings, Saint-Malo and the distress of working at the field hospital, a little enthusiasm and gratitude from strangers were no bad things. But for Eliza, the party fever only really kicked in after she read a note she received from Nora. It had been waiting for her at the hotel when they popped back in on the afternoon of the third day to freshen up.

Eliza

I ought not to have interfered in my brother's life. As you see, despite my best efforts to send him away, Alex has not gone. In fact, he seems to have become every bit as determined as I am to reach Germany. (Something about getting to Berlin?) He is miserable without you – without the thought of ever being with you – and tolerating his misery is not my idea of a pleasant time.

The thing is, you have cast a spell on my dear sibling, Lady Arbuthnot, do you know that? I suppose you do. Something happened to him in Cornwall, something wonderful, and he is on the path to becoming the man I used to know … at least, he was, until I persuaded you to say goodbye to him. (I know that is why you did it, and I am grateful.)

He is leaving Paris tomorrow morning, and I know that he would dearly love to see you. I ask you to please go to The Ritz Hotel tonight – I hear there's a party on – and give my name at the door. (I don't believe for one second that you are staying there so no need to keep up the façade.) I shall make sure Alex also finds his way there and what happens after that is entirely up to the two of you.

I'll be heading up the Paris bureau from now on, but if you need anything as you move forward with the Red Cross, I will remain your main point of contact, so do find a way to get a message sent back to me and I'll do what I can. I will definitely cross

*the Siegfried Line myself someday soon but, for now,
maybe I need to cut the apron strings and leave Alex
to move on east without me.*

All best wishes,
Nora

In the early evening, Eliza and Nancy settled themselves
at an outside table at the Café Royale just a few hundred
yards from The Ritz. They were sipping red wine when
Nancy said, 'You know what this reminds me of?'

Eliza rolled her eyes in mock exasperation.

'It's bound to be a film. Let me think for a moment ...'

But Nancy shook her head. 'No, it's not a film this time,
at least, I don't think so, because I'm not entirely sure what
it reminds me of exactly, I just know that it does, somehow.'
She glanced around to absorb the atmosphere while
thinking. 'No, it's gone. It was there a moment ago, a glimpse
of a memory, but now – poof! It's gorn!'

Eliza patted Nancy's hand. 'I think you've had too much
champagne, or sunshine.'

Nancy shook her head. 'Not at all. At any rate, I've only
had the same amount to drink as you. No, this is one of
those situations where you look around and you just know
that there is something familiar about a place, even though
you've never been there before. Perhaps it's something about
the people that are there with you, or maybe it's the *feel*
of the moment, or the atmosphere, like you've experienced
it all before, and you have no idea when, or where, of *if*,

even. But still, it's familiar. Maybe an ancestor was here and I'm feeling it through the blood?' Nancy picked up her glass and chinked it with Eliza's. 'You're right. I'm losing my mind. It's the booze, obviously.'

Eliza took a sip and said, 'You're not losing your mind. That's exactly how I feel when I'm with Alex.'

'Like he's more familiar than he should be?'

'Exactly that.'

Nancy pushed back the cuff of her shirt and glanced at her watch. 'Well, Cinderella,' she said, 'with any luck, you'll be seeing him again very soon.' She knocked back the last of her wine. 'We ought to set off pretty sharpish, though. You wouldn't want to miss him.' Nancy tilted her head to assess Eliza's outfit. 'You're not thinking of going dressed like that, are you?'

Eliza, who had just put her glass to her mouth, spat out her wine because of course she was going dressed like this.

'Oh, Nancy!' Eliza reached a hand out across the void. 'Am I an awfully wretched person to go?'

Nancy scrunched her face. 'No, you are not. And you are going even if I have to drag you there – and I could, by the way, easily. For goodness sake, you haven't seen Arthur properly for months – years – and you've already walked out on Alex once, and then you wrote that blasted note ...'

'You wrote the note,' corrected Eliza.

'... saying to forget you, and yet here he still is, waiting.

Love like that, Eliza ...' She didn't need to finish the sentence.

Eliza took a deep contented breath. 'I'm so grateful you're here,' she said. 'You nursed me when I was wounded, and now you're guiding me when I'm confused. What on earth would I have done these past weeks without you?'

Nancy batted Eliza's emotion away good-heartedly. 'Golly, I don't know. You would have stayed sober last night for a start, I should say. What would I have done without you, that's the question!'

They held hands as a violin struck up within the café. Neither woman knew the tune, but they continued to simply hold hands and look about them, taking in the street and the people and the music. It was a beautifully mournful tune. Full of loss and grief and longing.

'In my next life,' began Eliza, thoughtfully, 'I'm going to play some kind of instrument. I can't imagine anything could be more wonderful.'

Nancy smiled. 'I bet you will, too. But best not to head off to that life too soon, eh?'

Eliza shook her head. 'No, not so very soon,' she repeated.

And then the music silenced them. It stilled them. Eliza closed her eyes but the visions of the past few weeks – the past few years – came anyway. Good visions and terrible visions, the light and the dark, all merging together to create a kaleidoscope of grief. The inevitable tears came, edging over her lashes like a gentle brook. Nancy squeezed Eliza's hand.

'Let them come, old thing,' she said. 'Let them come.'

They arrived at The Ritz at seven, Nora's name the only ticket they needed to get in.

'You'll never guess!' said a breathless Nancy, emerging from the powder room. 'Hemingway – *the* Hemingway, you know, the writer – is throwing a bash upstairs, and Marlene Dietrich is up there too. I nearly wet myself when I heard! Shall I try to get us in? I could tell them that you're a great lady and all that?'

Eliza guided Nancy away from the stairs. 'Not a chance. Nora must have meant the main party in the ballroom, not a private bash. Come on, let's go in.'

They followed the noise of a band into the ballroom where the party was in full swing. A host of uniformed men danced to 'Boogie Woogie Bugle Boy', swaying and swishing with their Parisian partners beside them. The lights were low and the crystal sparkled. Eliza stood on the periphery with an eye on the door, all the while trying to appear nonchalant, as though she didn't have an eye on the door at all. Nancy did a tour to assess the room. She reappeared two minutes later with a champagne glass in each hand.

'Well, the eats are poor,' she said, 'but the booze is flowing like a river. They must have had secret stashes of champagne everywhere. That's the French for you. Got their priorities right, I'd say.'

Eliza took a glass from Nancy. 'What baffles me is how they got a band together so quickly. And they're awfully good, too. I don't suppose things like art and music and literature can ever really be quelled though. They just become a coiled spring, ready to bounce back the moment they're released.'

Nancy raised her glass. 'Well, it's certainly been released now!'

'What shall we toast to this time?' asked Eliza, getting into the mood.

Nancy stuck out her bottom lip. Eliza smiled. She'd paint it sometime.

'How about "To absent friends"?'

Eliza scrunched her nose. 'Too morbid.'

'All right, then, how about "To all the men we've loved before"?'

Eliza shook her head. 'Too twee. And anyway, I haven't.'

'Haven't what?'

'Loved that many men,' Eliza confessed. 'Just two, in fact.'

'Reeeeally?' Nancy was clearly shocked at this. 'But you give off such a different impression!'

'Nancy!'

'No, what I mean is, you're so glamourous. You're Lady Arbuthnot, which means that you simply glide along looking like a woman who has known great ...'

Eliza waited for her to finish, an amused smile spreading across her face. 'Great?'

Nancy shrugged. 'Well, great sex, to be honest.'

'Nancy!'

Nancy laughed outrageously before holding up her glass and saying, 'All right, here's my final offer: "To new loves and passionate kisses".'

Eliza smiled. 'Perfect.'

She glanced towards the door again.

'A watched pot never boils, my love,' said Nancy, following Eliza's gaze. 'He'll come, don't you worry. Best to enjoy the party and have the look of a gorgeous siren about you when he arrives. You're Ingrid Bergman in *Casablanca*, remember – demure, aloof, wonderful. Basically, don't look too keen, as t'were. And I'll tell you this, my estimation of that Nora woman has gone up a thousand-fold.' She raised her voice to be heard above the band. 'And if anyone can get him here, it's her. Mark my words, he'll pitch up around nine – that's what I would do if I were him. What you need to do in the meantime is dance with some chap, or some "guy" as these fellows from America would say, just as he walks in.'

'Which guy?'

'Any, doesn't matter, but it needs to be a slow dance, a waltz, preferably, then Alex will arrive, see you in another man's arms, go green with envy, then tap the chap on the shoulder and say something like "This is my dance, I think." You will acquiesce with demure grace, the GI will disappear (glumly, because you're a catch) and Alex will take you in his arms and tell you that he loves you and you're to get married immediately ... well, once you've sorted things with Arthur. The rest is history, as they say. I've seen it a thousand times at the Pally. You're Maureen O'Hara and he's ... Actually, I'm not sure who Alex is but it'll come to me.' She put a hand to her mouth. 'Ooh, what if he can't dance? That would be dreadful!'

Eliza, feeling the need to halt Nancy's imagination, took her friend's glass and placed it down on a table. She held out her hand. 'Well, *I* can dance even if he can't, and this is exactly my kind of a song. Would you care to dance the American way, m'lady?'

Nancy said that she would. 'Absobloodylutely,' she would.

At nine-thirty, Eliza began to worry. Many men had asked her to dance, all of whom she refused politely, much to Nancy's disappointment. But then she received a tap on her shoulder that delighted and shocked her in equal measure.

'Say, if this dance isn't taken,' the soldier said. 'Maybe you would like to dance with me?'

Recognising the voice, Eliza turned around and threw her arms around the man standing next to her.

'It's you!' she said. 'But what on earth are you doing here?' She stood back to take him in.

'They fixed me up pretty quickly after a bit of a blow on the beaches. I've been out with the First for a couple of weeks now.'

Eliza couldn't believe it. It was one of the Idaho boys she had painted in Portsmouth. And here he was, in Paris, back in the fight.

'So, will you dance?' he asked.

'Of course I will,' she said. 'I'd be honoured.'

The band struck up with a new song, a fast Glenn Miller number. How wonderful it was, Eliza reflected as she was spun around the dance floor, to be in Paris and yet dancing an American dance with an American GI. They danced two songs but then the music slowed to a song the whole room seemed to know – 'I'll Be Seeing You' – and when the words began, Eliza was sure she recognised the voice of the woman singing. She looked over her partner's shoulder to find Nancy looking perfectly at home, back where she belonged, on the stage.

And then came a tap. Her heart stopped. Her face flushed. Could Nancy be right after all? She turned around. But it wasn't Alex, it was Nora, and she had the manner of an urgent messenger about her.

'You need to leave,' shouted Nora above the noise of the band. 'I've a driver waiting to take you to the station.'

Eliza stopped dancing, gave her excuses and followed Nora into the foyer where, her ears ringing, she could finally hear.

'What's happened?' she asked. She put a hand to her mouth. 'Oh, my God. Has something happened to Alex?'

Nora shook her head. 'Nothing has happened to Alex except that he's become the main whipping boy for General

296

Patton, that's what. He's to travel to Calais tonight to report on something big – something that Alex won't even give me a sniff of, which I'm really annoyed about! He's catching the train' – Nora looked at her watch – 'in half an hour. I've told Alex to watch out for you at the station.'

Eliza's mouth gaped open. She simply couldn't keep on the same page as Nora, who always moved just a little too fast.

Eliza looked back towards the ballroom. 'What about Nancy?'

'I'll look after Nancy. And the driver will wait for you at the station and bring you back. If you don't go now, you'll miss him. Come on, Eliza. Move yourself!'

Nora turned without waiting for an answer. Eliza dashed after her and reached the road just as Nora put two fingers to her mouth and whistled. An open-topped American jeep driven by a pretty WAAC screeched up and Eliza jumped in.

'To the train station,' shouted Nora, hitting the jeep on the side. 'And don't spare the horses!'

Eliza shouted, 'Wait!' and leant out of the jeep. She took Nora's face in her hands and kissed her full on the lips. 'Thank you!' she said, her eyes bright, her heart racing. She turned back to the WAAC. 'You heard the woman,' she said, 'drive on!'

The carriage doors were slamming shut as Eliza ran along the length of the train, looking in each carriage, desperate to catch a glimpse of Alex. But when she reached the very last door there had still been no sign of him. She turned around and glanced down the length of the platform, one hand holding her chip hat by her side, the other hand running anxiously through her hair.

A group of GIs were boarding the train halfway back along the platform. As they dispersed, a man wearing a leather flying jacket, carrying a kitbag and a portable typewriter – and a very broad smile – began to walk quickly towards her.

It was Alex. Her Alex. And he *was* hers, and always would be, she knew that now. How could she not when all she could see was his beautiful face – his beautiful smile – beaming full of absolute joy at the sight of her.

'Nora told me what she said to you,' he said, 'and about the letter. She thinks you only wrote it because of her. Am I right to have hope?'

Eliza touched his face. 'I'm so sorry. I thought I was doing the right thing. But my life with Arthur is over. There's no going back now, whatever happens with ...'

'Us,' he concluded, softly.

'Yes,' she agreed, 'with us.'

'I'm sorry I couldn't make it to The Ritz ...' he said, putting down his things.

Eliza smiled. 'Well, there were no trains there, so it wasn't the right place for us to meet, clearly.'

Alex laughed. 'I think you're right,' he said. 'But if I had been able to go to The Ritz tonight ...' His face was coy.

His eyes were dancing. 'I would have asked if you cared to dance.' He held out his arms in invitation. Eliza, not caring a jot that she was on the platform and the passengers on the train had begun to stare, fell into his arms, and Alex began to waltz them across the platform. He leant forward to whisper into her hair. 'And then I was going to ask if I mightn't have every dance tonight ...?' Eliza glanced up, her entire body swimming – beaming – with happiness. 'And then every dance after that,' he said, 'for as long as we both shall live.'

The whistle blew. Eliza stopped dancing. Alex released her from his hold. He opened a carriage door, jumped in and pushed the window down. Eliza stepped onto the footplate as the train began to move. They looked at each other. It was a look that was the awakening of complete understanding. A look that said: welcome home.

They kissed. She pulled away. The train was moving too quickly to hold on now. Alex waved wildly. He put his hands to his mouth and shouted, 'Farewell, brave Theodora! Stay safe, and don't forget, I want every dance, for ever.'

'I shan't forget!' she shouted back, before adding in a whisper, 'As long as we both shall live.'

Chapter 25

Ellie

Bodmin to Par

It was well gone midnight when the D-Day Dames took a moment to ask everyone to stand and hold hands in a circle (or a rectangle, Joe said, due to the shape of the carriage) for the finale.

Ellie, who had exerted more energy in one evening than she would usually exert in a whole month, was exhausted. But she didn't want to be exhausted, she wanted to party until dawn like the rest of them – the nurses, the doctors, the Land Army girls, the soldiers and the sailors. Even Winston Churchill and Yoda were dancing – together – at that moment. But she was done for. She sat down and glanced at Joe, who looked so happy and so full of energy that the real world came crashing down on her just as the introduction to the last song of the evening began to ring out, which was, exactly as Ellie had predicted, 'We'll Meet Again'.

Joe turned to Ellie with a smile as the first bars of the introduction began. 'You nailed it!'

He went to put a hand in his pocket but Ellie took his hand to stop him. 'You already paid up front, remember? The tip, on the platform ...' She released his hand.

Joe pushed himself onto his feet. 'Well, it's the last dance,' he said, 'and I've decided that this is "our" song. You called it, after all.' He held out a hand. 'Shall we?'

Ellie looked up at him, her big blue eyes full of longing and regret. Dreaming of falling in love was one thing, as was having fun with Rihanna and behaving like any other young (or older) woman who did so much want to fall in love. This man was wonderful. He was everything she wanted him to be – handsome, funny, generous and kind. But what about Joe? What did he want the woman in his life to be? All of those things too, she imagined, but most particularly – and it wasn't a big ask – Joe would want the woman in his life to be *in* his life for many years to come. This man deserved a love to last a lifetime. Ellie couldn't be certain she could give him that. In fact, she was pretty certain that she couldn't. But for all of this worry for the sake of Joe's heart, mainly she was worried for the sake of her own. This wasn't a man to fool around with for a few days or weeks and then wave a cheery goodbye to, this was a man she could – would – lose her heart to, and she was simply too frightened to let it go.

'I'm sorry, Joe,' she said. 'But I'm so tired. I've had such a wonderful evening. It's been the time of my life – I mean it. But I'm afraid it's time for Cinders to go to bed.'

Joe helped Ellie to her feet, his face a picture of anti-climax and his shoulders sagging with disappointment.

'But ...'

She stood on her tiptoes and pecked him on the cheek. 'Goodnight, Joe from Leeds,' she said, her eyes misting over. She raised a hand to his face. 'You're wonderful.' She picked up her shoes, her clutch and the journal and walked to the door. Florence Nightingale (wrong war, but it didn't matter) tried to pull her back and encourage her to join in with the sing-song, which was now in full swing.

'But won't I see you at breakfast?' shouted Joe after her as she reached the door, which opened automatically as she approached.

Ellie didn't turn back. It was too late – the carriage door had already shut behind her. Ellie Nightingale had done what she always did, and would, one day, do for ever. Slowly, regretfully, she drifted away.

Chapter 26

Eliza

December 1944

My darling, Eliza
By the time you receive this letter the press camp will have retreated. I pray this is a temporary blip, because surely all that we have gained so far – and all that we have lost – cannot have been for nothing. Little has changed. My days roll on exactly the same: each day I tag along with the General or his Chief of Staff and head to the front to capture in five hundred words the horror of this bloodbath. Half of it won't make it past the censors, but I have to try. Conditions have been changeable, sometimes decent enough, sometimes hellish, and we're a shoddy lot of reporters – battle scarred and exhausted – and yet we're still prepared to rush ahead of the next chap if we come across a sniff of a scoop. We have become bloodhounds and I am starting to wonder what it is that

motivates us onwards. I am embarrassed to remember my sanctimonious preaching on the train.

Nora tells me your artwork has become quite abstract and much sought after at home. I am delighted to be able to report that she has developed an incredibly deep respect for your work. You capture much more with a brush, she feels, than I manage with paper and ink, which is quite the compliment from my sister.

Speaking of Nora, I have news that may bring a smile to your face … she's here, in the camp, with me. You will not be surprised to hear that she simply could not bear to miss out on the action and has found someone else to head up the Paris bureau. My face must have been quite the picture when she sashayed into the press camp, bright as a button and determined as all hell!

I am still reeling from Paris – from the thrill of seeing you and the disappointment that our time was so short. But I have a wonderful recurring dream of our future that keeps me going through these terrible times. In my dream we have returned to Porthcurno, to our beach (I've claimed it as ours, you will note) and we replay that wonderful day last April, only there is no wire this time, no flamethrowers. It's just you and me and the plovers – who mate for life, did you know that? Then, in my dream, we head back to Penberth – to our home – where we sit by the window and watch the sun set beyond the cove.

Counting the days until I see you again. If only we knew how long that would be.

With all of my love,
Alex

Having re-read the letter for the tenth time, Eliza kissed it and tucked the envelope safely into a jacket pocket. She then put on every layer of clothing she possessed — which wasn't many — and her helmet. She hauled her backpack over her shoulders, grabbed her satchel and headed out into the rain, thinking of Paris.

Paris. The utter joy and celebration of Paris with Nancy and then — blissfully, briefly — with Alex were short-lived. The following months saw the Allies push the Western Front eastward with gusto.

Eliza and Nancy travelled east with the field hospital, Eliza continuing to paint the humanitarian effort while also feeding intelligence to … well, she had no idea who, exactly, but she did what she was asked to do and no one had yet complained. The Red Cross unit she and Nancy were affiliated to now supported the American First Army, which, by December, was firmly established in the Ardennes, a key location on the border between France and Germany that was a densely wooded area Hitler saw as the weak link in the Allied Western Front, a weakness he now fully intended to capitalise on.

The stage was set for an all-out bloody fight … and it was bloody.

With the hospital established on the grounds of a convent near the town of Spa, Eliza found herself nursing more and painting less, such were the numbers of casualties pouring into the wards, hour after hour, day after day. All the while, the supply lines were stretched to the limit, meaning that rations became sparser and Eliza and Nancy, facing exhaustion, suffering from battle fatigue, became desperately thin.

But two things in particular kept Eliza's spirits up during that grim, cold, wet November, a November that lead into an even colder and nastier December. The first was Nancy, who, although run ragged, with her hair now half mousy-brown and half peroxide blonde, still managed to be an all-round trouper and good egg. The second was the thought of Alex.

They had not met since Paris, the press camp being established some distance away in an abandoned chateau near Liege, but still she checked the faces of the wounded constantly. War correspondents were every bit as much in danger as the soldiers they travelled with, and even though, like Eliza, Alex wore an armband which provided non-combatant status, Eliza knew – everyone knew – that the enemy was unlikely to care about that, and if caught, Alex would be imprisoned or shot along with the soldiers he travelled with.

And so she worried.

It was early evening when the hospital staff made ready to pack up and leave. The German counter-attack was pushing the Allies back and the First Army had no choice but to fully retreat. The field hospital was also required to move back by several miles and it needed to move quickly.

Eliza took a moment to sketch Surgeon Smythe again. He was sitting in the mess hall at a table, his head resting in one hand as he slept. An American major appeared by Eliza's side and said he had received instruction that Eliza was to pack up her kit immediately so that he might drive her to a location where she could retrieve a message. She had no choice but to say yes, and with the painting of Surgeon Smythe incomplete on paper but firmly lodged into her mind, she left him sleeping, quickly got her kit together and jumped in the jeep. The major explained that his commanding officer was extremely anxious to see her before retreating west himself, and they would have to drive quickly to reach him before the Germans closed in. They headed off alone in the dark in an easterly direction, deep into the forest, which unnerved Eliza somewhat.

'We have reports that Tiger tanks have broken through in this area,' said the major as they sped through the forest, leading Eliza into a whole new realm of fear. She had been shelled many times, of course, the hospital often having been bombarded in the early days, but with this journey she was heading into uncharted territory – emotionally and geographically. 'It's a godawful hell show.' He was straining to see in the dark as they sped along. 'Jerry could be anywhere about, so keep a good lookout. We need to keep an eye out for infiltrators, too.' His shoulders were tense, his hands were clutching the wheel tightly, and his eyes darted left and right, his attention not as fixed on the empty black road as Eliza would have liked. Fir trees turned from real things highlighted in the headlights to black menacing giants running down the side of the jeep. Eliza tried to maintain a sense of calm, one hand clutching the dash in front of her, the other resting on the kitbag that sat between her knees.

'Infiltrators?' she asked, doubtfully. 'What do you mean?'

'Nazis dressed up as Yanks,' he explained. 'They must have gotten their hands on some of our tanks and jeeps. Uniforms, too, the whole kit and caboodle. A unit had to abandon its position by Aachen – they must have taken the lot. We had one bunch of guys who were heading back to town when they came across a troop of GIs who flagged them down. They must have thought they were safe with their buddies and then – bam! – Jerry shot them. Ploughed them all down where they stood.'

'You mean that the Germans – Germans dressed as Americans – shot them, the GIs?'

'That's right, Ma'am. Murdering bastards!' He took his eyes off the road momentarily to glance across at her. 'I'm sorry for the language, it's just, fighting in a war is godawful enough, but that kind of thing ... it's against every kind of military code.'

Eliza gasped as he took the next bend a little too aggressively.

'Don't be sorry,' she said, regaining some composure. 'But do keep your eyes on the road for now. Let's survive this particular journey at least.'

She was in the jeep for twenty-five minutes – a surreal oddity of travelling to an unknown destination with a man who increasingly seemed to be on the edge of keeping it together. Despite all the possible threats – German troops, infiltrators, mines and booby-traps, not to mention the major's haphazard driving technique in the dark – they arrived safely at their destination, which was a Hansel and Gretel cottage in the forest. They walked past two guards at the door and stepped into a dimly lit parlour – the windows were blacked-out using hessian sacks. A small group of officers were huddled around a table, looking at something – a map, Eliza guessed. They didn't see her at first, but continued to look down. Eliza committed the scene to memory. The men glanced up and assessed her briefly just as she had assessed them, her helmet on, her dark hair escaping underneath the rim, her heavy backpack hanging off her dipped right shoulder, her artist's satchel hanging loosely from her left arm. Everything about her said 'woman' but Eliza was past caring. It was all so surreal, this tableau – the cottage, the lamplight, the dankness and stale smell of damp – and she was now part of the tableau, too. The scene must have seemed every bit as surreal to them as it did to her.

One of the men smirked. She remembered her advice

to Nancy that day in the orchard – 'never let anyone carry your bag or see that you're tired or struggling.' She straightened up. A colonel with kind but tired eyes moved towards her and held out his hand. They were soft hands, which surprised her.

'You must be the artist.' His breath condensed between them. He turned to his men. 'Give me a minute,' he said, before picking up a paraffin lamp and ushering Eliza into a separate room, a room that was once a basic kind of kitchen but was now a dumping ground for used ration packs and kitbags. He closed the door behind them, took a notepad from his top pocket, ripped out a page and handed it to Eliza.

'Here,' he said. 'Do whatever it is you do with it.'

She warmed her hands by the lamp then sketched a scene from the evacuation of the hospital, all the while kneeling on the floor, resting her sketchbook on a wooden milking stool, swiftly incorporating the coded message into the painting. The colonel watched on.

'Is that it?' he asked when she stood and put her things away.

'It's enough for now,' she said. 'I'll finish it tonight. I always sketch out a scene first and reproduce it with paints later. I'll make sure it's dispatched by the usual means tomorrow.'

'Tomorrow will be too late. The courier is coming here tonight, any time now, in fact.'

'Here?'

'You'll have to finish it now,' he said. 'You have twenty minutes until we all leave. Have you anything with you to add colour? If not, the black and white sketch will be swell.'

Eliza floundered a little and reopened her satchel. 'I have some coloured charcoals, of course, but I can't guarantee it will be my best work.'

He threw in a good-humoured eye roll. 'Lady, we ain't looking for a Rembrandt. Come through when you're done.'

As ordered, twenty minutes later, with everything packed up for a second time, Eliza edged her way back into the parlour to find the men ready to move on.

'Right then, Major.' The colonel looked directly at the man who had driven Eliza to the cottage. 'You know your orders?'

The major nodded smartly. 'Sir, yes, Sir.'

'After the courier arrives, get this young lady away from here immediately. Take her back to her unit and then wait for us in Spa. No point coming back here.' He turned to the other gentleman. 'Ready to move on, too, Adjutant?'

A young man, no more than twenty-two, nodded. 'Yes, Sir!'

The colonel said his goodbyes to Eliza and approached the door, but as he went to step out two other people stepped in, and for some reason – call it second-sight, or déjà vu, or just plain old common sense – Eliza knew that the course of the rest of her life had been determined right there and then.

Chapter 27

Nora walked in first, with Alex only two marching paces behind her.

Nora? Of course. Who else would be the courier? But Alex? As delighted as Eliza was to see him, why on earth was he here?

Nora walked straight over to Eliza.

'Do you have it?' she asked.

Eliza handed over the charcoal sketch. Nora crossed to a lamp to look at it.

'I can touch it up now, if ...'

'No.' Nora rolled the paper carefully and turned towards the door. 'Thank you,' she said. 'It's fine as it is.' She turned to the colonel. 'I need to get to Malmedy tonight. Can the man who drove us here take us on?'

'He can.' The colonel gave a nod in the direction of their driver. 'Best get on your way, too, Major,' he said to Eliza's driver. 'The road will be overrun by midnight.'

They all turned to leave. Alex, who had recovered slightly from the shock of seeing Eliza, seemed determined to at least say 'Hello.' He positioned himself to step outside alongside her. Their hands brushed as they headed to their respective jeeps.

'Ships in the night, again,' he said.

Eliza was about to answer when another jeep came screaming to a halt outside the cottage. A soldier jumped out and dashed over to the colonel. They exchanged words. The colonel turned to the assembled group.

'They've taken the roads to the south and to the east.' He directed his speech to Nora. 'The road to Malmedy is still secure. Take the artist with you, she'll not get back to the hospital the way she came. You'll have to drive yourselves, or I'll never get my man back. You know the way?'

Nora said that she did.

'In that case, go.'

'You said you knew the way!' Alex reversed the jeep up a country track and started off down a more significant road again. He was clearly not impressed with Nora.

Nora shone a torch onto a compass. 'It wouldn't have mattered if I'd said I didn't. They couldn't spare a man.' She peered closer to assess the dial better. 'We'll be fine, so long as we keep heading northwest. All you have to do is keep driving.'

Eliza remained silent in the back while Alex drove and Nora directed. Despite Alex's doubts, they eventually arrived in the small town of Malmedy by moonlight. Fearing the return of the Germans, the local people had closed their shutters and taken cover. It was a ghost town save for one small dog, a type of terrier, who barked through the dead of the night. The jeep edged along the road while Nora looked out for a house that belonged to one of her associates in the French Resistance, Philippe.

'Here,' she said, hitting the dash. 'Right here. Pull up this track. This is it.'

Alex steered off the road onto a track that ran alongside the next row of cottages then round to the back and into a thicket of trees. A barn came into view with big double doors, a man standing outside, illuminated by the light of his cigarette. On seeing the jeep he put out the cigarette and opened the doors. Nora told Alex to drive straight into the barn.

'Leave everything to me,' she said as they jumped out. 'And you' – she addressed Alex directly – 'none of this is to be written about. Understand me?'

Alex turned to Eliza and winked, his face highlighted by torchlight. Eliza wondered why it was that the close proximity of one person was able to make another so happy, even though – although out of the actual physical woods – they were very clearly not out of danger.

They followed the man, who was well into his dotage, through a back door into one of the cottages. There was a need for explanations all round and Alex began the inquisition once the man, whom Nora had spoken to in hushed words as they walked into the cottage, backed out of the parlour. It quickly became clear that this was the first Alex knew of Nora's connection to intelligence work.

'Would either one of you care to explain any of this to me?' he began, turning to Nora, who lit up a cigarette, inhaled, rested her bottom against a sideboard and answered, 'No, not really.'

Eliza stepped towards him. The last time they had spoken had been at the train station, such a wonderful memory, and now here they were and they couldn't be themselves because they were not lovers just at this moment, but a war artist and a couple of reporters on the run. 'For my part,' began Eliza, 'there really isn't much to tell. But if Nora can't explain, then I'm afraid nor can I.'

'And since when, exactly, have you had friends in the French Resistance?' he asked Nora.

'Since forever,' she said, 'but that's not important right now.'

'Really? Do illuminate me as to what is important, then.'

'Getting out of here, before the Germans move in. They can't get hold of Eliza. She has information in her head that I can't risk them torturing out of her.'

Alex burned red. 'What? I can't believe I'm hearing any of this! What have you done?'

His anger was irrelevant to Nora.

'Philippe is organising a safe passage for the morning.'

Alex shook his head. 'No. We need to go right now. Jackboots will be marching down this road at any moment.' He gestured towards the kitchen. 'Let Philippe hand it over, whatever it is that Eliza has sketched for you. Grab your things and jump back in the jeep. This is not open for discussion, Nora!'

Nora sighed. 'I can't.'

Alex began to argue.

'Please, Alex, just this once, don't feel that you have to protect me ...'

'That's rich from you, sister dear. Speak to Philippe, tell him what he needs to do, and then we'll go. We need to head west or it will be too late.' He turned to Eliza, who thought the idea made perfect sense. 'Let's get to the jeep,' he said.

'There's no road out. Philippe told me.' This from Nora.

'What?'

'There is no direct road to the west from the town, and the road north was taken by the Germans this evening. The only road out is the way we came, and we can't do that. It's too late.'

Eliza watched while Alex wrestled with the absolute anger bubbling within him.

'We have to grab our things from the jeep and stay put,' she said, 'at least for the evening. Philippe will take it further into the woods and cover it over, just in case. He's hoping to get you out at first light, and I'll follow on.'

Alex crossed to stand within a hair's breadth of Nora. His jaw tight, his eyes narrow, he asked in a whisper, 'How do you know you can trust him?'

'One never knows completely,' she said. 'But I'm pretty certain I can.'

At this, Alex laughed out loud and shook his head.

'I can't believe I'm hearing this. Jesus, Nora, what the hell have you got yourself caught up in?' He turned to Eliza. 'And got Eliza caught up in, too, clearly.'

Eliza shook her head and tried to explain but Alex would have none of it. Nora cut him off by saying, 'I told you not to come.' She turned to Eliza. 'I very clearly told him not to come.' She turned to Alex again. 'But you thought I was onto a scoop and you wanted in on it. I only let you come because I knew Eliza would be here and thought it would be ...' She paused.

'Would be?' Alex's face creased into a picture of frustration and confusion.

'Well, nice for you. For the two of you. To see each other. We were supposed to meet at the cottage, drop the message here, then get the hell out. Easy. I had no idea the Germans were as close as they are. If I'd known, trust me, you wouldn't be here.'

'But Eliza would?' he pressed.

'Eliza would.' Nora stubbed out her cigarette and flopped into a chair.

'Can't we take our chances across the fields tonight?' Eliza dared to ask. 'You know, keep clear of the roads and make our way west in the dark? It can't be more than ten miles to safety and we could do that, surely. Couldn't Philippe find a guide?'

Nora bit her lip. 'That won't be possible.'

The siblings continued to bicker while Eliza looked on,

watching the room through the eyes of an artist, the eyes of a friend, the eyes of a lover.

'Look, Alex,' began Nora, softer now. 'There will be time for explanations later, but for now, we need to grab our kit out of the jeep, eat something – Phillipe will probably have a little bread and cheese we can have – get some rest and prepare for tomorrow, which is going to be the bloodiest kind of day, I shouldn't wonder.'

Nora handed the sketch back to Eliza and told her to quickly do another one – one without a military feel, or any link to the Allies. If they were captured it would be scrutinised, she said, and perhaps decoded. Eliza took out her sketchpad and drew a charcoal painting of a country scene. It was the garden from the collecting station she had visited with Surgeon Smythe, with hollyhocks and sweet peas and roses growing near and over the door, but without the macabre scene of the amputation in the room beyond. There were numbers on the door and letters on a road sign. Nora took both sketches and took herself (and her cigarettes) into the kitchen.

'I need to drink strong coffee and talk with Philippe,' she said, before disappearing out of earshot, leaving Eliza and Alex alone to talk. They sat side by side, edging into conversations tentatively while physically edging towards one another, like two electric currents desperate to touch but afraid of what might happen if they did.

'Did you receive my letters?' asked Alex.

'One.'

'Only one? I sent tons. Never mind. They'll catch up with you one day, I should think.'

Lit by candlelight, Alex reached into his backpack and took out a little clock. Eliza recognised it immediately.

'You brought it with you?'

'You said that our lives could begin again once it was fixed ... So as far as I was concerned, the sooner I got it working, the better. I hoped to work on it at the quiet moments, but ...'

The hands were still fixed at three-fifteen. 'I take it you haven't had many quiet moments.'

'Not as many as I'd thought,' he said. 'It's been my good luck charm, although I have taken out an insurance policy for the two of us, just in case I don't make it home.'

'An insurance policy?' questioned Eliza.

Alex opened the back of the clock and took out a folded piece of paper. He handed it to Eliza.

1 November 1944
To whomever this may concern. I once met a beautiful woman on a beach in Cornwall – at Porthcurno Beach. If you are reading this note then I am asking you to go to that beach at three-fifteen on any day (if destiny works it won't matter) and know that the only woman you will ever love will be standing there. I write this note to myself in the future, in the knowledge that if we cannot be together in this lifetime, then we will more than make up for it in the next. What are you waiting for, man? Go!

'Oh, Alex. What a wonderful idea. I love it. But how ...?' She handed the note back, searching for the word.

'Romantic?' he said.

The word she was looking for was 'sad', but she didn't say so. 'Yes,' she said. 'Romantic.'

Alex put the clock and the note on the floor and pulled her in close.

'Of course, nothing actually is going to happen to me. One day I'll put that clock on your kitchen windowsill,' he said, 'and when that day comes I'll fix it. This life we're living now, it's just a grotesque play that we're all having to sit through, but it won't last for ever, and then, at Penberth, we'll start time again.' He glanced down at her. 'If that's what you want, too?'

'I do,' she said, as he brushed his lips with hers. 'Absolutely, I do.'

Daylight arrived around seven-thirty and slivers of light began to pierce through gaps in the closed shutters. Nora arrived with coffee and woke Alex and Eliza – who were lying sleeping in each other's arms on the sofa – explaining that the sketch had to be taken to Spa to be handed over to another agent. The original plan had been for the agent to meet Nora at Philippe's house, but as the agent had not arrived in the night, the advance of German troops was more severe than they had hoped.

'I'm sorry, Eliza,' said Nora, 'but you'll have to put on civilian clothes – Philippe has some – take the sketch and go on without us. And you need to go pretty much now. Philippe has a cart ready. You can go with him as far as you need to and he'll arrange safe passage for you after the drop. He's making coffee and has a little breakfast for you, but then ...'

Alex jumped up once the words had sunk in, leaving Eliza somewhat disoriented on the sofa.

'What? Are you mad? I'm not having it. I'll go with her.'

Nora held up her hand to quieten him. 'No. We're Jewish, Alex. We can't go out there.' Nora gestured to the shuttered window. 'Not until we know we have a safe escort. It may be that we have to wait until the Allies move east again. No one will notice Eliza riding along with Philippe. She even looks French ... sort of. And even if she is caught and they look at her papers, they'll know that she's a non-combatant – an artist – and she'll be fine. Well, if not fine, then ... not shot, I shouldn't think.'

Alex was incandescent with rage.

'No!' he shouted. 'She will not be fine and you bloody well know it! Why do you think artists and correspondents wear uniform with the armband, Nora, you bloody fool? It's to declare that they are unarmed, merely there to report.'

'Don't call me a bloody fool. It is you who are the fool. Of course I know what the danger is, but the code in the sketch – yes the code, seeing as how I have had to tell you after all – could alter the course of the war back into our favour. It's a message from a German officer working for us, Alex – a double agent. He is a man who has risked everything – many lives, not just his own – to get that message passed on, and the only person who can get this whole bloody mess sorted out is Eliza.'

'You're not seeing things rationally, Nora!' He ran his hands through his hair in desperation.

'You're wrong. I'm the only one of us who is able to see things rationally here, and Eliza knows it too, don't you Eliza?'

Eliza turned to Alex and nodded regretfully.

'That painting has got to be delivered this morning and then word can be sent back that two correspondents are trapped,' said Nora.

Alex stepped forward and spoke quietly to Nora. 'And Philippe,' he said. 'What does your instinct say? And do not even begin to lie to me, Nora Levine, because I shall know it.'

Nora did not waver. 'That he is a good and decent man who deserves better from you.'

Alex began to walk around in circles. 'But it's the uniform and the armband – the A and the C – that prevent us all from being shot as spies,' he said, stopping in front of Nora to protest. 'Can't you see that? If Eliza is captured wearing civilian clothes, they'll look at her papers and they will not believe that she is an artist. Trust me on this. They will shoot her as a spy – on the spot, probably.' He turned to Eliza. 'Please,' he begged. 'Don't do this. We'll head across the fields tonight. Fuck the war!'

'Alex!' shouted Nora. 'Stop this!' She turned to Eliza.

'I'm very sorry, Eliza, but we truly have no choice.' Philippe arrived just then with a pot of coffee. 'Have some breakfast and then I'll tell you what you need to do. And take off your wedding ring. Today you are simply Philippe's unmarried daughter.'

Alex turned away while Eliza slipped the ring off her finger. She handed it to Nora, knowing with certainty that she would never wear that ring again.

A short while later, Eliza walked to the door wearing an assortment of *paysanne* clothes belonging to Philippe's niece. Her face feigned the kind of bright optimism Alex had chided her for, that night on the train, but what else could she do now? And anyway, for some reason she really did believe that she would be fine. She had faith in having faith, just as she had said, and somehow she would get through the next twenty-four hours alive, she knew it. Alex took her hand and Nora turned away to award them a little privacy.

Try as he might to express his emotion, Alex, it seemed, had no words.

Eliza did. 'I'll see you in Berlin,' she said, 'or if not Berlin, Penberth. And whatever happens now,' she raised a hand to touch his cheek, 'remember what I said on the beach last April ...'

Alex shook his head, clearly struggling to comprehend the direction their lives had taken so quickly. 'We said lots of things,' he whispered.

'All shall be well,' she said. 'Remember?'

He smiled and rested his forehead on hers. She stepped back, her eyes bright, her face a picture of hope. 'I have absolute faith that we will stand together on that beach again one day, Alex, and all of this ... this madness will be just a memory.'

He shook his head. 'I wish I had your faith.'

'You can,' she said. 'If you choose to.'

He embraced her then, and it was his tears, not hers, that dampened their lips as they kissed.

Chapter 28

Ellie

Par to Penzance

It was 6 a.m. when Ellie popped her head around her cabin door and whispered, 'Rihanna' after hearing the sound of footsteps hurrying along the train corridor.

Rihanna scurried back towards her, delivering a barrage of questions such as, 'What on earth happened? Why did you run off?' as she walked.

Ellie ushered Rihanna into her cabin and closed the door. The two women sat down on the bed.

Rihanna patted the unruffled duvet. 'You haven't slept, have you?'

Ellie shook her head. 'Can you read this for me, just to see if I've got the tone right? It's for Joe, and I don't want him to think that I read more into last night than I ought to have.'

She handed a letter – written on *Cornish Riviera* complimentary notepaper – to Rihanna.

Rihanna sighed and sat for a moment staring at the note.

'But didn't you like him?' she asked. 'Maybe ... Did he upset you, or something? Because, honestly, the man is an angel, and he was completely deflated when you left. I felt so sorry for him, just standing there like a lemon, and after he'd asked for the last song to be played for you especially ...'

'He asked for it?'

'Yes.'

'"We'll Meet Again"?'

'Yes.'

Rihanna really wasn't making this any easier.

Ellie put her face in her hands and shook her head. She came up for air. 'Please, just read the note and tell me what you think. I want him to remember me fondly, having had a lovely night. I shouldn't have flirted, not even a bit. I got carried away without thinking it through ... Please ...'

Rihanna let out a short sharp sigh.

'All right, but then I do have to get on. They'll all be getting up for breakfast soon.'

She opened the note.

Dear Joe,

I wanted to write to say how wonderful it was to meet you this evening (although it will be 'last night' for you by now) and to thank you for making the first night of my Cornish adventure so special. Lying on my bunk as the train trundles on, I have replayed the specialness of the night over in my head like a favourite film, but as the train edges closer to its final destination, the reel keeps sticking at one particular point – the point at which I walked away – and I wanted to explain why I did that. Firstly, I left because I was genuinely very tired. Secondly, because during the course of the evening I became quite smitten with you, and I think that you might even have grown to quite like me.

The thing is, I could not allow the evening to run on to what might have been its natural conclusion, because it would be unfair on you. I didn't tell you everything about my heart. In childhood, I was diagnosed with congenital structural heart disease. I was prone to infection, had poor resilience and, frankly, wasn't expected to make it to adulthood. I had surgery twice, which led to bursts of a more normal life. Last year I underwent yet more surgery, which was, almost certainly, my last unless a donor is found. With all this behind me, you can't know how wonderful it felt to be a normal person last night, able to laugh and talk and dance and sing.

When I got back to my cabin I could have kicked myself for walking away. 'Go back!' I said to myself. 'Don't waste the best evening of your life, Ellie, you mad fool.' But I made a decision a long time ago not to allow more people than absolutely necessary to become too close to me, and I began to see that you might, perhaps, be starting *to feel for me in the way that I was starting to feel for you. And so despite having had the most wonderful evening, and despite having been hopeful at first that the attraction might be mutual, in the cold light of day (or cold light of night, as it turned out) I woke up from my dream, and remembered the reality of my life.*

Perhaps if I hadn't known about the letter in the clock I would have stayed, but I am a great believer in fate and destiny, and I have no doubt that a wonderful woman will be standing on Porthcurno Beach waiting for you today, or tomorrow, or whenever it is that you choose to go. A woman who is healthy and resilient and strong. That woman is who you need to be spending time getting to know and having a wonderful, adventurous holiday with.

All that is left to say is: thank you for the very best night of my life. I shall remember it always. Go find your true love, Joe. I can't explain it, but something deep within my soul tells me that she'll be standing there, on the beach, waiting for you at three-fifteen.

Ellie x

Rihanna sighed, folded the letter in half and put it down on the bed. 'Oh, Ellie,' she said, 'I'm so sorry.'

Ellie shook her head. 'Don't be. I don't know what I was thinking, encouraging you. Encouraging Joe. I suppose I loved the idea of being like any other single woman, but the reality always comes back to whack me in the face.'

Rihanna stood.

'Please could you find an envelope and give this to Joe, but not until after he's had breakfast?'

'But can't you ...'

Ellie shook her head. 'No. Absolutely not. As soon as we arrive at Penzance, I'm going to dash off the train, and if you could waylay him somehow, that would be helpful.'

Rihanna put a hand on the door handle.

'Don't you think you ought to give Joe the option of whether or not he wants to get to know you first? It's his choice after all.'

Ellie didn't answer and busied herself by putting the finishing touches to her packing, searching around the tiny cabin for a missing high heel, which was the only remaining thing to pack.

'Joe Burton is adorable. He's a sweet, kind and funny man,' she said, while systematically lifting the duvet, the pillow, her violin case, and putting them down again, frustrated that the shoe was nowhere in sight. 'Trust me, the last thing he needs right now is me around, dragging him down! Have you seen a green high heel, by the way? I can only find one.'

'But you don't actually know that he fancied you,' pleaded Rihanna. 'What on earth would be the harm in spending time with him this week? Just having a wonderful week together in Cornwall, no strings? He's not asking you to marry him, Ellie ...'

Ellie noticed the journal lying on top of the green dress in her open suitcase.

'A very special lady also met a man and fell in love on this train and she did exactly that – decided to have one week of fun with him, no strings, no emotional attachment.'

'And?'

Ellie finally made eye contact. 'When two people fall in love there is no such thing as "let's just have a week of fun then forget about it", and trust me, after another day, I would definitely have fallen head over heels for Joe, or just one heel, actually, as I can't seem to find the other ...'

Rihanna began to protest but Ellie wouldn't listen. 'Thank you so much for everything, Ri, but just give him the note when I've gone.' Ellie stepped forward to give Rihanna a hug. 'You're brilliant, you know that? But all I really need right now, is room service – a cup of tea and a croissant if you have any going – and to find my shoe.'

Rihanna scrunched her nose. 'No new hat for me then?'

Ellie shook her head. 'No.'

Chapter 29

Eliza

20 December 1944

The road leading out of the village of Malmedy was not a smooth one. Eliza, sitting side by side with Philippe on the cart, felt every stone and bump and gully as the horse, who was as old as the cart by the looks of the poor thing, lolloped its way out of the village. For the next few hours they were father and daughter heading to tend a sick aunt at her house near Spa before Christmas.

Eliza had never travelled so light. With all of her kit abandoned at the cottage, she was stripped bare. Nora had decided at the last moment that Alex was right; Eliza was better off travelling without any papers, because if she was searched and uncovered as a war artist, they would never believe that she was not involved in espionage of some kind – and they wouldn't be wrong. And so her papers were left behind and she travelled only with the clothes she wore – thick woollen trousers, a heavy winter coat – too big but she was grateful for its warmth – and a red headscarf, which was far too fancy for the rest of the outfit, but was all Philippe could find. She wished she had gloves, but made do by pulling the sleeves of the coat over her hands. The main problem was her boots – Philippe had not been able to provide footwear, and so she wore her issue boots, which were hidden beneath a sack placed by her feet.

The only thing she kept of her own (which neither Alex nor Nora knew about) was her journal. She knew keeping it was madness, and it put both her and Philippe at great risk if she were caught, but she simply refused to part with it. She had hidden it in the lining of the coat, believing that if things became complicated enough that her coat was taken from her and the lining searched, then she was probably beyond saving anyhow.

The horse sauntered on through the misty winter morning, pulling awkwardly at the reins now and again, presumably angry at being made to work so hard, so early. The painting – the message – had been placed inside her sketchbook, which had been ripped to nothing but blank pages with any previous sketches burned in the grate. The sketch book had been placed in Philippe's knapsack along with their meagre offering of lunch – it would look more authentic that way. If the Germans searched them they would look as if they were simply a daughter and father on the road for a Christmas visit, the sketchbook taken with them purely a gift for the aunt with a single image drawn by the niece.

They made good progress and by lunchtime they were just six miles from Spa, having come across only a handful of other local folk who were going about their business, their anxious faces refusing to make eye contact, unsure as to who was in charge of them now – was it the Allies or the Germans? Either way, the mistrust was evident, with everyone they passed merely nodding an acknowledgement in their direction or hurrying along on their way without looking up.

Halfway to Spa, their horse, having been unfastened from the cart to be walked down a slight embankment to a stream for a drink, lost a shoe and became lame. Philippe's curses echoed around a thicket of trees, stark and bare in their winter nudity. Eliza, having jumped off the cart to join horse and driver by the stream, was hushed by Philippe who put a finger to his lips and cocked his head to listen Eliza heard something too, the unmistakable sound of a motorbike heading in their direction.

'A German bike,' he said, shooing her up the embankment. 'I recognise the sound. Quickly, get onto the cart and cover your feet. And remember, speak only French.'

The motorbike, as they had feared, belonged to a German soldier, and he pulled over by the cart. He was an older man than Eliza was expecting and not an officer, she was sure, and despite wearing a uniform associated with evil and pain, the glow around him, Eliza could see, was a warm one.

She sat, mute, on the cart while Philippe slapped the behind of the lame horse to encourage him up the embankment and to cause a distraction. If Eliza had been concerned about Philippe's loyalty beforehand, she was not concerned anymore.

The soldier smiled warmly at Eliza before speaking directly to Philippe. His French was perfect.

'You are having some difficulty with the beast, Monsieur?' The soldier stood atop the embankment and looked down.

'He is lame,' said Philippe, looking up. 'My daughter and I will have our lunch here and set off shortly after. There is a blacksmith a mile further on. I know the man. He will help me. That is if I can move the beast up this blasted hill first!'

The German laughed. He turned to Eliza.

'Come, Madam ... or perhaps it is mademoiselle?' He waited for an answer.

Eliza cleared her throat. 'Mademoiselle,' she said, softly.

'Jump down from your seat and we shall help your poor father or you shall not be home before Christmas!'

It was the worst possible situation. Those damn boots! Philippe began to protest light-heartedly but she had no choice but to jump down. The soldier noticed her boots at once. His manner changed from jovial to considered.

'Those are some sturdy boots you have there, Mademoiselle,' he said. 'Where did you find such a pair?'

Philippe, who had let go of the horse and begun to walk up the embankment, spoke first. 'First the Germans came,' he began, 'and then the Americans, and now, here you are again. While the Americans were here – you know what they are like, Monsieur – they gave us things and I managed to acquire a pair of boots for my daughter. I'm sorry. We did not mean to offend you by taking the boots, but my daughter, like the horse, has not been properly shod since the war began.'

The soldier's face remained considered.

'Your papers, Mademoiselle,' he said, the horse now forgotten and Philippe's attempt at joviality stepped over completely. 'You too, Monsieur.'

Philippe grabbed the canvas bag that contained his papers. The soldier held out his hand.

'I'll take the bag,' he said.

Philippe shrugged and handed it over.

The very first thing the soldier removed was the sketch-book. Eliza wrapped her coat closer around her. He put down the bag to open the book.

'Why have all the pages been removed?' he asked, his face not aggressive, not kind, just completely straight.

'My daughter is an artist – a *very* talented artist. It's all she cares about. No time for love, no time for babies, eh?' He turned to Eliza and beamed. 'She will be famous one day, isn't that right, my love?'

Eliza, playing along, adopted a coy approach. 'Oh, Papa, don't ...'

'And the torn pages?' the soldier asked, again.

'Were gifts to family and friends. Portraits, and so on ... and some were sold, to gain us a few francs, here and there ...'

'And this one?' He held up the sketch.

'Is a Christmas gift for her aunt.'

'And where does this aunt live?'

'Near Spa.'

'You cannot go to Spa.' It was an order, not a suggestion. 'You have to stay this side of the river.'

Philippe turned to Eliza. 'Never mind. We would not have made it to your aunt's at any rate, not with a lame horse and' – he glanced up to the sky – 'I feel that the weather will turn soon.'

The soldier handed the sketchbook to Philippe and searched further in the bag. He found Philippe's papers but not Eliza's.

'Your papers?' he said, directly to Eliza. 'They are where?'

Eliza glanced at Philippe. Having eaten little, she suddenly felt exceptionally weak. Alex had been right. This had been a thoroughly foolish undertaking. She was sure to be caught now.

'I'm sorry, Papa,' she said, addressing Philippe, not the German, her eyes swimming with tears, not for herself, but for the compromised safety of this lovely old man. 'I forgot them.'

The German soldier took a deep breath, put the bag

down and picked up the sketchbook again. 'Where did you study art?' he asked.

Eliza had a split second to make a decision.

'I am self-taught, mainly, Sir.' She thought of her neighbour as a child, Mrs Kelly, in Penzance. 'Although there was a lady in town who had studied in Paris years ago and she taught me some techniques. She is dead now.' Eliza crossed her chest. 'God rest her soul.'

The soldier sniffed. He shook his head. 'I am an artist myself, Mademoiselle,' he said. 'I studied in Berlin for three years before the war, and I tell you now, this is no sketch by the daughter of a French *paysanne*. And your accent ... is not local.' He handed the book to Eliza who was now sitting in the cart, her boots visible – what was the point in hiding them now?

The German turned to look down the road.

'You are trying to get to Spa, yes?' He spoke in English now. Eliza looked desperately at Philippe.

'The old man cannot help you now, Mademoiselle. The horse is lame but you are not. You have good boots and you will need them, because only you can save your life now.'

She still dared not respond. A French peasant's daughter would not know fluent English and would not speak in a flawless English accent even if she did. What he said next surprised Eliza to the core.

'You must run now,' he said, again in English. 'More Germans are headed this way. They will not be as lenient as me. My officer is not a tolerant man. This stream will lead to the river. Follow the water; it will lead to Spa. Cross the river early, at the oxbow turn. Two rivers meet there and once it widens you will not be able to cross. There are boulders part of the way across and the water will only reach your waist.'

'What about the bridge?' asked Eliza.

'It has been blown. Keep low. If you hear vehicles, take cover in the embankment and do not move until nightfall.' He turned to Philippe. 'I will help you with your horse, Monsieur, but you are walking a very fine line. Go to your blacksmith friend and if you can, stay there. No German will believe that you were out visiting your aunt, not with the counter-attack in progress.'

Eliza jumped down from the cart.

'I thank you for your extreme kindness,' she said, speaking in English. 'What is your name?'

A smile crossed his lips. This was no Nazi, but a very kind man indeed. 'Why do you ask?' he said.

'Because, when I draw a sketch of you, I should very much like to know the name of the man who spared my life.'

'Leo,' he said, handing Philippe his bag. 'My name is Leo.'

Eliza jumped down from the cart, taking the sketchbook when Leo offered it to her. Such a little thing to have caused so much trouble. 'You have offered me such kindness, both of you,' she said, speaking in French once more. Philippe quickly took out the lunch they were to share and a small flask of water.

'Take it all,' he said. Eliza began to protest but Philippe insisted. 'You will need it, Madam.'

She stuffed the bread and a little cheese into her coat pockets and with an uncertain nod, turned on her heel and dashed down the embankment, lifting her coat to cross the shallow stream beyond the horse. She began walking at a pace along the stream. Part of her wondered if they had been tricked, and waited for a shot to ring out, but the shot never came, and with her heart beginning to settle a little, Eliza Grey – or Lady Arbuthnot, or whoever else she had become now – set off on the next leg of her journey and did not dare to look back.

Chapter 30

It was the coldness of her hands that made the journey so painful. She feared frostbite every bit as much as she feared capture, because as an artist she was nothing without her fingers.

The German had said that all she needed to do was to follow the river and not be seen. A task that seemed straightforward enough when the relief of being set free was new, but it was an undertaking that in reality proved to be the most challenging and exhausting task of her life. She had witnessed the Normandy landings, nursed at the front lines and been trapped in Saint-Malo, but in all those other circumstances she had never once had to face such a harrowing ordeal alone.

Following the stream to the river was the first challenge. The water's edge was pure bog, but she dared not leave the shelter of the scrappy hedgerow that ran alongside it. She waded through icy water up to her knees while looking ahead and all around constantly with the hope of keeping out of sight. She also hoped that the stream would lead her away from the danger of the road. This landscape was flat, with mile after mile of pasture fields that were wide open for all to see. Any trees and hedgerows were denuded down to their winter skeletons, and so it took longer than she expected to reach the river.

The weather, as Philippe predicted, turned for the worse. She had been walking for about an hour, spending half of that time hiding in hedgerows at any sound of a vehicle in the distance, when the sky morphed from an overcast grey into a dense blanket of white. Snow was coming – Mother Nature knew it and had softened and quietened the landscape in preparation for its arrival. Eliza, her heart having fallen into her soaking boots, knew it too.

Her spirits lifted a little when she reached the river. A large beech tree growing on the bank had a hollow beneath its roots and Eliza scurried into it, trying to ignore the growing numbness in her toes. She slipped her hands from her sleeves and took out the bread, struggling to tear off a piece with her frozen fingers. She placed the rest in her pocket and then ate, her hands and shoulders shaking from cold and nervous exhaustion.

From midday, soft, fat flakes fell and the world around her turned white. All except Eliza, who knew that her black coat would prove to be even more conspicuous, silhouetted against the white of the snow, as she moved along the river bank. The red headscarf was wrapped tightly around her neck beneath the coat. She wanted to wrap her head in it so very much, but red against white would only act as a beacon flashing as she ran, and so her head remained uncovered, except for the snowflakes that melted into her hair.

She made good ground after the stop at the beech tree, thanks to the cover of a dense mixed hedge of holly and elder, but reaching an oxbow bend she stopped. Leo had said to cross there.

The narrowest point was obvious as it was no more than fifteen feet wide. She saw the boulders and realised that for the first part of the crossing she could remain dry, but so what? By the time she reached the other side she would be wet. Regardless, the best thing to do – the only thing to do – was to get on with it.

Deciding it best to keep as many items of clothing as dry as possible, she mustered all of her strength and courage and, with trembling fingers, stripped down to near-naked. She kept on her boots as they were soaked through already. With her body shaking with a violence she had not known possible, Eliza placed all of her clothes inside the coat and held it above her head. She jumped from boulder to boulder quickly and was soon halfway across, but then the moment came that she could prolong no further and without allowing herself a moment to consider, Eliza looked down and noted the depth of the river – no more than waist deep as Leo had said – and jumped in. It was beyond cold. Standing in the water she feared she had entered into shock, but then her survival instincts kicked in and it took her less than a minute to cross.

Scrambling up the far embankment, her limbs scorched red from the cold, Eliza grabbed some of the dryer died-back bracken from the undergrowth and rubbed the worst of the wet from her legs, arms and chest. Dressing proved nigh-on impossible. Her hands simply refused to work. But she eventually managed to pull on her clothes and, now even more grateful for the oversized coat provided by Philippe, she gave herself a moment to wrap herself in its residual warmth before she moved on, like a fox who knows the hunt is coming.

A mile upriver and feeling a little warmer, Eliza assessed the situation with growing despair.

The river was about to cross open land – for a mile or so, at least. There were areas of sunken mud where cattle had once ambled from the field to the river to drink, but no vegetation to hide within or shelter by.

Eliza hid under an arched hawthorn and listened. Somewhere in the distance, muffled by the falling snow, she thought she could hear a motor car. She blinked the snow away from her lashes and blew on her hands. She needed to keep moving – moving was the only thing that kept her relatively warm. But to follow the river here, in daylight? It was too open – too risky. There was no choice, she realised, slumping further into the prickly tree, but to wait. Wait until nightfall, or dusk at the earliest, when she could befriend darkness and find safety hiding in the shadows. She wrapped the scarf around her head, leaving not even a slit to see through, and pulled her arms to the inside of the coat. She closed her eyes, tried to stop the shaking and turned her thoughts to home. But not even thoughts of Porthcurno, and Alex and picnic blankets, and balmy summer days, could warm her. She doubted she would ever know the comfort of warmth again.

It was dusk when Eliza realised her body had begun to freeze. Ideally, she would wait another hour before moving, but she knew she would perish if she didn't try to move on as any residual heat the earth might have clung onto would soon be lost. It had stopped snowing and the skies had cleared. The almost-full moon was up, which meant that, on the one hand, it would help to guide her along the way, but on the other, it would act as a spotlight as darkness fell.

She jumped down from the safety of the hawthorn to the river bed. The embankment was high and Eliza made use of this, hugging the right-hand bank while staying low. It was exhausting work. Should she scurry, she wondered, or take it in stages? She weighed the risk on all counts and decided to scurry, running for a mile or so, eventually crossing the open farmland, always keeping the river immediately to her right. As she ran, she wondered: would she hear the shot that killed her before it hit?

But no shot came.

On reaching the safety of a copse of fir trees, she stopped for a moment, her hands falling to her knees as she caught her breath. Hearing a noise, she glanced up. A deer was standing deeper inside the copse, watching her. The snow had settled on the fir trees, but the ground was a bed of soft pine needles and the combination of the deer, the snowy green branches, the last of the twilight and the stillness that only fresh snow can bring brought a sense of calm wonder to Eliza. It was as if she had entered into a wonderland – a safe, otherworldly wonderland – with the deer acting as her guide – her protector. For a moment, she wondered if she was dead.

The deer soon scampered and the moment passed, but the beauty of the scene had lifted her, and Eliza felt a revived sense of survival – of warmth, of energy. The worst was over. Beyond the copse the black outline of a town was silhouetted in the moonlight. She had made it. All she had to do was find a safe way across the fields and pray that this was the town of Spa, and that the Allies had not yet been forced to surrender it.

Chapter 31

Eliza

Eliza could not remember crossing those last fields, nor did she remember any of the faces of the British patrol that found her, prostrate on the road, taken for dead, half a mile short of the town. The men mistook her for a daring French woman who had taken it upon herself to escape the clutches of the Germans by fleeing across the river to safety, and in a way they were right. They had no way of knowing that it was the body of Lady Eliza Arbuthnot they lifted gently into the truck, a lady who by her own volition had made a conscious decision to stop taking the easy route in life, and should not only also be a woman in uniform, but wearing the armband of a non-combatant, too.

And so Eliza, hovering in a place somewhere between life and death, was not taken to her own military hospital and to the tender care of Nancy, who, at that very moment, was caring for yet another tranche of bloodied soldiers who had fallen into the ward several miles west, but to

a cottage hospital staffed by French local volunteers established in the town hall. Most of the volunteers had little
or no medical knowledge or experience, but what they
lacked in training they made up for in goodwill and
diligent care, and despite the fact that Eliza had no iden-
tity papers on her person and no one had any idea who
she was, her carers took her in as one of their own.

A woman called Francine was assigned to care for Eliza
throughout the night. With respect and grace she peeled
away the layers of Eliza's soaked clothing and wrapped her
in sheets and blankets before taking her ice-cold hands in
hers and praying to God. She thought Eliza would die in
the night, but somehow, when all hope for this frozen
woman seemed lost, Francine, feeling an inexplicable
strength of connection to her patient, refused to leave Eliza's
side, and slowly, gently, mindfully, warmed her back to life,
all the while wondering how this woman had found herself
in such a terrible situation, almost dead, lying in the middle
of the road, carrying no papers, no food, no money, nothing
at all. Nothing, at least, except a soaked sketchbook with
a loose-leafed blurred painting inside, which, as it lay on
a table next to Eliza's bed and began to dry, revealed nothing
of the original scene, and nothing of the sacrifice that had
been made by so many to create it.

Eliza was feverish and delirious for two days, but on
Christmas Eve, Francine's efforts and faith were rewarded
when Eliza's temperature returned to normal and she
opened her eyes. Her clothes, or, rather, Phillipe's niece's

clothes, had been carefully folded by Francine once dry and sat on the table next to the bed. The sketch, also now dry, its edges curling, had been placed on top of the clothes. When Eliza turned her head and saw the blurred, indecipherable image, the events of her last waking hours came flooding back, and quietly, in the arms of the stranger Francine, she sobbed.

Hitler's counter-attack was effective while it lasted, but it did not hold the Allies back for long. Like a rugby scrum that is determined to powerhouse its way back into the other team's half, the weary but determined Allied armies of the Western Front regrouped, reassessed and forged on.

And somehow, so did Eliza.

She had nothing left to call her own, of course – no clothes, no canvases or sketching paper. No charcoal or pencils or paints. Just her boots, which she clung onto as others might cling onto a rabbit's foot for luck.

Once well enough, she returned to her affiliated hospital and to Nancy, and began working harder than ever to capture the work of the Red Cross. She coped with the nub of a pencil and any paper she could get her hands on until Nora's replacement in Paris sent out fresh art supplies. Nancy requisitioned battledress for Eliza from an American WAAC who was being sent home on compassionate leave. The uniform was too big, but Eliza didn't particularly care.

In February, Nancy was transferred to the 120th Evacuation Hospital, which had also retreated to Spa. It would be moving east as the troops pressed on. Eliza immediately sought affiliation with the 120th, too, and followed close on Nancy's heels, not only because heading east might bring news of Alex, but since that day by the river in December, when Leo had let her go, she had begun to feel quite vulnerable, as if she had used up all of her nine lives in one day.

From the moment of waking in her hospital bed, Eliza sought news of Alex and Nora, but none came until the day the 120th passed through Malmedy, now safely back in Allied hands, when Eliza persuaded Nancy to accompany her to Phillipe's cottage. She knocked on the door but no answer came. A neighbour stepped out into the street and through heartfelt sobs told Eliza her story.

A troop of Germans – Germans dressed as American soldiers, the neighbour noted – had entered the town on the afternoon Eliza left with Philippe. Nora, on seeing the soldiers, ran out into the street to ask for help. She was taken prisoner immediately, along with her brother, who had walked out into the street with his hands up to join her once he knew she had been taken. Brother and sister were taken away, but the man who had sheltered them – the wonderful Philippe – had been killed upon his return to Malmedy, his body left on the street as a warning. With her story complete, the woman collapsed into Eliza's arms and wept.

Eliza coped by throwing herself into her work and repeating her mantra as if on a permanent loop inside her head. 'All shall be well,' she repeated whenever her mind drifted to Alex, 'and all shall be well.'

In March, Eliza got word from a correspondent for *The Times* that two British correspondents had been taken prisoner. Alex had always been a favourite of General Patton and, unbeknown to Eliza, a great deal had been done to trace him. He was in Germany, the correspondent told her. No one could be certain, of course, but he was believed to be in a place called Buchenwald – Buchenwald prison camp.

With this knowledge, Eliza developed a newfound hope. A prison camp was a dreadful place to be, but at least it meant that there was a chance they were alive. She simply had to sit tight until the Allies arrived to free them. She had discussed the idea of hope with Alex on that lovely day when they sat chatting on the stepping stones at Penberth. He had wondered if it had been a bad thing that Pandora had left Hope in the jar, if doing so had made accessing her impossible. But Eliza knew now that this was not the case, and as she thought of the possibility of Alex and Nora surviving the camp, she delved deep into the jar and took out all the hope she needed.

By April, the Allies had crossed into Germany. Eliza thought of Alex as she crossed the border. *I'll see you in Berlin*, they had said.

The hospital was established in the grounds of an old school in Frankfurt on Easter Sunday. On arrival, they found the city destroyed both physically and emotionally. Only a third of the local population were still alive. Twenty thousand slaves who had been working in the munitions factories were freed by the liberating army, all of whom raided German food stores immediately upon their release, resulting in a humanitarian crisis of epic proportions.

Eliza stumbled through her days by doing what she always did, painting and nursing. Her nights began the same way: kneeling by her cot, her crucifix in her hand, praying to anyone who would listen that someday very soon Alex and Nora would be found safe and well, or if not well, then at least alive. Please God, she said, let them be alive. And as for her paintings, they became darker by the day. The scenes she sketched and painted varied wildly now.

She still accompanied Surgeon Smythe from time to time. He had moved to the 120th with them. On one particular day he took her into the city to paint a street lined with white hospital sheets used as surrender flags. It was on this occasion that he introduced Eliza to an American general. The general asked Eliza if she had the stomach to paint something his soldiers had just happened upon across town. It was a tableau of a family scene he thought should not be missed. When she saw the tableau Eliza genuinely wondered how she would find the strength to carry on. And even then, she did not falter. She set up her easel in front of the family – a German family, dressed in their finest clothes, sitting at a table set for a meal. They had all committed suicide, and had done it just moments before the Allies had marched in.

Was this the type of work she had anticipated creating

when sitting in the office with Cartwright when he had said that this was no job for a woman? Not at all. But spring will always find a way through to warm the soul, and it was a bright sunny morning – the first that year – a morning that spoke of the promised heat that summer would bring.

Eliza and Nancy were sitting quietly in the hospital garden watching a female blackbird skit about in the grass when the ward sister – Sister Jenkins, who had known Eliza since Normandy – emerged from the school building and walked at a pace towards them. She had a pile of tatty envelopes in her hand and a broad smile across her face.

'I think these have chased you halfway around the world, Eliza, by the looks of them. Better late than never though.'

The handwriting was unmistakable.

'Alex?' Nancy asked.

Eliza nodded.

Sister began to walk away but changed her mind and turned back.

'Oh, I meant to say, there's a meeting in the assembly hall in ten minutes.'

Nancy spoke for both of them. 'What about?

Sister Jenkins sighed. 'We're looking for volunteers for something quite unpleasant, I'm afraid.'

'What kind of volunteers?' asked Eliza, glancing up.

'I'm not entirely sure. Major Smythe is going to clarify it all at the meeting, but it seems that one of these so-called camps they've been looking for has been found. We're the closest hospital to the site and I'm guessing we'll be needed to set up a response unit. It will be grim, I'm afraid.'

'You don't happen to know the name of the camp, do you, Sister?' asked Eliza.

Sister looked away to think. She took a deep breath and eventually said, 'It sounded like Bruckenland, or something like that?'

'Buchenwald?' asked Eliza, praying to God that it would be.

'Yes, Buchenwald. That sounds right.'

'Well, I don't mind volunteering,' said Nancy. 'They'll need all the help they can get, I shouldn't wonder.'

Sister nodded and began to walk away. Eliza jumped up.

'Sister,' she said, calling after her. 'Do you think I could go, too? I could help with the nursing, and the liberation of the camp should be recorded on canvas.'

Sister looked at her doubtfully.

'You want to paint it? Are you sure? Reports are that these camps are worse than anyone could have imagined.'

'What do you mean?'

Sister put her hands together and began to wring them. 'They're camps where people seen as, well, undesirable to the Nazis were put. Word is that the Jews have been ... Well, it won't be pleasant and it won't just be the Jews, either. There are probably more people dead than alive, put it that way.'

Eliza realised that her idea of the nature of Buchenwald camp had been naïve.

'Still,' she said, 'I'd like to go. I've painted some terribly grim things so far. It's my job, I'm afraid.'

Sister nodded. 'All right. The nursing staff will need your help anyway, I should think. Thank you, Eliza. And thank you, too, Nancy.'

Nancy looked up at Eliza when the sister was out of earshot. Eliza's hands were shaking, holding the letters.

'Buchenwald? That's where they think Alex is, isn't it?'

Eliza nodded.

'Will you open them, do you think?' she asked, nodding to the letters.

Eliza didn't need to answer as she had already chosen a letter at random and had begun to open it. A leaf of paper fell out of the envelope. She smiled and her eyes filled with tears. The leaf had the Julian of Norwich quote written on it. Eliza read the first couple of paragraphs of the letter with joy in her heart and a smile on her face. Half of the detail was blacked out by the censor, but Alex had written of how he had hated to leave her in Paris and that he couldn't wait until this thing was all over and they could go home, to Penberth.

Eliza put the letter back in the envelope. They sat for some moments before Nancy said, 'Do you ever wish you'd saved your heart from everything that's happened?'

'That depends. Do you mean from Alex, or from the war?' answered Eliza. She had returned to watching the blackbirds, two of them now, one male, one female, hop around the grass.

359

'Either? Both? You could have hidden away in Scotland with Arthur, played the role of the great lady and saved yourself from all the heartache, the distress, the ... not knowing.'

'Sometimes, yes, I do,' she answered honestly. 'Sometimes I do wonder ... If I had never caught the night train, if I had never invited him in to my cottage – I did try to, you know, not with any great determination, admittedly, but I did try to – then it would have been easier. But Alex, he ...' Eliza paused.

'He?'

'Let's just say that my work is better because of him.'

After a pause, Nancy took the envelopes from Eliza's knee, placed them on the grass and took both of Eliza's hands. 'Listen, I'm not sure you should go to the camp tomorrow. He might not even be there. It was only supposition that he was. I've heard that there are loads of these camps dotted around. He could be at any one of them ...'

'Then I'll go from camp to camp until I find him. I'll paint them all. The rest of the world is going to need to know about all of this. Oh, Nancy, don't you see, whatever we find, it can't be as bad as not knowing.'

Realising the case was lost, Nancy picked up the envelopes and handed them to Eliza with a smile. She linked her arm through Eliza's and led her indoors, the two of them not realising that they would soon find themselves walking, not through pretty garden gates into the hospital, but through twisted, macabre gates into hell.

Chapter 32

Eliza

Buchenwald Camp, 11 April 1945

Eliza and Nancy travelled to Buchenwald in a convoy of trucks carrying medical staff, equipment and stores. It was a long journey with little conversation. The camp had been liberated by the Americans only the day before and they were to prepare themselves, Major Smythe said, to witness atrocities beyond any human comprehension. The liberating party had discovered that Buchenwald had been a place of slavery, starvation and mass murder. Some survivors had the strength to greet their liberators, while most were found inside the barracks, their bodies nothing more than skin and bone, lying in bunks – four bodies to a rack – some of them dead already, the others barely alive. The living had tried to find the strength to raise their arms to greet the incoming soldiers, but their arms were weighed down by the gravity of starvation and neglect.

The trucks, having wended their way through a forest for quite some miles, turned off the road and followed a track until coming to a halt next to a railway siding, where a long line of cattle carriages sat on the track. Eliza and Nora jumped out of the truck and began to look around.

Eliza's role, she knew, would be threefold. Firstly, she would search for Alex and Nora among the survivors. Then, she would also help to nurse – to try to breathe new life into the lungs of the living dead. And when all that was done she would take out her paper and paints and she would record it. She wouldn't – she couldn't – look away at this final moment.

They walked forward with a group of medics and the stench of the camp soon became overpowering. Nancy pulled her neckerchief – made of parachute silk and offered as a gift from a grateful airman – up to her face. They were about to pass through large iron gates when Eliza saw something that made her gasp. A board sat on a chair at the entrance to the camp, '3.15' painted on it. Eliza turned to speak to a GI who was standing at the gates.

'Why three-fifteen?' she asked.

'That's the time we liberated the place yesterday,' he said. 'The Colonel wanted it to be noted.' He took off his helmet and ran a hand through his hair. 'Marking the time that we arrived was the one good thing we could find to keep us going after living through a day that had been such a godawful mess. To be honest, Ma'am, it was the only ray of hope we had.'

So there it was. She didn't have to look for the light at all, someone had already found it for her. And the time? It couldn't be a coincidence; it was, quite literally, a sign. Eliza smiled. Hope had not deserted her after all.

With her heart beating out of her chest she walked on. Once through the gates she turned back to read the sign above them – *Jedem Das Seine*. When everything else had been done, she would paint an image of the numbers on the board. It would be a painting that would symbolise her hope, her faith, and her love for Alex. Moreover, it would symbolise her faith in destiny. Her faith that at some time in the future, at three-fifteen precisely, a man and a woman would meet on a beach in Cornwall and nothing that the world could ever throw at them – not now, not ever – could possibly get in their way.

Chapter 33

Ellie

Penberth, Present Day

The bus dropped Ellie half a mile short of Penberth. She walked the last part of the journey down a narrow lane that cut through a wooded valley. It was a cloudy but dry day and Ellie felt her shoulders begin to relax as the beauty of the valley began to seep into her aching, sleep-deprived limbs. She stifled a yawn but smiled at the sight of flower-bedecked stone hedges either side of the lane. Cornwall was so lovely at this time of year; the pink campions, the foxgloves, the wild garlic and the ground lilacs all offering the perfect welcoming bouquet for Ellie's arrival. She reached out a hand now and again to collect a stem, eventually reaching the flower farm, where a number of spectacular posies were offered for sale on a table.

That last half a mile down the lane to the cove was as wonderful as ever, but Ellie's broadest smile was reserved for the moment she passed a pretty thatched cottage on her left and the cove came into view. Her neighbour's lobster pots and a collection of bright orange buoys were scattered, as they always were, outside the house on the cobbles, and the front door into the cottage – freshly painted in lilac blue – stood fast as always, welcoming her home.

Ellie took a deep breath and sighed.

Penberth.

Meadowsweet.

Home.

She spent several hours busying herself airing the old place through, sorting through the online food delivery she had ordered, cleaning the kitchen and catching up with welcoming neighbours. She wouldn't allow herself to linger on thoughts of Joe. This was, after all, her first time at the cottage – *her* cottage – entirely alone and it felt wonderful to be so free, even if the night before insisted on replaying in a loop in her mind.

With her chores for the morning complete, Ellie made a cup of tea, wandered through to the lounge and, with her eyelids suddenly quite heavy, sat down on the settee and decided it was probably best to sleep a while.

She woke, still fully dressed in dungarees and a lilac cashmere jumper, and her thoughts immediately returned to Joe, and – inevitably – to regret. She sighed, pushed her toes into flipflops and sauntered into the kitchen, noticing as she passed that a note had been pushed under the door.

Dear Ellie. Please meet me on Porthcurno Beach at three-fifteen today. I have a surprise for you. Do come. Joe

Ellie didn't know what time it was. There wasn't a single clock in the blooming house and she never wore a watch! She dashed upstairs to where her phone sat on the bedside table (next to a toggle from a duffle coat), and when she turned on the phone she was shocked to see it was 6 p.m.

She had slept for seven hours!

Ellie picked up the toggle and flopped backwards onto the bed.

She had missed him. The disappointment ripped through her like a knife. But when the dust settled she wondered, would she have actually gone to meet him, even if she had read the note in time?

She shook her head. Maybe, maybe not. Maybe this way was best – the decision taken out of her hands. Anyhow, it didn't matter. The moment was gone.

Ellie put the toggle on the kitchen table and, having grabbed a snack, pulled up a chair to sit at the front window. Two books sat on the table – Eliza's journal, of course, and another book that Ellie had found, not on the bookshelf, but on the bedside table next to Great Granny Nancy's bed. It was called *Women in History That Other*

Women Should Read About. It sounded like a decent enough read, decent enough to keep her mind off Joe at least.

She spent the next half-hour flicking through the pages of a story about the comings and goings of a Byzantine Queen, and even though there were some good nuggets in the story, Ellie's mind (drifting all by itself without any help from her) returned to Joe. She looked up from the book and stared blankly out of the window. She thought of him waiting on the beach, miserable to have been let down.

She shook the thoughts of Joe away and returned to the brilliant Byzantine empress, Theodora, a rebel whose father was a bear-keeper in Constantinople's hippodrome. There were, Ellie thought, aspects of Theodora's personality that might be viewed as a little extreme (a fondness for torturing and murdering, to begin with) but it must have been very tricky to be an empress at that time (at any time, really) so she glossed over that bit and decided that she might like to have been Empress Theodora for a day or so, if only for the crown (and the beard).

Ellie stared out of the window and wondered what Theodora would have done about Joe. She smiled – she'd have ravished him, definitely. One hundred per cent. And he really was quite sexy. Sexy and yet ... sweet, gentle and – most importantly – kind.

Oh, what had she done?

Nothing, that's what she had done. Why, oh why, had she not embraced her inner Theodora more? Rihanna was right,

Joe wasn't asking for a lifetime of commitment, just a bit of fun. Ellie glanced at Eliza's journal and remembered another two people who had fun at this cottage ... and hadn't their lives been uncertain at the time, too? Alex and Eliza had no idea what the future would bring either when they met and yet here they had been, prepared to grab their moment, falling in love.

What a fool she was.

Given that it must be getting on for seven o'clock, Joe would almost certainly be long gone from the beach by now.

'Come on, Ellie,' she said aloud, 'for once in your life, *do* something!'

She grabbed her coat and decided to knock on every single door in the village in the hope of a lift along the coast to Lamorna, to Joe's hotel. The mountain wouldn't come to Mohammed, after all (especially as she had abandoned him twice already), but Mohammed could definitely go to the mountain.

Chapter 34

Joe wasn't at the hotel in Lamorna as he had already checked out after having arrived only that morning. 'And just twenty minutes ago,' the receptionist said, trying to be helpful.

'And did he mention where he might be staying next?' asked Ellie, trying not to look too desperate but feeling utterly wretched.

The receptionist shook her head. 'I'm sorry,' she said, offering the indifferent shrug of a woman more than used to the unpredictable comings and goings of her guests, 'he didn't say much at all, I'm afraid.'

Ellie turned the key in the front door at *Meadowsweet* just as the sun was setting behind the steep cliff beyond the cove. She walked into the kitchen and saw the two books on the table, books capturing the stories of remarkable women, women who would no doubt be rolling their eyes in frustration at Ellie right now. She put the books away in a kitchen drawer – story time was done for the day –

and took a seat at the window once more. The room was wonderfully quiet now. It was that special kind of quiet that seems more noticeable somehow at the edges of the day. A beautiful golden twilight caught a crystal elephant that sat on the window ledge and suddenly the whole room was filled with refracted light.

Awash with peace and tranquillity, and yet longing for something she would now never have the chance of again, Ellie decided to turn to the one thing that always brought her comfort in times of stress, no matter how worried or disappointed or lost she felt: music.

She opened her fiddle case, turned her back on the window, smiled at the posy of wildflowers sitting in the vase on the table, and rested the violin under her chin. An image of Joe sitting with Paddington at the station came to mind and she smiled again, but then the tears began to edge onto her lower lashes. She sniffed them back. 'Come on, Ellie,' she said, 'get in the zone.'

She gathered herself. But what to play? With her mind's eye still focusing on Joe sitting all alone at Paddington Station, she remembered one of the songs they had danced to on the train, 'A Nightingale Sang'. She put bow to string and began to play, which was when there was a knock at the door.

'Hiya,' said Joe, Ellie's shoe in one hand, a posy of flowers in the other, the setting sun bouncing off his head to create a halo. 'I thought you might want this back,' he said, holding up the green silk high heel. 'No point just having the one.'

She took the shoe and the posy, her hands shaking. 'Thank you,' she said, her heart racing far too fast for a woman whose heart goes tickety tick tock rather than plain old tickety tock.

Speak, Ellie, she said to herself, *just speak*.

Joe pushed his glasses up his nose. 'I'll be off then,' he said, turning to leave. She was just about to say, 'No, don't go,' when he turned back and said, 'Oh, I've got something for you ... a gift.'

He put a hand in his duffle coat pocket and took out the little brass clock. 'I fixed it. It was quite easy to fix, as it turned out. I'd like you to have it. You said on the train that you'd like it for the kitchen, didn't you?'

'I did ...' she said. She put down the shoe and took the clock. 'You made it tick again ...'

'Well, I thought about it, and decided that it's definitely time for the old thing to move on from three fifteen. You can't make a moment last for ever, Ellie, and I really don't think you should try.'

Ellie continued to stare at the clock.

'Right, then ...' He nodded towards his hire car, parked along the way. 'I'll toddle off. But ... before I do, I just wanted to say ...' Ellie glanced up at him, knowing her green eyes were wider than ever. 'I just wanted to say that ... well, "Ellie Nightingale, for one night only" isn't enough for me, and not for the rest of the world, either. Don't hide away, go out there and grab it – at your own pace and in your own time – but grab it.'

With these words, he walked away.

Ellie, finding her voice finally, shouted after him.

'Joe, wait!'

He turned around.

'I was wondering,' she began, 'I mean, I understand if you're busy, but I was wondering if you fancied going to the beach tomorrow, maybe in the afternoon sometime?'

'What time were you thinking of going?' he asked.

She looked at the clock and smiled. 'Shall we say ... three-fifteen? Only, I've got a clock now, so I won't miss you this time.'

Joe laughed. 'It sounds like the perfect time to go. Till tomorrow, then.' With a last smile he turned to leave.

'Oh, and Joe ... Joe from Leeds ...'

Joe stopped, but didn't just turn around this time. He walked back to face her, smiling.

'Yes, Ellie Nightingale?'

'I just wanted to say ... I just wanted to say ...'

He leant in then. He leant in very close indeed.

'Go on ...' he whispered.

She rubbed her nose. 'Well, I was just about to put the kettle on. And I wondered if you fancied one? A cup of tea, obviously. Aaand, you could look at that book of paintings of Eliza's I told you about, and I've got a Victoria Sponge that needs eating, too ... so ... why don't you just ... I don't know, come in now?'

He frowned, which threw her. 'I'd love to. But is it

Yorkshire Tea? Because you know, that's a real deal-breaker with me ...'

She laughed. 'I know it is,' she said. 'I bought it in, especially ...'

They walked into the kitchen then. Ellie threw out her own posy and put the flowers from Joe in the vase. She placed the clock on the windowsill. Joe took off his coat and, picking up the toggle that sat alone on the table, he looked across at the clock.

'It looks at home there,' he said. 'Like it belongs.'

He took a seat by the window and let out a very contented sigh and it seemed to Ellie at that moment – a moment she knew she would remember all of her life, however long or short a time that might be – that maybe it wasn't just the clock that had found a home, but everyone.

Epilogue

Alex

Christmas Day, 1944

The train moved on. Never, in all of his life, had Alex felt so completely alone. Crouched like a frightened dog in a corner of the carriage, with his knees up to his chest and his face pressed against the shattered wood panel, Alex knew that if this train ever stopped it would be almost impossible to find the strength to walk. The journey, which must surely be almost at an end soon, had only been bearable by dreaming of Eliza, but even the most pleasant thoughts had turned around to haunt him.

He had been thinking about how he wished he had got things right with Eliza, right from that very first night. But there was no going back now, he concluded, his eyes staring out into the black of the cattle carriage. It was done for. *He* was done for. And it was only now, at this moment of reckoning as the train powered on to what must surely be Alex's final destination in this war, that he – like every other man who found himself facing the iron grasp of Destiny far too soon – realised that he had thrown away far too many of the simple but precious moments that life had sent his way.

He slept then. Another hour passed by.

His head began to nod in and out of consciousness and his mind – his delirious, troubled mind – wandered from night train to night train, with Eliza always a carriage away, her green dress floating down the aisle, the door closing behind her. They had said that they would meet in Berlin one day, when it was all over. Berlin! He shook his aching head. What was Berlin but a castle in the clouds? He imagined now he was on a night train to Berlin. It would be a journey of comfort, no doubt, of wonder and of hope. It would take its passengers – Alex and Eliza – into the light where they would finally – thankfully – arrive at their much-longed for destination – that destination being nothing more than simple peace. But, now he thought about it, hadn't they been on the train to Berlin all along, ever since he had waved to her as she stood on the dock-side, both of them, the eager children that they were, heading to the Normandy beaches, desperate to make a difference, to 'do their bit'. Yes, that was when they had begun their journey to Berlin, and the train hadn't been a place of comfort at all, quite the opposite. It had been a vehicle of destruction.

The train's brakes began to screech, causing the limp

body next to him to press even harder into his side. Something sharp dug into his ribs suddenly.

From somewhere he managed to force his dry and cracked lips to smile. It was the clock that had woken him. Eliza's little clock was still inside his jacket pocket. It must have slipped and one of the little feet had jabbed into his side. It was a sign, surely? A message from Eliza, perhaps. Had she just given him the prod he needed to waken him from despondency? Was she telling him to keep strong, to find courage – to find faith? Yes, he decided, she was. And he must. He must find his faith. He must find hope. He searched around in the confusion of his mind and remembered a note – an insurance policy – he had written for the two of them. It was a silly notion perhaps, but it had given him something to focus on in those first dreadful hours after Eliza had left for Spa with Phillipe. With an overwhelming sense of dread that he would never see Eliza again, Alex had written a short note and placed it inside the clock. In doing so he had embraced Eliza's faith in destiny and in the power of everlasting love ...

To whomever this may concern. I once met a beautiful woman on a beach in Cornwall – at Porthcurno Beach. If you are reading this note then I am asking you to go to that beach at three-fifteen on any day (if destiny works it won't matter) and know that the only woman you will ever love will be standing there, waiting for you. I write this note to myself in the future, in the knowledge that love never dies and if we cannot be together in this lifetime then we will more than make up for it in the next. What are you waiting for, man? Go!

The End

About the author

About the book

Read on

Insights,
Interviews
& More...

Meet Melanie Hudson

© Marte Lundby Rekaa

Melanie Hudson was born in Yorkshire in 1971, the youngest of six children. Her earliest memory is of standing with her brother on the street corner selling her dad's surplus vegetables (imagine *The Good Life* in Barnsley and you're more or less there).

After running away to join the British armed forces in 1994, Melanie experienced a career that took her around the world on exciting adventures. In 2010, when she returned to civilian life to look after her young son, she moved to Dubai where she found the time to write novels. She now lives in Cornwall with her family.

Melanie's debut, *The Wedding Cake Tree*, won the Romantic Novelists' Association Contemporary Romance Novel of the Year 2016 and her second novel, *The Last Letter from Juliet*, was a *USA Today* bestseller. ꙮ

Author Q&A

1. When did you first start writing stories? Did you write as a child or was it a passion and ambition that came to you in adulthood?

I did write as a child and it was always a dream of mine to write novels one day, though it turns out it had to be once I had lived a bit (lot).

2. Who are your favourite authors? Do you have a favourite book, or are there any particular books that have inspired you?

My two favourite authors are Elizabeth Von Arnim and Kate Atkinson and my favourite book is *The Enchanted April*, which is a masterclass in characterisation and basically just a wonderful, witty, inspiring book to read. Both authors have influenced my writing.

3. Ellie is a beautiful violinist and her playing brings joy to the commuters at Paddington Station. What music do you enjoy? Do you ever listen to music while you write?

I trained as an operatic singer in my early twenties, but only for relaxation rather than performance. I also play the piano (badly). Music is vital to my writing and when I start writing a first draft, I set up two – one for classical music and one that is more like an old fashioned mixed tape. I listen to the classical one when I'm writing to set the emotional mood and the mixed tape when I'm driving for inspiration and to absorb the emotion so that I can then portray that same feeling in the story.

4. If you had to pick one song or album to accompany this book what would it be?

I can't pick just one! The theme music to *Schindler's List*, Glasgow Theme from *Love Actually* and *A Nightingale Sang in Berkeley Square* are the tunes I associate the most with this book.

5. What hobbies do you like to do when you're not writing?

Hiking, I'm an avid walker, and gardening are my big passions – and I'm partial to a glass of wine in front of the telly!

6. What advice would you give to aspiring authors?

Don't hold back. If you think it, write it down and open your heart completely. Also, a finished novel is unlikely to be the story you write at first draft so remember that it's simply a way of edging into the makings of a story for the first time.

7. Where did your inspiration for the book come from?

I live near the Telegraph Museum at Porthcurno in Cornwall. Eliza was originally going to be a telegraph operator, but I simply couldn't uncover enough information about deployed female telegraph operators. During that research, however, I stumbled across the work of war artists and I realised that I'd found Eliza's vocation.

8. Ellie shares a close relationship with her grandmother. Did any of your own family history inspire your writing?

I only knew one of my grandparents so, not really, no but my own experience of being a woman at war, when I served with the Royal Navy in Iraq, undoubtedly influenced my writing.

9. What lasting feelings, themes, or emotions do you hope readers are left with after finishing *The Night Train to Berlin*?

The story is about faith, hope and somehow being able to dig deep enough to find strength during the most challenging times. It's about cherishing the special moments and not necessarily expecting more. It's about the consideration of the idea that 'all shall be well' in that, what we define as being 'well' in life might not be the gold plated solution we first aspire to, and that wellness is a state of mind, of acceptance of each other and of absolute love, whatever the circumstances.

10. The world today is still such an uncertain place and sometimes it can be difficult to see the light in the darkness. What gives you hope?

Hope comes to me by connecting with nature and mainly when I'm alone with my dog during my daily walk. I'm lucky enough to live in a beautiful place by the sea and there's something intensely spiritual about that kind of life. Growing plants for the garden is also a very hopeful thing to do and very mindful. I'm also able to be hopeful by surrendering, too, by not being too attached to outcomes. My time serving in the Armed Forces in conflict when I truly did not know if I would live another day changed my outlook on life completely. I feel that we are children who are given a beautiful planet to play on for a while, we just don't know how long it will be before the bell rings to beckon us back inside, but when it does ring, I want to know that I've made the most of my time in the sunshine, however long or short that may be.

Author's Note

Much of the inspiration for *The Night Train to Berlin* came from the work of women war correspondents and photojournalists of the Second World War, a cadre of women about whom far too little is known, which is ironic considering that they broke boundaries within their professional sphere in order to make sure that plenty was known about the work of others. When war broke out in 1939 journalists from all over the globe (and particularly from America) were desperate to get a piece of the action, but for women, despite some having proven their metal reporting from the front during the Spanish Civil War, the road to the battlefield was not an easy one, leaving many to cook up quite elaborate plans in order to be officially affiliated to Allied Forces. In her book, *The Women Who Wrote the War*, Nancy Caldwell Sorel provides a vital and fascinating record of the bravery and determination of these women reporters in order to get the job done.

Take, for example, the American photographer Margaret Bourke-White, who was the first woman allowed to work in combat zones during the Second World War. Often under fire, she was active in Moscow when the Germans invaded, was in North Africa and Italy with the American Army and she was the first female photojournalist to fly on a bombing raid with the American Air Force. She not only survived a helicopter crash but also survived the sinking of a troopship she had boarded. This woman was a born survivor, with nothing but guts and grit flowing through her veins. Most importantly, in terms of providing inspiration for my novel at least, Margaret was one of the first people to arrive at Buchenwald concentration camp after liberation. She later said, 'Using a camera was almost a relief. It interposed a slight barrier between myself and the horror in front of me,' which was a coping mechanism I gave to Eliza in the book.

Another source of inspiration was Lee Miller. In 1942, rejecting advice to return home, the American devil-may-care photographer was living in England while working for *British Vogue*. For countless reasons (one of which was to take advantage of shopping at the PX) Miller applied to the US Army for accreditation and was accepted. Her new uniform opened up access to areas of journalism that would otherwise have been restricted. Like my Eliza, Miller began by posting upbeat stories about life on the home front. Gradually, like Eliza, her portrayal of the war became grittier, showing, for example, the true reality of London under constant attack from the air.

It was D-Day, acting like a flame to a moth, that attracted a new tranche of women to the fore; women who were desperate to be allowed to do their bit and

Author's Note *(continued)*

get in on the action. It was in June 1944, at the time of the Normandy landings, when women reporters and photographers such as Lee Carson, Catherine Coyne, Ruth Cowan and the indomitable Martha Gellhorn rushed to the English south coast to try to find a way across the Channel. There was a movement by now for women to be seen not necessarily as token reporters, kept back and only able to get to the action through subterfuge, but as having merit in their own right in terms of reporting the war from a female, perhaps more human, perspective. As a result, many American newspapers rushed to have their women reporters accredited and sent across the Channel to Europe, and yet even when they arrived, women were still not allowed to get too close to the action, with many senior military leaders refusing to have women on board – though such a minor detail did not prevent the more dedicated, individualistic type of woman from getting the story she was after. Eliza's decision to volunteer to assist the British Red Cross, thereby gaining access to the action via other means was inspired by the story of gritty reporter Virginia Irwin of the *Saint Louis Post Dispatch* who, after her newspaper refused to try to accredit her, took a sabbatical and joined the American Red Cross overseas as a means of getting her typewriter closer to the action. Eventually, when the *Dispatch* saw that they were being left behind by having no accredited reporter, the War Department approved her accreditation, purely on the basis that she was already at the front, albeit as a nurse, her ruse having come to fruition.

Further inspiration for Eliza's story came from the antics of the fabulous Martha Gellhorn. On D-Day plus one, Gellhorn snuck onto a hospital ship and hid in a lavatory until well underway. She went on to witness the D-Day landings at their peak and produced some of the most inspired reporting of the whole war, writing of the heartbreaking operation of recovering the wounded from the beaches and from the sea. Gellhorn, like Eliza, put down her notebook to wade out and help carry the wounded back to the ship. On her return to England she was arrested and confined to an American nurses' camp, where, refusing to bow down, she promptly escaped and hitched her way by road and by air to Naples, where she carried on reporting.

Such bloody-minded determination and frankly, blind bravery, was commonplace amongst these women, many of whom, by hook or by crook, found the ways and means to cross the Channel to get to the action during the summer of 1944. Like Eliza and Nora, many got themselves attached to the Women's Army Corps (who really did march along French roads singing the Marseillaise), or to field hospitals. Also

Author's Note *(continued)*

like Eliza and Nora, they were not granted
the freedoms their male colleagues enjoyed,
in that they were not allowed to go to the
press camps, not allowed to go further
forward than the nurses, and not allowed to
send their stories home via the usual, faster
routes. All of which meant that they could
not do the job properly, a job that they were
desperate to do. But such petty restrictions
were never going to stop them, especially
Lee Miller, who, like Eliza, found herself
wandering into St. Malo, having been told
that the town had been liberated, only to
find herself in the rush of the action, taking
the kinds of photographs that her male
colleagues could only dream of.

But my Eliza was not a photographer, or
a writer, she was an artist and yet I found
that it was to the work of the reporters I
had to turn to in order to find the nuggets
of historical detail I needed because so little
is written about any women commissioned
as war artists. Despite more than four
hundred artists being taken on by the War
Artists' Advisory Committee at the start
of the war, only two women were given
overseas commissions and only one of them
was paid – Evelyn Dunbar – who was on
lower pay and given far less publicity than
her male colleagues. There was a point
during my research when I thought that
my desire to create a story about a female
war artist would have to be dropped, that

it simply too unrealistic a concept, but then I stumbled across an article about a woman called Doris Zinkeisen, a society painter who, having been a VAD nurse during the First World War, volunteered to nurse again during the Second, and ultimately, like Eliza, was commissioned to follow the British Red Cross across Europe and capture their work on canvas. I do not believe I have seen or read any other work that captured the humanitarian effort of the war so perfectly and honestly portrayed in her paintings.

In a way, my Eliza embodies the strength, bravery and commitment of all of these women. They were the groundbreakers who followed the troops across Europe, often finding ingenious ways to position themselves much further forward than supposedly allowed. They were the groundbreakers who produced an account of events that would have been tragically missed if not for their tenacity. The female perspective from the battleground gave readers at home – mothers who waited anxiously for news of their sons – a more human angle on the war. They proved, without question, that they were unflinching in their determination to not look away but to face the horror of such a terrible and incredible period in our history and to record it in their own way – the woman's way. ᘓ

Reading Group Guide:
Discussion Questions for
The Night Train to Berlin

1. Discuss the book's structure. *The Night Train to Berlin* is written in a dual narrative told from the perspective of two women, Ellie and Eliza. To what extent do the narrators serve as an entry point for the reader into the story? How do Ellie and Eliza compare?

2. The Prologue and Epilogue are the only two points narrated by Alex and provide the reader with a glimpse into his thoughts and feelings. What do you think is the purpose of this change in narrator? How do you think the book might have been in different if another character was telling the story?

3. Do you have a favourite passage from the book? What is it and how does this particular passage relate to the story as a whole? Does it reveal anything specific about any of the characters or illuminate certain aspects of the story?

4. At the heart of the book is the bond between Eliza and Alex, the solace they find in that bond, and their will to survive for each other. How does this relationship develop over the course of their journey? What other relationships are there in the book and how do they impact the story?

5. What did Joe and Ellie's timeline add to the book? How did the author use this relationship to highlight key themes? Which couple did you prefer – Eliza and Alex or Joe and Ellie?

6. What part does Nancy play in both timelines? What does her friendship with Eliza bring to the story?

7. Part of *The Night Train to Berlin* is set during the Second World War. How well does the author convey the era? How does she bring that time period to life for the reader? Did you learn anything you didn't previously know about this significant historical event?

8. The end of the book is left open to interpretation. How did this make you feel? What do you think happened to Eliza and Alex? ᕙ

Prologue

Read Me

This is a note to yourself, Juliet.

At the time of writing you are ninety-two years old and worried that the bits and bobs of your story have begun to go astray. You must read this note carefully every day and work very hard to keep yourself and the memories alive, because once upon a time you told a man called Edward Nancarrow that you would, and it's important to keep that promise, Juliet, even when there seems to be little point going on.

In the mahogany sideboard you will find all the things you will need to keep living your life alone. These things are: bank details; savings bonds; emergency contact numbers; basic information about you – your name, age and place of birth; money in a freezer bag; an emergency mobile phone. More importantly, there are also your most precious possessions scattered around the house. I've labelled them, to help you out.

Written on the back of this note is a copy of the poem Edward gave you in 1943. Make sure you can recite it (poetry is good for the brain). And finally, even if you forget everything else, remember that, in the end, Edward's very simple words are the only things that have ever really mattered.

Now, make sure you've had something to eat and a glass of water – water helps with memory – and whatever happens in the future, whatever else you may forget, always remember … he's waiting.

With an endless supply of love,
Juliet

Chapter 1

Katherine

A proposal

It was a bright Saturday lunchtime in early December. I'd just closed the lounge curtains and was about to binge-watch *The Crown* for the fourth time that year when a Christmas card bearing a Penzance postmark dropped through the letter box.

Uncle Gerald. Had to be.

The card, with an illustration of a distressed donkey carrying a (somewhat disappointed-looking) Virgin Mary being egged on by a couple of haggard angels, contained within it my usual Christmas catch-up letter. I wandered through to the kitchen and clicked the kettle on – it was a four-pager.

My Dear Katherine
  Firstly, I hope this letter finds you well, or as well as to be expected given your distressing circumstances

*of living alone in Exeter with no family around you
<u>again</u> this Christmas.*

Cheers for that, Gerald.

*But more of your circumstances in a moment because
(to quote the good bard) 'something is rotten in the
state of Denmark' and I'm afraid this year's letter will
not burst forth with my usual festive cheer. There is at
present a degree of what can only be described as civil
unrest breaking out in Angels Cove and I am at my
wits' end trying to promote an atmosphere of peace
and goodwill in time for Christmas. I'm hopeful you
will be able to offer a degree of academic common
sense to the issue.*

*Here's the rub: the Parish Council (you may remember
that I am the chair?) has been informed that the village
boundaries are to be redrawn in January as part of a
Cornwall County Council administrative shake-up. This
simple action has lit the touch paper of a centuries-old
argument amongst the residents that needs – finally –
to be put to rest.*

*The argument in question is this: should our village
be apostrophised or not? If 'yes', then should the apostrophe come before or after the 's'?*

It is a Total Bloody Nightmare!

It really isn't, Gerald.

At the moment, Angels Cove is written without an apostrophe, but most agree that there should be an apostrophe in there somewhere, yet where? The argument seems to rest on three questions:

1. Does the cove 'belong' to just one angel (the angel depicted in the church stained glass window, for example, as some people claim that they have seen him) or to a multitude of angels (i.e. the possessive of a singular or a plural noun).

2. Does the cove belong to the angels or do the angels belong to the cove? (The minority who wish to omit the apostrophe in its entirety ask this question.)

3. Does the word angel in Angels Cove actually refer, not to the winged messengers of the Divine, but to the notorious pirate, Jeremiah 'Cut-throat' Angel, who sailed from Penzance circa 1723 and whose ship, The Savage Angel, was scuppered in Mounts Bay (not apostrophised, you will note) when he returned from the West Indies at the tender age of twenty-nine?

As you can see, it's a mess.

Fearing the onset of a migraine, I stopped reading and decided to sort out the recycling, which would take a while, given the number of empties. An hour later saw me continuing to give the rest of Gerald's letter a stiff ignoring because I needed to get back to *The Crown* and plough my way through an ironing pile that saw its foundations laid in 1992. Just at the point where Prince Philip jaunts

5

off solo on a raucous stag do to Australia (and thinking that I really ought to write a letter to the Queen to tell her how awesome she is), I turned the iron off (feeling a pang of guilt at leaving a complicated silk blouse alone in the basket) poured a glass of Merlot, popped a Tesco 'extra deep' mince pie in the microwave and returned to the letter...

I expect you will agree that this is a question of historical context, not a grammatical issue.

I do not.

As the 'go to' local historian (it must run in the family!) I attempted to offer my own hypothesis at the parish meeting last week, but can you believe it, I was barracked off the stage just two minutes into my delivery.

I can.

But all is not lost. This morning, while sitting on the loo wracking my brains for inspiration, I stumbled across your book, From Nob End to Soggy Bottom, English Place Names and their Origins *in my toilet TBR pile (I had forgotten you have such a dry wit, my dear) and I just knew that I had received Divine intervention from the good Lord himself, because although the villagers are not prepared to accept my opinion as being correct, I do believe they would accept the decision of a university professor, especially when I explain that you were sent to them by God.*

So, I have a proposition for you.

Time for that mince pie.

In return for your help on the issue, please do allow me the pleasure of offering you a little holiday here in Angels Cove, as my very special present to you, this Christmas. I know you have balked at the idea of coming to stay with me in the past (don't worry, I know I'm an eccentric old so-and-so with disgusting toenails)...

True.

...but how do you fancy a beautiful sea view this Christmas?

Well, now that you mention it...

The cottage is called Angel View (just the one angel, note) and now belongs to a local man, Sam Lanyon (Royal Navy pilot – he's away at sea, poor chap). He says you can stay as long as you like – I may have mentioned what happened to James as leverage.

Gerald!

The cottage sits just above the cove and has every-thing you could possibly need for the perfect holiday (it's also a bit of a 1940s time capsule because until very recently it belonged to an elderly lady – you'll love it).

The thing is, before you say no, do remember that before she died, I did promise your mother that I would keep an eye on you...

It was only a matter of time.

... and your Christmas card seemed so forlorn... Actually, not forlorn, bland – it set me off worrying about you being alone again this Christmas, and I thought this would be the perfect opportunity for us to look out for each other, as I'm alone too since George is on a mercy mission visiting his sister in Brighton this year. Angels Cove is simply beautiful at Christmas. The whole village pulls together (when they are not arguing) to illuminate the harbour with a festival of lights. It's magical.

But?

But ... with all the shenanigans going on this year, I'm not sure the villagers will be in the mood for celebration. Please do say you'll come and answer our question for us, and in doing so, bring harmony to this beautiful little cove and save Christmas for all the little tourist children.

Surely this kind of thing is right up your Strasse?

My idea is that you could do a little bit of research, then the locals could present you with their proposals for the placement of the apostrophe in a climactic final meeting. It will be just like a Christmas episode of The Apprentice *– bring a suit! And meanwhile, I'll have a whole programme of excitement planned for you – a week of wonderful things – and it includes gin.*

Now you're talking.

Do write back or text or (God forbid) phone, straight away and say you'll come, because by God, Katherine, you are barely forty-five years old, which is a mere blink of an eye. You have isolated yourself from all your old friends and it is not an age at which a person should be sitting alone with only their memories to comfort them. Basically, if anyone deserves a little comfort this Christmas, it's you. I know you usually visit the grave on Christmas Day, but please, for the build-up week at least (which is the best part of Christmas after all) come to Cornwall and allow yourself to be swaddled by our angels for a while (they're an impressive bunch).

I am happy to beg.

Yours, in desperation,

Gerald.

P.S. Did I mention the gin?

Sitting back in a kitchen chair I'd ruined by half-arsedly daubing it in chalk paint two weeks before, I glanced around the room and thought about Gerald's offer. On the one hand, why on earth would I want to leave my home at Christmas? It was beautiful. But the energy had changed, and what was once the vibrant epicentre of Exeter's academia, now hovered in a haze of hushed and silent mourning, like the house was afraid of upsetting me by raising its voice.

A miniature Christmas tree sat on the edge of the dresser looking uncomfortable and embarrassed. I'd decorated it with a selection of outsized wooden ornaments picked up during a day trip to IKEA in November. IKEA in Exeter was my weekly go-to store since James had gone. It was a haven for the lost and lonely. A person (me) can disappear up their own backside for the whole morning in an unpronounceable maze of fake rooms, rugs, tab-top curtains, plastic plants and kitchen utensils (basically all the crap the Swedes don't want) before whiling away a good couple of hours gorging themselves on a menu of meatballs and cinnamon swirls, and still have the weirdest selection of booze and confectionary Sweden has to offer (what on earth is *Lordagsgodis*, anyway?) to look forward to at checkout.

And we wonder why the Swedes are so happy!

But did I really want to spend the run-up to Christmas in IKEA this year? (Part of me actually did – it's *very* Scandi-chic Christmassy). But to do it for a third year in a row, with no one to laugh out loud with when we try to pronounce the unpronounceable Swedish word for fold-up bed?

(That was a poor example because a futon is a futon in any language and I really did need to try to control my inner monologue which had gone into overdrive since James died – I was beginning to look excessively absent minded in public).

But did I want to spend Christmas in IKEA this year? Not really, no.

But the problem (and Gerald knew this, too) was that if I left the house this Christmas, then it would mark the beginning of my letting go, of starting again, of saying that another life – a festive one – could exist beyond James. If I had a good time I might start to forget him, but if I stayed here and kept thinking of him, if I kept the memories alive, re-read the little notes he left me every morning, if I looked through photographs on Facebook, replayed scenes and conversations in my mind, then he would still be here, alive, in me. But if I go away, where would that lead? I knew exactly where it would lead – to the beginning of the end of James. To the beginning of not being able to remember his voice, his smell, his laugh – to the beginning of moving on.

And I wasn't sure I was ready for that.

But still...

I knocked back the last of the Merlot while googling train times to Penzance and fished out the last card in a box of IKEA Christmas cards I'd abandoned to the dresser drawer the week before. It was an exact replica of the one I'd already sent him, a golden angel. I took it as a sign and began to scribble...

Dear, Uncle Gerald,

You are quite correct. This kind of thing is indeed 'right up my Strasse'. Rest assured there will be no need to beg – I shall come!

I arrive in Penzance by the 18.30 train on the 17th and intend to stay (wait for it) until Boxing Day! By which time I am confident that, one way or another, I will have found a solution to your problem. DO NOT, however, feel that you have to entertain me all week. It's very good of you but actually – and quite selfishly – this trip could be a blessing in disguise. I have been wracking my brains for an idea for a new book – a history project to keep me going through the rest of the winter – and I have a feeling that hidden deep within the midst of Cornish myth and legend, I might find one.

Please thank Mr Lanyon for the offer of the use of his cottage – I accept!

How are the cataracts, by the way? Are you able to drive? If so, I wonder if you could meet me at the station?

With oodles of love,

Your, Katherine

P.S. Wouldn't it be funny if 'The Cataracts' were an old couple who lived in the village and I would say, 'How are the Cataracts, by the way?' And you would answer, 'Oh, they're fine. They've just tripped off to Tenerife for Christmas.'

P.P.S. Take heart in knowing that there is nothing simple about the apostrophe. It is punctuation's version of the naughty Cornish pixie, and seems to wreak havoc wherever it goes. There is a village in America, for example, where the misplacing of the apostrophe led to full-scale civil unrest and ultimately, the cold-blooded murder of the local sheriff. Let us hope for your sake that the situation at Angels Cove does not escalate into a similar scale of brouhaha!

P.P.P.S. Gin? I love you.